The
Kew
Gardens
Girls at War

The
Kew
Gardens
Girls *at* War

Posy Lovell

ORION

An Orion paperback
First published in Great Britain in 2021 by Orion Fiction
an imprint of The Orion Publishing Group Ltd
Carmelite House, 50 Victoria Embankment
London EC4Y 0DZ

An Hachette UK Company

1 3 5 7 9 10 8 6 4 2

A CIP catalogue record for this book is
available from the British Library.

ISBN (Mass Market Paperback) 978 1 4091 9332 6
ISBN (eBook) 978 1 4091 9333 3

Typeset by Input Data Services Ltd, Somerset

Printed and bound in Great Britain by Clays Ltd, Elcograf S.p.A.

www.orionbooks.co.uk

For Darren, Tom and Sam

Chapter One

Kent, Summer 1940

Louisa heard the engines before she saw the planes. They were high-pitched and droning like bees. Angry bees, she thought.

She straightened up, rubbing the small of her back because she wasn't as young as she'd once been and bending over the plants in her garden always made her ache, and peered upwards.

It was a glorious day. The sky was bright blue, with little puffs of white clouds. Louisa shut her eyes for a second, enjoying the feeling of the sun on her face, then opened them again almost immediately as the droning engines grew louder.

And suddenly there they were, right overhead. Two planes – no, three, four – spinning and spiralling, silhouetted against the cornflower-blue sky as they dived down.

Louisa felt a little thrill of fear and excitement. The war often seemed far away from her sleepy Kent village, but not today.

'Teddy?' she called to her husband. 'Teddy, come and see.'

The noise was louder now, engines screaming and guns crashing. The planes swooped downwards and Louisa gasped, thinking that surely they couldn't come this low, but then they were shooting upwards again, into the clouds.

She could hear voices around her, as the village children crowded out into the street. She knew they'd be running to the fields, hoping to find some bits of shell or shrapnel. Part of her wanted to go and see what they would find, but she couldn't tear her eyes away from the battle in the skies.

One of the planes came powering across the horizon, with another in pursuit. Louisa couldn't tell which was German and which British. She narrowed her eyes, squinting against the sun. German in front, she thought, and a Spitfire closing the gap from behind.

'Good lord.' She turned to see Teddy standing next to her, his nephew Christopher at his side. Teddy frowned as he saw the planes and Louisa immediately regretted calling him outside to look. Teddy's son had been killed in the last war and he'd been devastated when this conflict had begun. Devastated.

Without taking her gaze from the sky, Louisa reached for Teddy's hand and squeezed his fingers in hers, letting him know she was there. Teddy was resigned to the war now. He knew that Hitler had to be stopped, but that didn't mean he liked it. He refused to do anything that supported the fighting; instead, he was the billeting officer for the evacuees that had flooded the village.

Overhead the sky was criss-crossed with contrails as the planes raced across the blue. The droning of the engines was peppered with gunfire so loud that Louisa almost wanted to put her hands over her ears to drown it out.

Her stomach was fluttering. It was scary and exhilarating to watch these pilots battling it out over their heads. But then, she'd always liked a bit of drama.

'He's been hit,' Christopher said, pointing to the German plane, which had a trail of thick smoke coming from the wing. 'He might bail out. Look for a parachute.'

Louisa breathed in sharply. 'He's turning round.' The plane streaked across the sky leaving wisps of inky-black smoke in the blue. 'Look!' She took her hand from Teddy's and pointed upwards. 'Look, he's going back the way he came.' She laughed in excitement. 'Our boys have seen him off.'

Teddy gave a little shudder and walked back up the garden towards their cottage without a word. Louisa felt a moment's regret for enjoying this dogfight as much as she did. She looked at Christopher. 'Poor Ted,' she said. 'This is tough for him.'

Christopher nodded. 'Every day must bring back memories of Philip.'

Overhead the planes were disappearing into the distance, the sound of gunfire fading as they went. Louisa wondered if the German pilot would make it back to France safely or if he would bail out. She was surprised to realise she hoped he would be all right and smiled to herself. That was what marriage to Teddy did, she thought. She remembered how passionate she'd been during the early years of the last war, gobbling up every bit of news from the Front and even, she swallowed down a burst of shame at the thought, abusing the men who didn't fight. She and Teddy had very different memories of the last war. Very different.

Louisa looked towards the house, where she could see Teddy getting his bicycle out of the shed at the side of the cottage. 'It helps when he's busy,' she said to Christopher. 'He'll be off to see his evacuees now.'

Christopher sat down on the lawn with a thump. Louisa looked round at him. He was a funny chap, Christopher. Forgetful and distracted, tall and ungainly and always falling over, but loyal and honest and with a real talent for growing plants. She was very fond of him, as was Teddy – whose younger sister was Christopher's mother – and they'd been delighted when he'd got a job as a farmhand nearby.

'Do you wish you were more involved?' he asked bluntly. 'More involved with the war, I mean?'

With a small grunt and a rather graceless motion, Louisa sat down next to him, wondering how to explain how she felt. 'I do,' she admitted. 'I feel rather . . .'

'Useless?'

3

'That's it exactly.' She smiled at Christopher. 'Last time round I was doing my bit.'

'At Kew Gardens?'

'You've heard all my stories a thousand times.'

'I like them.'

Louisa sighed. 'I know it was hardly the same as what Philip did, or the other men who fought at the Front, or the women who nursed or supported the troops in other ways. But by keeping the gardens going we freed up the male gardeners to go and fight.'

'I'm thinking about joining up,' Christopher said. Louisa turned to look at him, surprised. He'd never mentioned this before now.

'Really?'

'I know I'm probably no use to anyone,' he said, giving a small, self-conscious smile. 'I'm so clumsy. But I just feel . . .'

This time it was Louisa who said: 'Useless.'

'All the lads from back home, friends from school or the ones I used to play with growing up, they've all gone, Louisa. I should be doing my bit.'

'Farming is a reserved occupation,' Louisa pointed out. 'You're fighting the war in the fields.'

'I know that,' Christopher said, nodding vigorously. 'But even so.'

'What would you do?'

He shrugged, his skinny shoulder blades pushing against the fabric of his shirt. 'Army, probably. I wouldn't last five minutes in a plane and I get seasick.'

Louisa laughed but Christopher looked serious. 'Do you think Uncle Teddy would be upset?'

'I think he'd understand,' Louisa said carefully, though she wasn't sure she was telling the truth. She glanced at where her husband was crouched down next to his bike, prodding the tyre, out of earshot of their conversation.

'And what about you?'

'What about me?'

4

'Do you think I should enlist?'

Louisa felt a little prickle of something that she thought might be envy. 'I can't tell you what to do, Christopher.' She plucked at a piece of grass.

'What would you do?' Christopher said. 'If you were me?'

Louisa thought about the charming village they lived in, where she knew everyone's name and everyone knew her. She thought about her friends in the Women's Institute, strong capable women who kept the village running smoothly. She thought about the rolling fields and the beautiful hills and woodlands where she could walk, and about her carefully tended garden.

And then she thought about the last war, when she worked so hard at Kew that she would be asleep each night before her head hit the pillow. She thought about her friends Ivy and Win – the Kew Gardens girls, they called themselves – who supported each other and fought for each other when things went wrong. And she thought about her time as a Suffragette, battling for the vote and doing things she'd never have thought herself capable of.

'Louisa?' Christopher said. 'What would you do if you were me?'

'I'd enlist.'

'Thought so.'

Louisa felt a lurch of fear. She adored Christopher but she wasn't blind to his flaws. She knew he was being honest when he said he was clumsy. She couldn't imagine him with a gun in his hand. 'Don't do it because of me,' she said quickly. 'And don't rush into anything, will you? This is a big decision.'

Christopher bit his lip, making him look like the little boy he'd been when Louisa and Teddy had got married.

'You're needed on the farm,' Louisa added. 'Mr and Mrs Oliver would be lost without you.'

'They're getting some Land Girls,' Christopher said with a shrug.

Louisa doubted that Land Girls – good as they might be – would know with a glance at the soil what crop would thrive there and what would fail as Christopher did, but she smiled. 'Do what you think is best,' she said. 'No one else can make this decision for you.'

Up at the cottage, Teddy had stopped fiddling with his bicycle tyres.

'Off to see my evacuees,' he called cheerfully. 'Save some lunch for me.'

Louisa waved. 'Will do.'

'Uncle Ted wouldn't enlist,' Christopher said, as Teddy sailed round the side of the cottage and out onto the street, ringing his bicycle bell as he went.

'No.'

'And he wouldn't want me to either.'

'No.' Louisa felt uneasy, as though she were being disloyal to Teddy even having this conversation. She curled her legs to one side and stood up – with some difficulty, because she was almost sixty, after all, and women of her age were not supposed to sit on lawns like schoolchildren. 'I should go and get lunch ready.'

Christopher looked at his watch, which had a large crack across the face. 'Oh blow it, I was supposed to be picking up some wood to mend the fence up at the farm,' he said. 'I totally forgot that was why I came down to the village. I saw Uncle Teddy at the window and waved, and he invited me in for a cup of tea, and the fence totally went out of my head.' He slapped himself on the forehead with his sizeable hand. 'I'd better go.'

He got to his feet much more easily than Louisa had, and bent down to kiss her on the cheek. 'Thanks, Louisa,' he said. 'You've really helped.'

And with that, he darted off, leaving Louisa wondering whether she actually had helped or if she'd just made everything a whole lot worse.

Chapter Two

'Do you, Daisy Dobson, take this man . . .'

As the vicar spoke, Daisy gazed at Rex. He was so handsome, she thought, with his blue jacket bringing out the colour in his eyes. His hat was tilted at an angle, giving him a slightly cheeky look, which Daisy liked. That, together with his freckles, made him look more like the boy she'd fallen in love with when they were both still at school than the man he now was, despite his RAF uniform. She had a sudden memory of watching him share his lunch with Scruffy Nev, a boy in their class who would come to school in bare feet because his family couldn't afford to buy shoes. Rex's parents didn't have much back then – no one did – but he still shared what little he had. That was one of the reasons Daisy loved him so much.

'Daisy?' Rex whispered.

She blinked. She'd been so busy staring at her husband-to-be that she'd stopped listening to the vicar. 'Sorry,' she said, grinning. 'Is it my turn?'

There was a murmur of laughter from the congregation. Daisy glanced at her mother Ivy in the front pew. Ivy rolled her eyes at Daisy fondly – at least Daisy hoped it was fondly – and next to her, Daisy's father Jim gave her a wink.

Brimming with happiness, Daisy turned her attention back to Rex.

'I do,' she declared, and Rex threw his arms up in triumph, like he'd scored the winning goal in the cup final.

This time the laughter around the church was louder, and even Reverend Osmond joined in.

'I now pronounce you man and wife,' he said and Rex gathered Daisy into his arms and kissed her so firmly and proudly that Daisy felt her legs go weak.

Hand in hand with her new husband, she walked down the aisle, waving to the friends and family who had come to wish them well.

'I'm sorry it's not the perfect wedding day,' Rex said.

Daisy squeezed his fingers. 'It's not what we would have planned, but it is the perfect wedding day anyway,' she said. 'Because we got to say our vows.'

They reached the church porch and paused. Rex touched his nose to Daisy's. 'You're a soppy old thing, Daisy Dobson.'

'Daisy Cooper,' she said, trying out her new name for the first time. 'Mrs Daisy Cooper.'

Rex beamed and pushed open the heavy wooden door, so they and their guests could spill out into the small churchyard.

'Are you ready for a photograph?' Daisy's father Jim asked.

Daisy made a face. 'I'm not sure I want one,' she said. 'It will just remind us who wasn't here.'

Jim put his arm around his daughter. 'I know you wanted your brother to be here.'

'I know it was impossible but it still feels odd, doing this without Archie. If we'd waited, then perhaps he would have been home on leave.' She screwed her face up. 'But I suppose if we'd waited, Rex would have gone.'

'I'm glad we did it today, even if it was a bit rushed,' Rex said. 'When the war's over, we'll have a big party and Archie can bore us all with his stories about army adventures, and Poppy can be a proper bridesmaid—'

'Thank you,' said Daisy's younger sister, who'd been furious there hadn't been enough time to get a new frock for her to wear.

'And perhaps my mother will have stopped crying by then,' Rex added in Daisy's ear. Sure enough, her new mother-in-law was sobbing into a lacy handkerchief. Daisy – who'd known Rex's parents for donkey's years – hoped it was just the emotion of the day that had caused her tears and not that she'd secretly been disliking Daisy all this time.

'And Louisa and Teddy can come,' Ivy said adjusting Daisy's veil around her face. 'And Bernie.'

Daisy grinned at the mention of her godmother. 'Louisa would have a hip flask in her handbag.'

'Almost certainly,' Ivy said. 'Now come on. Let's have a picture. You're only going to do this once, and it's important to remember it.'

In Rex's arms, smiling at the camera, Daisy thought she would never forget today. And yes, it wasn't perfect. She missed her brother, and she was wearing a dress that had once belonged to her mother, altered to fit and with the neckline changed, along with Rex's mother's veil. Her shoes pinched, and she wished Louisa was there to dispense an occasional tot of brandy along with sage advice about married life. But they'd been lucky to arrange this wedding so fast.

Her cheeks hurt from smiling and she focused on the feeling of Rex's arms around her shoulders, instead of dwelling on why Rex was so keen to tie the knot.

'I might not come home,' he'd said seriously. He'd finished his RAF training and was going to join Bomber Command as a navigator. Daisy was fiercely proud of him and absolutely terrified, at the same time. 'And if something happens—'

'Stop,' Daisy had said. 'Don't say it.'

But Rex had been firm. 'If something happens, I want you to be looked after.'

And so Daisy, thrilled at the thought of being Mrs Cooper, no matter what the circumstances, had agreed.

With only a handful of guests, they weren't having a party. Instead, Ivy and Rex's mother Margaret, had collected their coupons for butter and sugar and made a cake and some sandwiches, and they were all going back to Ivy's and Jim's little terraced house in Hackney.

Daisy and Rex didn't have a home of their own. Not yet. They would find somewhere together when the war was over and for now Daisy would stay with her parents and Poppy. She didn't mind really. It would be nice to have company while Rex was away.

With the photographs done, everyone piled into the Dobsons' house for tea and cake. Thankfully, the weather was bright and warm, so even though there wasn't much room in the house, people could spill out into the small but beautiful garden. Daisy wandered out outside and ran an appraising eye over the Anderson shelter she and her father had built at the bottom of the lawn. It was looking good, she thought. She knew all about Anderson shelters because she worked at the Home Office and spent all day every day sending out leaflets about how to construct them. Not that anyone used them. Her father had filled theirs with spades, forks and a few old tools.

Daisy sat on a deckchair, with a slice of cake on a plate on her knee and let the sun warm her face. She breathed in the scent of the flowers, many of which she'd planted because she enjoyed gardening just as much as her parents did and they were often too busy growing fruit and veg in their market garden to spend time on the roses and honeysuckle in their own backyard.

She had to remember this moment, Daisy told herself. Remember being here, with her family around her and Rex at her side, the bees buzzing around the flowers, and the sun shining. Right at that moment, everything was perfect.

'Having a good day?'

Daisy looked up to see her mother standing beside her chair. She beamed at her. 'The absolute best day,' she said. 'I've just been sitting here, trying to imprint it all onto my memory forever.'

Ivy sat down in the chair next to her. 'I like doing that too,' she said. She smiled at Daisy and Daisy thought how pretty her mother was. How the problems she'd endured over the years didn't show themselves on her face. 'Taking a moment to remember the good times.'

To her total surprise, Daisy suddenly felt close to tears. 'I'm scared this is the happiest I'll ever be,' she whispered.

Ivy took her hand and stroked it gently. 'None of us knows what's around the corner,' she said. 'But you're doing the right thing, living in the moment. We're lucky to have today.'

Daisy nodded. 'We are.' She looked over to where Rex was standing chatting to Jim and Poppy. 'I'm the luckiest girl in London. I just don't know what I'm going to do when he's away.'

Ivy slapped her hand to her forehead. 'That reminds me,' she said. 'I got this letter today.'

She jumped up from her deckchair and disappeared back into the house, re-emerging a second later clutching a white envelope. 'I've read it but I wanted to make sure I'd got it right. Can you have a look?'

'Course,' said Daisy. Her mother wasn't a confident reader or writer. She always said the letters wiggled about on the page. She didn't like people to know, and never admitted finding it hard, so she always asked Jim or Daisy to read letters for her.

Daisy took the envelope as Ivy sat down again.

'What is it?'

'Have a look.'

Daisy unfolded the letter. 'It's from Kew Gardens,' she said, impressed. She loved hearing her mother's stories about her time as a gardener in the last war, and her adventures as a Suffragette. She scanned the typewritten note.

'They're recruiting women to take over as gardeners,' she said in delight. 'And they want you to go back to work there. Oh, Ma, this is wonderful.'

But Ivy shook her head. 'I can't do it,' she said. 'I've got the market garden, and we're already growing more than we were. Plus Snow I've joined the Women's Voluntary Service I'll be kept busy with that. And there's Poppy to look after. I know she thinks she's proper grown-up already but she isn't. She still needs her ma keeping an eye on her—' She paused. 'Besides, you can't go back, can you?' She sounded thoughtful. 'Best to keep moving forward.'

Daisy was disappointed. 'So you're not going to do it, then?'

'Fraid not,' Ivy said. 'It's not for me. Not this time.' She gave Daisy a sideways glance. 'But I think you could do it.'

'Me?'

'Why not?'

'I'm not a gardener.'

'Nor was I, before I went to Kew. Anyway, you've grown up with a trowel in your hand and dirt under your fingernails. You probably know more than all the other gardeners put together.'

'I don't think so.' Daisy made a face and Ivy frowned.

'Give over, Daisy. You're always talking yourself down.'

Daisy rolled her eyes. 'Anyway, I've got a job.'

'A boring job.'

Daisy looked down at the letter she was still holding. 'Do you really think I could do it?'

'I know you could do it. I think you'd be a real asset to the gardens.' Ivy grinned at Daisy. 'And more than that, I think being out there, working in the borders or planting out seeds, will be good for you.'

She sat forward on the deckchair and looked straight at Daisy. 'Gardening's special like that, you see. Because you're always look-ing ahead so it makes the days whizz past.' She glanced over at Rex and Jim. 'That helps, when you're missing someone. Planning for next summer, or thinking about what you're going to do over winter, makes you understand that time is passing.'

Daisy gave her a small smile. 'What happened to living in the moment?'

'Live in the moment at Kew Gardens,' Ivy said.

'What about Kew Gardens?' Rex looked round at them and Daisy's heart lifted as her husband's eyes met hers.

'Ma's been asked to go back to work at Kew,' she said. Her father nodded, and Daisy realised he'd already read her mother's letter. She thought they'd probably discussed this already and that made her feel a bit prickly.

'I said Daisy should do it,' Ivy jumped in. 'She'd be great.'

Rex looked delighted. 'That's a brilliant idea. You love being out in the garden and you've got ever such green fingers.'

Daisy preened at his praise. 'Do you reckon?'

'I do.'

Jim nodded. 'Rex is right, Daisy. You've definitely got the knack. Why not give it a go, eh?'

Daisy bit her lip. She couldn't deny that the thought of being outdoors all day, getting her hands dirty, was appealing. It sounded much more her cup of tea than sitting in her gloomy office in Whitehall, stuffing Anderson shelter leaflets into envelopes. But she had a lot to live up to. Her parents had both worked at Kew. Her mother had obviously made an impression in the time she'd worked there, because they'd asked her to go back. What if Daisy wasn't good enough? She didn't want to let anyone down.

She took a breath and grinned at her parents and at Rex. 'I'll have a think about it,' she said. 'Right, who wants another drink? There are some bottles of beer in the kitchen.'

Chapter Three

Beth considered herself to be a calm person, generally, but right now she didn't feel that way.

'I'm afraid the answer's no,' her father said, pushing the form she'd given him back towards her and shaking his head. 'This isn't possible. I can't allow you to go to medical school.'

Beth had known deep down that he'd say no, but hearing the words so bluntly seemed unnecessarily cruel. Rage bubbled up inside her and she stared at her father through narrowed eyes and imagined clambering over his desk, grasping the lapels of his jacket – it was a good while since he'd worn a white coat to work – and shouting: 'This isn't fair!'

But, of course, she didn't do that. Instead, she clenched her fists behind her back and took a deep breath.

'I just don't understand,' she said, trying to keep her voice steady.

Her father took his glasses off and rubbed the bridge of his nose. 'Beth, darling, I know from bitter experience how hard it is to be a doctor. It's no life for a woman.'

Beth opened her mouth to argue but Dr Sanderson hadn't finished. 'It's exhausting and it can be brutal and upsetting and—' he gave a small laugh – 'rather cut-throat. It's a man's world.'

'But—'

'Lord knows, I had enough reservations about you becoming a nurse,' her father snapped, interrupting her again. 'Though I admit you have proved an asset to St Catherine's and we need all the nurses we can get at the moment. But you're twenty-one years old, Beth.'

'So?' Beth knew she sounded like a sulky schoolgirl, but she didn't care. 'It's not too late to train as a doctor. I've got a head start with my nursing experience, anyway, and if you look at the form, they've said—'

'That's not what I meant,' her father said. Beth could hear something that sounded like amusement in his tone and it made her even more annoyed. 'I meant it's time to start thinking about settling down. Have you discussed this with Paul?'

'No,' Beth said in disbelief. She didn't discuss anything with Paul. Most of the time she didn't have anything to say to him at all. Not that it seemed to bother him. He did more than enough talking for both of them. 'He's got nothing to do with this.'

Her father sighed. 'I think he'd disagree.'

'Daddy,' Beth said. Pleaded, in fact. 'Maybe I could leave the form with you and you can read it again?'

'No.' Dr Sanderson's voice boomed around his office and Beth jumped. 'No,' he said again, more quietly this time. 'This is my final word on the subject, Elizabeth.'

He put his glasses back on and picked up his pen and turned his attention to a document on his desk. 'Now, if you'll excuse me, I'm rather busy. There is a war on, if you hadn't noticed.'

Beth wanted to scream with frustration and fury. She was so angry she felt dizzy for a second and steadied herself on her father's desk as she picked up her application form. Dr Sanderson didn't look up. Beth's fingers touched something cold and she looked down to see her father's name badge. He hardly ever wore it now, because as director of the hospital, he was barely on the wards. And when he was, everyone knew who he was anyway. Without really thinking about what she was doing, Beth picked up the badge and dropped it into the pocket of her nurse's uniform.

15

'I'll see you at home,' her father said, his eyes still fixed on the papers in front of him. 'Close the door behind you, please.'

There it was again, that anger, spreading upwards from her belly, like the time she'd taken a huge gulp of hot chocolate when she'd been out carol singing one Christmas only to discover it was laced with brandy. Only then the heat had been welcome and comforting. Now it was burning with a ferocity that alarmed her.

She glared at the top of her father's head.

'This isn't over,' she said.

Her father signed his name with a flourish at the bottom of the page he'd been reading. 'The door, please Nurse Sanderson.'

Swallowing a growl of frustration, Beth turned and marched out of the office, letting the door slam shut behind her. She ignored her father's secretary, who was hammering away at her typewriter, pretending she hadn't been eavesdropping, and pushed her way into the hospital corridor. She looked down at the little upside-down watch she wore pinned to her uniform – a present from her mother when she'd qualified. At least one of her parents was proud of her. She had half an hour before she was due on the ward. Perhaps she should take a moment, calm down a bit before she came face to face with her patients.

She put her hand in the pocket of her dress and pulled out the name badge. *Dr Sanderson*, it said. Beth put her finger over the part underneath where it said *Director* and gazed at it.

'Dr Sanderson,' she said aloud. It sounded so much more 'her' than Staff Nurse Sanderson. Though she admitted she liked that too. 'Hello,' she whispered, 'I'm Dr Sanderson.'

Her anger had vanished now, replaced with wave after wave of self-pity. She wiped away a tear from her cheek and dropped the badge back into her pocket. Goodness, she had to get a grip before she went onto the ward. Her father's office was – of course – right at the top of the building. And at the end of the corridor was the door that led to the roof. Every night since war had been declared, teams of fire watchers had worked in shifts, making sure no bombs had fallen onto the hospital, putting patients in danger. So far, there had been no raids.

Suddenly longing for fresh air, Beth pushed the bar that opened the door and went out. She went up the metal stairs and onto the roof.

It was warm outside, and the sun was shining brightly. It made Beth blink and it took a second for her eyes to adjust from the gloomy corridor. She walked to the edge of the building – there was a metal fence so it was safe – and looked out over London. If she'd been feeling more cheerful, she'd have enjoyed admiring the view because she could see for miles, the river twisting its way through the buildings and glittering in the sunshine. But instead of gazing at the horizon, she took the name badge out of her pocket again and looked at it. How was it fair that her father had been allowed to train as a doctor? No, not just allowed. Encouraged. Lauded. And she was not. Just because she was a woman and that meant marrying and having babies and supporting her husband in his job. She thought about Paul and imagined sitting next to him every evening while he talked about his day and she made him a drink and told him he was wonderful. She groaned in horror at the thought, and the sound echoed around the rooftop and made her feel better. So she did it again, shouting her frustration out over the London skies.

'I want to be a doctor,' she screamed at the top of her voice. 'I want to be a doctor.'

'You too, huh?'

Shocked at being caught in such a personal moment, Beth whipped round to see a man standing there. He was, perhaps, ten or so years older than she was. Tall, with a slightly confused smile. He was wearing a white coat, his hair was cut very short, and his skin was dark.

'What are you doing?' she said abruptly, her surprise making her sound rude. 'Why are you up here?'

The man smiled properly this time. He had a dimple in his left cheek. 'I came to shout at the heavens,' he said. Beth couldn't place his accent. It was like nothing she'd heard before. 'But I guess I need to wait my turn.'

Amused and much less embarrassed than she'd been just a minute before, Beth stood back. 'Be my guest,' she said.

The man stepped forward, gripped the edge of the railing, and bellowed: 'I want to be a doctor!' so loudly that several pigeons were startled into swooping upwards from where they'd perched nearby.

'Better?' Beth said, watching him with interest.

'Much.'

The man sat down on the roof with his back to the railing. Beth knew she should go downstairs to the ward, and get ready to start her shift, but she was intrigued by this man with his strange accent.

'You're wearing a white coat,' she said, sitting down next to him. 'But you're not a doctor?'

'I work in the pharmacy.'

'You're a pharmacist?'

'No,' the man said through gritted teeth. 'I'm a doctor.'

'But you just said—'

The man sighed. 'Back home, in Jamaica,' he began. Beth nodded, understanding now where his accent was from. 'I am a cardiologist.'

'Nice,' Beth said. She had been doing a lot of reading about the heart recently. 'But here?'

'I am not allowed to see patients.'

'Why not?'

'Because,' the man said in exasperation, 'some of them don't like being treated by someone who looks like me. And one or two people complained. And now I have to work in the pharmacy instead.'

'Can't you go back to Jamaica?'

The man snorted. 'I wish,' he said. 'They asked me to come to London because of my knowledge of a new heart medication. So I came, and I shared my knowledge and then war was declared and now I'm stuck here because it's not safe to cross the Atlantic. So just because that nitwit Sanderson won't let me practise, my skills are being wasted at a time when I could really make myself useful.' He rubbed his head with the palm of his hand. 'Sorry, I'm being so rude,' he said. He held his hand out to Beth. 'Dr Gus Campbell.'

Beth shook his hand and smiled. 'Beth,' she said. 'Beth Sanderson.'

Dr Campbell's face dropped. 'Sanderson?' he breathed. 'Are you?'

'The nitwit's daughter? Yes.'

Dr Campbell jumped to his feet. 'I'm so sorry,' he said. 'Please accept my apologies for being so rude. I was just venting my frustrations. I didn't mean it.'

Beth held her hands out to him and got up too. 'Don't be sorry,' she said. 'Honestly, it's fine. I know what he's like.' She grinned. 'Why do you think I was up here?'

Dr Campbell smiled back at her. Beth liked the way his eyes crinkled up as he grinned. 'Because you want to be a doctor?'

'And who do you think is stopping me?'

'The nitwit?'

'The very same.' Beth laughed. Suddenly things didn't seem so bleak now she had someone who understood her predicament. 'I applied to medical school."

'That's good.'

Beth sighed. 'It is a first step. There are only a few universities that will accept women and those that do, require us to have permission from our fathers. My father won't give it.'

'Just like I need his permission to get back on the wards,' Dr Campbell said. He looked at her. 'What are you going to do?'

Beth threw her arms out. 'No idea,' she admitted. 'Keep nursing, keep reading medical books. Apply again next year and hope my father changes his mind? What about you, Dr Campbell? What are you going to do?'

'Call me Gus.'

'Gus.'

He grinned again. 'I've got an idea,' he said. He reached into the pocket of his white coat and pulled out a cutting from a newspaper. 'Kew Gardens,' he said.

Beth made a face. 'What about it?'

'They're forming a committee to research alternatives to medication,' Gus said, holding out the cutting. 'Drugs that can be produced in Britain rather than being brought in from overseas. It seems it's not just me that can't cross the Atlantic.'

Now Beth was interested. She took the article and scanned it. 'So they're recruiting people to join the committee? Botanists?'

'Not just botanists. Gus leaned over her shoulder and pointed further down the page. He smelled of soap. 'Doctors, too. Cardiologists.'

'Have you applied? You'd be so valuable as you've got a knowledge of pharmacy too.'

'This morning.'

'How wonderful.'

'You should apply as well.'

'I'm a nurse, not a doctor.' Beth frowned.

'Nurses have useful knowledge too,' Gus said, and Beth felt a little bit ashamed of herself. She nodded.

'That's true.'

'It would look good on next year's application to medical school,' Gus added.

'It would.' Beth smiled. 'And it would really annoy my father.'

Gus gave a loud bark of laughter. 'Keep the article,' he said. 'And let me know what you decide. You can come and find me in the pharmacy.'

'I will.' Beth tucked the piece of newspaper into her pocket next to the Dr Sanderson badge. 'Maybe I'll see you up here again. Next time you want to shout at the heavens.'

'Maybe,' said Gus.

Beth watched him walk across the roof and through the door that led back down into the hospital. And then, with her hand in her pocket, brushing the newspaper article he'd given her, she followed.

Chapter Four

Kent

Louisa was feeling unsettled. She'd woken up with a headache because she hadn't slept well and even a new jar of marmalade left on the doorstep by one of her WI friends hadn't lifted her mood at the breakfast table.

She kept fretting about her conversation with Christopher about him enlisting. More than once she'd thought about mentioning it to Teddy. Just casually. An off-hand comment that Christopher had said something and she'd assumed he'd talked to Teddy about it.

But no, Teddy wasn't stupid. He'd know at once that Louisa was fibbing because something as important as Christopher going to war would never be an afterthought. And now that their conversation was days ago and she hadn't brought it up, she felt even more like she was doing something wrong.

And yet.

She couldn't help thinking that Christopher should enlist, if he wanted to. Louisa had been a vigorous supporter of the Great War, at first. She'd been passionately patriotic and believed that everyone should do their bit for King and Country. But by the end of the war, she'd seen things differently, her pride in Britain tarnished a little.

This time, though, it wasn't just about being British. It was about putting a stop to Herr Hitler. Goodness knows, if Louisa could pick up a rifle herself and shoot him she would, so she couldn't blame Christopher for feeling the same.

And that was the rub, as they said. Because Louisa couldn't pick up a rifle and shoot Hitler, could she? Because she was an old woman. Old and useless and washed up. She was self-aware enough to know that was why she'd encouraged Christopher, and that just made her feel worse.

She sighed heavily. In the kitchen she could hear Teddy bustling about, making toast. The back door of the cottage was open and the morning sun was shining in through the windows. From where she sat on the patio, cup of tea by her hand, she could see her perfect lawn was shimmering shades of green and the borders were a riot of colour, attracting hundreds of bees and butterflies.

But she was still really rather grumpy.

She got up from the table and went into the house to pick up the newspaper, then sat back down again as Teddy appeared with the toast rack.

Louisa gestured for him to help himself to toast before her, then she opened the newspaper and shook it out, somewhat crossly, before she turned to the right page.

She stared again at the article at the top. She'd already read it twice. In fact, it was yesterday's newspaper and she'd read it twice then too, but there was no harm in scanning it once more.

'Something wrong?' Teddy asked mildly. His eyes were amused. Louisa glared at him across the small garden table.

'No,' she said.

There was a pause as Teddy spread some marmalade on his toast and frowned at the still-folded newspaper next to him on the table.

'Are you reading yesterday's paper?'

Louisa ignored him. 'Kew Gardens is re-opening,' she said with a sigh.

'Surely that's a good thing?'

'It is good.'

'But it's annoyed you because . . .?'

Louisa folded the newspaper in half and thrust it at him. 'Because they're recruiting women gardeners.'

In his slow, deliberate way, Teddy read the article, nodding at points and then – eventually – he looked up.

'Darling, I don't think that you—'

'I know,' Louisa wailed. 'I'm too old to be any use this time.'

Teddy reached out across the table and squeezed her hand. 'That's not true,' he said. 'You just have different skills this time.'

'I loved my time at Kew,' Louisa said, talking to herself, really, more than Teddy. 'Being part of something bigger than me. Doing my bit to keep the gardens blooming, while the men were off at the Front. Meeting Ivy and Bernie – and Win of course.'

There was a little moment as she and Teddy both thought fondly of Win, who'd passed away before war broke out. Thank goodness, Louisa thought. Win would have hated to know that the country was facing another conflict.

'But now I'm an old lady – far older than Win was last time – and they wouldn't want me anyway.' She screwed her face up. 'I would just love to feel needed again,' she said.

'You are needed, darling.'

Louisa scowled. 'To do the flowers in church.'

'You've been out of sorts since we saw those planes the other day,' Teddy said astutely.

'It's not the planes,' Louisa lied, because it was a bit. It was the planes, Christopher, Kew Gardens. The whole lot. 'I'm just feeling like an elderly woman with too much time on my hands and nothing to offer the war effort.' She groaned. 'I know I'm being foolish, but I just wish there was something I could do.'

'You could help me,' Teddy suggested, helping himself to more toast. 'This marmalade is excellent. I could really do with another pair of hands.'

'With your evacuees?' Teddy was responsible for the ragtag gaggle of children who'd turned up at the railway station in the early days of the war, looking frightened and out of place. As it turned out, dealing with the children's problems, questions, worries and fears, not to mention complaints or concerns from their new homes, as well as keeping track of every last one of them, had become almost a full-time job.

'Lots of them want to go home.'

'Is that safe?'

Teddy grimaced. 'I don't think so. Not after Dunkirk, and what's happening in France. I can't have those children on my conscience.'

Louisa had a wave of guilt so overwhelming that she had to close her eyes for a second. He was such a sweet man, her Teddy. Another war hadn't been easy for him to cope with, but he was working so hard for those children and there she was, trying to send his favourite nephew off to war. She took a mouthful of tea to hide her discomfort and then, with some effort, she smiled at him.

'I'd love to help you with the evacuees, darling,' she said. Perhaps helping Teddy would stop her feeling bad. And, for all she knew, Christopher had decided not to enlist after all. He didn't have to – as a farm worker, he wouldn't be called up. Maybe he'd changed his mind.

Louisa went along to the billeting office with Teddy that morning instead of spending time in the garden. She was glad of the distraction and, actually, she did quite enjoy it. She liked children and she had always been sad that she'd never had a child of her own. Her first husband, Reg, had been a violent man, who'd beaten her when she was pregnant and had caused her to lose her baby. Reg had eventually repented and written to say how sorry he was about the baby. And when he died shortly after the last war, his body ruined by years of drinking, Louisa had gone to his funeral to pay her respects. She had moved on, married Teddy who was worth a hundred of Reg, but the tiny bud of sadness inside about her lost child never left her. However, she had plenty of nieces and nephews who she adored, and Christopher of course, and she had Ivy and Jim and their children, and now she would have the evacuees.

'There's a lot of admin,' Teddy warned her, brandishing a pile of letters from mothers eager to have their children back with them. Louisa winced and Teddy grinned. 'You can choose between replying to all these, or dealing with these.' He picked up another pile of notes.

'What are those?' Louisa asked suspiciously.

'Complaints from billets.'

Louisa groaned. 'I'll do the complaints.'

With a broad smile and a visible show of relief, Teddy handed them over. And so, Louisa spent the morning cycling around the village, visiting the homes where the evacuees had been put up. She soothed frazzled nerves, comforted worried children, and came up with solutions to problems.

On her final visit, the evacuee – a little girl called Julia – was nowhere to be seen.

'She's not eating,' Mrs Stevenson, the lady of the house, said in a quiet voice. 'She's barely speaking. She's so tiny and quiet, and so very sad. She's missing her mother terribly and I really just want to be sure she's all right.'

'Where is she now?' Louisa said, thankful that the Stevensons had been the ones to take in Julia and not one of the boisterous farming families which might not have been so tolerant.

'In the garden. Shall we go and see her?'

'Please.'

Mrs Stevenson led Louisa round to the side of the house and into the pretty cottage garden. Louisa ran her eyes over the borders and the fruit trees approvingly, and nodded at the beehive.

'Bees?'

'Oh yes. I've had them for years.'

'I fancy getting myself a hive. I've always had a liking for bees.'

'I can help, if you're interested.'

Louisa nodded and the women carried on their chatter, pretending not to have noticed the little girl who was crouched down in a bare patch of earth at the side of the garden. She was digging with her bare hands and patting down the soil gently.

'Do you know who gave her those seeds she's planting?' Mrs Stevenson said softly, pretending to be showing Louisa one of the apple trees.

'Who?' Louisa was interested to know who'd encouraged this quiet child to push her hands into the soil, because it was exactly what she'd have done, if she'd thought of it first.

'Your Christopher,' said Mrs Stevenson.

'Oh how sweet.' Louisa was delighted and not surprised.

'I wasn't sure she'd want to do it, but it's the only thing she's shown any enthusiasm for.'

'Growing things is very healing.'

'I agree.' Mrs Stevenson smiled.

'If she likes being outdoors, then maybe we could get her growing some vegetables?' Louisa said thoughtfully. 'It might encourage her to eat? And she could help you with the honey. Not collecting it, obviously, but putting it in jars?'

Mrs Stevenson nodded. 'It's worth a try.' She looked over at the small girl and spoke more loudly. 'Julia?' she said. 'This is Mrs Armitage.'

The little girl looked at Louisa with wide eyes, but she didn't speak.

Louisa crouched down next to her. 'What have you planted?'

'Sunflowers.'

'When I lived in London I lived in a basement flat,' Louisa said. 'Do you know what that is?'

Julia gave her a disdainful look. 'Course. Downstairs.'

'I grew sunflowers in a pot and they grew so tall that their faces peeked through the railings and I could see them when I walked along the street.'

'In London?' Julia said. 'I never knew you could grow stuff in London.'

'It's much easier to plant seeds here, mind you,' said Louisa, kicking herself for mentioning London. 'Things grow beautifully in the countryside.' She touched the girl's back very gently. 'Would you like to plant some more things?'

'Like what?'

'Potatoes? Carrots?' said Louisa. 'Strawberries?'

Julia smiled. 'Food,' she said.

'And then you can eat it afterwards,' Louisa told her. 'Food that you've grown always tastes better than stuff you buy from a shop.'

'Does it?'

'It does.'

Mrs Stevenson cleared her throat. 'I need to collect some honey from the beehives,' she said. 'I wondered if you'd help me, Julia?'

'Will the bees sting me?'

'You can stay indoors while I take the honeycomb from the hive, so the bees won't bother you, and then we can get the honey out together.'

'Will the bees mind if we take their honey?'

'Not one bit,' Mrs Stevenson assured her.

Julia thought for a second, then she nodded, getting to her feet.

'And I'll bring you some more things to plant tomorrow, if you like,' Louisa said, thinking about the veg she had growing in her own garden that might take root if she moved them.

'Yes please,' the little girl said. She grinned suddenly, a gappy smile that made Louisa's heart twist in the hope that this sweet child was going to be all right. 'Fanks.'

With Julia and Mrs Stevenson happily heading towards the beehive, Louisa got back on her bicycle and pedalled home as fast as she could. Their discussion about how growing plants could be healing had reminded her of something, and she was eager to see if she could find it.

She whizzed round the corner and up the garden path, then she jumped off her bike and with her heart hammering against her ribs, somewhat alarmingly, she had to admit, she tried to catch her breath as she found yesterday's newspaper again. She leafed through the pages until she'd found the article about Kew Gardens and then she sank down into the armchair by the window to read it for the hundredth time.

And there it was, right at the end. A mention that a committee was being set up to research the medicinal uses of plants.

'Healing,' Louisa said to herself, feeling her heart rate return to normal, thank goodness, as she thought.

The Vegetable Drugs Committee would work on finding alternatives to imported medicine, Louisa read. And they would use plants and shrubs grown in the English countryside. They were hoping to get the people of Britain involved in growing and collecting the plants.

With a tiny smile on her face, Louisa looked out of the window at her garden. Then she got up, walked to the front of the cottage, and looked out at the hedgerows.

'Healing,' she said again.

Two women walking along the road waved to her as they past. She waved back. They were two friends from the WI. One of them stopped to admire Louisa's peonies and, watching her, Louisa smiled to herself, all the cogs in her brain spinning wildly.

She ran her finger along the bookshelf next to the fireplace until she found what she was looking for. A battered hardback book, with a peeling cover, called *Medicinal Plants of Great Britain*. She'd bought it at a church jumble sale for a ha'penny a few years ago, and hadn't so much as opened it. But now she was glad she had it. She sat back down again and opened the book. She had just had the most wonderful idea.

Chapter Five

St Pancras Station was full of men in uniform – a sea of khaki and blue. It was hot and smoky and noisy and Daisy thought it had to be absolutely the worst place in all of London to say a proper goodbye. She gripped Rex's hand tightly as they ducked through the crowds, not wanting to lose him in the throng. She still couldn't quite believe it was happening, that she was saying goodbye to Rex without any guarantee of when she would see him again. Or, indeed, if she would ever see him again. She suppressed a sob; she had to be brave for Rex. She didn't want him to know how scared she was.

Past the ticket office, Rex paused and turned to Daisy.

'That's me,' he said, nodding his head towards a group of airmen. He tried to smile and didn't quite manage. Daisy didn't even try. She just put her arm through Rex's, feeling the rough fabric of his uniform on her bare skin, and concentrated on taking in everything about him – the warmth of his body, the smell of his hair oil, the smoothness of his freshly shaved cheek against hers.

'I'm going to go,' Rex said into her ear. 'And when I go, I'm not going to look back because if I do, I won't be able to leave.'

'Then don't,' Daisy said fiercely. 'Don't leave. Stay here with me.'

Rex held her tightly. 'You know I can't.'

'I know, I know. You have to do your duty.'

'Well, yes. There's that,' said Rex, looking at her with a

mischievous glint in his eye. 'Plus that awful Frank Fletcher from school is over there and you know he'd never let me forget it if I tried to make a run for it. He's still going on about the time I missed an open goal in the second-form football tournament.'

Despite herself, Daisy giggled. 'Is he RAF?' she said. She'd been so proud of Rex when he'd enlisted in the air force. It hadn't been an easy selection process but they'd seen Rex's potential.

Rex made a face. 'He is. Mechanic.'

'Then you'll never see him,' Daisy reassured him. 'You'll be up in the clouds, far away from him.' The horror of goodbye hit her suddenly once more and she clutched Rex again. 'I can't bear it,' she said.

He kissed her gently. 'Me neither.'

'I'll write to you every day.'

'And I'll reply every day.'

They held on to one another for a few minutes and then the sound of a train's whistle reminded them where they were and slowly, reluctantly, they let go. Rex turned away slightly and Daisy could see his eyes were damp and he was dabbing them subtly. She did the same, then, with a huge effort, she turned to her husband with a dazzling smile.

'Goodbye, then, my darling,' she said.

'I'm glad we got married,' Rex said, putting his hat on his head and giving her a silly salute. 'Bloody glad.'

'Me too,' Daisy said. 'It was the best day of my life.'

Rex slung his knapsack onto his back and blew her a kiss. 'I love you, Mrs Cooper.'

'I love you too, Mr Cooper.'

He gave her the silly salute again, turned away and then he was gone, swallowed up by the crowds of men wearing identical blue uniforms.

Daisy watched for a few minutes, trying to pick out Rex, but she couldn't. He was just another airman now. Another one doing his bit. She felt the tears begin to fall again and, keeping her head

31

down so that no one would see her streaky make-up, she hurried through the station to catch the bus back to her office.

When Daisy told people that she worked at the Home Office, they always thought it sounded terribly important. But generally, she spent her days bundling up instruction leaflets for Anderson shelters and sending them out to local councils. Sometimes she had to answer the phone and write down how many leaflets a particular council needed. Sometimes, she had to count them into bundles. None of it was remotely interesting. Occasionally, she had to stand in for one of the typists, but that was tricky because Daisy's typing was slow and she made a lot of mistakes, so she found it stressful and boring at the same time. No one wanted to build an Anderson shelter in their garden, apart from her dad, so she didn't even feel like she was doing anything important. Not like Rex.

She pushed away the thought of him, trying not to wonder where he was or what he was doing, and concentrated on counting leaflets into envelopes. Occasionally, she stopped to admire the ring sparkling on her wedding finger. Because they'd got married in such a hurry, they'd not had an engagement, but she was so pleased to have a wedding ring. It had belonged to Rex's nan and Daisy had been touched when his mum had given it to her. She was ever so pleased to be Mrs Cooper. It made it all official – even though they didn't have a house of their own or anything like that yet. Rex had said that once the war was over and he came home, they could find somewhere in between Daisy's parents in Hackney and his family in Poplar. Though Daisy thought she'd really rather just stay in Hackney.

The day dragged but, eventually, the clock ticked round to five o'clock and Daisy could head home.

She let herself in wearily, feeling exhausted by the day.

'Daisy,' said her mother, appearing in the hall. 'Oh sweetheart, you look done in. Have a sit down and I'll put the kettle on.'

Daisy tried to smile but she burst into tears instead, and her mother pulled her into her arms. 'I know,' she soothed. 'I know, love.'

The awful thing was, Ivy did know. And somehow, thinking of her father off in the trenches and her mother waiting for news that he was safe, when they were both so young, made it worse. Daisy couldn't believe that after all the heartbreak her parents had been through, all the horrors and loss they'd faced, that it was happening again. So she let herself cry on her mother's shoulder for a minute, but then she pulled herself together. She was a grown woman, for heaven's sake. A married woman, no less. Thousands of other women were going through the same thing, just as her mother had.

'He's ever so clever, my Rex,' she said. 'He'll be right as rain.'

'Course he will,' Ivy said. 'Come and have a cuppa.'

'Where's Dad?' asked Daisy as they went into the kitchen and she sat down at the table.

Ivy made a face. 'ARP meeting.'

Daisy smiled. Her father had volunteered to be an Air Raid Precautions Warden as soon as war had broken out and he took it very seriously. She thought he was a bit disappointed that the injuries he'd got in the last war stopped him enlisting, and this was his way of making a difference.

'And Poppy?'

'Having dinner at her friend Lizzie's house,' said Ivy with a grin, filling the kettle and putting it on the stove. 'So it's just you and me for now.'

Daisy was pleased. She liked spending time with her mother, just the two of them. Not that they'd had much chance to do it lately, with Daisy busy with Rex and their wedding plans, and Ivy rushed off her feet with delivering fruit and veg all over East London.

'So he got off all right, did he?' Ivy said, putting a mug of tea in front of Daisy.

'St Pancras was full of soldiers and airmen. All those lads, Mum, going off to fight. And some of them will never come back.'

She felt close to tears again and swallowed, trying to be brave. 'I'm really going to miss him.'

'I know, love.' Ivy squeezed her hand. 'It's awful.'

'And it's all looking so bad,' Daisy said. 'Dunkirk, and then France surrendering.'

'We'll get through it, Daisy. We've done it before.'

Daisy nodded, but she wondered if this time it would be too much for tiny Britain? If France had fallen to the Nazis, then what was to say they wouldn't be next? She felt sick at the thought.

'I don't know if I can do it, Mum,' she whispered, looking down into her mug of tea. 'I don't think I can keep going with Rex away.'

'You can, sweetheart, because you have to.'

'You did it last time.'

'I did.' Ivy looked far away for a second. 'Because I had good friends and a job to keep me busy.'

Daisy knew what was coming. 'Are you thinking about Kew Gardens again?'

'Are you going to apply?'

'Oh Mum, I don't know. I'm not sure it's my thing.'

'It's a damn sight more your thing that sitting in an office all day,' said Ivy. She leaned over the table and looked at Daisy intently. 'When your dad was off last time, I got real comfort out of seeing things grow and bloom and die back in the winter, only to bloom again when the weather changed. It was . . .' She cast around for the word. 'Reassuring.'

'Reassuring?' Daisy repeated. She couldn't see how. 'Didn't it just remind you how long he'd been away?'

Ivy shrugged. 'Not really. Gardening's all about the future, isn't it? Planting seeds and waiting for them to grow.'

Daisy had never heard her mother be so philosophical before. She smiled. 'You really think it would help?'

'I do.'

34

'What if I'm no good at it?'

Ivy held out her hands, showing Daisy the callouses and ingrained dirt on her fingers from years of working in the soil. 'You're from gardening stock, sweetheart,' she said. 'There's no way you won't be any good.'

Chapter Six

Beth was so busy on the ward that she didn't have time to think about Dr Campbell, or the article he'd given her, until it was time to go home.

When, finally, she got on the bus, she reached into her pocket and pulled out the name badge she'd taken from her father's desk – she would have to find some way of returning it before he noticed it was missing – and the piece of paper. She smoothed the article out on her leg, as the bus trundled across Westminster Bridge, and read it more carefully this time.

Kew Gardens had been shut since the beginning of the war, but now it was reopening to visitors. They were recruiting women to take on roles as gardeners, replacing the men who'd enlisted, and also doctors and pharmacists to work on the committee which Dr Campbell – Gus – had mentioned.

Beth felt a little flicker of excitement. It was clear her father wouldn't give his permission for her university application this year. Just as he hadn't last year. Or, in fact, the year before. But maybe Gus was right. Maybe doing something like this for the war effort, and at a prestigious organisation like Kew Gardens, no less, would prove how serious she was to her father. And it might give her the edge over other applicants when it came to medical school, too.

She looked at it again. They weren't asking for nurses, that was a problem. Like she'd said to Gus, they wanted qualified doctors. Experienced pharmacists and cardiologists and anaesthetists. Experts in their field. People like Gus. She ignored the voice in her head that said 'men'. Men like Gus, not people, and not nurses. Perhaps, despite all the reasons to do it, it just wasn't worth applying.

Beth was confident in herself, sure of her abilities and determined to be a doctor, but the relentless fight to get to where she wanted to be had worn her down. She wasn't sure she had it in her to be rejected again. She thought about applying to this drugs committee at Kew, and being turned down and how that would make her feel, and shuddered. Perhaps she should just stick to nursing, read her medical textbooks in her spare time, and apply to university again next year. That sounded much less bruising than another failure.

She looked out of the window as the bus reached the top of Charing Cross Road and pushed the article safely into her pocket. She was almost at her stop so she rang the bell and jumped off at the back as the bus slowed down.

Beth lived in a large house in Bloomsbury, not far from the British Museum, with her parents and their housekeeper. They had wide stone steps leading to their big black front door with its heavy iron knocker, and from the back windows Beth could see the pointed roof of University College Hospital, where she hoped to train one day. Though in her darker moments, she thought she would prefer to go to Edinburgh or Manchester, where no one had heard of Dr Sanderson and where she would be accepted on her own terms.

She trudged up the steps to the front door, feeling weary all of a sudden, and let herself in. Perhaps she could have a bath, she thought. Her legs were aching after a busy day on the wards, and she was working again tomorrow. Yes, a bath and an early night sounded perfect. She took her jacket off and hung it up, and then – to her dismay – heard her mother calling her.

'Beth, darling? Is that you?'

'Hello,' she called, trying to sound cheerful.

'Come and see who's here.'

Beth looked at the stairs up to her bedroom and then at the door to the lounge, where her mother was, and thought about dashing up the stairs and hiding in her bedroom. But instead she plastered a smile on her face and pushed open the door.

There, on the sofa, was Paul.

'Hello, stranger,' he said pointedly. He put the glass he was holding onto the coffee table in front of him and stood up. He took Beth by the shoulders and kissed her chastely on the cheek. 'I've missed you.' Paul smelled of cigarette smoke from the tube, mingled with his aftershave and the whisky he'd been drinking and, for a small – disloyal – second, Beth thought of Gus and how he'd smelled as clean as a summer morning.

'Paul says you've been so busy at the hospital he's barely seen you,' Beth's mother said. She was sitting in an armchair by the window and also had a glass in her hand. Beth tried to keep smiling as Paul stood beside her, not touching her but somehow making his very presence next to her seem territorial.

'I find myself envying your patients,' he said.

Beth thought about the elderly gentleman who'd been admitted to her ward that morning, frightened and in pain after an operation on his kidney, and hid her face in Paul's shoulder so he wouldn't see her scowl.

'I'm here now,' she muttered.

'Paul's got some wonderful news,' Beth's mother said. 'Tell her, Paul. She'll be as delighted as I am.'

'Agatha, you're so sweet,' he said, making Beth's mother smile. 'I got the promotion, Betsy.'

Beth hated when he called her Betsy, her childhood nickname and a reminder that she and Paul had known each other forever, because their parents were friends.

Well, of course you did, she thought. She knew that Paul's father had friends in high places who would smooth his son's path to success. She smiled at him. 'Well done.' She wondered how it would be to be a man like Paul and go through life expecting things to go your way, because they always had and always would. 'What's your job title now, then?'

'Oh, I'm still a boring old civil servant,' he said modestly. 'Still heading off to the Ministry every day. I'm just a little bit more important now, that's all.' He gave her a sudden, genuine smile. 'I've got my own office now. It's got my name on the door.'

'That's great.' Beth put her hand in her pocket and felt her father's name badge. She wondered if she'd ever have her name on anything that wasn't a marriage certificate.

'It means Paul won't be called up,' her mother said. 'That must be such a relief.'

Until that moment, Beth hadn't admitted to herself that she was waiting for Paul to enlist. Now the possibility of him leaving London had gone, she felt – disappointed? That was awful. What kind of horrible person was she? Appalled at herself, because Paul really was a nice man and she was fond of him, she smiled broadly at him and gave him a quick hug. 'Such a relief,' she said. 'How marvellous.'

'I'm not ashamed to say I'm pleased,' Paul said. 'I don't think I'm really the military type.' A shadow crossed his face. 'Though I do feel a little bad. Our boys are off doing their thing, you know, and here's me skipping the action and staying safe behind a desk.'

'Absolute rubbish,' said Beth, her vehemence coming more from her horrible thoughts than any concern for Paul's state of mind. 'You're doing all sorts of important stuff at that desk.' She cast around for an example, and found she was worryingly vague about what Paul actually did at work. 'You're providing vitally important support to Mr Churchill. He's not fighting this war alone, you know.'

Paul looked extremely pleased. 'You're right,' he said.

'I was thinking that if Paul's here for the time being, you could spend lots more time together,' said Agatha.

'Absolutely,' Beth agreed. 'If I'm not too busy at the hospital.'

Agatha waved her hand as if dismissing all Beth's patients and the hospital itself. 'I know it's important to you, Betsy, but perhaps it's time to re-think this little nursing job of yours.'

Beth bit the inside of her cheek to stop herself glaring at her mother. 'They need me, Mother,' she said. She felt very sad suddenly, that the only person who'd supported her when she'd started nursing was suggesting she give it up for a man.

Paul – who could be very astute when he wanted to be – obviously saw her face drop. He put his arm round Beth's shoulders. 'I'm so proud of you, darling,' he said. 'And of course the patients need you. But don't forget we need you, too.'

Beth's mother, always incurably soft-hearted and who gobbled up romance novels at an impressive rate, clapped her hands with joy. 'Oh you two, you're perfect together,' she gushed.

'I can't argue with that, Agatha,' said Paul, looking at Beth fondly. She wanted to squirm away from his loving gaze but instead she just dropped her head so she wasn't looking directly at him. 'And now, I'm afraid I must go. Early start tomorrow after all.'

Beth smiled up at him, pleased he'd remembered that she was working the following day. But no, he hadn't been referring to her job.

'I've got a big meeting first thing – top secret, of course – and then I'm interviewing for my new secretary.'

'Busy, busy, busy,' said Beth.

'Perhaps we can have dinner on Friday night?' Paul said. 'Celebrate my promotion. Talk about the future. Make some plans.'

'That would be lovely,' said Beth's mother. 'Beth would love that.'

'I'm working a late shift,' Beth said. Paul's face fell and she felt guilty again. 'How about Saturday instead?'

'Perfect.' Paul picked up his hat. 'I'll book somewhere.'

He kissed Beth's cheek again and tipped his hat to Agatha. 'I'll see myself out, ladies.'

As soon as they heard the front door close, Agatha turned to Beth. 'I hear wedding bells,' she said, looking thrilled to bits.

Beth stifled a groan. 'Don't get ahead of yourself, Mother. Paul's got this new job and I'm busy at the hospital. I'm going to have a bath.'

Deflated by Beth's lack of enthusiasm, Agatha sat back against the sofa cushions. 'I'm right,' she called as Beth trudged up the stairs. 'You'll see.'

Beth went into her bedroom, where she took off her uniform and pulled on her dressing gown. Then, instead of filling the bath, she sat down at her desk and looked once more at the article Gus had given her.

She scanned the newspaper carefully for the right name. The director of Kew Gardens was called Sir Edward Horton. That would do. She nodded slowly as she took a sheet of writing paper and her pen from the drawer and, neatly, she began to write.

Dear Sir Edward, she wrote, *I'm writing to apply for a position on the Vegetable Drugs Committee at Kew Gardens . . .*

Chapter Seven

Louisa couldn't look at Teddy. She could feel the tension coming from him in waves. She wanted to reach out and take his hand but she thought he might pull away because he was nervous and irritable, and she couldn't bear that.

Christopher was leaving. It had all happened so fast. He'd enlisted in the army and here he was, just a couple of weeks later, going off to his basic training, along with two other men from the village. Well, they were boys really. Christopher was in his mid-twenties, but the other two were still in their teens and they looked like little children next to Christopher, who towered over them.

They were all stiff and uncomfortable in their unfamiliar uniforms as they stood on the station platform. The other two – Joe and Barney – were straight-backed and smart, but Christopher, in his usual way, managed to look scruffy despite his new short haircut. His jacket was slightly askew – just enough to make him look lopsided – and his trousers were too short because he was wearing the longest pair available but his legs were longer. Louisa looked at him and felt her heart break a little bit. What on earth had she done, encouraging him to join up? He belonged in the fields, his hands in the soil, not holding a rifle.

'Oh God,' she breathed. Beside her, Teddy glanced in her direction, but he didn't speak. His mouth was tightly shut and Louisa could see his lips were white.

'That's us, then,' said Christopher cheerfully, nodding down the track where there was a train heading their way. 'Uncle Teddy.'

Teddy took Christopher's outstretched hand and then pulled him close, hugging him tightly. Teddy wasn't a small man, but Christopher was much taller. It looked like an awkward embrace but Louisa could see there was a lot of love there. 'Just—' Teddy said.

Christopher nodded. 'I will,' he said. 'See you soon, yes?'

Teddy slapped his nephew on the back and turned away. Louisa knew he was hiding his tears. This is your fault, she thought to herself. And if Christopher dies, then that will be your fault too. She wondered if Teddy would ever find out and if he did, if he would ever forgive her, and thought with a deep and definite sadness that he probably wouldn't.

'Auntie Lou,' Christopher said, pulling Louisa into a hug. 'Look after Uncle Teddy for me, will you?'

Louisa nodded. She couldn't speak.

'Right, then.' Christopher picked up his knapsack upside down and Louisa caught it just before everything fell out.

'Christopher,' she mock-scolded, because she thought she was going to cry and she wanted to pretend she wasn't.

He took the bag from her, holding it in his arms like a wriggly toddler, and gave her a silly salute as the train pulled into the station.

Glad that talking was impossible over the noise of the engine, Louisa contented herself with giving him another hug. Teddy did the same, and then they both stood back as Christopher, Joe and Barney all boarded the train. Joe hung out of the window blowing kisses to a very pretty dark-haired girl who, Louisa assumed, was his girlfriend, while Barney called goodbyes to his enormous family who had crowded onto the platform. Christopher tried to open the window where he stood but couldn't manage it, so he just waved through the dirty glass as the train puffed away.

Louisa watched the train disappear into the distance, heading to London where gentle, clumsy Christopher would join the rest of the new recruits and be bundled off to learn how to kill.

'Everyone always expects more of him,' Teddy said suddenly. 'Because he's so big, you know? When he was a toddler, people thought he was already at school and tutted because he couldn't read.'

'I remember,' Louisa said softly. Christopher had only been young when she'd first met Teddy, and she knew what Teddy meant about people expecting too much.

'And then when he was at school, everyone thought he was some sort of thug,' Teddy went on. Louisa thought he wasn't really talking to her; he was sifting through his memories. It was like an elegy, she thought with a start. 'They tried to make him play rugby, remember that?'

'I do.' Louisa smiled. 'That wasn't really Christopher's thing, was it?'

Teddy gave a small nod. 'Not at all. He's such a gentle lad, Louisa. Always rescuing baby birds and looking after stray dogs.'

Louisa shuddered. 'I remember that summer when he carried a mouse around in his pocket.'

Teddy looked stricken and Louisa felt his pain piercing his own heart.

They were still on the station platform, though the other families had drifted away and they were the only ones left now. Teddy sat down on one of the wooden benches where passengers waited for their trains. He took his hat off and rubbed his head. He had very little hair now and he was self-conscious about it but Louisa rather liked it. She thought it made him look dignified. At the moment, though, with his face twisted with sadness, it just made him seem vulnerable. She sat down next to him and took his hand and, to her relief, he let her.

'I don't understand why Christopher didn't come to me,' Teddy said. 'Why he wouldn't talk to me about what he was planning to do.'

'I think perhaps he knew what you'd say.' Louisa chose her words carefully. 'You would have told him not to go.'

'Damn right I would have.' Teddy's anger flared for a second and Louisa winced. 'After what happened to Philip, I would have told him straight.'

'But Christopher isn't Philip and this wasn't your decision,' she pointed out. 'Christopher had to make his own mind up. Just as Philip did.'

Teddy's guilt that he had pushed his son to join up haunted him still. Louisa thought he would always carry it with him, despite the lives he'd saved by helping conscientious objectors during the last war, and all the good he'd done since. And despite the fact that he wasn't to blame. Louisa had never met Philip, but she had heard a lot about him and she suspected he'd have gone to war whatever his father had said. Or perhaps she was just telling herself that, because hadn't she done the same to Christopher?

'Why didn't he say anything?' Teddy said again. 'Simply announcing that he'd enlisted was so unlike Christopher. I can't believe he didn't mention it. Did he say anything to you, Louisa?'

He turned to her and Louisa felt trapped. She'd never lied to Teddy and she wasn't about to start now. She took a breath. 'He did,' she admitted.

Teddy's eyes widened. 'What did he say?'

'He asked what I would do in his position.'

Teddy's shoulders slumped. 'And what did you say?' he asked, though he looked very much like he already knew the answer.

'I told him I would go.'

She braced herself for anger from Teddy but instead he looked defeated. 'Of course you did,' he said. 'You and your zeal.' He spat the last word as though it were something to be ashamed of. 'You have no outlet for your passions and so you inflict them on everyone else.'

'Teddy . . .' Louisa protested, feeling this was awfully unfair, given that he'd been telling her just a few weeks ago that she

45

was fine as she was. But he didn't let her speak. Instead, he stood up, put his hat on, and turned and walked away without looking at her.

Louisa got to her feet and went after him to the gate that led from the platform out onto the road, but he had already got into his car and was starting the engine. They'd driven to the station together and she, naturally, had assumed they would return home together. But Teddy obviously didn't want to share the car with her. She raised her hand to wave as he pulled away. Teddy, though, kept his eyes fixed on the road ahead.

Louisa felt terrible. Her legs were wobbly and she felt close to crying. She hated arguing with Teddy, mostly because they didn't disagree often. But also because it stirred up memories of her first marriage to Reg, who'd been quick to anger and who drove his point home with his fists. Many years had gone by since then, but Louisa thought that just as the guilt Teddy felt about Philip would never leave him, the memories of Reg would never leave her.

But despite all this, she also knew that she had been honest about her own feelings and she was glad she'd told Teddy the truth. She would have to walk home, which was no bad thing. A stroll along the lanes back to the village would make her feel better, help her gather her thoughts and, hopefully, by the time she got back, Teddy would be less cross.

She set off towards home, feeling the sun on her face. It was another glorious day. The birds were singing and the sky was bright blue and the war seemed very far away.

As she walked, though, a shadow fell over the path ahead. She looked up to see four planes in formation, high up in the sky, blocking the sun. Perhaps the war was never far away. Not really. She thought of Christopher and wondered if he was scared. And she thought of Teddy, terrified that what happened to his only son would happen to the nephew he adored and she felt ashamed of herself. She should have told Christopher to speak to Teddy, she thought. She should have warned Teddy herself that Christopher was thinking of enlisting. Given them a chance to talk about it.

She felt tears in her eyes. She'd made such a mess of everything, and not for the first time. Her zeal, as Teddy had so rightly called it, had caused her problems before. It had upset friends and hurt people and still she hadn't learned her lesson.

She'd reached the village now. Up ahead she could see their cottage and Teddy's car parked outside. But Louisa couldn't face going home – not yet. Instead, she sat down on a bench next to the war memorial and thought with icy-cold certainty that there would soon be many more names etched in the stone there. She put her face in her hands and let herself cry quietly for a moment or two. And then she lifted her head and wiped her eyes with her handkerchief.

'You silly old woman,' she said aloud to herself. 'Put this right.'

The trouble was, she didn't know how to.

'Are you sad?'

Louisa turned to see the little evacuee – Julia – standing a little way from her. She was holding a small posy of wildflowers and she looked worried. 'You was crying.'

Never a fan of lying to children, Louisa chose to nod. 'I was,' she admitted. 'I did something wrong that hurt someone and I'm feeling bad about it.'

Julia came closer. 'Did you pinch someone?'

'No. I didn't talk to my husband about something important.'

The little girl frowned. 'You kept it secret?'

'In a way.'

'That's why you're sad?'

'Yes.'

'I don't think that's nothing to be sad about.' The child shrugged. 'Just say sorry.'

Louisa smiled at Julia's East End twang. It reminded her of her friend Ivy when she'd first met her. 'That's very good advice.'

She looked at the little girl more closely. She had colour in her cheeks now and looked much better than she had when Louisa had first met her. 'How are your vegetables doing?'

Julia grinned. 'They've grown a lot, and my sunflowers are as tall as my knees. Want to see?'

Louisa found that she did, very much, want to see. 'Yes please.'

She stood up and was touched when the little girl took her hand. 'Come on,' Julia said. 'Come and see.'

Louisa let her lead her along the road towards Mrs Stevenson's house. As she went she glanced over to her own cottage and saw, with a start, Teddy standing in the front garden watching her. She raised her hand and gave him a little wave with her fingers and to her relief, he nodded back. Perhaps all was not lost.

'Come and see,' Julia said again, tugging Louisa's hand.

In the garden, Mrs Stevenson had given Julia a small section all of her own. She'd planted carrots and lettuces – donated by Louisa from her own vegetable patch – and she had her sunflowers, and a little bunch of lavender.

'The bees like the smell,' Julia said as Louisa bent down to rub the leaves and enjoy the scent. 'The bees come and then they help the vegetables grow.' She smiled proudly. 'We've got a club.'

'What kind of club?' Louisa asked straightening up again.

'A gardening club. At school. There's me and Ginny, we're the main ones. And then Robert Reynolds comes too and sometimes his sister Lucy, but she's a bit whiney. And Ginny's dad said we can plant potatoes.' She took a breath and grinned at Louisa. 'I never grew nothing in London.'

'A gardening club,' Louisa said thoughtfully. 'How wonderful.'

'Ginny's dad said we can grow flowers too but I don't want to. I want the things we grow to be useful.' Julia puffed her chest out. 'Doing our bit for the war effort.'

The embers that had been smouldering in Louisa's brain since the day of the dogfight suddenly sparked into flames.

'A gardening club,' she said again, with more excitement this time. 'A gardening club, Julia.'

48

'Yes, a gardening club,' the little girl said, frowning as though Louisa was a little soft in the head.

Louisa gave Julia a hug. At first the child stayed stiff in her embrace but then she relaxed and hugged Louisa back. 'You're terribly clever, Julia,' Louisa said. 'A gardening club.'

Julia preened. 'No one's never called me clever before.'

'Well, you are extremely clever,' Louisa told her adamantly. 'And now I must go.'

She waved goodbye to the little girl, who'd already turned her attention back to her plants, and set off for home as fast as she could.

'Zeal,' she muttered under her breath as she went. 'I have found an outlet for my zeal.'

Chapter Eight

'There's a letter for you,' Matron said to Beth as she finished her handover at the end of her shift. 'I put it in your pigeonhole.'

'Thank you,' said Beth, trying not to sound too excited. Finally! She'd been waiting to hear from Kew Gardens for weeks and she'd almost given up. She'd put the address of the hospital on her letter of application partly because it looked more professional and mostly because she didn't want her parents to see any reply she might receive. She'd tell them when she was ready.

She hurried into the nurses' room and found the envelope. It had the Royal Botanic Gardens, Kew on the back flap. Beth ripped it open and pulled out the letter.

'Dear Miss Sanderson,' she read out aloud to herself. 'Thank you so much for your letter expressing an interest in the Vegetable Drugs Committee here at the Royal Botanic Gardens, Kew.' Impatiently, Beth shook out the paper, as though it would help her read faster. 'Blah, blah, blah . . . all the positions have been filled. However, we are recruiting gardeners and wondered if you would be interested?'

Gardeners? Beth snorted. At the end of the letter, a date was given for an interview for a gardener position and a request for her to reply with a photograph of herself. Beth rolled her eyes. She did not want to be a gardener. It wasn't Kew she was interested in as such, it was the drugs committee. Crossly she crumpled up the letter and dropped it into the waste-paper basket. She took off her apron and her cap and put them in her locker. She took out her handbag, trying to pretend she didn't care that all the positions had been filled. If that was even true.

She wondered if Gus – Dr Campbell – had heard about the role he'd applied for. She'd not seen him since their meeting on the roof. Once or twice she'd volunteered to go to the pharmacy for Matron, but each time she'd been disappointed to see that Gus wasn't there.

She wondered if he'd been offered a job as a gardener instead. Unlikely, she thought. Feeling a sudden rush of anger, she took the letter from the bin again and scrunched it up in her fist. She knew what she was going to do with it.

Replacing her handbag in her locker, she hurried out of the ward, along the corridors and up the stairs to the entrance to the roof. She was going to tear up this stupid letter and throw it over the railings and watch it drop like confetti onto the London rooftops. Kew Gardens could get stuffed, she thought.

She pushed open the door that led to the roof and ran up the stairs and outside. It was warm up there, because it caught the light. And there, lying in a patch of sun, outstretched on a low wall that surrounded an air vent, was Gus, with his eyes closed.

'Oh,' said Beth.

Gus opened his eyes. 'I like the sun,' he said. 'I miss the sun.'

Beth liked how he said what he was thinking. 'I'm not surprised,' she said. 'Though we're having a lovely summer, aren't we?'

Gus made a face. He sat up and put his feet on the ground. 'Lovely,' he said sounding as though it was anything but. 'Right.'

'I got my letter from Kew Gardens,' Beth blurted out.

'Me too.' Gus produced a pristine envelope – the same as the one Beth had found in her pigeonhole. 'I've been asked to join the committee. I'm working on the cardiology drugs.' He looked at her. 'Where's your letter?'

Slightly ashamed, Beth opened her fist and showed him the

scrunched-up ball that had once been her letter. 'They said no,' she explained. 'I was going to throw it away.'

Gus looked disappointed. 'That's a real shame.'

'It's good news for you, though,' Beth said. 'Is it full-time?'

'No, I'll be staying at the hospital too.'

Beth was pleased to hear it. 'Working at the pharmacy might seem less arduous if it's helping your work with the committee.'

'That's true.' Gus looked at her closely. 'Are you upset?'

Beth tested her feelings, then shook her head. 'I was at first,' she admitted. 'But I'm used to things not working out the way I planned.'

'But you were going to throw the letter off the roof?'

'I was cross because they asked if I wanted to be a gardener instead,' Beth said, feeling grumpy again just thinking about it. 'They've offered me an interview.'

Gus frowned. 'Show me.'

Beth handed him the crumpled letter. 'It's at the bottom.'

He scanned the page and Beth watched him. He was very nice to look at, she thought. He had beautiful cheekbones and his dark brows framed his eyes perfectly.

'You should do it,' he said, looking up at her and interrupting her admiration. She felt her cheeks flush as though she'd been caught doing something she shouldn't have been doing.

'What?'

'You should do it,' he said, handing her the letter. 'Take the job as the gardener.'

'Really?' said Beth, who'd never so much as planted a seed in her life.

'Why not? It would get you to Kew and I bet once you're in, you'd be better placed to get a role on the committee.'

'I'd have to get through the interview first.'

Gus shrugged. 'Clever woman like you, pretty, nice accent, hard working. It won't be hard.'

Beth was absurdly pleased that he'd called her clever. And

pretty. She tried to hide her smile. 'I've never done any gardening.'

'It says they'd train you. It would be useful to get some knowledge about plants.'

'I suppose.' Beth was doubtful. 'What if I make a fool of myself?'

'When I was asked to come to England and talk at the conference, I was very nervous,' Gus said. 'I'd never been this far from home before, and I was scared I wouldn't be good enough. And my mother said I could stay at the hospital in Kingston and never try anything new and that would be fine. But how awful would it be to always wonder how it would have been.'

'Wise woman,' Beth said. She gave a small smile. 'Bet she's regretting saying all that now you're stuck here, though.'

Gus put his head back and laughed loudly. 'You are right,' he said. 'But that's no reason for you not to go to this interview.'

'Maybe.'

'No maybe. Say yes. Go to the interview, see what the job is all about. It can't do any harm.'

Beth gazed at him in wonder. 'You're a doer,' she said. 'You don't wait for things to happen, you just get out there and do them.'

Gus made a face. 'I have only been in England for a year, but I learned very quickly that unless you speak up for yourself, you'll get nowhere.'

Beth thought about Paul's promotion and how his father had asked a friend to 'put in a good word', but she nodded anyway.

'All right,' she said. 'I'll go to the interview. But I'm still not convinced I'm a gardener.'

Gus slapped her on the back. 'Excellent,' he said. 'I think this is a good choice.'

'Perhaps,' Beth said. 'The thing is . . .'

Her words were drowned out by the scream of an aeroplane's engine as it came soaring from behind them, so low that Beth could see the pilot silhouetted in the cockpit and the colours on the wings and the tail that showed it was British. She let out a little shriek of shock and clutched Gus's arm.

Together they watched as the plane swooped overhead and headed east, following the river towards the docks. Another followed and another. It was so clear that they could see them for ages, long after the roar of their engines had faded away.

'Heavens,' said Beth. 'My heart's thumping. They gave me such a fright.'

'Me too,' Gus agreed. He took Beth's hand and put it to his chest. She could indeed feel his heart pounding away, the warmth of his skin under his shirt, the firm muscles and the suggestion of hairs beneath her fingers. Her own heart thumped again in response and she took her hand away.

'I should go,' she said, flustered. 'My shift is finished.'

'And mine is about to begin,' Gus said. 'But you'll go to the interview at Kew?'

'I will.'

They smiled at each other and Beth's heart hammered inside her chest again. 'I'll let you know how it goes,' she said.

Beth led the way down the stairs from the roof and out into the corridor. She stopped as her father emerged from his office at the same time.

'Hello, darling,' he said. 'Have you come to see me? I'm just dashing off to a meeting.'

'Oh.' Beth was disconcerted to see him, though she wasn't sure why. 'Erm, no. I was just—'

Gus came through the door from the roof behind her and her father frowned. 'Campbell,' he said.

'Dr Sanderson.'

'Have you been on the roof?' Beth's father asked. 'Together?'

Beth and Gus exchanged a glance. They'd not done anything wrong and yet Beth felt like she'd been hauled up in front of the headmaster. From Gus's expression he felt the same way, though he had assumed a more bullish air. 'Did you hear the planes, sir?' he said. 'Four of them there were, heading east. Spitfires. I heard the engines and went to have a look.'

Dr Sanderson nodded. 'I saw them,' he agreed. 'Impressive engineering.'

'And brave men flying them,' Gus said.

'Oh undoubtedly.'

'Many of my countrymen have enlisted,' Gus went on. 'Eager to serve.'

Dr Sanderson frowned. 'Good for them.'

'If you'll excuse me, I have to get back to the pharmacy,' Gus said. 'Good day to you both.'

He sauntered off down the corridor and Beth watched him go, marvelling at how polite he'd been while making his dislike of her father quite apparent.

It seemed the dislike was mutual. Her father was also watching Gus walk away, but he had a decidedly disdainful expression on his face.

'Everything all right?' Beth said sweetly.

Her father gave her a sharp look, then glanced at Gus's retreating back again.

'Everything's fine.' He checked his watch. 'I'll see you later,' he said. 'Will you be at home this evening?'

'I will,' said Beth. 'I have a letter to write.'

Chapter Nine

Daisy had been to Kew Gardens a hundred times before. She'd spent hours there as a child when her dad was still gardening at Kew, and even when he left to start the market garden business with Ivy, the family still visited often. She'd been there with her parents, and with her godmothers Louisa and Win, hearing about their escapades as young gardeners during the last war. It was almost as though Daisy had grown up on the lawns of the gardens. She had such fond memories of running around the grass with Archie, and then Poppy, of hiding among the trees and jumping out on her parents and giving them a fright. She remembered a snowy visit when she and Archie built a snowman bigger than they were and stole their father's hat to put on his head. And she remembered coming with Rex to wander hand in hand round the lake and watch the sunshine sparkling from the greenhouses like diamonds.

But even though she knew the gardens like the back of her hand, she was a nervous wreck when she and Ivy set off for her interview.

Daisy had devoted the last few days to brushing up her knowledge of plants. She would get home from work each evening, get changed and head out into the garden at the house or sometimes go and find her father at the market garden. She quizzed Jim and Ivy about Kew and made notes. Ivy was impatient but her father was a calm, engaging teacher. Daisy suspected he was drawing out his lessons to keep her busy. Because the war had finally begun in earnest, and to Daisy's utter horror, it was being fought in the skies.

Every day brought news of more attacks by the Luftwaffe on Britain's coastal defences, and every day Daisy ached with fear for Rex. They heard the planes screaming up the Thames, and Daisy had learned to tell which were German engines and which were RAF, just from the sound. She would look up and wonder if Rex was in one of the aircraft that swooped overhead. She knew he would be right in the heart of the action and she hated to think about it. So concentrating on learning about plants turned out to be exactly what she needed to take her mind off her worries.

Her parents had told her about the day her mother became a gardener at Kew and it sounded much less formal than now. She'd had a letter asking her to attend Kew Gardens on 9 August at 10 o'clock, and to send a photograph of herself with her reply. Ivy had raised an eyebrow at that, but Daisy had been photographed when she started at the Home Office, too. It was an easy way to keep track of employees, she thought. She'd had to ask for time off from bundling up Anderson shelter leaflets for her interview and, thankfully, it hadn't been a problem. She'd worried about what to wear and in the end she'd gone for a neat skirt and blouse. She hadn't been sure whether she should focus more on the interview aspect, or the gardening part. She hoped she wouldn't be asked to weed the herbaceous border in her stockings and skirt.

'I feel like I should have worn overalls,' she said to her mother as they walked through the large black iron gates into the gardens. They had to walk a little way to the building where Daisy's interview was going to be, but Ivy had said it would calm her nerves being in the gardens.

Her mother laughed. 'We wore long skirts when we first started. Later on we swapped to trousers, but imagine us digging the rose garden in our frocks. It seems very old-fashioned now.'

Daisy looped her arm through Ivy's. 'I'm so glad you came with me. I'm so nervous.'

'No need to be,' Ivy said with confidence. 'They'll be lucky to have you, mark my words.'

After a few gorgeous weeks of weather, the skies were heavy with rain clouds but Kew still looked beautiful. Ivy lifted her head, taking it all in as Daisy watched fondly.

'This is my favourite approach to the Palm House,' Ivy said. 'I love coming from the side, so you don't really see how wonderful it is until you're right there.'

They strolled along arm in arm and then the path curved round and there was the Palm House in all its glory, its panes of glass twinkling in the sun that had broken through the grey clouds.

'Oh my,' said Daisy. 'It never gets boring, does it?'

'Never.' Ivy stopped walking and gazed at the huge glasshouse. 'It's simply extraordinary.' She smiled at her daughter. 'You know, we weren't allowed to work in there at first?'

Daisy, who knew this because she'd heard it many times, shook her head. 'You weren't?'

'No, we women were only trusted with the borders for a long time.'

They carried on walking. 'Over there is the rock garden,' Ivy went on. 'Louisa and I hauled lots of the rocks into position. Our head gardener—'

'Mac,' said Daisy.

'Mac,' agreed Ivy. 'Mac was quite impressed we managed to pick the rocks up, I think.'

Daisy grinned at the thought of her mother and Louisa winning over the male gardeners.

'And that's the Orangery,' Ivy said, as they got closer to the buildings. 'And the winter garden just in front of it.'

Daisy felt a little flutter of excitement. It really would be something to work here and spend her days outside instead of at a desk. Following in her parents' footsteps seemed daunting but it also seemed like something she had been born to do. She clutched Ivy's arm. 'I really want this job,' she groaned. 'I hope I don't mess it up.'

Ivy gave her a kiss on her temple. 'Of course you won't. Ready?'

'As I'll ever be.'

Ivy didn't like offices much anyway, and she said the ones at Kew held some bad memories for her. So she stayed on a bench under a tree, while Daisy went inside. She gave her name to a woman at the reception desk and was shown to a corridor to wait. Her nerves were back and she sat on her hands to stop them trembling. She wasn't shy generally, not backwards in coming forwards, her mum always said. But she often doubted her own abilities and today felt important. She wasn't sure why.

Opposite her sat a woman, perhaps a few years younger than Daisy. She was very pretty, with shiny dark hair and well-polished shoes. And she was also, it seemed, wearing a nurse's uniform.

The woman caught Daisy's eye and looked down at herself. 'Is it really obvious?' she said. 'I had to come straight from work.'

Daisy was intrigued. 'You're a nurse?'

'I am.'

'But you want to be a gardener?'

'Sort of.' The woman smiled, making her look even prettier. 'I want to be a doctor.' She glanced around, but there was no one else there. She took in Daisy's bewildered expression. 'But I'm not sure wearing my uniform is the best way to prove my commitment to Kew.'

'Maybe we could do something with your collar?' Daisy said, looking at the woman carefully. 'If you could unbutton it, it would look different. Oh and try this—' She untied the narrow scarf that she'd been wearing round her head and showed it to the woman.

'Oh thank you,' the woman said. She had a nice voice. Refined and clear, with an undertone of laughter.

The woman unbuttoned the top fastening of her dress, opening out the collar.

Daisy nodded approvingly. She held out the scarf and the woman took it, looping it round her neck and tying it to one side. Suddenly she was transformed from a nurse in uniform to a stylish young lady. Daisy was rather envious.

'I'm Daisy,' she said.

'Beth,' said the other woman. 'Where's everyone else?'

Daisy shrugged. She'd been wondering that herself. Surely Kew needed more than two female gardeners? 'Perhaps we're the only interviews today?'

'Perhaps,' Beth said.

'I'm so nervous,' Daisy confessed suddenly. 'Look at my hands – they're so shaky.'

She held them out to show Beth how her fingers trembled and the other woman smiled at her.

'You're wearing a ring. Are you married?'

Daisy beamed. 'I am,' she said. 'Me and my Rex managed to tie the knot before he went away. He's in the RAF. He's a navigator.'

Beth looked impressed and Daisy brimmed with pride. 'Have you got a fella?' she asked.

'Paul,' Beth said. She looked a bit sad when she said it and Daisy felt a wave of sympathy for her.

'Has he gone?' she said. 'It's awful, isn't it? My brother's in the army, too. I just feel scared all the time.'

'Paul works at the War Office.' Daisy thought she looked uncomfortable suddenly, but she didn't understand why.

'Lucky you,' Daisy said. 'Having him here.'

'I am lucky,' Beth said in a mechanical tone. Daisy pursed her lips. She didn't look like she was pleased about it. Daisy would be over the moon if Rex was still here.

'Daisy Cooper and Elizabeth Sanderson?' An older woman stood by one of the heavy wooden doors that lined the corridors.

'That's us,' said Beth.

Daisy was pleased at the interruption because she'd been beginning to feel rather prickly. She caught Beth's eye and the other woman gave her a small supportive smile and stood up. Daisy returned the smile – perhaps slightly more forced – and did the same.

'This way please,' the woman said. They followed her along the corridor and she showed them into a room at the end, and then left without a word. Two men were standing together, studying a piece of paper. Neither of them looked up as the women entered.

'I think it's about four feet deep,' one man said. 'There, look. It says the dimensions right there. The hole needs to be seven feet, six inches long; six feet wide and four feet deep.'

The other man peered at the page and Daisy fought the urge to go and look over his shoulder. Those measurements sounded remarkably familiar to her.

'So there should be plenty of room?' the second man said.

'Undoubtedly.'

Daisy cleared her throat and the men looked up. 'Are you talking about Anderson shelters?' she said.

'We are,' the first man said. He was in his fifties with a thick, grey moustache and a Welsh accent. 'How did you know?'

'I send out those leaflets,' Daisy said with a chuckle. 'All day, every day, I'm putting them in envelopes. I know everything there is to know about those blooming things.'

The other man, a younger chap wearing overalls, laughed loudly. 'Well, I never,' he said. 'We want to create a sort of model allotment in the gardens so people can come and have a look and get some advice about what they can do in their own backyards. Huw here's worried there won't be enough room if we put in a shelter.'

'Oh there'll be plenty of room,' said Daisy. 'Because they're strong, see? You can pile earth on top of them – for extra protection really – but that means you can use it for planting.'

'How much earth?' the man in overalls asked.

'Three feet.'

He nodded. 'There you go, Huw. We can plant on top.'

Huw smiled. Daisy wondered if his moustache tickled his nose and made him want to sneeze. 'Go on, then, Will. You get your Anderson shelter.'

Will grinned at Daisy and then looked shocked. 'I'm so sorry,' he said, folding up the leaflet and stuffing it in his pocket. 'You must be the new recruits.'

Feeling a little off-balance, Daisy looked at Beth, who gave her a look that said 'Who knows?'

'I'm Daisy Cooper,' said Daisy.

'Elizabeth Sanderson,' said Beth. She stepped forward and held out her hand to Huw. He looked at her properly for the first time, then he shook her hand firmly and looked at the other man – Will – who nodded.

'You know about Anderson shelters?' he said to Daisy.

'I do.'

'And you, well—' He made a sort of sweeping gesture towards Beth which Daisy suspected was a way of saying how pretty she was without sounding lecherous, though why good looks were an asset for a gardener, she wasn't sure.

Huw went over to the table in the room, leafed through some papers and produced what Daisy recognised as her application letter, with the photograph they'd asked for, paper clipped to the top.

Huw looked down at the paper. 'And which one of you works in the family fruit and veg business?'

Daisy raised her hand. 'That's me.'

Will chuckled in delight and Huw leaned against the table with a triumphant look.

'It's perfect,' he said. 'They're perfect.'

Again Beth and Daisy looked at each other in confusion.

'For?' Daisy said. Her voice had a slight edge. She hadn't come here to teach men about Anderson shelters and watch them admiring her fellow recruit's pretty face.

'Oh Lord, I'm sorry, we just got carried away, didn't we, Will? And I forgot, you didn't have the foggiest what we were talking about.' Huw grinned at them, tickling his nose with his mous-tache again. 'You explain, Will.'

'For the Dig for Victory model allotment.'

Still none the wiser, both Daisy and Beth looked at him blankly.

'You've heard of the Dig for Victory campaign, of course?' said Will. The women both nodded and he smiled. 'We want to have a place in Kew where we can grow the perfect example of an allotment or back garden, growing enough fruit and vegetables to feed a family all year round. We want people to be able to come here for advice and ideas, to ask questions, get inspiration. And we want to give the campaign a bit of publicity too. We looked at the application forms and we thought you two stood out as the perfect pair to take charge of it.'

'Us?' said Daisy, overwhelmed by the idea.

'You're ideal,' Huw said. 'You've got the knowledge, and you're both young and strong and friendly. No one will be intimidated by you. You're approachable.'

'I can be quite intimidating when I want to be,' said Daisy but she was only joking, because she was really flattered by the offer.

'Won't it be a lot of work?' Beth said. She sounded nervous. 'For two of us?'

'That's the beauty of it,' Huw said. 'We want to show families what they can do themselves. What women can do. After all, lots of the menfolk are off and the women are fending for themselves. You girls will be an inspiration for them – we want you to be the faces of the Dig for Victory campaign. Getting stuck in. Getting your hands dirty. And doing it all with a smile on your pretty faces.'

Daisy was cross. Were they only here because they looked nice? She opened her mouth to argue but Beth jumped in.

'What sort of help will we have?' she asked.

'Will here will oversee it all, of course, but otherwise it's all down to you.'

'And it'll really be just the two of us, growing the allotment?'

'Like I said, that's the whole idea – to show families that they can do it all themselves. There are lots of mothers who need to feed their children. They might think they can't possibly do all the gardening themselves, but you'll show them they can.'

Daisy felt a tiny thrill. 'We'll be making a real difference.'

'Definitely,' said Huw. 'You'll be a role model to women all over Britain.'

A role model? Fancy that. Working on the allotment sounded like a lot of hard work, but that was, Daisy thought, exactly what she needed to keep her mind off Rex. And it would be very welcome after months sitting on her backside stuffing envelopes.

Daisy smiled. 'I accept.'

'Excellent,' said Huw. 'And how about you?'

He turned to Beth, who was looking very pale.

'I don't think I can do it.'

Daisy was oddly disappointed. She'd been imagining doing this as part of a team, with Beth by her side. 'Really?' she said. 'Why not?'

'Because I'm a nurse,' Beth said. 'I can't possibly grow food and work at the hospital. It just won't work. I thought I could do both things but it's obvious now that I can't. I'm sorry to have wasted your time.'

She picked up her bag and walked out the door, leaving Daisy staring after her.

Chapter Ten

Beth felt a bit light-headed. Why on earth had she come here? She didn't know the first thing about gardening. She'd been so caught up in Gus's idea that this could help her get to medical school that she'd applied without thinking. Then the beauty of the gardens and the buildings and the astonishing glass houses, and the kindness of the other woman – Daisy – with her flaming red hair and sweet smile, had been so overwhelming that she'd just gone along with everything.

She paused at the top of the stairs. This wasn't at all what she'd imagined when she'd written the letter asking for a role on the Vegetable Drugs Committee. She hadn't a clue about planting veg or allotments or any of it. Mind you, these men – Huw and Will – knew that. They had her letter, which spelled out her experience – or lack of it. Beth had seen it on the desk when she entered the room, so she knew they'd read it. And, for whatever reason, they didn't seem to mind. So who was she to argue? She looked out of the window at the huge, sprawling gardens and shivered in excitement. Or fear. She wasn't sure which. She imagined going back to the hospital and telling Gus she'd given up. Fallen at the first hurdle. She thought he'd be disappointed and she couldn't bear that idea.

Maybe she could do this, she thought. Maybe it could work.

Before she had a chance to talk herself out of it, she spun round on her heel and marched back to the office. Huw and Will were showing some paperwork to Daisy. They looked up as she entered and Daisy gave her a broad, beaming smile.

'I need to carry on working at the hospital,' Beth said. 'I can't stop nursing.'

'All right,' said Huw, straightening up. 'We can work around that. Perhaps you could do three days a week here? And fit your nursing shifts in too?'

Beth thought. She generally worked three days or nights at the hospital so that could work. 'I might need to be flexible with my days, depending on my night shifts.'

'That would be fine.'

There was a pause. Beth felt Daisy's eager eyes on her and worried she was going to end up regretting it. She nodded. 'I'll do it. But could we go and have a look at where the allotment's going to be?'

'Of course,' said Will. He seemed pleased that she'd asked. 'Is it all right to take them now, Huw?'

Huw nodded. 'Mrs Atkinson will get all your paperwork in the post to you,' he said. 'And you can start at the end of the month?'

Beth thought about the shifts she was due to work at the hospital and bit her lip, but Daisy squeezed her arm. 'We'll work it out,' she said in Beth's ear in a low voice.

Beth swallowed down the nerves she was feeling. 'Next month is fine,' she said.

Will took them down the wide staircase of the grand building and out of the door that led directly into the gardens. Beth caught her breath as she stood looking at the view. It spread out before her, as far as her eyes could see. The colours were startlingly bright despite the gloomy day – the vivid greens of the lawns and the trees, rosy pinks and reds in the borders, and yellows and oranges in the bushes. It was glorious. She breathed in deeply, appreciating the fresh air. Central London may only have been a few miles along the river, but it seemed very far away.

'One minute,' Daisy said. Beth watched as she dashed over to where an older woman with the same red hair as she had was sitting on a bench. The pair spoke, using identical hand gestures, and then with a cheerful wave, the older woman got up and wandered off towards where the Palm House could be seen in the distance.

'My mum,' Daisy said, coming back to where Beth and Will stood waiting. 'She worked here in the last war.'

Will looked impressed. 'I read that in your letter of application,' he said. 'And your father too?'

'S'right.' Daisy grinned. 'Gardening's in my bones.'

Beth swallowed, feeling out of her depth again. There was no garden at all at the house in Bloomsbury, though the people who lived on their square were allowed to use the green space in the centre of the street. Someone else tended that garden, though. Beth had seen an older man and a young lad sweeping leaves in the autumn and digging in the borders. For the first time, she wondered who they were and who employed them.

'This way,' Will said, reminding Beth where she was. He set off at a cracking pace and the women scurried along after him. As they walked, Daisy turned to Beth. 'What do you think?' she murmured.

'I think I may have bitten off more than I can chew,' Beth admitted.

'I'll help you. You're really going to keep nursing?'

'Definitely,' said Beth. 'I want to be a doctor.'

Daisy gave her a quizzical look. 'I don't see how Kew will help you with that.'

Briefly, Beth explained about the Vegetable Drugs Committee. 'I've a friend who's working on it. He said I should apply. He thought it would be good experience and maybe help when I apply to university next year.' She didn't add that she'd been applying for years now and this felt like her last chance. Instead, she gave Daisy a little smile. 'It was a good idea.'

Daisy shook her head. 'Except this isn't the committee?'

'They wrote back and asked if I'd be interested in gardening instead,' Beth said with a shrug. 'I was going to say no, but Gus talked me into it.'

'I thought he was called Paul.' Daisy looked confused and Beth's cheeks flamed.

'Gus is just a friend,' she said, embarrassed. 'He's a doctor. Paul's my, erm. Paul's working in the War Office.'

Beth winced inwardly as Daisy gave her a look that made her cheeks flush even more. Flustered, she changed the subject. 'I understand why they chose you to do the allotment,' she said. 'But why me? I've never grown a thing in my life.'

'You really don't know?'

Beth shrugged and Daisy laughed. 'You're beautiful, Beth.'

Beth stopped walking. 'Do you think that's why?'

She knew she was pretty enough. She got a lot of attention from men, and compliments from other women who often asked where she'd got her dress from, or how she curled her hair in a certain way. But as far as Beth was concerned, how she looked had absolutely nothing to do with who she was.

Daisy looked her up and down. 'They said they wanted people to be the face of the Dig for Victory campaign, didn't they?' she said. 'I reckon they wanted someone with your looks to look good in the photos.'

Beth felt deflated. She started walking again, following Will. Was it only her appearance that had bagged her this job?

'And, they must know how clever you are,' Daisy added. 'They would know from your application letter that you're a quick learner.'

'I am a quick learner,' said Beth feeling reassured. 'That's true. And I work hard. I'm very keen.'

'Look at this,' Daisy said as Will stopped walking. 'Oh heavens above. Just look at this.'

Will was standing in a spot next to the Orangery, spreading his arms out to show them this was the place.

'Here we are, girls,' he said. 'This space is all yours.'

Beth turned around slowly, taking it all in. It was an area the size of a largish backyard, and it was in a prime location. Everyone coming to visit Kew Gardens through the main gate would have to walk straight past.

'The Ministry of Agriculture wants us to create an allotment that will provide a family of five with year-round fruit and vegetables,' Will said.

Beth felt light-headed again. Where on earth would they begin?

But Daisy was grinning. 'I grew up in a family of five,' she said. 'And we only ever ate the fruit and veg my parents grew.'

'Really?' Beth breathed. 'Goodness.'

She was starting to feel intimidated by Daisy. She was so confident and knowledgeable. She thought about how she'd walked into that room and interrupted their conversation about Anderson shelters that way. And she'd understood straight away why Beth had been offered the job, while Beth had been clueless. And now she was already telling Will what they should plant.

'We should get lettuce in as soon as we can,' she was saying. 'Turnips and carrots, definitely. Maybe beetroot? Some runner beans, perhaps. And cabbage, of course.'

'Oh dear,' Beth said to herself. 'What have I got myself into here?' She didn't even know how to cook a carrot, let alone how to grow one. She had no idea how much food a family of five would eat. She was an only child, and often her parents were out for dinner in the evening, so she ate alone, or in the kitchen with their housekeeper, who was a lovely woman called Nessa and who, Beth suspected, felt sorry for her.

'Oh dear,' she said again. This was impossible. It had sounded so straightforward when Huw had worked out her shifts. But this was about more than fitting in Kew and the hospital. This was about Beth not being up to the job. She had been a star pupil at school and won every prize at prize-giving each year. She had got top marks in her exams. She was a good nurse and she knew she would be an even better doctor. But she wasn't sure she'd be a good gardener. And she didn't like the idea of not being the best at something. It made her feel unsettled.

Daisy was nodding and laughing at something Will had said.

'I'll leave you to have a look at it all and I'll be back in a while,' he said, raising his hand to say goodbye to Beth. She raised hers in response and gave him a weak wave. Then, when he was out of earshot, she turned to Daisy and gripped her arm.

'Daisy, I can't do this,' she said. 'Not even with the allowances they've made for me to carry on nursing. I'm just not a gardener. I think I'll go back to the office, make my apologies and go. They've recruited a whole bunch of women to be gardeners. I'm sure they'll easily find someone to replace me.'

She expected Daisy to roll her eyes and good-naturedly accompany her back to find Huw. But that didn't happen. Instead, Daisy looked at her in horror, then she sat down with a thump on the grass and started to cry.

Beth was aghast. But she'd been a nurse long enough to know how to deal with an upset patient or relative or even colleague. She sat down next to Daisy, pulled a handkerchief from her pocket and offered it to her.

'Thank you.' Daisy sniffed. She wiped her eyes. 'Oh look at me, what a goose I am.'

'What's the matter?' said Beth. 'Do you not want to work at Kew either?'

'Oh no, I do,' said Daisy. 'I really do. And I was so looking forward to doing this allotment with you. I was thinking we could have a laugh together and it would take my mind off Rex.'

She trailed off and Beth felt bad for her. She'd been so wrapped up in her own selfish worries and so busy envying Daisy's confidence that she hadn't, for one minute, thought she was fretting, too.

'You can tell me all about him, if you think it'll help,' Beth said. She used the straightforward, kindly tone she used at work. 'Sometimes it feels better to talk about things.'

Daisy wiped her nose with Beth's hanky. 'I bet you're a really good nurse,' she said. 'Good bedside manner.'

'Good vegetable-bedside manner,' joked Beth and found she was pleased when Daisy managed a small laugh.

'Our wedding was lovely,' Daisy said. 'We did it all in a rush because Rex had some leave.'

'But you said he's gone away now?' Beth asked cautiously.

Daisy nodded. 'I'm worried sick, obviously. And I know I'm not the only one in this boat, but it's hard not to think about it all the time, when the planes are going over the house, flying up the river – I'm always wondering if he's up there.'

'Heavens,' said Beth, with a shiver. She realised how lucky she was, having no one she loved off fighting, but hearing Daisy talk like this really brought it home.

'He's actually in Bomber Command,' said Daisy looking proud. 'So he's not in those planes. But that doesn't seem to stop me worrying. I know it's only a matter of time before he's sent off to do his bit. And then there's Archie – my brother. He's in North Africa. Can you imagine? I can't even picture it because I've got no idea what North Africa looks like. He draws us pictures on his letters because my mum – well, my mum likes the pictures. And he drew a camel. I thought it would be lions and monkeys.'

Beth was quite touched that Daisy was telling her so much. She must have needed a shoulder to cry on.

'I can't imagine how hard it is having two people you love away fighting,' she said.

Daisy looked at her. 'No, because your Paul is still in London,' she said sharply and Beth, who'd been leaning forward with concern, felt wounded. She drew back and Daisy pulled a face.

'Gosh, I'm sorry. It's not your fault.'

Beth was sympathetic. 'I'm not surprised you want a bit of distraction.'

'My mum worked at Kew, you know? During the last war.'

'You said. That's wonderful. Is that why you applied for the job?'

'Mum suggested it. She said growing plants helped her think about the future, while she waited for my dad to come home.'

'And he came home,' Beth said with confidence, because hadn't Daisy mentioned both her parents before?

'He did.' Daisy smiled properly this time. 'He was injured but he came home safe and sound, just before I was born.'

'That's a good sign, I reckon,' said Beth.

Daisy bit her lip, but she nodded and Beth felt relieved. She liked this woman with her freckles and her wide smile and her confidence.

'So will you stay?' Daisy asked.

'Stay?'

'Here at Kew? Will you stay and work on the allotment with me?'

Beth looked around at the space they were going to be expected to fill with vegetables and fruit and scratched her nose. 'I have no idea what to do.'

'It'll be fine,' said Daisy. 'Mum and Dad will help. They know everything about growing veg.' She nudged Beth. 'They can do all the work and we'll take the credit.'

Beth laughed. She felt a little kernel of warmth – a little seed of friendship – take root inside her. She didn't have many friends. She'd found the social side of school quite difficult and she preferred her own company most of the time. And she had no siblings. She just had Paul, who she always felt she had to be a certain way with. But now she had Daisy. She nodded, quite slowly, but deliberately. 'I'll stay,' she said.

Daisy looked absolutely thrilled. She threw her arms round Beth and squeezed her, and Beth let her. 'We're going to have the best time,' said Daisy. 'I can't tell you how pleased I am to see the back of those blooming Anderson shelter leaflets.'

'I'm nervous about it,' Beth admitted.

Daisy clapped her hands. 'It's fine,' she said. Beth wished she had her new friend's conviction that they would make a success of this. 'Are you working this evening?'

'No,' said Beth, who was looking forward to an early night with her textbooks.

'Then why don't you come back with me and Mum to Hackney? We can have our tea together, and I'll show you the market garden and we can have a chat with Mum and Dad about the allotment.'

Beth was absurdly pleased to be asked. 'Won't your mum mind?'

'Course not.'

'That would be nice.' Beth grinned.

'It's a bit of a trek from here, mind you. Where do you live?'

'Bloomsbury,' said Beth and then felt embarrassed when Daisy raised an eyebrow, impressed. 'Should we go and find Will before we go?' she said hurriedly.

Daisy got up from the grass and brushed off her skirt, and Beth did the same. They both stood for a second, looking at the patch of bare earth.

'This is going to be the best model allotment Kew Gardens has ever had,' said Daisy.

'I think it's going to be the only model allotment they've ever had,' Beth pointed out with a smile.

'Oh shush.' Daisy linked her arm through Beth's. 'It's going to be perfect.'

Chapter Eleven

Ivy had gone home after Daisy had finished the interview. Daisy could tell her mother was itching to come and see the allotment with them but she'd gently encouraged Daisy to go with Beth on her own. Daisy thought that was very clever of Ivy. She always knew when to hold Daisy's hand – metaphorically speaking – and when to let her go it alone. Even though Daisy was now a married woman, she was always grateful for her mum being by her side.

'I need to pop in to see Marge at the WVS,' Ivy had said. She'd joined the voluntary service early in the war and, predictably, had thrown herself into providing support for the ARP wardens and firefighters, and all the other people doing their bit. 'I'll jump on the tube now and see you back at home.'

She'd given Daisy a kiss. 'I'm proud of you,' she'd said and Daisy had beamed. She was proud of herself. Apart from that little wobble when Beth had said she was going to pull out, she'd done it. She'd got the job and she was already thinking about what they could do with the allotment. And, best of all, she'd made a new friend.

Though, if she was completely honest, Daisy was already regretting inviting Beth back to hers. She was so nicely spoken, and her skirt wasn't faded and patched like Daisy's was. Her shoes weren't worn down, and her handbag wasn't scuffed. Suddenly Daisy saw her life through different eyes and she felt a little bit embarrassed.

Her parents weren't poor. Not at all. They were just – normal. They worked hard and they put food on the table. Daisy knew that was something to be proud of and she felt guilty for worrying what Beth would think of them. But still. Beth was from Bloomsbury. Daisy wondered if she lived in one of those big houses with the black railings and the huge front doors. Mind you, they'd probably taken the railings now to melt down for munitions, she thought. War seemed to be a leveller of sorts.

'You're quiet,' Beth said as they sat together on the tube, rattling east through the tunnels. 'Are you all right?'

Daisy smiled. 'I'm fine.' She was fine, really. She was just being silly. She was relieved that Beth had agreed to work with her on the allotment because she liked her and she knew that Beth's good looks and nice accent were an asset. From what Will said, the bosses at Kew and the Ministry of Agriculture wanted the model allotment to attract a lot of attention. Daisy's work on the Anderson shelters meant that she knew how important information was to the war effort so she understood that they wanted this to work, so she had a sneaking suspicion that her knowledge of gardening wasn't as important to them as Beth's appearance. Still, Daisy wasn't afraid of hard work and, goodness knew, she needed the distraction.

As they approached Mile End, Daisy picked up her bag. 'This is us,' she said. 'It's a bit of a walk from here, but it's the easiest way home, just sitting on one tube the whole time.'

'I like watching all the people,' Beth said. 'Wondering about their lives.'

'Me too,' said Daisy as the doors opened and she steered Beth towards the exit. She didn't say that she looked at all the women, wondering if their husbands or sweethearts or little brothers were off fighting; if they spent most of every day and night worrying that they'd never see them again. And how knowing that they probably were, and they probably did, made her feel less alone.

They walked away from the station, along the main road towards Hackney, chatting about everything and nothing – about Huw's moustache and Will's enthusiasm for the allotment, and about Daisy's parents meeting at Kew.

Daisy shot a glance at Beth every now and then. She seemed to glow against the dreary grey of the terraced houses they were walking past. She was so – shiny. She shone with health and wealth and contentment. Daisy couldn't really imagine her wearing gardening overalls and clogs. Perhaps this was going to be a disaster? Perhaps Beth wouldn't get stuck in? She sneaked another look at her. She was wearing gloves, for goodness' sake. Gloves! Maybe Beth would be too la-di-da to get her hands dirty, and Daisy would be left doing all the graft.

'And so I told Matron where I was going, and I think she'll be all right with it all. Huw didn't seem to think it would be a problem,' Beth was saying. Daisy blinked. The way Beth talked about the hospital it sounded like she was a real nurse. Daisy had sort of assumed she just helped out. Maybe she was one of those nice women who went to read to the patients and serve them tea?

'We're just along here,' she said, showing Beth the turn-off to her road. 'About halfway along.'

As they got closer to home, Daisy could see a group of boys racing up and down the street on their bicycles. She turned to Beth. 'Don't seem like five minutes since that was me and my brother and sister,' she said.

'I used to pretend I had a brother and sister,' Beth admitted, looking slightly embarrassed. 'I'd set up a game of cards around the table and play all the hands. I'd move from chair to chair.'

'That's so sad,' Daisy said. 'I'm not sure whether to laugh or cry.'

'Laugh,' said Beth. 'I was a very odd child.'

Daisy did laugh. 'It was a good use of your imagination – oh!'

She gasped as one of the boys up ahead hit a hole in the road and flew off his bike, over the handlebars. He landed hard and lay, horribly still, on the road.

Daisy clutched Beth's arm. 'Oh my goodness,' she said.

Beth dropped her bag and before Daisy had even realised she was gone, she ran to the boy who was now roaring with pain. Daisy picked up her new friend's bag and raced after her to where the lad lay on the ground. His arm was at a very strange angle and his face was grey. His friends gathered around him.

'Stand back,' Beth said sternly to the other boys, who all obeyed immediately. 'What's his name?'

'Mickey,' one of the boys – Daisy thought his name was Walter – told Beth breathlessly.

Daisy turned to the lad who'd spoken. 'Walter, can you get his mum?'

Walter ran off to Mickey's house and Daisy watched nervously as Beth bent down to the injured lad. 'Mickey,' she said gently, 'Don't try to move. I'm just going to check you over. Make sure you've not damaged anything." She ran her hands over his neck and shoulders, and he winced. Beth nodded. Then she checked both legs, asked him to wiggle his toes, and looked in his eyes. 'Did you bang your head?'

'Nah,' said Mickey. 'Just my arm.'

'Do you think you can sit up?'

Mickey struggled and Daisy crouched down on his other side and helped support him.

Beth turned to one of the other boys and barked some orders. 'I need bandages, and something to make a splint from. A rolled-up newspaper would do. And some water and a cloth to clean his wounds.'

With Mickey leaning against Beth, Daisy stood up, feeling a bit like a spare part. She picked up the bicycle and put it on the pavement, leaning it up against a garden wall.

The boys were coming back with all the things Beth had asked for, followed by several women, including Mickey's mum, Dawn, who was looking worried.

'What's happened?' she said.

'Mickey fell off his bike. I think he's broken his arm. But Beth's looking after him. She's a nurse,' Daisy explained, feeling quite proud that Beth was her friend.

'It hurts,' Mickey said. Dawn bent down next to him and talked to him quietly as Beth bathed his grazes and bandaged his arm swiftly. Daisy watched, impressed by her skills.

'I think he'll be all right,' Beth said to his mum. 'But he needs that arm looked at properly. It might need to be re-set and plastered.'

'A plaster cast? Wizard,' said Mickey, trying to force a smile. 'It doesn't half hurt now though.' He swayed as Dawn helped him to his feet. And then, while Daisy watched in horror, he turned green and vomited, all down Beth's skirt.

Beth, to her credit and to Daisy's amazement, didn't even flinch. She just rubbed the lad's hair gently. 'Poor you,' she said. 'You must be feeling grotty. Into bed, I think, and wait for the doctor.'

Dawn thanked Beth and said sorry for her skirt, and Beth waved off the apology.

'Do you think I could borrow something of yours to wear?' she asked Daisy quietly as they went up the path to Daisy's house. 'I can't meet your parents covered in sick.'

An hour earlier, Daisy would have worried that Beth wouldn't want to wear one of her frocks, but now she thought she wouldn't mind one bit. She grinned at Beth. 'Course you can,' she said. 'What with that and my scarf, you'll have my whole wardrobe soon enough. Come round the back and we'll get you cleaned up in the kitchen.'

With a few buckets of water, a borrowed dress, and a lot of soap, Beth was soon presentable again. Ivy, Jim and Daisy's younger sister Poppy all thought it was hilarious that Mickey had vomited on poor Beth – much to Daisy's despair.

'You helped him and he was sick?' Poppy said, giggling, as they all sat at the table to eat the food Ivy was dishing up. She'd not been at all fazed at having to feed another person – as Daisy had expected. She'd simply added more carrots to the pot and stuck another potato into the mash.

Daisy scowled at her sister. 'Don't you have any homework to do?'

'It's the summer holidays, birdbrain.'

'Girls,' said Ivy mildly. 'We've got a guest. Be polite.'

'I didn't mind, really. I'm used to being covered in all sorts at work.'

'Beth's a nurse,' Daisy said. 'A real one.'

Beth gave her an odd look and Daisy felt embarrassed. 'I thought you might have just been helping out,' she admitted. 'Doing your bit for the war effort, you know?'

'It's a good job,' Ivy said. 'What made you want to be a nurse?'

Beth dug her fork into her mashed potato and grinned at Ivy. 'I don't really want to be a nurse,' she said. 'I want to be a doctor. That's why I've applied for the job at Kew.'

Ivy looked astonished. 'A doctor? How will working at Kew help you there?'

Beth sighed. 'My father is a doctor. And my grandfather. Medicine is in my blood.'

'My grandfather sold flowers at Columbia Road market,' Daisy said, looking at her mother, who nodded and rolled her eyes because Daisy's grandfather had been too fond of drink. 'Gardening's in mine.'

'Ah but there's a difference, do you see?' Beth said, looking sad as she glanced from Daisy to Ivy and Jim. 'Because your parents encouraged you to follow in their footsteps. Mine tried to stop me.'

'Stop you?' Daisy couldn't imagine having parents who weren't supportive.

'My father wouldn't approve my application to university. He said medical school wasn't suitable for women.'

Ivy snorted and Daisy hid a smile. Her mother did not like hearing about what women couldn't do.

'He said women are more caring and nurturing, while men are clinical,' Beth said. Daisy felt she wasn't really talking to them anymore. Beth was somewhere else in her mind, looking out of the kitchen window as she remembered. 'So I said that he was very clever to point that out, and that he'd made me realise I had to find something to do that played to my strengths. My caring skills—' Beth paused. 'I told him I was going to become a nurse.'

'And what did he say?'

Beth gave the ghost of a smile. 'What could he say? I told him it was all his idea. He wasn't keen, but he couldn't argue.'

'Good for you,' said Ivy.

Beth looked at her and smiled. 'My mother is on my side. More so than my father, at least. She was really proud of me when I qualified as a nurse. I think she wishes she'd done more, last time—' she looked up at the ceiling – 'but now she wants me to settle down. I think they would have made me stop nursing if the war hadn't come along.'

'War changes things,' Ivy said.

Beth nodded. 'I've not given up, though. I've applied three times now and I'm going to apply again. I thought working at Kew would prove how committed I am to being a doctor one day.'

Daisy didn't doubt it for one minute. She felt a bit uncomfortable, as though she'd misjudged Beth.

Ivy was frowning. 'I still don't understand why Kew will help?'

'I applied to work on the committee studying medicinal plants. I've a friend who's working there. But they asked me to be a gardener instead. I'm still going to try to get onto the committee, though.'

There was a small, slightly stunned silence around the table as Daisy and her family all stared at Beth.

'So you're nursing, you're working on this model allotment with

Daisy, and you're going to try and get involved with this plants committee?' said Ivy.

Beth nodded. 'That's right. Do you think I'm being silly?'

Daisy exchanged a look with her mother and raised an eyebrow. Ivy smiled.

'I think,' she said, 'that you're the perfect addition to Kew Gardens.'

Chapter Twelve

Daisy wrote to Rex every day. Sometimes she wrote twice a day. She was so used to seeing him all the time, of being able to fill him in on every little detail of her day – and hearing about his, too – that not being able to share her thoughts was strange. So she wrote down all her worries about starting at Kew instead, and poured out her heart about how much she missed him. She knew Rex was busy. Bomber Command were right in the thick of the fighting now, giving support to the planes that were defending Britain from Hitler. Daisy would stop whenever she heard engines overhead, looking up to the skies and wondering if Rex was high above her and if he was all right. She knew all the planes now – she could recognise Spitfires and Hurricanes, or the larger Bristol Blenheims, which she knew Rex flew in, from their silhouettes against the clouds. Rex wrote back, of course, but it wasn't the same as being able to chat to him.

Some days she felt fine; she could distract herself with thinking about Kew and making plans. On other days she felt like she was in a dark tunnel of despair. She would spend hours reading the casualty lists in the newspapers and tormenting herself about the horrors Rex was experiencing. One day she felt so bleak that she could barely drag herself out of bed. She fibbed that she had a headache and spent the day huddled under the blankets in a fog of sadness.

But Kew was helping, already. Even though she had a week or so before her job at the Home Office ended and she started at the gardens, just knowing she had work to do was giving her something to get up for. It was a focus for her mind, and it helped to take away the dark thoughts or make them recede a little, at least.

She threw herself into planning for the allotment. She drew little diagrams of the garden, and thought about the best place to plant each vegetable. She wrote out a calendar and spent hours considering which crop to plant and when. Ivy and Jim were busy all the time, but they kept sticking their heads round the kitchen door when Daisy was working at the table, surrounded by bits of paper, and saying things like 'What about peas on a trellis?' or 'Is there space for a tree?'

When Daisy was done and she had a bundle of notes, her sister Poppy – who, like Archie and their mother, was a beautiful artist – swooped in and took all the bits of paper, all the drawings, and gathered them together. She tied the pages up with ribbon, put cardboard covers on the front and back, and drew the loveliest picture of a vegetable patch on the front. Daisy was quite touched when she presented it back to her.

'It's been a real family affair,' she wrote to Rex. 'I am so pleased I listened to Mum when she suggested I get a job at Kew. I feel part of something at last.'

And then, finally, it was her first day at Kew. And instead of getting dressed for work at the Home Office in a smart skirt and blouse, Daisy tied her hair up in a scarf, put on her overalls and set off across London, feeling a strange mix of nerves and excitement in her stomach.

Beth was waiting by the gardeners' break room when Daisy arrived, wearing the same overalls as Daisy and looking terribly nervous.

'I have no idea where to start,' she said, before Daisy had even said hello. 'Is this going to be a disaster?'

'Chin up, Beth,' said Daisy cheerfully, pulling her notes out of her bag. 'I've got it covered.'

The first few days passed in a blur. Beth and Daisy were so busy, they barely had time to draw breath. Will – who was the head gardener – was helpful, and Huw – who, it turned out, worked for the Ministry of Agriculture – was around, but mostly they were left to their own devices.

Unused to such physical work, Daisy flopped into bed each night feeling her shoulders aching from digging, and her legs complaining about all the bending down. Her cheeks were ruddy from the sun, her appetite – which had all but disappeared when Rex left – came back and she found herself feeling happier than she had for weeks. Not completely happy – how could she be, when Rex was still risking his life up in the air? – but happier.

Beth was working just as hard. She was carefully listening to everything Daisy told her, reading up on plants when she had a moment (which wasn't often) and generally proving herself useful.

After they'd been at Kew a few days, and had planted five neat rows of winter cabbages, Daisy stood for a second, leaning on her spade and admiring their hard work. What had been just a patch of bare earth only a few days ago was starting to look like a vegetable patch.

'I'm good at this,' she said under her breath. 'I really think I'm good at this.'

She felt a rush of pride, which she'd never felt when she'd put leaflets about Anderson shelters in envelopes. They were doing something really useful here. Something important. She grinned.

'It's definitely coming on,' she said.

Beth was kneeling down sorting out poles for some runner bean plants that they were going to transplant into the allotment. 'I can't believe how much we've done already.'

'Ready for those beans?'

Beth got to her feet, clutching the stakes. 'How many do we need?'

'We can plant two for each pole, so maybe about ten?'

Beth counted them out and the women began pushing them into the earth.

'How far apart should they be?' Beth asked.

Daisy thought. 'About six inches, I reckon.'

'I've always thought you should only put one plant per pole?' said a voice. Daisy turned round to see two women watching them with interest. 'Ooh, sorry to interrupt,' one of them said. 'That was ever so rude of me. I've just dug my own garden up, you see, and me and Maureen – this is Maureen—' the other woman gave Daisy and Beth a cheery wave – 'we thought we'd come here and see if we could get a bit of inspiration for our own backyards.'

'I said we'd not get any help from here, because we've hardly got any space and Kew is enormous,' said Maureen. 'But Edie here said I should listen to her, and I reckon she's right, because here you are.'

Daisy and Beth exchanged thrilled glances. 'Here we are,' said Daisy.

'So it's all right to put more than one plant per pole, then?' asked Edie.

'Absolutely. You can put two for each pole,' Daisy said.

She started showing Edie and Maureen how to plant the beans, and soon they were joined by some other onlookers, who asked all sorts of interesting questions. Daisy found she was enjoying herself enormously.

'What's next?' shouted one onlooker when they'd finished with the beans.

'Christmas dinner,' said Daisy with glee. 'We can do some brussels and swedes.'

Because she'd spent ages poring over the information from

the Ministry of Agriculture, Daisy found she was sharing all the knowledge she'd absorbed.

'The aim is to grow vegetables for your family to eat every week of the year,' she told the gathering crowd. 'Even in the smallest space.'

'I can see how that works in summer, but in winter?' said one man, looking dubious. 'I don't understand how we'll get enough.' He puffed his chest out a bit. 'You can't keep planting on the same patch over and over anyway,' he said to Edie and Maureen, who looked concerned. 'Because the soil will run out of nutrients.'

Daisy tutted. She didn't like being told she was wrong. 'The ministry has worked out a crop rotation schedule,' she said. 'It's going to work. We're going to do it here and you can keep visiting and see how it's going. We've got some leaflets about it, if anyone wants one.' They had a tiny shed on their allotment, where they kept some tools, and inside they had a bundle of information leaflets Huw had given them.

The man rolled his eyes. 'You're not gardeners,' he said, looking down his nose at Beth and Daisy. 'You're just decoration.' He turned and spoke to the small crowd that was still watching. 'Someone else is doing the hard work for them,' he said confidently. 'They don't know what they're talking about.'

Daisy looked at Beth, who gave her a sidelong glance and a smile.

'Did someone have a question about the broccoli?' Beth called. 'Lady with the grey blouse, was it you?'

As Beth chatted to the woman about planting out brassicas, impressing Daisy with the knowledge she'd picked up in just a few days, Daisy hid her own smile. Beth clearly didn't like being belittled either.

The know-it-all man looked grumpy as he listened to Beth's chatter and Daisy felt a swell of pride.

'If you've got any questions about anything, we can answer

them,' she said, raising her voice so everyone could hear. 'We're here to help.'

Beth began handing out the leaflets while Daisy told the people watching about how to plant carrots this late in the year without them going wrong. And then someone else asked a question about watering, and someone mentioned caterpillars. It was non-stop and, at some point, the grumpy man disappeared off into the gardens. Daisy didn't even notice that he'd gone because she was too busy telling someone else that you could eat the leaves from beetroot as well as the roots.

I didn't think about you all day, Daisy wrote to Rex later. *That sounds dreadful because you are always with me, and heaven knows I can't forget how scared I am when I hear the planes going over. But when I was at the Home Office, I would sit and fret every hour of every day. I had nothing else to think about, you see? Nothing to occupy my mind. Now I'm so busy I don't have time to worry. And I'm always thinking ahead. Planting carrots that won't be ready until Christmas. Will you be home by then, Rex? Home by Christmas?*

She paused, tapping her chin with her pen.

Remember how we thought the war would be over by last Christmas? How wrong we were and how long ago that seems now. I reckon that it won't be finished this year either. I wonder when you will get leave and come home for a visit? I'm longing to see you, Rex. I miss you very much. But I know you'll be back in my arms soon and I can tell you all the things I've been doing at Kew. Mum says I'm a chip off the old block and I guess I finally am. When we get our house together after the war, we'll have to put a veg patch in the garden. Anyway, I am tired now and my eyes are drooping. I'd like to say that I'm looking up at the stars and thinking of you, but really I can't see out of the window because of the blackout blinds, and even if I could, all I would be looking at would be a barrage balloon swaying overhead. But I am thinking about you, Rex. Stay safe, my darling.

All my love, your Daisy

Chapter Thirteen

Beth was always rushing now. Rushing from home to the hospital. Or to Kew. Or in the other direction. Her first week at the gardens flew by and she barely had time to sit down. On the nights when she wasn't working, she fell into bed – sometimes before it was even properly dark – and was asleep before her head hit the pillow. It was really hard work; her muscles ached from the physical labour at Kew, and her brain ached from switching between nursing and gardening and reading medical textbooks in between. But she was loving every moment. She felt as though a fire had been lit under her.

She'd not seen Gus. She was desperate to bump into him at the hospital, where she knew he was still working – juggling his two roles just as she was – or at Kew, and to tell him all about her new job. And she was keen to hear about the committee, too. But there was no sign of him. She even went up to the roof of the hospital, hoping to see him there, but she didn't catch him.

At the end of her first week at the gardens,, Beth was hurtling down the street from the hospital towards Paddington station one morning when she felt a hand on her shoulder.

'Beth,' Gus said, sounding slightly out of breath. 'I thought it was you. Have you just finished a night shift?'

Even though she'd been hoping to bump into him, Beth was surprised by just how delighted she was to see Gus. She wondered if he'd run to catch up with her and that was why he was gasping a little. She found herself grinning at him. 'No, I've not been working. I just had to come and check the rota for the next few weeks so that I can arrange my shifts at Kew.'

'It's good to see you,' Gus said. He smiled at her and Beth felt her stomach give a little flutter as she admired the way his eyes crinkled when he found something funny.

'And you,' she said.

They stood there on the pavement for a second, looking at each other. Beth felt as though she should say something but she wasn't sure what to say and she was worried that if she spoke, she'd say something totally inappropriate like, 'I've been longing to see you.' So she kept her mouth closed until a bus trundled past, belching out fumes, and broke the strange moment between them.

'So where are you off to?' Gus asked, sounding slightly awkward as though he was making small talk at a party.

'I'm going to Kew.'

'You've started?'

'I have.' Beth found herself standing up a bit straighter with pride. 'I'm working on the model allotment. It's part of the Dig for Victory campaign.'

'Good heavens,' Gus said. Beth basked in the glow of his admiration. 'Growing vegetables?'

'Mostly veg, but a bit of fruit too.' She adopted a BBC-style voice. 'We're showing the nation how to feed a family of five from one small plot, all year round.'

'Well, isn't that something. Are you enjoying it?'

'I really am. It's hard work though. And look, I'm sure I've got muscles already.' Beth was wearing a summer dress with short sleeves and she bent her arm at the elbow, showing Gus her arm like a circus strongman.

Gus laughed loudly and Beth was pleased she'd amused him.

'I'm going to Kew now too,' he said. 'Shall we travel together? You can tell me all about this Dig for Victory campaign.'

'I'd like that.'

They strolled down the road together, into the station and down into the underground and onto a train, chatting about Kew Gardens the whole way. Gus, his eyes dancing with passion, filled Beth in on the work of the Vegetable Drugs Committee.

'We know what we need,' he explained, 'but they're hard to come by and we can't pay commercial growers for them because they take a long time to grow.'

'So what will you do?' Beth asked.

'Some of the plants are to be grown in special plots at Kew. Belladonna, for instance.'

'And the rest?'

Gus looked thoughtful. 'Well, there's the rub,' he said. Beth liked the way the very English expression sounded in his Jamaican accent. 'We're not sure yet.'

'You'll work it out.'

'I hope so. Everyone's putting in a lot of effort and I'd hate to see it go to waste.'

'It sounds fascinating,' Beth said. 'Do you think I could come and see what you're doing?'

'I have already asked.' He looked slightly sheepish. 'I've told them all about you.'

'You have?' She smiled at him again and there was that flutter once more. 'What have you said?'

'That if they don't let you have a nose around, you'll come anyway.'

Beth pretended to look cross, but then she shrugged. 'You're probably right.'

Gus laughed again. Along the train, a few seats away, a small girl sitting with her mother and another woman stared at him. Gus caught her looking and made a silly face. The little girl looked surprised for a second and then made an even sillier face back.

Gus gave her a mock-stern look and she held his gaze and then collapsed into giggles as he stuck his tongue out and crossed his eyes. Her mother, who'd been chatting, turned round to see what had made her daughter laugh and widened her eyes as she took in Gus. She said something sharply to the little girl and then to her friend and they all got up and moved to the other end of the carriage.

Beth felt uncomfortable suddenly. Was this how it was for Gus all the time? People treating him with suspicion because of how he looked? She wondered if he'd noticed. Of course he had. How could he not? She and Gus sat silently for a second, awkward for the first time, then they both talked at once.

'My friend Daisy—'

'Will you have a busy day?'

They both stopped speaking together and Gus smiled. 'You go.'

Feeling the mother's eyes on them, Beth told Gus all about Daisy, and her parents who had met at Kew Gardens, and their fruit and veg business, and her husband being in the RAF and how worried she was.

'They sound like a lovely family,' Gus said. 'Reminds me of my own parents and siblings in Jamaica.'

'Do you miss them?' Beth asked. 'Do you miss home?' She had no idea what Jamaica was like and she found that she wanted to know more.

He thought about it. 'I miss the sunshine and my mother. And the ocean. London is so far from the water.'

'It isn't really,' Beth said. 'I should take you to Brighton one day and you can dip your toes in the English Channel. Though I imagine it's quite different from the sea around Jamaica.'

'The Caribbean Sea,' said Gus. 'The water is bright blue and warm like a bath. And calm. And it's so clear you can see the fish darting about. When the sun shines on the surface, it sparkles like a thousand diamonds.' He sounded dreamy. 'And the sand is white and fine and you can lie down in the sun and warm your bones.'

Beth was enchanted. 'It sounds wonderful.' She smiled at Gus. 'The sea at Brighton is often choppy and freezing cold, and sometimes blue, but mostly a sort of murky grey. And the beach is stony, not sandy. Actually, it's all closed, because of the war, and I believe there are barricades there now, in case the Germans invade. So I can't take you there after all.'

'Maybe I will take you to Jamaica.'

Beth felt her cheeks flush and Gus, perhaps realising that there was a world of difference between a day-trip to Brighton and a voyage across the ocean to the West Indies, looked uncharacteristically flustered.

To her utter relief, Beth realised that the next stop was Kew Gardens. 'Here we are,' she sang and Gus leapt to his feet.

'Let's go,' he said.

'You should come and see the allotment on your way in,' Beth told him. 'We've done so much already.'

'You really are enjoying it.'

'I love it,' Beth said honestly. 'I really didn't expect to love it so much. But seeing our hard work growing before our very eyes is astonishing.'

'I shall come by this afternoon.'

'They were putting in the Anderson shelter this morning,' Beth added. 'They weren't sure about putting one on the plot but Daisy asked them to do it. She wanted to show visitors how they can grow vegetables on top of it.'

'Sounds impressive.'

Gus went through the ticket barrier, showing his pass to the guard. Beth fumbled a bit for hers and lagged behind.

'Come on, slow coach,' Gus grumbled.

Rolling her eyes, Beth flashed her ticket at the man in the booth, and shoved it back into her bag.

'Excuse me, miss?' a voice said. She turned to see another man in London Underground uniform looking concerned. 'Could I have a word?'

Beth glanced at Gus, who indicated he'd wait. She smiled at the gentleman. 'Is everything all right?'

The man took her elbow and steered her to one side. Alarmed, Beth snatched her arm away and stared at him. 'What's going on?'

'I just wanted to check you were all right, miss,' the man said, looking over her shoulder to where Gus stood waiting. Beth followed his gaze, admiring how straight-backed and professional Gus looked in his smart shirt, carrying his black doctor's bag. She frowned at the man. 'I'm fine, thank you,' she said hesitantly. 'What seems to be the problem?'

The man looked at Gus again and lowered his voice. 'I thought you might be in trouble. I thought you might have been forced to go along with that—' he looked at Gus – 'that man.' He made the word 'man' sound like it was in italics. 'I wasn't sure you were safe.'

Beth felt a rush of anger. Here was Gus, who was a sweet, kind, clever man, from what she knew of him. First there was the woman on the train and now this man, both judging him – she assumed – because of his skin colour. Because he didn't look the same as most other Londoners.

She gave the man her sweetest smile and put on her loudest, most piercing, cut-glass accent. The one she used when her mother forced her to join her and her father at dinner with guests.

'This man?' she said clearly, her voice carrying across the station concourse. She flung her arm out to gesture towards Gus. 'This man here?'

The London Underground man looked genuinely frightened. 'Shh,' he said. 'He'll hear you.'

'I'm just checking that you mean my good friend Dr Campbell?' The man blinked. 'Doctor?'

'I am a nurse and we work together at St Catherine's,' Beth said. Out of the corner of her eye she saw Gus looking half amused, half appalled at her gumption. 'He's a respected cardiologist from Jamaica and I can assure you I'm safer in his company than in most other people's.'

The London Underground man opened and closed his mouth but he didn't speak. Beth span round on her heels and marched over to Gus. She very deliberately put her arm through his and pulled him out of the station exit and along the road towards the gardens.

'Well,' said Gus once they'd crossed the road. 'Well.' He pulled his arm from hers and Beth felt a sudden cold sensation where his skin had been close to hers. She felt prickly and cross though she wasn't sure why. 'Well, what?'

'I don't need you to fight my battles for me,' Gus said softly.

Beth's stomach lurched. She felt like she'd done something wrong. 'I'm sorry.'

Gus stopped walking. He tipped his hat down over his eyes and Beth couldn't read his face anymore. 'Sometimes it's not a fight you can win. You could have put yourself in a sticky situation.' He paused. 'And I don't need your protection.'

Beth felt a bit odd, as though she'd upset him by doing something she'd thought was right. She swallowed. 'I consider you my friend,' she said. 'Friends look out for each other. I'm sorry if I misjudged the situation.'

Gus sighed. 'I am your friend.' He smiled at her suddenly and Beth felt her worries disappear almost immediately. 'And you're right. Friends do look out for each other. Which is why I'm asking you to be careful.'

'I will,' said Beth. 'But I won't stop standing up for you.'

Gus gave her a curious look. 'Nobody can tell you what to do, can they?'

'Nobody.'

Chuckling quietly, Gus started walking again and Beth had to scurry to catch up with him.

'Nobody,' he muttered.

Beth was a little distracted all day. Daisy teased her about it mercilessly.

'Potatoes,' she said, holding up one of the Ministry of Agriculture leaflets and showing Beth a picture. 'This is a potato. Do you know what they are?'

Beth giggled. 'Stop it, Daisy,' she said, pretending to be cross. 'I'm sorry to be so flaky today.'

'Your head's in the clouds,' Daisy said. 'What's got you like this?' She narrowed her eyes and stared at Beth. 'Are you thinking about your Paul?'

Beth felt her cheeks flush again and she bent over her spade so Daisy wouldn't see. 'How deep does this trench have to be?'

'Two inches,' said Daisy. 'I remember when Rex and I were first together. I was still at school, and I scribbled his name all over my arithmetic book. I couldn't think of anything else. Tell me about Paul.'

Beth didn't want to talk about Paul. She pretended not to hear and instead looked over to the other end of the allotment. 'Oh look. They've finished the shelter.' She pointed to the end of the allotment where Will and another man, ably helped by a group of female gardeners, had been shovelling earth onto the top of the structure.

To Beth's relief, Daisy was thrilled. 'It looks marvellous,' she said, leaping over a row of cabbages to get to the shelter.

'We can plant some veg on top later,' Beth said.

Will was standing admiring his handiwork. 'Marrows, I reckon,' he said.

Daisy snorted. 'Too late for marrows. We can put some savoys in there for now, and maybe some of the beetroots we were about to sow down there.'

Beth looked at the bare expanse of earth across the top of the shelter. It was bigger than she'd expected, but because most of it was buried, it wasn't too much of an eyesore. At least, it wouldn't be once it was planted over.

'Perhaps we could put some flowers on it for now?' she asked. 'Maybe on the sides? Just to brighten it up a bit.' She looked at one of the other women – a nice girl called Melanie. 'You could do that, couldn't you?'

Melanie nodded thoughtfully. 'We're thinning out the borders this week so I can plant out some of the flowers we take from there. And later I can plant some bulbs, if you like? For a bit of colour in the spring.'

'Perfect,' said Beth. She looked around at the allotment. It didn't look much like the rest of Kew, which was full of dazzling colours from the bright green of the lawns, to the deep pinks and shining yellows of the rose garden. Their allotment was just neatly dug rows of tiny plants, a patch of tomatoes in one corner that they'd transplanted from one of the greenhouses, some poles for beans in another, and now the shelter. It was utilitarian, Beth thought. That was the word. But she was very proud of it.

'What shall we do with the inside of the shelter?' Daisy asked. 'Can we use it for tools and stuff? We can take down our other shed if so. Give us more room for veg.'

'If you like. You're in charge,' said Will mildly. 'Melanie, can you take your lot back to the borders?' Melanie and the other women drifted off. 'And you two—' he nodded over to where a group of visitors was gathering – 'have an audience to impress.'

Beth grinned at Daisy. 'Shall we put some cabbages and beetroots on the shelter, then?'

'Let's do it.'

Beth and Daisy had – which was something of a surprise to Beth – become quite the double act. Beth asked lots of questions, which were often silly, and Daisy answered, pretending to become increasingly irritated with her partner to make the crowd laugh while they were teaching them about the plants. Beth had felt uncomfortable at first but Daisy seemed to be a natural performer. She even played up to her appearance, messing up her red hair and unfastening one strap of her overalls so that she looked unkempt and scrappy next to tall, neat Beth. Now Beth ran a hand over her own hair, making sure it was all pinned in place, and straightened her collar.

'Surely we can't plant anything on top of an Anderson shelter?'

97

she said loudly, picking up a spade. 'There isn't enough earth for the roots.'

The crowd watched as Daisy ran up the side of the shelter and stood on top, hands on hips, her hair blowing in the breeze. 'We can and I'll show you.'

'What will we plant?' said Beth. 'An apple tree?'

A ripple of laughter encouraged her to go on. 'Raspberry bushes?'

Daisy gave an over-exaggerated sigh of frustration and the crowd laughed again. They were all paying attention, Beth thought. That was exactly what they wanted. She looked over to where the people were watching and with a start saw Gus join the back of the group. She felt heat in her face again and saw Daisy notice. She followed Beth's gaze over to where Gus stood and her eyes widened as she saw him.

'If not an apple tree, then how about some daffodils?' Beth said. She watched as Daisy pulled her attention back to her.

'Daffs are pretty to look at, but they're not going to feed a family, are they?' Daisy said. 'How about some savoy cabbages?'

'Sounds good,' Beth said.

She felt Gus's eyes on her the whole time they were planting, and knew she was putting on a good show to impress him. She and Daisy worked hard, answering questions from the crowd, making them laugh, and getting all the cabbages planted, too. Beth kept glancing over to where Gus stood, checking he was laughing or listening or watching. He always was. Until, eventually, he gestured to his watch, gave a regretful shrug towards Beth and a cheery wave, and sauntered off back towards the main building where the committee was based.

Beth watched him go. They'd finished their planting now and the crowd was chatting among themselves, moving away to admire the flowers and wander around the gardens, or looking at the rest of the allotment and making their own plans.

'Who's that?' Daisy appeared at Beth's side, watching her watching Gus walk away. 'Is that Paul?'

Beth wasn't sure what to say. She pinched her lips together and looked at Daisy helplessly.

Daisy looked confused and Beth didn't know where to begin.

'That's not Paul,' she admitted, feeling her cheeks redden once again. 'It's Gus.'

Daisy looked slightly awkward. 'Your friend from the hospital?'

'That's him.'

'But he's—'

'I know,' Beth said. She felt a stirring of the annoyance she'd felt earlier on their journey to Kew and looked straight at Daisy with defiance. 'So?'

Daisy looked annoyed too. 'Do you like him? Gus? I saw how you were gazing at him.'

Beth went very still. 'No,' she said weakly. 'Of course not.'

'What about your Paul?'

Beth opened her mouth and then closed it again.

'Paul's here,' Daisy said. Her face had gone a bit red. 'He's here in London, safe, and you're making eyes at some other man.'

'No,' Beth protested. 'That's not it at all. Paul's a nice man. I like him a lot.' She felt ashamed of herself. 'I've not seen enough of him recently, what with working at the hospital and coming here. I've been neglecting him. I'll arrange to see him this weekend.'

Daisy didn't reply. She just stuck her spade into the ground with force.

'Gus is a friend, that's all,' Beth said. 'Honestly.'

'We need to get on with these cabbages.' Daisy turned away and Beth felt half sorry she'd upset her and half relieved that she didn't have to talk about Paul anymore.

She looked over to where Gus had vanished into the distance. Paul was the man for her, she told herself, trying not to think about the flutter she felt in her stomach when Gus smiled. Every-one said so. Her parents had always told her they were perfect together. Paul's parents said so, too. The girls at school had sighed about how lucky she was to have a ready-made boyfriend waiting for her. Yes, she thought, ignoring the butterflies she felt when she thought about Gus, Paul was the one for her.

Chapter Fourteen

Louisa and Teddy were talking again, but barely. Teddy had taken on a lot of extra billeting duties and was now helping Land Girls find positions locally, as well as finding homes that had space to accommodate officers from nearby army bases. It meant he was terribly busy and most nights he stayed up late, going through paperwork. Louisa liked to be in bed at a reasonable hour, and was an early riser, so they'd hardly seen each other. They hadn't even shared a meal since Christopher had left because they were rarely at home at the same time. Louisa felt wretched about the whole thing but she had a strong feeling that she just had to let Teddy work it all through in his own time. She'd apologised and she knew she'd done wrong. Now she had to wait and see if he could forgive her. She hoped, desperately, that he could.

It was Saturday, so Teddy had less work to do. He was in the house, and Louisa had taken herself into the garden to deadhead her roses, wanting to stay out of his way. So she had a good view when some planes came over – just as they had that day when Christopher had made his decision. This time, though, there were more of them. Louisa stood up and shaded her eyes so she could look upwards. The noise of the engines and the gunfire shook the ground where Louisa stood and she felt a lurch of fear. They were so low, and so close.

There were two British planes. No, three. And two German. Twisting and turning in the air, almost like they were dancing. It would be beautiful, she thought, watching the trails snake round the blue sky, if it wasn't so frightening. If she didn't know that inside those tiny planes were boys just like her Christopher, or Ivy's Archie, or Daisy's Rex. It all seemed much more real than it had the last time they'd watched a dogfight. It wasn't a thrill today, it was just terrifying.

One of the British planes swooped down low overhead. Louisa could see the colours on its wing clearly and the shape of the pilot's head. Her heart pounded and another burst of gunfire from one of the German planes made her shriek. Suddenly Teddy was beside her.

'They're too close,' he said in wonder. His voice shook a little. 'Too low.'

Louisa didn't want to watch anymore but she couldn't tear her eyes away. The gunshots were bursts of orange in the sky. Teddy put his arm around her. 'We should go indoors,' he said gently. 'It's dangerous to be outside when this is happening.'

Nodding, Louisa turned to go, enjoying the feel of her husband's arm on her waist. But a coughing sound overhead made them both stop and look back. The German planes were whizzing away with two British planes in pursuit. But the other British plane was in trouble. Its engine was spluttering and smoke was pouring from its tail.

'He's hit,' Teddy shouted. 'He's hit and the others have gone. They don't know.'

With a whining drone the plane plummeted towards the ground, heading for the fields behind Louisa's and Teddy's cottage.

'He's going to crash into Mr Farthing's field,' Louisa cried. 'Come on.'

Without hesitation she dashed down to the end of the garden and out of the gate onto the path at the bottom. She didn't need to look back to know that Teddy was right behind her and she was glad. The plane was shrieking now, plunging so fast that it was a blur of smoke. 'Why can't he parachute out?' Louisa gasped, scrambling over a stile and into the field. 'Perhaps he's unconscious,' Teddy jumped over the gate with the energy of a much younger man, 'or . . .'

Louisa didn't want to think about the 'or'.

Behind them she heard a rumble and, frightened that something had fallen from the plane, she turned. But it was Mr Farthing, who owned the field, arriving in his tractor. Louisa could see his face glowing pale in the cab, his mouth a dark circle of shock. He'd been in the trenches, last time, she remembered. She wondered if he was all right and thought she should check but the noise was ear-splitting now and the plane was closer still.

'Here it comes,' she gasped. She made to run forward but Teddy caught her arm and yanked her back.

'Stop!' he yelled. 'Wait.'

With a roar and a huge gust of hot air that blew Teddy's hat from his head and whipped Louisa's hair around her face, the plane crashed into the field just yards from where they stood, sending a shower of soil and bits of plant and hedge and goodness knows what else over them. The plane came to a halt and, for a second, there was a shocked silence as Teddy and Louisa looked at one another. Teddy's face was brown with dirt and dust and Louisa thought hers must be the same.

'We need to get the pilot,' she said, starting to run. Teddy didn't hesitate or argue; he ran too.

'Careful,' he warned as they reached the plane. 'Just be careful.'

The plane had hit the ground at an angle. One wing was buried in the ground, while the other stuck straight up in the air. The tail, which was where it had been hit, was gone – Louisa didn't know where – and smoke was billowing out. Was it on fire? She didn't know, but she did know they had to act fast.

She tugged Teddy's arm and, trying to ignore the shaking in her legs, she went round to the side of the plane where the wing was stuck into the earth. 'I can get up,' she said, her breath ragged. 'I can climb up.'

She didn't wait for Teddy to answer, but simply pulled herself up onto the wing and clambered up. The pilot was slumped in his seat, his head lolling to one side, and Louisa felt sick. Were they too late?

'We need to get into the cockpit,' she shouted. 'The glass is cracked but we need to break it enough to get him out.'

Teddy disappeared under the wing and re-emerged a second later with a large rock. He followed Louisa up the wing, holding it under his arm. 'Stand back,' he said. 'I'm going to hit the glass.'

With the end of the rock, he thumped one side of the cockpit. More cracks were added to the ones already there, and then, with another thump, it broke completely. Louisa was wearing a cardigan over her blouse but now she took it off and wrapped it round her hand so that she could clear the broken glass from the window without cutting herself to ribbons.

She wriggled into the cockpit with her legs still on the wing, Teddy holding her steady around her thighs. 'Hello?' she said loudly to the pilot. 'I'm Louisa and this is Teddy. We're going to get you out of here.'

She reached in and undid his harness, then pressed her hand to his chest. 'He's breathing,' she cried in delight. 'He's alive.'

But the smoke was thicker now and the air in the cockpit was thin. With some difficulty, Louisa managed to get her hands under the man's arms and then she pulled. He didn't budge.

'Teddy, you need to help,' she said over her shoulder, coughing as the smoke hit her throat. 'When I say pull, give us both a big yank.'

'Hurry,' Teddy said. His voice was small and scared.

'Pull!' yelled Louisa. She tugged at the man's arms, feeling Teddy pulling her legs, and suddenly, like a cork being released from a bottle, the pilot came free from his seat. Teddy tumbled backwards off the wing with a thump and a cry of pain. Louisa slid down the wing with the pilot on top of her, hitting the earth so hard it took her breath away.

'Quickly,' Teddy begged again. He was already on his feet. Louisa saw his head was bleeding where he'd hit the ground as he fell. But he didn't seem hurt. He simply held his hand out to help her up and together they dragged the pilot upright. Each taking an arm, they half ran, half stumbled across the field to where Mr Farthing had made it out of his tractor and was running towards them.

As they reached the tractor, the plane burst into flames with a whoosh. Louisa tripped over her own feet and fell onto the earth and found she had no energy to get up again. Teddy gently laid the pilot down next to her.

'He's breathing,' he gasped.

Mr Farthing was holding a flask of water. Without speaking, he crouched down and gently put his arm under the man's shoulders, raising him up, and dribbled water onto his lips.

'Come on, mate,' he said. 'Come on. You're safe now, mate.'

Louisa held her breath for what seemed like minutes but was probably only a few seconds and then the pilot spluttered and coughed and his eyes flickered open.

'Oh thank God,' she said. 'Thank bloody God.'

Mr Farthing was talking to the man in a low, steady voice, reassuring him that help was coming. Louisa managed to reach out a hand and give the pilot a pat on his arm and then the adrenaline deserted her and she began to shake as the horror of what had just happened started to sink in.

Teddy sat down next to her. 'All right?' he said casually, as though they'd just been to the shops or to church.

'I'm not sure.'

'Me neither.' He smiled at her suddenly, his teeth looking very white in his dirty face. 'What a thing to happen, eh?'

Louisa reached down and took his hand in hers.

He squeezed her fingers. 'Here comes the ambulance,' he said.

They sat there on Mr Farthing's field as the ambulance arrived, followed by a police car and then some RAF officials in a truck. The pilot, who was talking now and seemed to have escaped his ordeal largely unscathed, was taken off in the ambulance to be checked over and the RAF men went over to the plane and frowned a lot and wrote things down in their notebooks. Teddy gave the details of what had happened to the police, and Louisa and Mr Farthing added their own information and the police joined the RAF men at the plane. Eventually, Mr Farthing chugged off in his tractor and suddenly it was just Louisa and Teddy left standing by the hedgerow at the side of the field.

'Cup of tea?' Teddy said. He held out his arm and Louisa took it. Together, they went back along the lane and through the gate into their back garden. Louisa's secateurs were still on the grass, next to a small pile of deadheaded roses. It seemed like hours had passed since she had been gardening but it was still morning – not even lunchtime. She was still very shaky. She felt wrung out.

'One of the reasons I love you so much,' Teddy said as they walked towards the house, 'is the way you grab life with both hands.'

Louisa stopped walking. She looked at her husband and gave him a small smile. 'It's more like I jump in with both feet,' she said. 'And I don't always stop to think first. Sometimes that's the right thing to do. Like today. But sometimes it isn't.' She swallowed. 'I was wrong not to talk to you about Christopher and I'm sorry.'

'I was wrong to be angry,' said Teddy. 'Christopher's his own man and he makes up his own mind. And—' he chuckled – 'I knew what you were like when I married you.'

'Zealous,' said Louisa, looking at him with a glint of mischief in her eye. 'I have zeal.'

'It's not a bad thing. I was wrong to imply it was.'

'No, not bad.' Louisa was thoughtful. 'It just needs direction.'

They started walking again, across the patio and into the kitchen. Teddy looked at Louisa with what she could only describe as trepidation. 'I would suggest helping with my billets, but I know that look and I think you've already found a direction for your zeal.'

Louisa lifted her chin. 'I think we both need a large mug of sugary tea,' she said. 'And then I will tell you all about it.'

Chapter Fifteen

Louisa was wearing her best dress and a wide-brimmed hat and she was regretting it slightly, because it was an unseasonably warm day and the train was sticky and dusty. But she wanted to make a good impression when she got to Kew Gardens.

She had a plan – a good plan. At least, she thought it was a good plan and Teddy agreed and it seemed the people in charge at Kew thought so too because when – encouraged by her husband – she'd written to them, they'd asked to meet her. In fact, she had an appointment with the director himself, which was why it was so important that she pulled this off.

Teddy had dropped her at the station that morning and had given her a kiss.

'Good luck,' he'd said. 'Not that you need it. I think you're really on to something here.'

Louisa hugged her bag containing all her plans to her chest nervously. 'Oh I hope so.' She smiled. 'I feel really fired up about this. I think it could be something important.'

'Looking forward to seeing the gardens?'

'I am. And I'm going to find Daisy, too. Ivy says she's really enjoying working at Kew and I'm so pleased.'

'Must be in her blood,' Teddy said with a smile. 'You'd better go, the train will be here any minute.'

*

Louisa had deliberately planned to get to Kew early for her meeting. She didn't get up to the gardens as often as she liked anymore, so she wanted to take some time for herself. It was a good decision. Rather than going through the main Elizabeth Gate, she decided to go through the Victoria Gate, so it was a longer walk through the gardens to the offices. Almost as soon as she stepped through the impressive entrance, she felt herself breathing more deeply, her shoulders relaxing, and her face turning towards the sun like a flower. It was like coming home, she thought. She felt more comfortable here than almost anywhere else in the whole world. She strolled slowly towards the Palm House, admiring the neat borders and smiling as she saw female gardeners tending the plants. There were so many of them, she thought.

In a sheltered spot by the rose garden she found what she was looking for. A wooden bench with a simple plaque attached.

In loving memory of Lady Winifred Ramsay, who adored Kew Gardens, it read.

Louisa smiled. Her friend Win, whom she'd met when they'd worked in the gardens together during the last war, had passed away last year and she and Ivy missed her hugely. They'd arranged for the bench to be put in, close to the roses that Win had loved so much.

She sat down and inhaled the heavy scent of the flowers.

'I'm back, Win,' she said out loud. 'Back in Kew, where I belong.'

Goodness, there were so many memories here. Memories of herself and Ivy working hard, digging in the earth and planting flowers; of their fight to be paid the same as the male gardeners; and of their friend Bernie, who'd worked alongside them and who'd been fighting his own battles.

Louisa smiled. Good memories, she thought. Happy times among the horror of the war and the sadness of Win losing her beloved husband.

'Daisy's working here now,' she told Win. 'The next generation. Her Rex is in the RAF so it's a good distraction.'

Win had adored all of Ivy's children – especially Archie, who was named after her husband – and they'd all loved her too.

'Wish you were here, Win,' Louisa said. A tear trickled down her cheek and she wiped it away quickly, hoping it hadn't streaked her make-up. 'But I hope I do you proud today.'

Checking to make sure no one was looking, she stood up and went quickly to a yellow rose bush. She opened her bag, pulled out a small pair of scissors and snipped off a bud, attaching it to her lapel with a pin she'd brought with her for that very reason.

'A yellow rose for friendship,' she said aloud. 'And for good luck.' She touched the little flower gently. 'I'll take you with me, Win.'

Feeling as though she had her friend by her side, she straightened her hat and her jacket and walked quickly through the flowers to where the offices were in the imposing beautiful building at the edge of the gardens.

'Louisa Armitage,' she told the woman on the front desk. 'I have an appointment with Sir Edward.' Her voice shook slightly as she said his name. During the whole time she'd worked at Kew she'd never met the director – not even when she, Ivy and Win had fought their campaign for equal pay. But now here she was, being shown up the sweeping staircase that would forever remind her of herself and Ivy waiting at the bottom, watching Win make her way down after receiving the news that Archie had been killed. She touched her yellow rose again, took a deep breath and followed the woman to Sir Edward's office.

'Mrs Armitage for you, Sir Edward,' the secretary said. She gestured for Louisa to go inside and withdrew, leaving Louisa in a large room with huge floor-to-ceiling windows showing the most glorious view of the gardens.

'Oh, my,' Louisa breathed in wonder, forgetting herself for a moment, 'isn't this wonderful? You can see right across to the Palm House.'

'It really is something to behold, isn't it?'

She turned to see a man, a little older than her, with a grey beard and kind eyes and she flushed, embarrassed by her reaction.

'Sorry,' she mumbled.

The man – Sir Edward – grinned at her, making his eyes crinkle. 'Never apologise for appreciating Kew Gardens,' he said. He held his hand out for her to shake. 'Sir Edward Horton.'

Louisa shook it. 'Louisa Armitage.' She smiled. 'I remember we dug up the Palm House Parterre to plant onions during the last war.'

'So I've heard,' said Sir Arthur. 'Marvellous.'

There was a desk at one end of the room but instead Sir Arthur invited Louisa to sit on one of two armchairs in front of the windows.

'I like to sit here when I'm thinking,' he said. 'I find it helps.'

'I'm sure it does.' Louisa liked this man, who clearly loved Kew as much as anyone she knew.

'I was most intrigued to receive your letter,' Sir Edward said. 'It sounds as though you have worked this out in a most detailed fashion. Could you tell me all about it?'

Louisa had expected to be nervous, but now that she was here – back in the family of Kew Gardens – and now that Sir Edward was so nice and interested in what she had to say, she found she wasn't anxious at all.

'A while ago, I read about the establishment of the Vegetable Drugs Committee,' she began.

'Marvellous idea to use the resources at Kew,' Sir Edward said. 'We have all sorts of clever chaps working on the committee. One fellow's come from Jamaica, would you believe?'

Louisa nodded, eager to say what she wanted to say. 'I know that you have the expertise here at Kew to work out which plants are needed for which medicines,' she said. 'But I also know that you can't possibly grow everything you need here.'

'That is true.' Sir Edward stroked his beard. 'Which is why I was so interested when I got your letter. Tell me exactly how you think it would work.'

'Women,' said Louisa. 'You need to use the women.'

'I looked at your file when I received your letter,' Sir Edward said. 'You were one of the women who campaigned for the female gardeners to be paid the same as the men.'

'I was.' Louisa lifted her chin slightly and waited for Sir Edward to carry on.

'Remarkable,' he said. 'I believe we underestimate women at our peril.'

Louisa smiled. She was warming to Sir Edward.

He carried on: 'You believe women are the solution to the problem of how to grow medicinal plants?'

'I do.'

'How?'

'We use the Women's Institutes,' Louisa said. 'They're the backbone of Britain already. These women are competent, keen to help and many of them are talented gardeners. And they know a lot about the plants that grow wild around the countryside. We can simply piggyback on the structure they already have and create groups or committees – I thought we could do it according to counties – to pick the plants that are growing wild, or grow the ones you need more of.'

'County committees,' Sir Edward said thoughtfully.

'You'd need someone to oversee it and to make sure everyone was growing what they needed to grow. And I thought perhaps the people at Kew could provide us with information leaflets about what to look for or what to plant?' Louisa went on. 'But then the actual growing could be done at local level.'

'Would the WI be willing?'

Louisa smiled. 'I wrote to the woman in charge – the general secretary, she's called – before I wrote to you. I knew there was little point in making these plans if they weren't on board.'

'And?'

'She said they would love to be involved. She's already started mentioning it to people and lots of the women are keen to get started. You just have to say the word.'

'Good,' said Sir Edward. He looked straight at Louisa. 'You've thought of everything, haven't you?'

'I felt a bit useless,' Louisa admitted. 'I'm not doing anything for the war effort really. Just helping Teddy – that's my husband – with his evacuees. I wanted to get my teeth into this.'

'Well, you've certainly done that,' Sir Edward said. Louisa thought he looked amused. 'We are going to need an enormous amount of plants. I think perhaps the picking would be an issue. We will need a huge workforce and I can't for the life of me work out where we would get it. The farmers are all busy and the Land Girls have work to do.'

Louisa had thought of this, too, thanks to little Julia back in the village.

'I thought schoolchildren? Cub Scouts and Brownies perhaps? Evacuees? As long as they're told what to do, they'd be a great help. Then the plants could be sent for drying and for making into medicine.'

Sir Edward got up and went to his desk. He took a pencil from a pot and drew on a sheet of paper, then came back and handed it to Louisa.

'Like this?'

He'd drawn a sort of chart starting with the letters 'VDC' at the top and then with arrows spreading – like the roots of a tree – into what he'd called County Herb Committees, then WIs, and then Cubs and Brownies.

Louisa breathed out. He'd understood it perfectly. 'This is it exactly,' she said. 'Do you think it could work?'

Sir Edward sat down again, tapping his pencil against his chin. 'I do,' he said slowly. 'But it would have to have the right person to oversee it. Someone who really grasps what we're trying to do here. Someone who has the organisational skills, the horticultural knowledge, and an understanding of how these WI groups work.'

Louisa made a face. 'I thought there would be someone here already who could take on the job – someone who's working on the VDC, perhaps?'

Sir Edward waved his hand. 'They're all doctors and pharmacists,' he said dismissively. 'I'm fairly confident none of them would know where to find a Cub Scout or a Brownie and they certainly don't understand the inner workings of the WI.'

Louisa thought that was probably a good thing, because in her experience the WI could be rather a distraction, but she didn't say that. Instead, she frowned. 'Do you think you'll be able to find the right person? It might be quite tricky.'

'Tricky?' said Sir Edward. 'Goodness me, no. I think it's going to be very easy. I have just the person in mind.'

'Who?'

'You.'

Louisa stared at him. 'Me?'

'Well, of course. You know about plants. You know about Kew. You know about the WI. You're the obvious choice.'

It wasn't often that Louisa was struck dumb but she was now. She couldn't think of the right words.

'I'm not as young as I was,' she stammered eventually.

Sir Edward shrugged. 'But fit as a fiddle.'

'I live in Kent.'

'Seems like as good a place as any for the County Herb Committees' HQ.'

There was a pause. Louisa looked out over Kew and thought hard. This wouldn't be easy. Putting together her plans to present to Sir Edward had taken hours; running the committees would be a full-time commitment. It would involve enormous amounts of hard work, she understood that. But she had no other job to make demands on her time. She and Teddy had a spare bedroom, so she could use that as a study, somewhere she could keep all her paperwork. She pictured the room and wondered if she could fit a desk in there. She thought she probably could. And perhaps a big noticeboard on one wall, so she could keep track of everything. That would be a good idea. She rubbed her nose gently, as she always did when she was thinking. Her friend Margot ran the local WI federation so she had an insight into how the organisation worked. It had been Margot who'd put her in touch with the general secretary, in fact. Louisa thought she'd be a good person to recruit as her right-hand woman . . .

'Mrs Armitage,' Sir Edward said, jolting Louisa out of her planning. 'Are you still with me?'

'Sorry, Sir Edward,' she said, flushing again. 'Of course I'm with you.'

He smiled. 'And are you *with* me?'

'To run the County Herb Committees?' Louisa said. He nodded and she gave him a broad smile. 'I'm with you.'

Chapter Sixteen

After a slightly overwhelming afternoon being introduced to the men running the Vegetable Drugs Committee, Louisa was glad to escape back out into the gardens and get some fresh air.

She'd gone over her plans for getting the WI involved with a man called Dr Bloomberg and some of the other members of the committee, including one chap who looked about thirty and who, from his appearance and accent, she judged to be the doctor from Jamaica. They'd shown her the lab where they were testing different types of medicines made from plants – it was fascinating. She was pleased that all of the doctors and pharmacists she met were supportive, with just one exception. One of the younger gentlemen – a pharmacist, she learned later – tutted as she mentioned using Cubs and Brownies to pick the plants.

'How will they know what to pick?' he said.

'We'll show them, with the help of the experts, of course.'

' "We" being the ladies of the WI?'

Louisa had bristled. 'Indeed.'

The man snorted and then – much to Louisa's irritation – he had spoken over her to Sir Edward. 'I really don't think this is a good idea, Sir Edward,' he said. 'I understand we're strapped for manpower but recruiting a bunch of women whose skills lie in jam-making and hymn singing is hardly the solution.'

Sir Edward looked at him sternly. 'This is the solution, and if you don't like it, I will have someone show you out.'

The pharmacist shut his mouth quickly, muttering an apology.

'You've made the same mistake many people make,' Louisa told him politely, shooting a mischievous glance at Sir Edward. 'Including many people at Kew Gardens, actually.'

'What's that?' said the pharmacist looking alarmed.

'You've underestimated the women.'

She followed Sir Edward out of the lab, chuckling to herself as she heard Dr Bloomberg say: 'She was a Suffragette, you know? Worked here during the last war . . .'

Hearing the men discussing her, Louisa stood up a bit straighter. She was feeling more like herself than she had for ages. Fired up. Ready for action. She was the new agricultural advisor for the VDC and she was going to make it a success.

Out in the gardens, the air was cooler and the stifling heat of the day was easing. She asked one of the gardeners where the model allotment was.

'It's down towards the Elizabeth Gate,' the gardener said, standing up and wiping her brow. 'Do you need me to show you?'

Louisa smiled. 'Not at all,' she said. 'I know the way.'

She headed down the path towards the Orangery, wondering how on earth an allotment would work, right beside one of the main entrances to the gardens, and then, there it was. It looked out of place among the beauty of the other plants. The grey corrugated iron of the Anderson shelter and the brown earth stood out in their dreariness. But it was attracting a great deal of attention and suddenly she realised why it had been put where it was – people coming into the gardens would find it immediately. It was prominent because it was so important. She felt a little flush of pride in Daisy – her god-daughter – who was carrying on her family's links with Kew in such a commendable way.

There was a crowd gathered at one end of the allotment and Louisa joined them to see what they were all watching. There was Daisy, looking full of energy and vigour as she raced about the plot, talking about their tomato crop, and a younger, startlingly pretty woman, who was making a confused face and scratching her head.

'But there are so many of them,' she was saying. 'Surely one family can't eat this many tomatoes? Won't it be a terrible waste?'

'That's the brilliant thing about tomatoes,' Daisy said, beaming at the crowd. 'You can make them into chutney and use them all winter. We haven't got a full harvest this year, because we're only just starting, but if you all follow the plans that the ministry has worked out, then next year you'll have marrows, carrots, potatoes, beans – all sorts.'

Louisa watched as Daisy answered the people's questions about when they should be planting carrots, and how to make sure they got the best potato crop, and marvelled at her enthusiasm. She looked just like her mother, dashing about the place with her hair flying behind her and her overalls askew. Her East End accent wasn't as pronounced as Ivy's was, but there was still no mistaking her roots. Louisa liked that.

The younger, elegant woman obviously didn't have the same knowledge as Daisy but her fingers were deft as she picked the tomatoes. Louisa thought the pair of them had probably fallen into this routine of asking questions and answering them, so they could help share the information with the people watching.

'Clever,' she murmured.

As the women finished picking the tomatoes and the crowd began to thin out, Daisy spotted Louisa. She ran over and Louisa found herself being squeezed tightly.

'Auntie Louisa, it's so good to see you,' Daisy squealed. 'Gosh, it's been ages. How are you? How's Teddy? Have you seen the allotment?'

Louisa untangled herself and smiled at her god-daughter. 'I'm really well, thank you. So is Teddy.' She looked around at the patch of earth where they stood. 'Why not show me what you've been doing?'

Daisy took her arm and led her to the far side of the allotment. 'This is where we're going to plant most of the vegetables, in the spring,' she began.

Louisa listened carefully as Daisy told her all about the plans for the allotment and the Dig for Victory campaign.

'It sounds as though you're really enjoying the challenge,' she said.

'I am,' Daisy admitted. 'When Mum first suggested it, I wasn't sure. But she was right. It's such a good distraction and planning ahead to the next crop, or the next lot of seeds we need to plant, helps the time pass.'

'Missing Rex?'

A shadow crossed Daisy's face. 'Every minute of every day. And I can't decide if it's worse or better that he's based nearby at the moment. I know some girls whose sweethearts are off in Europe and Africa – hundreds of miles away. Like Archie is. And that's awful. Rex is just across London but it feels just as bad.'

'It doesn't matter how far away he is, if you can't see him.'

'Do you see it?' Daisy said suddenly. 'Do you see the fighting in the sky?'

Louisa thought about lying and saying there was nothing to see, but Daisy was a clever young woman and she'd know.

'We do,' she said.

'Is it awful?'

Not wanting to upset her, Louisa answered carefully. 'I find it rather frightening,' she said. 'We had a Spitfire shot down, you know? In the fields behind our cottage. That was very scary.' Daisy looked horrified and Louisa added hurriedly: 'The pilot was fine. Barely a scratch.' She took Daisy's hand. 'Some of the youngsters in the village like seeing the planes. They think of the pilots as heroes and they cheer them on as they fly over.'

Daisy gave an enthusiastic nod. 'They are heroes.' She breathed in deeply. 'Rex is in Bomber Command, so he won't be in any dogfights.'

'That's something,' Louisa said, vaguely. Truthfully she didn't think there was anything to choose between Fighter Command and Bomber Command when it came to danger, but she didn't want to say so.

There was a pause as they both thought about Rex.

'I pray for him,' Daisy said suddenly. 'I've not even been to church for months and months, but I still pray for him. Don't expect it helps him but it helps me.'

Louisa nodded. 'Sometimes just taking time to think about things helps quieten your mind. Eases the worries.'

Daisy looked at her, with her head to one side. 'Did Bernie teach you that?'

Bernie was another friend of Louisa's and Ivy's from their time at Kew. He was a Quaker and he'd taught Louisa a lot about the value of silence and stillness. Now she nodded. 'He did.'

'He's very clever,' Daisy said.

'So are you.' Louisa looked around at the allotment. 'This is marvellous. I can't believe how much you've done in such a short time.'

'We pinched the tomato plants from elsewhere,' Daisy said with a grin. 'And we've had a lot of help from the Ministry of Agriculture.'

'You're attracting quite a crowd.'

'I know.' Daisy laughed. 'It's what they wanted all along, I think. That's why they put us here – right where everyone has to walk past.' She glanced over her shoulder at the other woman and lowered her voice. 'And I think it's why they chose Beth. She doesn't have any gardening experience but she's got the face.'

'She's very pretty.'

'She's really something. Come and meet her.'

Pleased that though Daisy was obviously missing her husband

hugely, she seemed to be coping with him being away, Louisa followed.

'Beth, this is my godmother, Louisa Armitage,' Daisy announced, making Louisa feel like she was a visiting dignitary.

'Pleased to meet you, Mrs Armitage,' Beth said. She stuck out a hand and then quickly pulled it back again as she realised her palm was filthy. 'Sorry.'

Louisa laughed. 'I remember when my hands looked like that. Isn't it wonderful, really getting stuck in?'

'I'm enjoying it so much,' Beth said. 'It's a world away from my work at the hospital.'

'Beth's a nurse,' Daisy put in.

'You're nursing and working here at the same time?' Louisa was impressed. 'That can't be easy.'

Beth made a modest face, which Louisa suspected downplayed just how hard she was working. 'What brings you to Kew?' she asked. 'A trip down memory lane?'

'Actually no,' Louisa said. She felt nervous suddenly, as though telling Daisy and Beth about her new job would make it real. Which was silly, because it was already real. 'I came to see Sir Edward.'

The younger women both looked at her, impressed.

'What did you want with him?' Daisy said in awe.

'I wanted to discuss something with him.'

Daisy raised an eyebrow 'What?'

'Here at Kew they're doing some research into making medicines from plants we grow here in Britain,' she began. To her surprise, Beth nodded vigorously.

'The VDC,' she said. 'I know all about it. My friend Gus from the hospital is working on it. It's fascinating.'

'That's it.' Louisa was pleased that Beth was so interested. 'I came up with an idea of how to grow and pick the plants that we'll need and I've been asked to put it into practice.'

'Well done, Auntie Louisa,' said Daisy. 'What was your idea?'

'To get the WI involved in growing the plants, and schoolchildren to pick them.'

'That's brilliant.' Daisy bounced on her toes in excitement. 'Simple and brilliant. They're perfect for the jobs.'

Beth was gazing at Louisa. 'Did you see the lab?'

'I did.'

'What's it like?'

'Very slick. Impressive. They know what they're doing.'

'I wish I could be part of it.'

'Beth came to Kew because of the VDC,' Daisy explained. 'She asked for a job there but they wanted her to be a gardener instead.'

Louisa rolled her eyes. 'They thought your nursing experience would mean you were more useful in the vegetable patch?'

'Apparently so,' said Beth drily.

'The foolishness of the men who run this country knows no limits.'

'Auntie Louisa,' Daisy said, laughing but sounding a little shocked.

'She's right,' Beth said. 'I want to be a doctor but my father is—' she made a face – 'unsupportive.'

'And you think getting involved with the VDC would help change his mind?'

'Not as such,' Beth said. 'I just think the more experience I can get, the better. And Gus says it's fascinating. I thought being here as a gardener would help me get into the committee but now I'm here, I'm not sure how to get involved.'

'Gus hasn't put a word in for you?'

Beth shook her head. 'I don't want him to.'

'Well then you need to ask them yourself,' Louisa said

'Ask the committee?' Beth looked alarmed. 'I don't know about that..'

'Don't ask, don't get.'

'You make it sound so simple.'

'Isn't it?'

'No.'

Daisy gave Beth a violent nudge that made Louisa smile. 'My mum and Auntie Louisa were Suffragettes,' she said. 'You can't say no to them.'

'You were a Suffragette?' Beth said in wonder. 'Seriously?'

'Seriously.'

'And you think I should just go and ask to be involved.'

'I'll take you over and introduce you, if you like?'

'Would you? It would be easier if you're there.'

'I'd be glad to,' said Louisa. She liked the steely determination she could see in Beth's eyes. It reminded her of her own younger days.

'Can we go now? I'll just fetch my bag from the shelter but I'm ready.'

Louisa laughed. 'Of course. Just one bit of advice for you, Beth.'

Beth looked at her questioningly. 'What?'

'I'd give your hands a wash first.'

Chapter Seventeen

Beth was already completely smitten with Louisa. She'd never met anyone like her before. So bold. So unafraid. So determined to make her mark on the world. So absolutely unlike Beth's mother.

She shot little glances at Louisa as they walked to the lab. She looked like any other woman of her age. Neat hair, nice summer frock, sensible shoes. But underneath that refined exterior was a woman who'd been a Suffragette, for heaven's sake. And who was the reason Beth and Daisy were being paid the same wages as the male gardeners. It gave Beth a thrill just to think about it.

'Tell me about your plans,' Louisa was saying.

'There's not much to tell,' Beth said, doing a little trot to catch up because while she'd been daydreaming about Louisa's days as a Suffragette, she'd fallen behind. 'I need to go to medical school.'

'I believe they are more welcoming of women these days.'

'They are,' Beth said glumly. 'But my father just won't allow it. I need his permission for the application, which seems ridiculous, frankly, but it's how it is. But he won't give it.'

'Is he not keen on the world of medicine?'

'Actually, he's a doctor. He thinks it's not a suitable job for a woman.'

Louisa snorted. 'I'm not sure it's up to him to decide what's a suitable job for a woman.'

Even though she'd only known Louisa for an hour, Beth

decided right there and then that she was her favourite person in all of England.

'Do you think the committee will let me work with them? Even just for a couple of hours each week,' she said, her courage deserting her as they approached the buildings.

'We'll ask them in a way that makes it clear they can't say no,' Louisa said over her shoulder – Beth was lagging behind again.

Beth swallowed nervously. What did that mean?

Like a chick following a mother hen, she trailed after Louisa as she strode into the building, down a corridor, through some double doors and into the lab. Inside, a group of three men – Gus and two others – were looking at a complicated chemical structure scrawled on a blackboard. They were so engrossed that they didn't even acknowledge the women as they entered. Beth's legs felt wobbly.

'This is a mistake,' she whispered to Louisa. 'We should go.'

Louisa tutted. 'Excuse me, gentlemen,' she said.

The men all turned and looked at her.

'Hello, Louisa,' one of them said. 'Did you forget something?'

'Hello, Dr Bloomberg,' Louisa said.

The man, who had an imposing air about him, gave her a broad smile. 'Oh please, call me David.'

Beth hid a smile. Clearly she wasn't the only one Louisa had won over. She felt Gus's eyes on her and avoided his gaze. She was so nervous already and she knew she'd go to pieces if she looked at him.

'This is Beth,' Louisa said. She turned to Beth and there was a tiny pause as Beth tried to work out what Louisa wanted her to say.

'Oh,' she said. 'I'm Beth Sanderson.'

'Beth works here at Kew on the Dig for Victory allotment, and she is also a nurse at . . . ?'

'St Catherine's,' Beth said. 'I'm on a general surgical ward.' She thought that perhaps she and Louisa should have prepared what they were going to say. But the men didn't seem bothered by Louisa's lack of knowledge about Beth's experience.

'Beth wants to learn more about medicinal plants so I thought it would be good for her to work in the lab for a couple of hours each week. Perhaps on a . . .?' She turned to Beth again.

'Friday afternoon?' Beth said.

The imposing man – Dr Bloomberg – pushed his glasses up onto his head and looked straight at Beth for the first time. 'Surgical?'

'Yes, sir,' muttered Beth.

'So you know about wound care?'

'Yes, sir.'

He nodded. 'Good. We'll see you on Friday, then. Nice to see you, Louisa.' He dropped his spectacles down onto his nose and turned back to the equation on the blackboard.

Beth looked at Louisa, wide-eyed with amazement and she gave a very small clap of her hands.

'See you on Friday,' Beth managed to say. She caught Gus's eye and he gave her a smile so wide she thought his face would split in two. 'Well done,' he mouthed.

Beth stood up a bit straighter and followed Louisa back out of the lab. 'If you don't ask, you don't get?' she said, as they emerged into the gardens once more.

'A lesson to live by,' Louisa said. She patted Beth on the arm. 'See you soon. Good luck at the lab.' And off she went in her sensible shoes, her handbag hooked on her arm.

Beth watched her go, still reeling from everything that had happened. Then she bounced a little with excitement and dashed off to find Daisy and tell her the news.

Her first afternoon with the VDC, just two days after Louisa's visit to Kew, was exhilarating and terrifying in equal measure. The laboratory team was all men, and some of them barely glanced at her when she entered. Thankfully, Dr Bloomberg was there to show her the ropes and give her a tour, though no one thought to show her where the ladies was – and she was too embarrassed to ask – so she was desperate for the loo by the end of the afternoon.

Gus was over in one corner. He was working on heart medicine made from a chemical taken from foxgloves. He looked up at Beth as she walked past with Dr Bloomberg and gave her a supportive grin. She smiled back.

'Dr Campbell is a renowned heart specialist in Jamaica,' Dr Bloomberg said. 'We're lucky to have him.'

'I know Nurse Sanderson from St Catherine's,' Gus said. 'We're lucky to have her.'

Beth flushed with pride. 'Thank you, Dr Campbell,' she said. 'I hope I don't let you down.'

They smiled at one another and, for a second, Beth felt as though they were the only two people in the room. Dr Bloomberg started telling her about the work they were doing with finding an antidote to poison gas from deadly nightshade, and she dragged her attention away from Gus and back to the lab.

'I thought we could use you with the team working on wound care,' Dr Bloomberg said. 'It's by far the most important area we're working on and we could do with some support. It'll be taking notes, mostly. Some filing of research documents. And I imagine the gents could do with a cup of tea occasionally.'

Beth felt a glimmer of disappointment that she was being treated as a secretary when she'd imagined getting stuck into the research side of things. But she pushed away her negative thoughts. What would Louisa do, in this situation? She would prove herself. That's exactly what Beth was going to do.

She spent the afternoon listening carefully to everything that was discussed. She paid attention to everything, did everything she was asked, and took careful, detailed notes, scribbling down everything that was said as Dr Bloomberg and some of the other members of the committee talked. Because the committee was in its very early days, they were still working out which plants to prioritise, which would be most useful and which would be easiest to grow. Beth found it fascinating to hear these clever, passionate men arguing about whether it was possible to collect enough yarrow flowers to soothe wounds, or if it was even realistic to consider growing fields of foxgloves in order to have enough of the precious ingredients that would make the heart medication Gus was working on.

She could barely write fast enough as they talked, but she didn't care about her aching hand. She was learning so much.

'One thing the doctors found in the last war was that the men were often very agitated and that obviously didn't help their blood pressure,' said one doctor, leafing through a journal and pointing to the relevant piece of information. 'They found there was little use in giving them the medication. So I'm wondering if we should focus our attention elsewhere?'

Gus sighed. 'High blood pressure will lead to other problems. We can't ignore it.'

There was a pause. Beth shifted on her stool. 'Sleep,' she said quietly.

Dr Bloomberg turned to her. 'Pardon?'

Beth swallowed as she felt the weight of the committee's eyes on her. 'You need something to help them sleep. Then the other medicine will be able to work while they're resting. We focus a lot on getting patients to sleep on the ward. Matron is a real stickler for it.' She looked round at the men who were all staring at her and gave a nervous smile. 'The thing is, the doctors don't see patients when they're sleeping – they only come on their rounds once everyone's awake. So you might not realise how important it is.'

She caught Gus's eye and he gave her an approving nod.

Dr Bloomberg was looking pleased. 'Sleep,' he said thoughtful-ly. 'Of course.'

One of the other men had gone to the bookshelves at the side of the room and was running his finger down an index. 'Valerian,' he called. 'Aids sleep.'

'Easy to grow,' one of the botanists said.

'Add it to the list,' Dr Bloomberg instructed. He beamed at Beth. 'Well done, Nurse Sanderson,' he said. 'I look forward to hearing more from you.'

Beth bent her head over her notebook to hide her proud expression so that no one thought she was gloating. She was doing what she intended – proving her worth. Now all she had to do was to keep it up.

'I think they were all rather pleased with me,' she told Paul later. They were having dinner with Beth's parents at home and Beth was trying to explain what she was doing at Kew. No one seemed very interested, though. Her father was tired and grouchy and her mother was distracted. At least Paul was listening – sort of.

'The chap in charge, Dr Bloomberg, said he wanted to hear more from me.'

Paul frowned. 'Bloomberg? Is he related to Victor Bloomberg?'

Beth had no idea who Victor Bloomberg was. She shook her head. 'I don't know.'

'Nice chap,' Paul said, jabbing a potato with his fork.

Beth's father looked up. 'I remember him. Played cricket for Middlesex.'

'Dr Bloomberg did?' Beth pictured the man's thick spectacles and found she couldn't see him as a sporty type.

'Victor.'

There was a pause. Beth took a sip of water. 'Anyway, I'm so pleased to be part of the committee now.'

'You should come and work with me,' Paul said. 'I'm rushed off my bloody feet in this new job and my secretary's about a hundred years old. I could do with something nice to look at in the office.'

Beth's mother looked pleased. 'What a lovely idea, Beth,' she said. 'That would be much less stressful than nursing and gardening.'

'I'm sure the War Office is no picnic,' Beth said, annoyed that Paul had even suggested it. She looked at him across the table.

He grinned. 'I just don't see enough of you, that's all.' He stared into her eyes. 'I miss you.'

Beth was embarrassed. She always felt awkward with him being romantic when her parents were there. As though they were playing a game. But then she felt bad for him, because he was sweet to her. 'I know. The war's keeping us all busy, isn't it? Things are bad enough at the hospital and we're awfully hectic at Kew, too. Though Daisy tells me there will be less to do as autumn progresses. We're planting—'

'So what do you say?' Paul interrupted.

'About what?'

'About coming to work with me.'

Beth blinked at him. 'I thought you were joking.'

'Of course I wasn't joking. It'd be great. I can get you a job as a typist first off and then sneak you into my office.'

'I can't type.' Beth's voice was icy.

'You can learn.'

'I have a job.'

Paul patted her hand. 'I know, darling. But won't it be fun when we can spend our days together?'

'Beth,' her mother warned, 'Paul is just being kind.'

Suitably chastened, Beth took a deep breath. 'It sounds wonderful, but it's just not possible.'

Paul pouted. 'Darling—'

'You wouldn't want me to choose you over my patients, would you?' Beth said, shamefully exploiting his kind nature. 'The hospital is busier every day. Isn't that right?' She looked to her father, who nodded.

'We do need all the nurses we can get.'

'They really need me,' Beth said.

'So do I,' said Paul.

Beth leaned over the table and gave his hand a squeeze. 'But you have me,' she said. 'This lamb is delicious, Mother.'

She put a large forkful into her mouth so that she couldn't talk anymore and tried not to think about how unsupportive her boyfriend was proving to be.

Chapter Eighteen

September 1940

Bombs were falling on London and Beth thought she had never been so frightened in her whole life. The windows of her ward were criss-crossed with sticky tape to stop them blowing in with an explosion, so the bright lights of the raid left odd shadows on the floor, like the bars of a cage.

'So much for the bloody blackout,' one of her patients said cheerfully. 'Light as day out there. Jerry won't have any trouble seeing where London is.'

Beth took a deep breath and tucked his blanket in around him more tightly. 'I'll have none of that talk, thank you,' she said, raising her voice because the roar of the planes overhead and the bombs falling was so loud. 'Our boys are doing a marvellous job seeing them off.'

'I don't like this,' said another patient – a young lad who'd been hit by a car during the blackout and needed surgery on his leg. 'I don't like it one little bit.' His voice was tremulous and scared.

Beth turned her attention to him. 'Now then, Mr Buxton. Don't you worry. You know we'll take care of you. You just have to trust us.'

She gave him a brisk pat on the sheet that covered his good

leg and bustled off down the ward, trying not to wince as another bomb falling nearby made the whole room shake. Some plaster dust scattered down from the ceiling.

'Nurse,' an orderly called from the end of the ward. Beth looked up and he threw her a tin helmet. 'Put this on.'

Beth pulled off her starched white cap and replaced it with the helmet. It was cold on her scalp but as more detritus fell from the ceiling she was glad of it.

'It's so hard to keep chivvying them along,' she said in an undertone to another nurse on the ward, Gladys Rowntree.

'Worst bit, I reckon,' Gladys agreed. 'Trying not to show we're scared.'

There was another – louder – crash and the women clutched each other.

'Not sure we're doing a very good job of it,' said Beth laughing as she untangled herself from Gladys's arms.

'Wonder if we'll get used to it?' Gladys said.

'I hope it won't go on long enough for us to get used to it,' Beth said. The bombs had been falling every night for a week now and she was hoping this was it. Surely Hitler didn't have enough planes and explosives to keep bombarding London in this way?

'Brace yourself,' Gladys warned. 'Incoming.'

Beth turned to see the doors of the ward flung open and several patients being brought in on stretchers. The first of the evening's casualties were arriving, sent up from the triage area on the ground floor.

The nurses sprang into action.

'You take that one with Matron,' Gladys said, straightening her tin hat. 'I'll take this poor bugger.' A shadow crossed his face. 'Don't reckon I'll be long.'

She headed to where a porter was moving a badly burned man onto the bed. He was very still and quiet and Beth thought Gladys was right.

'Over here, nurse,' Matron called, gesturing her over to the other new arrival. Beth pulled a curtain round her new patient, ignoring Mr Buxton in the next bed as he wailed: 'Is he dead? Has he gone?'

The new patient wasn't dead, but he wasn't looking good. He was barely conscious, which Beth thought was probably a good thing, considering.

'He's waiting for surgery,' Matron said. 'Can you make sure he's comfortable and I'll call down to the theatre and check if they're expecting him.'

Beth nodded. She felt light-headed suddenly as she realised for the first time that the man's leg was almost gone.

'Trapped under some rubble,' Matron said in a low voice. 'Give him some pain relief and a sedative and we'll get him down to surgery.'

She bustled off, her tin helmet making her look faintly ridiculous.

Beth carefully gave the patient his medication and with the help of Gladys – whose patient hadn't made it – took off his shredded shirt and replaced it with a hospital gown. She cleaned a cut on his head and Gladys bandaged his hand which was badly grazed.

'Like rearranging the deckchairs on the *Titanic*,' said Gladys, nodding to the end of the bed where the poor man's leg was a pulpy mess under the sheet.

Beth could only nod as the room lit up again with flashes from outside.

'Is he dead?' called Mr Buxton.

'He's fine,' Gladys said loudly. Then she lowered her voice. 'But you'll be in trouble if you don't shut up.'

Beth chuckled despite herself.

'Nurse Sanderson, I can't get hold of the operating theatre,' said Matron, pulling back the curtain. 'Could you run down and see if they're ready for our patient.'

'Of course,' said Beth, feeling her palms start to sweat. She'd not been down to the new operating theatres that had been set up in the basement and she was frightened she would get lost.

'Follow the white rabbits,' Gladys said, reading her mind. 'They've painted them on the walls to show you where to go.'

Beth was confused, but, sure enough, when she got to the bowels of the hospital, there was a trail of white rabbits daubed on the corridor for her to follow.

It was dark and cold down there. The lights were dim and flickering but it was quiet – much quieter than the ward – because the sound of the bombs was muffled. Her footsteps echoed around the corridor and it was strange to know how much activity was happening overhead.

Running footsteps made her look round and a doctor she vaguely recognised hurried past. And then another. Perhaps it wasn't so calm here after all.

The corridor opened out into a sort of ward – a holding area, it seemed, for patients waiting for surgery. Beth grimaced at the rows of beds. It looked like their poor fellow with the squashed leg wouldn't be having his op any time soon.

She looked round, wide-eyed, and her gaze fell on Gus. He was handing a box of medication to a nurse, who hurried off with it.

'Beth,' he said. 'Are you working down here?'

'No, I just came to see when a patient might expect to be taken for surgery,' Beth said. 'Not tonight, by the look of it, poor sod.'

A nurse hurrying past stopped. 'Is he stable?'

Beth shrugged. 'His leg's in a bad way and I'm pretty sure he'll need it off. But he's sedated.'

'Keep an eye on him for infection, and bring him down in the morning. I'll add him to the list. Do you have a name?'

'No. He's male, in his thirties.'

'Which ward are you from?'

'Atkins.'

'I'll make a note.'

The nurse rushed off and Beth turned to Gus. 'I need to get back.'

'I'll come with you.'

Side by side, they walked quickly along the corridor – back past the white rabbits – and up the stairs to the main part of the hospital where Gus would go one way to the pharmacy and Beth would carry on up to her ward. As soon as they came out through the double doors, the horror of the night hit them once more. The noise was even louder now – crashes and whistles outside as the raid continued, and there were people everywhere.

'Oh lord,' Beth said. She pushed her helmet down firmly onto her head and took a deep breath.

Gus wiped his forehead with the heel of his hand. He looked wretched and Beth wondered if he was frustrated, being stuck in the pharmacy. 'Good luck,' he said.

He turned to go as a porter shouted behind them. 'Nurse!' he called. 'Doctor!'

Beth and Gus both turned. The porter was supporting a man in army uniform. He was buckling, folding in on himself as the porter tried to keep him upright. 'Help me,' the porter cried.

Beth looked round. They were close to the entrance to the outpatients department which was being used as a sort of overspill area. 'In here,' she said.

She and Gus dashed over to the patient and helped the porter carry him through the swing doors and into outpatients. To Beth's relief, there was a spare iron bed covered in a sheet, so together they lifted the man. He was conscious, moaning quietly, and he was very pale. There was blood on the front of his jacket. 'He walked in the front door,' the porter said. 'And then he collapsed. He's bleeding.'

'Let's take a look at you, shall we?' Beth said gently, finding his pulse in his wrist. It was weak and slow. 'What's your name?'

'Ralph,' the man said through clenched teeth. 'Oh shit, it hurts.'

Beth carefully peeled back the man's thick uniform jacket and tried not to react as she saw the large wound on his abdomen.

Blood was gushing from his injury and pooling beneath him on the bed.

'Dr Campbell, can you help?'

Gus stood slightly to the side of the bed. 'I'm not supposed to—'

'I need your help here, doctor.' Beth was firm. She gestured around the room where nurses and doctors were rushing around and patients were being treated. 'Everyone else is busy.' There was a pause and for a moment Beth thought Gus was going to say no, and she would be left with this man bleeding to death in front of her.

But then suddenly, Gus nodded. 'We need to slow the bleeding,' he said to Beth.

And for the next ten minutes or so it was a blur of instructions and finding equipment and bandages in the unfamiliar ward, and trying to keep poor Ralph's blood pressure from dropping while Gus pulled pieces of glass from his wound.

When the poor chap had been patched up enough to be admitted, a nurse from admissions came to record what treatment they'd given him. Gus went through what they'd done and she wrote it all down.

'And your names?'

'Nurse Sanderson,' Beth said. Gus stayed quiet and Beth nudged him. She knew he wasn't supposed to be treating patients but in these circumstances no one would be cross. 'This is Dr Gus Campbell.'

'What wards are you from?'

'I'm on Atkins,' Beth said. She turned to Gus but he'd already walked away.

The other nurse simply shrugged. 'Busy night,' she said calmly, raising her voice so Beth could hear her over the thuds outside.

Beth went back to her own ward, her apron covered in blood. She was exhilarated by saving Ralph's life but uneasy about how Gus had reacted.

'Nurse Sanderson,' Matron said as she came through the door. 'Clean aprons are by the nurses' station, then check vitals on bay two please.'

And Beth was so busy that she didn't have time to fret about Gus.

The raid stopped in the early hours of the morning but the nurses barely registered the wail of the all-clear siren. Beth had been working a night shift but she didn't finish at eight o'clock like she'd been supposed to. She wasn't even really aware of what time it was. She and Gladys, and the other nurses, simply kept going until things were calmer on Atkins Ward. The chap with the crushed leg went down to theatre. Gladys swept up some glass from a broken window. Beth calmed Mr Buxton, who was having trouble breathing and thought he was dying but really he was just panicking and Beth couldn't blame him.

Eventually, Beth and Gladys were sent home. Big Ben was bonging as they emerged. Beth found the familiar sound reassuring after a night of destruction.

'Wash, sleep, back to it, I suppose,' said Gladys as they went their separate ways.

Beth felt like she'd gone through exhaustion and out the other side. Wanting some fresh air, she walked across the bridge to catch a bus home and as she crossed the river, she looked along the Thames at the orange glow of the sunset behind Tower Bridge. No, hold on, she thought. That wasn't the sunset, because it was only lunchtime. And the sun set in the west, not the east.

She stopped walking and stared, realising with a jolt of horror that the bright glow on the horizon was actually the East End burning. It was the fires that she could see. She thought of Daisy and Ivy and their family in Hackney and prayed that they were safe.

She still felt dazed when she got home. She hauled herself up the steps to her front door and put her key in the lock as there was a shout from behind her.

'Beth!' Paul was walking along the road, looking clean and smart in a trilby hat. Beth looked at him in bewilderment, unable to understand why he was there. He stopped at the bottom of the steps and looked up at her. 'Christ, what happened to you?'

'Work,' Beth muttered.

'Your face is filthy.'

Slowly Beth touched her forehead and then looked at her fingertips which were black with dust.

Paul looked faintly disgusted but Beth was too tired to care.

'Come on, then,' he said. 'Get yourself cleaned up and we'll head off.'

'What?'

'We're having a picnic in Hyde Park, remember? I've got all the bits in the car.'

'I can't go for a picnic.'

'It's all arranged.'

Beth looked down at herself. Her dress was dirty and she had a hole in one of her thick stockings. Then she looked at Paul in his cricket jumper and jaunty hat.

'I'm going to bed,' she said. She turned the key and pushed open the heavy front door, letting it slam shut behind her with a bang and leaving Paul outside on the pavement.

Chapter Nineteen

Daisy was shattered. It was supposed to have been her day off, but there was a lot to do and it had been a long day at the gardens. There had been no sign of Beth for the last few days, even though she had been on the rota to work at Kew, and Daisy wasn't surprised. She knew the raids that had been happening since last week were putting enormous pressure on the hospitals in London so Daisy was happy to pick up the slack and Beth usually called the office and left a message when she wasn't going to make it to the gardens. Daisy didn't mind the extra work because she liked to keep busy but there was no denying that it was exhausting. There had been a whole week of bombing every night now. She wondered how long it was going to carry on. Surely not much longer?

As she emerged from the tube station into the gloomy evening, she noticed there were already families beginning to make their way down onto the platforms, ready to settle in for the night. Daisy shuddered. Never had she been so glad that they had a back garden. Their Anderson shelter may not have been the most luxurious place to sleep but at least they didn't have to take refuge on a draughty platform with hundreds of others.

She pulled her collar up against the wind and hurried along the road towards home. Her father had already gone out when she arrived. His ARP duties had changed from enforcing the blackout, to being out all night. Along with his colleagues he sounded the air-raid sirens, directed people to shelters, and did all sorts to help people during the bombings. Daisy hated to think about him being out in the raids but he was adamant that he had to do his bit.

The family had fallen into a routine over the weeks of bombing. They'd all eat together in the kitchen as soon as Daisy got home, then gather their things for the night and go down the garden and into the shelter. Daisy took her notepaper and a pen so that she could write to Rex, and a magazine to read, as well as some extra blankets because it was so cold in the shelter overnight.

Inside the shelter were narrow, hard, uncomfortable bunks, but, this evening, Daisy was so tired that she'd barely written a few words to Rex before she felt her eyes drooping. She curled up under her blankets and was asleep within seconds.

She woke a couple of hours later with a start, hearing the wailing of the air-raid siren. Her mother was sitting up on her bed, sketchbook in her lap but not drawing. Poppy was fast asleep in the bunk beneath Daisy. She peeked over at her snoozing sister and shook her head.

'She really can sleep through anything,' she said, smiling at her mother. Ivy always said Poppy's talent to nap in the noisiest environment was because she'd been born in the middle of a terrible storm with huge claps of thunder shaking the house and the wind shrieking through the trees.

Ivy gave her a small, forced smile in return. Daisy knew she was listening carefully to hear the first bombs falling. And there they were – in the distance for now, just muffled thumps, and the boom of the anti-aircraft guns.

Daisy took a blanket and clambered across to the other bunk so that she was sitting next to Ivy. She draped her blanket across their knees and they sat, huddled together, as the sounds got louder and closer and scarier.

'Planes,' said Ivy. Daisy took a deep breath. After just a few nights of raids they had already got to know that they could only hear the planes when they were close, their engines droning overhead like malevolent bumblebees. And sure enough, now the thumps of the bombs were louder. The pilots used the river to navigate, Daisy knew.

Poppy snored and turned over in her bunk, but didn't wake, as the explosions roared.

'Bethnal Green,' muttered Daisy.

And now it was constant, the whistles of the bombs coming nearer and closer together; the shelter was shaking.

Somewhere nearby glass shattered. 'Mr Pilgrim's greenhouse,' said Ivy.

'Albion Drive,' Daisy said, as another explosion thudded. And another. 'Middleton Road,' she added.

And then the planes were overhead and they were quiet because it was so loud they wouldn't be able to hear themselves speak anyway. Daisy hunched down in her blanket, holding Ivy's hand, and when she looked up, Poppy had woken and was curled up next to her mum. They all braced themselves as more bombs whistled overhead. They heard timber creaking and more glass shattering and the roar of a fire taking hold somewhere close.

'That's us,' breathed Ivy in horror. 'That's our house.'

Daisy shook her head. 'It's not, Mum. It's further along.' She tilted her head, listening. 'It's the Robinsons at number six.' She frowned. 'No, not them. It's maybe Dawn and Mike on the corner?' She wasn't sure she was right, though. It was so hard to tell, when the wind was blowing and the bombs were coming thick and fast. 'Dawn and Mike don't have a shelter,' she added. She knew where all the shelters were nearby. She'd delivered those leaflets herself.

'They'll be next door,' Poppy said sleepily. She rested her head on Ivy's lap and closed her eyes. 'They go next door when the siren goes.'

Another bomb landed, so close that they heard rubble fall, and they all winced.

'We're safe,' Ivy said. 'That's the main thing. We're together and we're safe.'

'Dad,' Poppy said, her eyes still closed.

'He'll be fine,' Ivy reassured her, stroking her hair. 'We'll see him in the morning.'

Daisy reached across Ivy and took her sister's hand, and they all sat there close together, listening to the bombs.

Somehow, eventually, they all slept and Daisy woke, stiff and cold, a few hours later. Ivy was awake already, gently shaking Poppy to rouse her.

'Time to face the music,' said Ivy. 'Come on.'

Poppy pushed open the door and out they went into the chilly morning, bracing themselves for what they were about to see. It never got easier; emerging from the shelter to see the damage each morning was always awful. Daisy thought perhaps there were some things you would never get used to. Perhaps things that you never should get used to.

The air was thick with brick dust and smoke. Poppy coughed as she came out into the murky light, ahead of Daisy, and together they trooped round the side of the house and out into the street.

'God,' said Ivy, blinking away tears. Daisy wasn't sure if it was the acrid smoke that was making her mother's eyes water or the devastation that surrounded them. 'You were right, Daisy. It was Dawn's and Mike's.'

Their street was intact, but the bombs had followed the line of the main road, taking out the houses on the corners. Dawn's and Mike's house was reduced to rubble, while the house next door had been neatly split in two. Daisy could see half of the lounge, and half of the upstairs bedroom where the electric light still swung, looking faintly ridiculous, from half of the ceiling rose.

She wondered what Rex would think when he came home. She couldn't imagine how he would feel to walk along the streets where he'd grown up, and see them changed so completely. Icy-cold fear trickled down her spine as she thought that perhaps he would never see the destruction. Never come home to her. Then she shook her head to dislodge such awful thoughts. This was no time to be wallowing in her own misery. No time at all.

Across the road, the other corner house was on fire but the firefighters were there, dousing the flames. All around them were their neighbours, some in their nightclothes, others fully dressed. Some looking dazed, others injured or bleeding, and some taking charge or helping their families.

'It's getting worse,' Daisy said in despair. 'How much more of this can we take?'

Ivy put a reassuring hand on her back. 'We'll get through it, sweetheart. We always do.'

Daisy looked at her mother, marvelling at her strength, despite her having already lived through one war. Or perhaps it was because she'd lived through another war that she was so strong. Daisy wasn't sure. But either way, she nodded. 'I guess you'll be busy today? Shall I walk Poppy to school? Make sure she's all right?'

Ivy smiled. 'That would be great,' she said. 'We'll have our hands full at the centre and no mistake.'

'I'll come back and help you. Will won't mind me missing a day's work at the gardens. He's ever so understanding and I've been putting in a lot of hours.'

'Are you sure?' Ivy frowned. 'I'm not saying we can't use an extra pair of hands, but I don't want you to get into trouble.'

'It's fine. Don't reckon Beth will make it today either, after a raid like last night's. She's bound to get called into the hospital, even if she isn't supposed to be working.'

'Thank you.' Ivy gave Daisy a quick hug and kissed her cheek. 'I'll go and check on Mike and Dawn, and then go to the centre and hopefully I'll find your dad on the way. Meet you there?'

Ivy hurried off, and Daisy went into the house to find her sister. Their front windows had shattered, she noticed. She should board them up and save her father a job. But she suddenly felt exhausted and rather lightheaded and instead of going to find some wood, she sat down on the sofa and rolled her eyes as a cloud of dust rose up. Nothing was clean anymore. The powdered brick and the smell of burning had sunk into every bit of furniture, every item of clothing. Even their hair always smelled of smoke and their eyes felt gritty all the time. 'Poppy,' she yelled, too weary suddenly to get up. 'Are you ready for school?'

Poppy appeared at the door in her uniform. 'I don't see why I have to go.'

'We need to keep things as normal as we can.'

'Nothing's normal anymore.'

'That's exactly why we have to hang on to the things that are,' Daisy said. 'Got your gas mask?'

Poppy swung the cardboard box off her shoulder so Daisy could see. 'You don't have to walk with me. I'm not a baby.'

'I know,' Daisy said. 'It's for Mum, really. Just so she knows you're in safely.'

Poppy rolled her eyes but she didn't argue. 'Come on, then.'

Daisy stood up, and the room span for a second. She closed her eyes and steadied herself on the back of an armchair.

'Daisy?' Poppy's voice sounded far away. 'Daisy?'

She forced herself to open her eyes. 'I'm fine,' she said. And, actually, she was feeling better now. 'Just stood up too fast.'

She saw Poppy was looking worried, and thought it was sweet that her younger sibling was looking out for her. 'I'm fine,' she said again.

By the time she'd dropped Poppy at school, she was feeling much better. Tired, of course, but they were all knackered, with their sleep broken by bombs and sirens every night. She waved her sister goodbye and headed off to find her mum at the centre.

Ivy had joined the Women's Voluntary Services for Civil Defence ages ago but after being quiet for months, the raids this last week meant she'd spent every spare minute – when she wasn't working at the market garden – helping at a centre looking after bombed-out families. She gave out food parcels, distributed vouchers from the War Office for replacement clothes, and did anything else that was needed.

Daisy wrapped her scarf across her face as she walked, partly because there was a real nip in the air, and partly because of the dust that was floating around everywhere. The sound of an ambulance speeding by made her think of Beth and she wondered what she was doing. It wouldn't be easy, working at the hospital and at Kew Gardens now that the war had brought such horror to London. Not to mention the stuff she was doing with the drugs committee. Daisy thought Beth was quite something.

A shout made her look up and, to her relief, she saw her father coming towards her, holding his tin ARP warden hat in his hands.

'Dad,' she said. 'What a bloody night, eh?'

'Worst so far.'

'I'm helping Mum today,' Daisy told him. 'You go and get some rest. Graham can handle things at the market garden this morning. That's why you gave him the manager's job in the first place, isn't it?'

Jim's face was streaked with dirt and he looked tired, but he still managed a smile. 'I'll pop by and check he's all right first. Poppy get to school all right?'

'Yep,' said Daisy. 'Watched her go in.'

'Good.' Jim's shoulders relaxed. Daisy thought it was because he knew where all his family were – all except Archie, of course, who could be anywhere and doing anything, she thought with a lurch of fear. She reached up and kissed her father on his cheek, feeling affectionate suddenly.

'Go home,' she said.

'Tell your mum I'll bring her some veg for the boxes later.'

'I will.'

Daisy watched him go, and then pulled her scarf across her face once more. There was a lot to do.

Chapter Twenty

Beth climbed the stairs from the cellar and held out her hand to help her mother up into the house.

'I really don't think it's necessary to spend every night down there,' her mother grumbled. 'It's so uncomfortable.'

'The raids are happening every night, so we need to stay safe, Mother,' Beth said through gritted teeth. She hadn't enjoyed hunkering down in the cellar either, on her first night off in what seemed like years, but was actually just a few days.

'It's not right, us all sleeping together. With Nessa as well. What do you think, Geoffrey? It makes me uneasy sharing a room with our housekeeper.'

'Agatha, you know it's the only option,' her father said to Beth's relief. Her mother listened to him. She tended to pay more attention to men – her husband in particular – than women. Beth had met a lot of patients like that at the hospital. Men and women who dismissed what she told them and then listened intently as the male doctors told them the same thing. Generally, she just smiled and went along with it, but today she was annoyed and couldn't help tutting as they went into the hall.

Dust caught in Beth's throat and her mother ran her finger along the bannister, showing Beth and her father that it was grey with dirt.

'Must have been a close one, to bring so much dust into the

house,' Beth said to her father. 'Should we go and see if anyone needs help?'

He nodded, grim-faced.

'Darling, could you have a word with Nessa, because this isn't really acceptable,' Agatha said, showing him her dirty finger again.

Beth groaned. 'For heaven's sake,' she said, throwing open the front door. 'Look at this, Mother. Look at what's happening under your nose. Bombs are dropping and people are dying and all you care about is a bit of dust.'

There was a stunned silence and Beth wondered if she'd gone too far. Agatha looked outside into the street, where an ambulance whizzed past, its sirens blaring.

'The sky is red,' she said in wonder. 'Why is it red?'

Beth winced. 'I think it's from the fires. People's homes are burning. You can smell the smoke.'

Agatha took a few paces outside onto the stone steps that led up to their large front door. Beth and her father followed, exchanging concerned glances. 'Last time, we went on holiday, would you believe?' Agatha said, in a quiet voice. 'My father was away, obviously, so my mother and I went to stay with a friend who lived on the south coast. You remember, darling?'

'I do remember,' Geoffrey said. 'I remember you telling me about it.'

'And I was on the beach one day, reading my book. And slowly I became aware of a sort of thumping sound in the distance. It took me ages to work out what it was . . . ' She trailed off.

'What was it?' Beth was interested. She'd never really heard her mother talk about the last war before.

'The guns,' said Agatha with a shudder. 'It was the guns in France.'

'Oh God.' Beth put her hand over her mouth.

'We went home that evening, actually,' her mother went on. 'We couldn't stay there once we knew. But then we came home and we were safe and the war seemed far away again. I know there were air raids back then too, but nothing like this.' She looked out into the street once more. 'Not like this. Not on our doorstep.'

Geoffrey put a hand on his wife's shoulders. 'Why don't you go upstairs and get changed?' he said. 'Nessa's making breakfast – I can hear her clattering away in the kitchen. Beth and I will nip out and check if we're needed.'

Agatha nodded and, without saying another word, she turned and went upstairs. Beth leaned against the doorframe and looked at her father. 'She's infuriating.'

'She is,' Geoffrey agreed. 'But be patient. The last war was difficult for her.'

Beth snorted. 'She stayed here, and rolled a few bandages while Grandpa was in France and you were off in the medical corps.'

Geoffrey gestured for Beth to go down the steps from the front door. She waited for him at the bottom, gazing around at their street. There was no damage close by, but the dust hung heavily in the air, making the light hazy, and Agatha had been right – the sky was glowing red.

'Well, now,' Geoffrey said, joining her at the bottom of the stairs and taking in their surroundings. Their street was quiet, though Beth could hear shouts coming from nearby.

'I rather think everything's in hand. No one in need of immediate help.'

'We'll be more use at the hospital, I think.'

'I agree.'

Beth felt the tug of a bond between her and her father for what was possibly the first time in her life. They were in this together, she thought.

A bus rumbled past the end of their road and she marvelled at how life just kept going. The bombs fell and the houses burned, and people got up every day and went to work with a quiet, unassuming strength that they'd never thought they had. It made her feel emotional suddenly, and she blinked away tears.

'I'll go and get my uniform on,' she said. 'I'm sure I'll be needed.'

She turned to go back inside. Her father stopped her with a hand on her arm.

'Could you check on your mother? Just make sure she's all right.'

Beth nodded. She went upstairs and without much energy, pulled on a clean uniform and tied her hair up. Then she knocked on the door to her parents' room. Agatha was dressed and sitting at her dressing table, brushing her hair.

'Come in or go out, Beth,' she said. 'Don't hover.'

Beth rolled her eyes, but she went into the room and sat on the bed. 'I just wanted to see if you were all right,' she said. 'It must be hard for you when you've seen war before.'

Agatha began pinning her hair up.

'Your grandfather was terribly affected by the Great War,' she said. 'He was changed completely and never really recovered.'

Beth only had hazy memories of her grandfather who had sat in a chair by the window most of the time and never spoke. She remembered being told to be quiet around him as he didn't like noise. 'Shell-shock?' she said now, suddenly understanding.

'I think so.' Agatha put a kirby grip in her mouth as she twisted her hair and then stuck it in firmly and patted it down. 'He was a lovely daddy, before he went away. When I was a little girl he was so much fun to spend time with. But when he came home from the war, he was different. I wouldn't even have recognised him when he arrived back if my mother hadn't been there.'

'Was he injured?'

'Not physically. But his mind was never the same.' Agatha looked at her reflection, turning her head from side to side to check for stray hairs. With a flash of insight Beth realised that the fussing about dust and the sleeping arrangements, and the nagging of Nessa, were all just her mother's way of feeling as though she was controlling something that couldn't be controlled. She'd been here before. Lived through a dreadful war and everything that happened was totally out of her hands. It wasn't easy for her. For anyone.

'So you're working at the hospital today?' Agatha said, standing up.

Beth tried to look enthusiastic and failed. All she felt was tired. 'I am.'

'I'm proud of you doing your bit,' her mother said. Beth was touched. If only her father and Paul felt the same way.

Geoffrey put his head round the door and smiled at his wife. 'All right?' he said.

'All fine.'

'Need a lift to the hospital, Beth?'

Beth blinked in surprise. Though she and Geoffrey both worked at St Catherine's, they never travelled together and she very rarely saw him at work – he was always closeted away in his offices on the top floor. It had always seemed to Beth as though he pretended she wasn't nursing – that if he didn't see it, then it wasn't real. But for the last couple of days Geoffrey had been back on the wards because it was all hands on deck, and he seemed suddenly to have accepted that his daughter was Nurse Sanderson.

'That would be good, thank you,' she said.

'Then we need to leave,' Geoffrey said, pointing at his watch. 'Let's go.'

The journey through the city streets showed Beth the full extent of the damage caused by last night's bombs.

'Oh heavens,' she breathed. 'How will London ever recover from this?'

'It will,' said her father, though he didn't sound as certain about it as Beth would have liked.

'Every night,' Beth said, feeling close to tears. 'Every night is awful.'

Her father reached over and patted her knee. 'I know.'

There was quiet for a little while and then he spoke again. 'I heard you helped a chap with an abdominal wound.'

'Two nights ago,' Beth said. 'He wasn't my patient. I was just there when they brought him in.' She frowned. 'How do you know about that?'

'The paperwork ended up on my desk because the nurse who made a note of the admission didn't know which department the doctor was from.'

Beth stiffened. 'Dr Campbell,' she said.

'Yes.'

Bracing herself to argue that Gus had done nothing wrong when he treated poor Ralph, and that it would surely have been unethical for him to stand by and watch the man bleed, Beth opened her mouth but her father wasn't finished.

'He did a good job, I heard. Chap survived?'

'He's on Robinson Ward now,' Beth said, marvelling at the – faint – praise for Gus from her father. 'My friend Priscilla, whom I trained with, works there. She said he's doing well.'

'Glad to hear it.' Geoffrey took a deep breath. 'Listen, Beth,' he said. 'I understand that Campbell is a good doctor. It's why he came here in the first place. And he did well to step in when he did.' He looked at her over the top of his glasses and then turned his attention back to the road. 'As did you, in fact.'

Beth smiled, pleased that he'd complimented her.

They had pulled up in her father's reserved parking space now. He turned off the engine, then looked at her again. 'Campbell's nice enough,' he said. 'But he needs to remember that he's not on the wards. Could cause problems for the hospital if he's seen to be treating patients.'

Beth rolled her eyes, thinking that her father would soon change his mind if he saw Gus in action.

'And Beth, it's probably better for you to keep a polite distance from Campbell.'

Beth widened her eyes innocently. 'Why?'

'Well,' her father blustered. 'It's better. Considering, you know . . . Anyway, I'm afraid you'll have to make your own way home. I've got meetings this evening.'

Beth didn't reply. She didn't like the way her father talked about Gus but she wasn't going to argue about it now. Instead, she just got out of the car. 'I'll see you at home,' she said shortly.

Chapter Twenty-One

'I'd take the chance to head home now the next shift has arrived,' Matron said to Beth later that day. 'Go and get some rest. We'll call you if we need you later.'

Beth looked around the ward and saw most of the patients were settled. For now at least. She'd handed over to the nurses working the night shift but it was hard to leave when she knew another night of raids inevitably lay ahead. She didn't argue, though. Because, once more, she was exhausted. She desperately wanted a good night's sleep and she knew she should get back home as soon as possible. It was getting dark already and she didn't want to get stuck if the siren sounded. She took off her apron and hat in the nurses' room and tried not to look at her reflection in the speckled mirror over the sink. Her hair was lank and there were dark smudges under her eyes.

She gathered her things and headed out of the hospital. She decided to get the bus, and she sat down at the bus stop with a thump. There was no sign of the bus. She leaned her head back against the shelter and closed her eyes.

'Beth?'

She looked up to see Gus standing over her, looking worried. 'Are you sick?'

She smiled – or at least tried to. 'Not sick, no. Just exhausted.'

Gus nodded. 'I understand.' He looked over the road and then back at Beth. 'I don't suppose you fancy a drink, do you? It's been a hell of a few days.'

Beth, who five minutes earlier had been too tired to even stand up, suddenly thought that there was nothing she'd like more than to sit in a warm pub with this kind, interesting man, and drink a gin and pretend that everything was normal. She smiled at Gus. 'Yes please,' she said.

They found a table in the corner and sat down. Beth saw a few people glance at Gus, some looked twice or three times, but no one bothered them.

'I don't mean to be rude, but you look very tired,' Gus said. He pronounced it 'tiyad'. Beth liked the way he said it.

'It's been quite a day.'

'Quite a week.' Gus took a mouthful of his beer.

'Can you believe how awful this is? I'd never have thought it could be like this when I was training.' She gulped her gin and orange. 'I imagine you're wishing you were safe in Jamaica now.'

Gus gave the ghost of a smile. 'Actually, I'm glad I'm here, if that doesn't sound too terrible. I'm being useful, finally.'

'They're letting you see patients?'

'Largely from necessity, I think, and only when things are desperate. No one has complained so far.'

'I'm sure patients won't mind what colour your skin is if you're saving their lives.'

'It's because of Ralph,' Gus said. 'Dr Sanderson knew I'd helped him and he said I was to be on hand if I was needed.'

Beth almost snorted because it was so typical of her father to make it sound like he was being magnanimous when really it was he who needed the favour. But Gus put his hand on hers on the table and suddenly she couldn't think of anything else other than the feeling of his fingers on hers.

'It's because of you,' he said. 'I helped Ralph because I was with you, and you told me to. And because I helped Ralph, I'm no longer stuck in the pharmacy.'

Beth's mouth was dry. She wanted a drink, but she didn't want to move because then Gus might let go of her hand. 'You'd have helped him even if I hadn't been there,' she said.

'Maybe.' Gus gave her fingers a squeeze and then let go. Beth's hand felt cold where he was no longer touching her. 'Maybe not.'

Beth felt like the plants at Kew that unfurled their leaves when the sun shone on them. She felt as though she was sitting up straighter because of Gus's attention.

And then the air-raid siren split the atmosphere between them with its violent screams and Beth jumped.

'Already?' she said, checking her watch. 'It's so early.'

Around them, people were gathering their things. They grabbed their coats and hats and bags and hurried out of the pub.

'Should we go back to the hospital?' Beth said, not sure of the best thing to do. But already the planes were overhead.

'We need to get to a shelter,' Gus said, tugging her sleeve. 'Come on.'

'Tube?' said Beth.

Gus nodded and they hurried out of the pub and followed the stream of people heading towards the underground. An ARP warden stood outside, making sure there wasn't a crush as people hurried down the stairs.

Beth fell in behind a group of women, their hair tied up in scarves. Gus put his hand on her back, which she liked because it meant she knew he was there, just behind her. But as Beth went down the first step, Gus's hand moved. She turned to see the ARP warden with his arm out, stopping Gus from going down.

'I'll wait,' she said, stepping back up. She thought the warden was stopping him to avoid a crush at the bottom and to allow the crowd to thin out a bit. But he shook his head.

'Keep going, miss.'

'We're together,' Beth said. 'I'll just wait for my friend.'

The warden gave her a hard look. 'No more space.'

'What?' Beth looked to the other side of the staircase, where people were still filing down towards the safety of the station. 'Then where are those people going?'

The warden just lifted his chin. 'No more space.'

The anti-aircraft guns were firing now and Beth thought perhaps she hadn't heard him correctly. But he was still holding his arm out, stopping Gus from entering the station. 'Don't make this harder than it has to be, mate,' he said. As if he and Gus were friends and he was giving him advice.

'This is outrageous,' Beth said. But Gus simply said: 'You go, Beth.' He gave her a gentle nudge, urging her to go down to safety and then he turned away. A flash from an explosion nearby lit up the street and Beth saw him silhouetted against the orange light, shoulders drooping in resignation.

Without thinking, she ducked under the ARP warden's still-outstretched arm and dashed after Gus.

'It's not safe,' he said as she caught him. 'Go back.'

'We'll go elsewhere. Come on.'

She took his hand and pulled him along the street. 'There's another entrance,' she said. 'We'll go in that way.'

Overhead, whistling told them another bomb was dropping. Gus pulled Beth into a shop doorway and they both crouched down, shielding their heads as it fell – further away, luckily, than they'd expected.

'Come on,' Beth said again. Her voice was steady, which surprised her because she was really very scared. 'We'll run for it.'

The streets were deserted now, everyone having taken shelter. She ran to the corner of the street, hearing the crashes as the bombs got nearer. 'This way,' she gasped. 'Just a little further.'

Another explosion right in front of them lit their way and they both shrieked in fear. 'Nearly there,' Beth said.

There was another ARP warden close to the entrance but he simply nodded at them to go in and then hurried off. Her heart pounding from fright and from running, Beth ran down the stairs on very shaky legs and stopped at the bottom to lean against the wall and catch her breath.

'You should have gone in the other entrance,' Gus scolded. 'Let's keep moving, it's not safe until we're deeper underground.'

'I wasn't going to leave you.' Beth was gasping but Gus wasn't out of breath at all.

He led the way down the escalator onto the platform.

The heat was stifling and the smell of hundreds of humans sweating in a small space was very unpleasant. But they were safe, away from the bombs, and that was the main thing.

'There's a tiny space up there,' Gus said. 'Can we squeeze in?'

They stepped over a family with two small babies and another toddler, who were all sleeping peacefully on a pile of coats, and wiggled themselves into the gap. Beth sat down with her back against the wall and took off her coat. 'I suppose we should get comfortable as best we can.'

Gus took off his coat too and sat down next to Beth.

'Lean on me,' he said. He put his arm around her and she rested her weary head on his shoulder. 'We'll be safe here.'

Beth thought she would be wide awake all night, but she dozed fitfully, off and on, her face squashed against Gus's shoulder, with someone's elbow in her side and someone else kicking her on and off throughout the evening. At one point there was a bit of a scuffle between two men further along the platform, which meant that everyone moved down and it became even more stifling and cramped. Beth felt sweat trickling down her back and wondered if it was possible for a human being to simply melt away like a snowman.

They didn't hear the all-clear but there was a gradual release of the crush and Gus shifted slightly. 'I think it's safe,' he muttered. 'I think people are leaving.'

Relieved, Beth managed to sit up straight and in a rather ungainly way, stood up. The blood flowing back into her feet gave her pins and needles and made her stagger. Gus put his arm out to steady her and she smiled at him.

Carefully, they picked their way along the platform, stepping over sleeping bodies and sprawled children and discarded bags and coats, until they reached the escalators and the blessed relief of the cool London morning.

It was very early so it was still dark; once Beth had taken a few gulps of the glorious air, she realised it was freezing cold. She felt the breeze drying the sweat on her body and shivered.

'What will you do now?' Gus said. 'Will you go home?'

Beth thought about it, then shook her head. 'What day is it today?' she asked. All the days were merging into one at the moment. Broken nights and long hours at the hospital were playing havoc with her sense of time.

Gus frowned. 'I'm not sure.'

'I think I'm supposed to be working at Kew today, so I'll go and have a wash at the hospital – if I'm needed I can help on the ward – and then I might go to the gardens by bus; I'll have to take more than one. I don't think I can bear to go underground again.'

Gus chuckled. 'I hear you,' he said. 'I'm going to go home, and then I'm working at Kew later too.'

There was a small, slightly awkward pause. Beth felt them shift from people who'd spent the night squashed up against each other, Gus's arm around her shoulder and her head on his chest, back to colleagues who liked and respected each other. It felt odd. Like putting on a pair of shoes that didn't quite fit.

'Thank you for last night,' she said again. 'I appreciated you looking out for me.'

'Any time,' Gus said. He gave her a quick kiss on the cheek. 'Any time.'

She watched him walk away from her, his long legs meaning he was quickly out of view. Then, feeling deflated, tired and very dirty, she turned and walked back to the hospital to get ready for the day.

The mood at Kew when she arrived several hours later, was sombre. A bomb had dropped at one end of the gardens, meaning that most of the gardeners were busy clearing the area and trying to make it safe. Daisy was sitting at the allotment, drinking tea from a tin mug, her breath making clouds in the frosty air and her usual jaunty smile missing.

'It's awful,' she said as Beth approached, not even bothering to say hello. 'It's awful. It feels as though the whole East End has collapsed into rubble. There are so many families without anywhere to live. Without anything at all . . .' Her voice shook. 'I love coming here because it's a break from it all – from the destruction. And now it's come to Kew, as well.'

Beth hurried over. 'I understand.'

Daisy looked at her. 'I know you do,' she said. She sounded slightly surprised.

'I spent the night in the tube station,' Beth said, wanting to let Daisy know that they were sharing the same experiences. 'It was horrible.'

'Did you get caught somewhere?'

'Gus and I went for a drink and the siren went off.'

'You went for a drink with Gus?'

Daisy's face darkened and Beth felt like she'd done something wrong. Defensive, suddenly, she changed the subject. 'Any more tea?' she asked.

Daisy shook the flask. Beth could hear the liquid sloshing about inside but Daisy shook her head. 'No,' she said.

There was a pause, the atmosphere frosty. But just as Beth was about to apologise for whatever she'd done wrong, Daisy spoke. 'Last night was another bad one, wasn't it?' she said, her expression serious. 'It made me think that we should make sure we encourage everyone who comes by today to build a shelter if they haven't already. Yesterday morning, Mum and I were walking home from the centre – you know, where they help the families that have been bombed out?'

Beth nodded and Daisy went on. 'We looked across one bomb site. It was still smoking. Broken glass everywhere. It reminded me of an awful version of the story 'The Three Little Pigs' – the houses were completely destroyed. And among all the rubble, we could just see the mounds that were shelters and I knew that all the people who'd been inside would have been safe.'

Beth could see how much Daisy had been affected by all this. 'Tell people that, then, today. Make sure they know how important it is.'

'I will.' Daisy made a face. 'Who'd have thought I'd suddenly turn out to be so passionate about Anderson shelters, eh?'

Daisy poured some tea from the flask into a cup and gave it to Beth and gratefully, she accepted. They sat quietly for a while. When they'd finished their tea, they got busy with their work, digging and planting, and talking to the crowd that gathered. Daisy gave some visitors a guided tour of the shelter and explained how strong they were, so clearly and in such an easy-to-understand way, that Beth could only watch in admiration.

As they finished one of their silly little skits, with Beth pretending not to understand how potatoes grew, and Daisy explaining how easy they were to grow, to the delight of the passers-by, Beth saw Will, the head gardener, standing nearby. She felt nervous suddenly. He'd rather left them to their own devices since they'd been at Kew. Occasionally, he would walk by and give them a nod of approval, but mostly he left it to them to follow the guidance from the Ministry of Agriculture. Now, though, he was standing watching, his sharp eyes flitting from the people watching, to Daisy and Beth, and back again.

'Will,' she said out of the corner of her mouth to Daisy, who raised an eyebrow.

They finished their little talk about potatoes and Beth was

chuffed when the crowd gave them a round of applause. She sneaked a look at Will and saw he was grinning; that was a relief.

'Ladies,' he said, coming over to them. He clapped his hands – in his gardening gloves – together. 'Great work. Really good. I knew Huw was pleased with you but I hadn't realised quite how well this was working.'

Beth beamed at Daisy who looked flushed with pride. 'We're a good team,' she said. Beth thought that was a little unfair, given that it was Daisy who brought all the knowledge to the allotment. She just did what she was told.

'I've got some exciting news,' Will was saying. 'The ministry is so pleased with how you girls are doing, that they want to feature you in a newsreel.'

Beth stared at him. 'Not an actual newsreel, though? Not one that gets shown at the pictures?'

'Absolutely an actual newsreel,' Will said, laughing. 'This was the aim all along – to get more publicity for Dig for Victory – but they weren't expecting it to take off as well as it has. That's all down to you.'

Beth exchanged a glance with Daisy. A newsreel!

'They're coming to film in a few weeks,' Will said. 'It's a team from Pathé, so they know what they're doing.'

'From Pathé?' Beth said faintly. 'Oh heavens.'

Daisy was looking rather pale. 'What will we have to do?'

'Just what you do every day,' said Will. 'Talking to the visitors, sharing your knowledge, being your usual, funny, charming selves.'

'What if we can't think of anything to say?'

'Maybe practise a few things ahead of time? You could write a script, even. Get it really slick.'

'Slick,' said Beth. 'Right you are.'

'They want you to wear your overalls but they'll do your hair and make-up,' Will said, frowning down at a piece of paper he was holding. 'All the details are here.'

He thrust the page at Daisy who took it, still looking worried.

'So, I can tell Huw that you're on board?' Will asked.

There was a pause.

'Come on, girls, you're doing a great job. We should tell everyone about it. It's a good way to raise the nation's spirits.'

Beth looked at Daisy and Daisy looked back at her, and then they both nodded.

'We're on board,' Beth said.

Pleased, Will hurried off to tell Huw, while Beth and Daisy fell into their deckchairs, laughing nervously.

'A newsreel?' Beth said. 'Goodness me. Tell you what, Daisy, I'll go and refill the flask with tea, shall I?'

Daisy didn't reply. Beth glanced over at her friend and was horrified to see her slumped over, her head between her knees.

'Oh my goodness, Daisy,' she gasped. 'Are you all right?'

'Just feeling a bit faint,' Daisy said, her voice muffled.

Beth swung into nurse mode. She sat Daisy up and felt her forehead – she was cold and clammy, which worried her slightly – and checked her pulse, and gave her some water to drink and then she put her coat down on the dusty floor of the Anderson shelter and made her lie down.

'There's not so far to fall if you faint,' she explained, propping her feet up on a plant pot. 'Stay still until you feel better. Have you eaten today?'

'Yes,' said Daisy.

'Has this happened before?'

Daisy didn't reply.

'Daisy? Has this happened before?'

'Once,' she admitted. 'Well, twice really. Maybe three times. I'm just tired, Beth. I feel drained.'

'You need some proper rest,' Beth said sternly. 'I find it impossible to sleep properly through the raids and it's worse for you, in the East End, than it is for me. Why not go home now and get some sleep? I can hold the fort here for the rest of the afternoon and maybe you'll feel better in the morning.'

She thought Daisy would argue – she normally argued about everything – but instead she just smiled. 'That would be great, if you don't mind?'

'Course not.' Beth swallowed the worry that Daisy must be feeling really awful if she was agreeing to leave early. 'Just go straight to bed, all right?'

She helped Daisy to her feet and found her hat and scarf while Daisy put on her coat. 'Don't come in tomorrow if you're not up to it,' she added. 'The allotment's fine.'

Daisy, who was still very pale but looking a little perkier, gave her a grin. 'I'll be back tomorrow,' she said. 'We need to get ready for the newsreel people.'

Relieved that she was clearly on the mend, Beth gave her a gentle nudge. 'Go home,' she said. 'I'll see you tomorrow.'

Chapter Twenty-Two

'We've still got a lot of work to do before the newsreel people come, but we're getting there,' Daisy told her parents over the breakfast table a month or so later. 'We're going to do a Christmas dinner thing – show them what veg they can grow for harvesting in the winter.' She paused and looked pleadingly at her father over her mug of tea. 'We've got some spuds, and carrots, but we don't have any sprouts growing, nor parsnips. I thought maybe . . .'

'You want to transplant some from the market garden?' Jim frowned. 'Not sure they'll be great. What do you reckon, Ivy?'

'Might be all right if we stick 'em in some pots,' Ivy said.

Daisy grinned. That was good enough for her. 'Can I come and get them this evening?'

'I'll get them ready for you.' Jim looked annoyed but Daisy knew he wasn't really. 'Come on, Poppy. Get a wriggle on.'

Poppy sighed dramatically and didn't move.

'Poppy,' warned Jim.

With considerable effort, Poppy unfolded her long gangly legs and got to her feet just as there was a knock at the door. Everyone looked up at her expectantly and she sighed. 'I'll get that then, shall I?'

Daisy chuckled, watching her sister drag herself out of the kitchen.

'And these newsreel people are going to do your hair, did you say?' Ivy looked amazed at the idea. 'Do it up all fancy?'

'Good luck to them.' Jim reached out and tousled Daisy's head and she ducked away like she had when he did it to her as a little girl, and laughed, and then she looked up and saw Poppy standing in the kitchen doorway, her face white.

'What is it?' Ivy said.

Poppy didn't speak, she just stood to one side and there, behind her in the hall, just by the front door, was the telegraph boy – young Malcolm from the Post Office.

Ivy and Jim stood up at the same time. Ivy's hand went to her mouth. 'Is it Archie?' she said. 'Is it my Archie?'

But Malcolm wasn't looking at Ivy. He was looking straight at Daisy.

The edges of Daisy's vision went blurry and she closed her eyes briefly. She heard someone say her name, but she wasn't sure if it was her father, or Poppy, or even Malcolm. Taking a deep breath, she opened her eyes and then slowly but deliberately she got up from the table and walked down the hall to where Malcolm stood waiting. She kept her eyes fixed on her feet. She was wearing thick socks because it was freezing being in the gardens all day and Daisy's toes always got cold. It was like watching someone else's feet walking the few steps from the kitchen to the hall. She wondered how it was that her feet were walking when she wasn't telling them to. She didn't want to go to Malcolm. She didn't want to take the envelope he held out. And yet, there she was, taking it from him and opening it and reading the awful words from the Air Ministry:

Regret to advise you that your husband Pilot Officer Rex J Cooper has lost his life as a result of air operations over Germany on 20 October 1940.

Daisy squeezed her lips tightly together and nodded. 'No reply,' she said.

'Very sorry,' Malcolm said, backing out of the door. Daisy watched him get onto his bicycle and head off down the street, swerving to avoid a pile of rubble. Then she shut the front door and stood for a second in the hall, gripping the telegram tightly.

'Daisy?' Poppy sat on the stairs, her face wet with tears. Daisy looked at her, finding it hard to understand why she was there, in her school uniform, her gas mask slung over her shoulder and her bag in her hand. Why was she pretending everything was normal when nothing was going to be the same again?

She looked away from her sister and instead looked at the telegram once more. The Air Council express profound sympathy, it said. Daisy didn't understand that either. Who were the Air Council? They didn't know Rex. Why would they offer their sympathy and why should she care?

'Daisy?' Her mother stood there, her face etched in sadness. 'Come and sit down, love.'

Daisy let Ivy lead her into the living room where she stood, still holding the telegram, until someone – her father, presumably – took it out of her hand while her mother gently pulled her down to sit on the sofa.

'Daisy, we're so sorry,' Ivy said.

She could hear the words and she knew why they were being said, but it was like they weren't going into her brain somehow. Rex was dead; her worst nightmare was happening. Poppy was crying on the stairs and Ivy was wiping away tears. Jim had his arm round her shoulders, comforting her and somehow, for some inexplicable reason, that made no sense to her; Daisy didn't feel anything at all.

'Will Rex's parents get a telegram, too?' she asked her father.

He looked startled, but then nodded. 'I assume so.'

'Good. They need to know.'

'They do.'

'Dad, could you put that somewhere safe for me please?' Daisy said, pointing to the telegram that was now being gripped by her father's fingers. 'I expect I'll need it.'

Without a word, Jim put the envelope carefully into the writing desk by the fireplace. Satisfied, Daisy tapped her hands on her knees and then she stood up.

'Where are you off to?' Ivy said. Her voice was thick with tears and Daisy almost felt envious.

'Work.'

'Sweetheart, you don't have to work today.'

'Why not?'

Ivy looked stricken. 'Because Rex has been killed, sweetheart. He's dead.'

Daisy nodded. 'I know,' she said.

Feeling their eyes on her, she went out into the hall and put on her coat. She thought that she would forever remember that this was where she had been standing when she found out her husband had been killed.

'I'm so sorry, Daisy,' Poppy said, still sitting on the stairs, tears falling down her cheeks.

'It's not your fault.' Daisy tried to smile at her sister but her lips wouldn't move properly. She pulled her scarf from the peg and slung it round her neck, then put on her hat. 'I'm going to work.'

She opened the front door and walked outside, feeling the icy wind on her cheeks and the dust in her eyes from last night's raid. Across the road, a fire was burning, with firemen shouting to one another as they doused the flames. A woman in a nightgown was crying, two small children huddled next to her. She needed to go to the centre, Daisy thought. They would look after her. She took a step towards her, planning to tell her that there were people who would help, but stopped as someone caught her arm.

'Daisy.' She turned to see her mother there, holding a pair of boots. 'You need these.'

Slowly, Daisy looked down and realised that she was standing on the path in her woolly socks.

'Oh,' she said. 'Silly me.' She started to laugh, even though it wasn't that funny, and then suddenly she wasn't laughing anymore but crying. Sobbing, huge shuddering wails that hurt her chest and made her double over with the pain of it all.

'Come back inside,' Ivy said. 'Come with me, my girl. We'll look after you.'

Chapter Twenty-Three

Daisy slept for most of the day, occasionally roused enough to be aware of voices downstairs, or of Ivy peeking round the door to check on her. She was grateful that her parents had taken charge. She didn't even want to think about having to tell people what had happened. She couldn't say the words.

Each time she woke she remembered all over again that Rex was dead, that she would never see his lovely face again, or hear his laugh and she would feel the tears start. She would bury her face in her pillow and cry until she slept.

Of course, that meant that when evening came and the family had to go to the shelter, Daisy couldn't sleep at all, no matter how much she longed to simply cover her head with a blanket and block out the world. Jim stayed at home that evening, making sure Ivy and the girls were settled in the shelter, but then he went off to do his ARP warden duties as usual, leaving Poppy and Ivy sleeping, and Daisy curled up under her blanket, pretending to snooze in the hope that if she faked it, sleep would come eventually.

But it didn't. The bombs were as loud as ever but somehow Ivy and Poppy slept on. Exhausted by the emotion of the day, it seemed.

Daisy sat up on the hard bunk bed, hugging her knees. She felt the thuds as the bombs fell around them and wondered what Rex had felt when he died. Had he been shot down? Or perhaps his plane had crashed? Was he scared? Did he know what was happening? Was he in pain?

She stifled yet more sobs in her sleeve and wiped her eyes. She tried to remember what Rex had said to her – every word – the day she'd waved him off at the station. Had she told him that she loved him? She didn't know. Had he known how proud she was of him? She couldn't recall their conversation. Her heart began to pound and she gasped for breath as she realised she couldn't remember what Rex looked like. Not really. She could picture his RAF uniform and his hair poking out from beneath his hat . But how many freckles did he have on his nose? How did his eyes crinkle when he smiled? She pressed her hand against her chest trying to control her breathing. She didn't know. She couldn't remember. She had photographs, of course, but they were all in her bedroom.

Perhaps she could get them? she thought. Suddenly the bombs seemed much less frightening than not knowing what Rex's smile looked like.

Was it safe to run into the house and back again? Probably not. But so what if it wasn't? She found she didn't really care about her own safety.

She slid off the bunk quietly and crept to the door of the shelter. Ivy and Poppy slept on so Daisy pushed open the door a crack and squeezed through, shutting it firmly behind. She may not be fussed about keeping herself safe, but she didn't want any harm to come to her family.

It was a cold night. Daisy was in an old pair of Archie's baggy pyjamas with thick socks on her feet, because it was cold in the shelter, but that was no match for the icy wind. Autumn was definitely here now, though the trees had been bare for weeks – any leaves blasted off by the explosions. Daisy shivered, but she quite welcomed the sensation of the chilly night air on her bare arms. The sky was lit up, glowing orange and flashing with anti-aircraft gunfire and the air was thick with smoke. Daisy looked around her in fascination and instead of going up the garden and into the house, she went round to the side gate and through it onto the street.

The pavement shook beneath her socks as she stood, looking at the devastation. Up ahead a house crumbled like a sandcastle when the tide came in, and a cloud of dust billowed up. Daisy felt the grit in her eyes and her throat. But she didn't move. She was stuck, watching in morbid curiosity as the world around her – once so familiar she could navigate her way through the streets with her eyes closed – changed.

Planes were overhead, high above the houses. She looked up, seeing an endless stream of bombs falling, one, two, three … She watched as they fell and then heard the thumps and roars as they landed close by. It was so loud her head pounded with every blast, but still she stayed where she was.

She could hear sirens and occasional shouts in between the bombs and a sort of weird silence after each explosion like the air had been sucked away for a second. She felt as though all her senses were on high alert. She could hear and see so much, she could smell the smoke and – was that gas? – feel the dust in the night air. It was starting to rain now and she felt the moisture on her arms and in her hair. That would help the firemen, she thought. And as if the cold water had woken her from a nightmare, she realised suddenly how foolish she was being, standing outside on the pavement in the middle of an air raid. She took a step back towards her house, just as there was a whooshing sound and she fell backwards and the world went dark.

When she woke she was on a stretcher in a white room that looked vaguely familiar. She sat up, feeling her head aching, and gingerly touched her hair. There was a big lump there.

'Don't try to stand up,' a voice said. There was a man standing by the door. He was older than she was, closer to her parents' age, and he was wearing a grubby white coat with a stethoscope round his neck. He looked very tired. Daisy felt a flush of shame for causing trouble for the people who were helping those in genuine need. Putting herself in danger.

'Where am I?'

'Community centre. Poplar Street.'

'My mum volunteers here,' Daisy said. No wonder it looked familiar. 'What happened?'

'Gas main went up.' The doctor sounded matter-of-fact. 'Not where you were standing, thank goodness, but you just got caught in the wind from the blast and it knocked you over. You'll have a headache for a day or two, but you're fine.' He paused. 'And so is your baby.'

Daisy stared at him. Her baby?

She couldn't speak for a moment and the doctor, who'd been bending over his notes, looked up at her. 'You're expecting a baby,' he said.

Daisy pinched her lips together.

'You didn't know?'

Daisy thought about the times she'd felt faint and queasy. She hadn't for one minute thought . . .

'How far along?'

'At least seven months, by my reckoning,' said the doctor. 'Maybe a little more.'

Daisy felt very foolish. How had she not realised?

'Are you sure?'

'Quite sure.' He frowned at her. 'You didn't know?'

Very slowly, Daisy let her hand drop to her abdomen. It felt firm and rounded underneath Archie's old pyjamas. She shook her head.

'You didn't even have an inkling?' the doctor asked. He looked a bit stern, like she'd disappointed him.

Had she had an inkling? Daisy thought about it and realised that actually she had, but she had simply pushed away any niggling thoughts that this could be happening. 'I think I did know,' she admitted. 'I've not been feeling great.'

The doctor gave her a sympathetic smile. 'Husband away, is he?'

Daisy nodded.

'He'll be chuffed to bits when you tell him, I bet. Give him something nice to focus on, eh?'

For a second, Daisy allowed herself to pretend that she would write the news in a letter to Rex. And he would read it and beam with pride – he'd tell all his friends in Bomber Command. And then the horrible reality overtook her and she remembered that it was too late. Rex would never know now that she was having his baby. She would never be able to tell him the news. Never give him something to focus on. Because Rex was dead and it was too late. She snatched her hand away from her curved belly.

'I have to go,' she said. 'Has the all-clear gone?'

'It has, but I really think you should wait for someone to come and walk home with you,' the doctor said, sounding concerned. 'Is there someone I can call?'

Daisy wondered if her mother had realised she'd gone. Ivy would be frantic with worry. She thought about her father, spending all night working through the raids, and how upset he'd be if he knew she'd been wandering around while the bombs dropped.

'I have to go,' she said again. She stood up, wobbling slightly, and arranged Archie's baggy pyjama top over her swelling abdomen. With a start she realised she'd been doing this for weeks, wearing loose clothes that disguised any hint of a pregnant belly. Perhaps she really had known all along. 'Thank you.'

She pushed past the doctor, out into the corridor and through the doors into the smoke and flames of the East London dawn.

Chapter Twenty-Four

Louisa was in a heavenly flurry of organisation. Within days of taking on the task of organising the WIs up and down the country to grow and pick the plants Kew needed, she'd realised the tiny spare room in their cottage wasn't up to the task. So she'd asked around and it turned out the local doctor had recently added an extra room to the side of his large house at the other end of the village, where he was going to have his surgery. His former office – a small building tucked away next to the pub – was empty. It had a small reception area, a largish room behind and a flat upstairs that the doctor had used for storage. It was perfect for what Louisa needed and he kindly said she could have it for a peppercorn rent. She moved in immediately and set about putting up shelves and pinning maps to the walls. It was a very enjoyable way to spend her time.

She'd been doing lots of research into medicinal plants, even though the committee were doing the actual work when it came to all that. It was fascinating stuff. She'd learned so much already and – she flattered herself – she'd known a lot about plants before she'd started. The committee sent her regular reports on what they had discovered. Louisa was pleased to see Beth's name mentioned in their notes. She'd suggested they concentrate on sleep, which was a marvellous idea, so the first plant they'd asked for was valerian.

Louisa had worked out where in the country it grew wild, and got in touch with the local WIs. They'd jumped at the chance to be involved and were on standby ready to get picking. It wouldn't be quite yet – winter wasn't the time to be out in the hedgerows looking for plants – but spring would be here before they knew it and Louisa was determined to be prepared. She was well aware that this was a vitally important job she was doing and she was going to do it properly.

She was arranging some of her gardening books on her new bookshelves – which she'd put up by herself and was very proud of – when there was a knock on the door of her office. Carefully putting her prized copy of *A Year in My Garden*, given to her by her good friend Bernie, on the shelf, she hurried through the reception area to open the door. Perhaps some houseplants would be nice in here, she thought, looking around the rather gloomy and rundown room. They would bring a bit of life to the place.

She opened the door and there, on the doorstep, was Mrs Worthing from the Post Office, holding a telegram. Louisa's stomach plummeted into her boots and she steadied herself on the doorframe.

'Is it Christopher?' she stammered. 'Is he . . .?'

Mrs Worthing put her hand out and patted Louisa's arm. 'I knew you'd think that. That's why I wanted to come myself.' She held out the telegram. 'It's not official.'

Numbly, Louisa took the piece of paper and slit it open. It was from Ivy. She'd never sent a telegram before and Louisa thought that Jim must have helped her with the words:

Rex killed in action. Daisy in bits.

'Oh,' she gasped, putting her hand to her mouth. 'Oh no.'

She swayed slightly and Mrs Worthing kindly caught her elbow. 'Let's get you inside.'

She bustled Louisa into the waiting area and sat her down on one of the worn chairs. 'Is there a kettle?'

Louisa, who'd bought a tiny primus stove and a kettle just the day before, looked over to the table under the window where it all stood, with a few chipped mugs, a ceramic teapot, a canister of tea and a sugar bowl.

'Milk?' Mrs Worthing asked.

'Windowsill.' Poor, poor Daisy, Louisa thought. She'd had no time with Rex. No time at all. War was so cruel.

Mrs Worthing deftly made a pot of tea and then sat down next to Louisa to wait for it to brew. She didn't ask about the telegram but Louisa told her anyway.

'My god-daughter has lost her husband,' she said carefully. She didn't want to say the word 'dead'. It seemed too final, which was ridiculous because that's exactly what it was. Final.

'I'm sorry to hear that,' said Mrs Worthing.

'They only got married in the summer.'

'Terrible business.'

'It is,' said Louisa, realising for the hundredth time just how terrible it was. She looked down at the telegram she was still clutching. 'It's a terrible business.'

Mrs Worthing gave a little nod. 'I bet you miss your Christopher something awful.'

Pleased to talk about something else, Louisa tried to smile and found she couldn't, so she nodded vigorously instead. 'We both do,' she said. 'He's so much fun to have around. He keeps us young.'

'Always getting into scrapes, isn't he?'

'Always.'

Mrs Worthing got up and poured the tea. She opened the window and took the bottle of milk from the window ledge outside where it was keeping cool and poured just enough into each mug, then put it back and closed the glass again. It was a cold day and Louisa shivered as the draught hit her and then again when the front door to the office opened. It was Teddy.

Louisa got up and went to her husband and told him about Rex and cried a little. And Mrs Worthing gave Teddy the mug of tea she'd made for herself and left them to it.

'I thought it was Christopher,' Louisa admitted. 'And then I was pleased it wasn't him and then I felt awful for having thought that in the first place.'

'When Philip was killed I would look at soldiers and think "Why are you alive when my son isn't?" which is a terrible thing to think,' Teddy said. 'I didn't really wish those lads dead, of course I didn't. I was grieving. Just as you weren't wishing anything bad on Rex, poor sod.'

Louisa nodded. 'I feel awful for Daisy. When Win lost her Archie in the Great War it was ever so sad, of course, but she had so many memories of them together. They'd been married for years and they'd built a life together. Daisy and Rex barely got started.' Her voice cracked. 'They were going to have a big party at the end of the war, you know? A second wedding, Daisy said. So they could invite everyone who'd missed out when they tied the knot.'

Teddy gathered Louisa into his arms. 'It's very sad,' he said. 'Rex was a lovely chap.' He looked around. 'Are you done here for now?'

'I suppose so.'

'How about we pop across to the pub? We can sit by the fire and get warm and toast Rex.'

'That sounds like an excellent idea.'

Louisa went to find her coat and they locked up the office and walked along the road, arm in arm, towards the pub. It was raining quite heavily now and a horribly murky fog had descended on the village, which sat in a little valley and was prone to being engulfed in mist.

'What an awful evening,' Louisa said, shivering. 'Horrible.'

But Teddy had stopped walking. He was staring through the gloom, an expression of disbelief on his face.

'What's the matter?'

'I thought for a minute—'

'What?'

And then, almost right in front of them, was Christopher. He was in his uniform, knapsack on his back. His hair was very short and he was propped up on crutches.

'Hello, Uncle Ted,' he said cheerfully. 'I was hoping I'd see you.'

Teddy and Louisa both rushed to him and threw their arms around him.

'We're going for a drink,' Teddy said. 'Want to join us?'

Christopher turned towards the pub, almost knocking Louisa over with his enormous backpack. 'Nothing I'd like more,' he said.

They settled in a little nook by the fire and Teddy went to the bar. Louisa filled Christopher in on what had happened to Rex. He'd met Daisy a few times when they were children and though he didn't know Rex, he'd heard a lot about him.

'Crikey, poor chap,' said Christopher. 'And poor Daisy.'

'What about you, Chris?' Teddy said, putting their drinks on the table in front of them and sitting down. 'What happened to you? Where have you been? I thought you were still training?'

Christopher tried to tuck his long legs under the table and couldn't manage it, so he shifted sideways on his seat and stretched them out instead. A woman heading to the ladies had to step over his sizeable feet as she went.

'You mean this?' Christopher said, gesturing to the enormous cast on his left foot.

'Yes, that.' Louisa frowned. 'How did it happen?'

'I was shot.'

Louisa had taken a mouthful of her sherry and now she spluttered in a most unladylike fashion. 'Shot?'

'Bloody hell, Christopher,' said Teddy in alarm. 'You've not been in the army five minutes. I really think they should be properly training lads like you before they send them off to see active service.'

'I didn't get that far,' Christopher said looking slightly shame-faced. 'I wasn't shot by a German, I was shot by a Brit.'

Teddy's face went puce. 'Even more reason for there to be proper training. Who shot you? Was it an accident? He didn't mean it, did he?'

'Oh it was an accident all right,' said Christopher. He swigged his beer. 'I was in the wrong place at the wrong time. We were in Holland. We'd only been there a week, and we were moving through this village. Really creepy it was. Totally deserted. Odd shadows everywhere. We thought there might be people hiding out so we were on edge, you know? We were all jumpy. We spread out and I was trailing behind. So I walked faster to catch them up and Timmins, nice bloke, he got a bit startled. He turned and boom! That was me done.'

Louisa blinked at him. 'You were shot by a friend?'

'Not deliberately, Auntie Lou. Just one of those things. Like I said, he's a nice bloke. He felt awful about it – had a bit of a funny turn afterwards. Or perhaps he was having the funny turn then and that's why he was so nervy. Anyway, he's been sent home too.' He grimaced. 'It's not for everyone, the army. Poor bugger.'

'Poor you,' said Louisa.

'I know!' Christopher exclaimed. 'It bloody hurt. I've lost some of my toes. I can't go back, I'm invalided out. Because I've lost three toes. If it had only been one, I think I'd have been all right.'

'Going back to the farm, then?' Louisa was sorry about Christopher's toes, but she felt huge relief. Utter sweet relief that he was home safely, if not completely in one piece, and wouldn't be going back.

'I think it's for the best, don't you?' said Christopher.

Chapter Twenty-Five

Beth was trying her best to be a good friend to Daisy, but she wasn't making it easy. She absolutely refused to talk about Rex. She had simply stopped mentioning him altogether. She didn't so much as utter his name. Sometimes Beth thought she was about to, then she checked herself and trailed off as if she'd lost her train of thought. It was as though she'd shut off that part of herself – put her sadness and her former happiness away.

Instead, Daisy had thrown herself into the preparation for the newsreel filming, so Beth decided to do the same. One of the main aims of the Dig for Victory campaign was to tell people that they could grow and harvest fruit and veg all year round. So with that in mind, Beth and Daisy were planning to show the visitors to Kew how they could grow all the veg for Christmas dinner to prove that there could be crops in winter as well as summer. They'd been writing a script and having a lot of fun putting it all together.

'We can make some hats,' Beth suggested. 'And sing carols.'

Daisy made a face. 'I'm not much of a singer. But we could wrap up some boxes to look like presents, perhaps?'

Beth had agreed, enjoying seeing her friend caught up in something, anything, that would relieve her sadness, even for a moment.

Daisy's dad, Jim, who Beth thought was a lovely, quiet, thoughtful man, had brought them some plants – parsnips and sprouts

– to put into the allotment. They were doing this while they were chatting, with Beth pausing every now and then to scribble down some ideas.

'Did Rex like Christmas?' she asked cautiously.

Daisy gave her an odd look, as though she didn't understand the question. 'I hope these parsnips take to being transplanted,' she said.

Beth got the message. It was clear Daisy didn't want to talk about Rex and, actually, she thought, why would she? They'd never had a Christmas as husband and wife and now they never would. Feeling awkward, she cast around for something else to say. 'I was working with Gus on Friday. I was telling him about what we're doing and he said that in Jamaica they have rum cake for Christmas, and they all dress up in scary costumes and parade through the town.'

'That doesn't sound very Christmassy,' Daisy said.

'That's what I said.'

Daisy looked like she was going to say something else but then she shut her mouth and picked up her spade instead. Out of the corner of her eye, Beth watched her. She looked so fragile and pale that the nurse in Beth was concerned about her.

Daisy stuck her spade into the earth, stood still for a moment, and then slowly, like a deckchair folding up after a day at the beach, she dropped to the floor in a faint.

'Oh, heavens above,' said Beth, looking around frantically. She dropped to her knees next to Daisy.

'Daisy, wake up,' she said. She lifted her wrist and felt her pulse, which was strong, thank goodness. Across the way, close to the Orangery, she saw Will chatting to another gardener. 'Will!' she called. 'Will, help!'

Will caught her worried tone and came hurrying across as Beth stroked Daisy's hair, trying to rouse her.

'Is she all right?' Will asked. 'Is she ill? Is this to do with her losing her husband?'

Beth didn't say that in her opinion, Daisy had been poorly for a while. Since before she heard the news about Rex. She didn't want to give him a reason to send her home to wallow in her misery, nor to dismiss her altogether. She thought going back to sending out leaflets about Anderson shelters might finish poor Daisy off completely. The truth was, Beth was convinced that there was something physically wrong with her friend. She was desperately worried about her and determined to get to the bottom of it. But, first of all, she had to get Will to help her up.

'I think she's just tired,' she lied. 'Could we get her into a deck-chair, do you think?'

With some gentle encouragement, Daisy managed to open her eyes and let Beth and Will take one arm each and put her into the chair, where she rested her head against the hard, wooden frame.

'I might see if any of the doctors at the VDC are around,' Will said. 'Give her the once over before she goes home.'

Beth thought that she could do that very well herself, but she knew Will was just being kind. 'Good idea,' she said, smiling. 'Thanks for helping.'

Will dashed off and Beth looked at her friend.

'Daisy,' she said quietly, not wanting to alarm her. 'I think there's something the matter with you and I think you should go to hospital.'

Daisy's eyes snapped open.

'I'm fine, Beth,' she said. 'Honestly, I am. I've just not been taking care of myself.'

Beth shook her head. 'No, I think it's more than that. People don't faint as often as you've been fainting just because they've missed breakfast, or slept badly.'

Daisy struggled to sit upright and she gave Beth a fierce glare. 'I faint all the time,' she muttered. 'I've always been a fainter.'

'Really?' Beth was doubtful, but it was possible. 'Perhaps you've got low blood pressure.'

'Perhaps,' said Daisy. 'So I wouldn't need to go to the hospital about that, would I?'

'You should probably see a doctor, though. Your family doctor would know what to do. Or I could ask someone at the hospital.'

'Beth?' Both women turned to see Will hurrying towards them, followed by Gus. Beth's heart – much to her alarm – did a little jump in a way it never did when she saw Paul.

'Hello, Gus,' she said, trying to sound casual. 'Daisy fainted. Her pulse is strong, if a bit fast, and her breathing was shallow but it's recovering.'

'Thank you,' he said. He looked at Daisy. 'May I touch you?' he said, and Beth's heart broke a little bit because he looked like he expected her to say no. But Daisy nodded and Gus reached out and took her pulse himself, checking his watch, before nodding. 'Still a touch fast. Do you have any pain?'

Daisy shook her head.

'No headache? Stomach ache? Ear ache?'

'No pain.'

Beth put her hand on Gus's arm. 'Her husband—' she said in a low voice.

Gus's eyes widened as he remembered what had happened to Rex. 'It could be low blood pressure,' he said, turning back to Daisy, looking sympathetic. 'But you must make an appointment to get checked over. There might be a reason for it.'

Will scratched his nose. 'Daisy, I can't have you working if you're poorly. I really think you should go home and rest. Especially with everything that's happened.'

Daisy gave him a fierce glare. 'Everything that's happened is exactly why I don't want to go home,' she hissed. 'Being here helps.'

'But—' Will began and shut his mouth as Daisy glared at him again.

'I feel better now,' she told Gus. Beth thought she sounded like a little girl asking if she could go out to play. 'Can I stay here?'

'How about a compromise?' Gus said. 'You make an appointment to see a doctor, Beth can check that you're all right each morning, and you do nothing strenuous for the rest of today? Does that work for you, William?'

Will looked worried but he shrugged. 'If you're sure.'

Gus was very clever, Beth thought admiringly. He knew that whatever was wrong with Daisy wouldn't make her feel as bad as being alone at home would. He was exactly the kind of doctor she wanted to be. Knowledgeable and kind. A good bedside manner.

'We can work on our ideas for the newsreel,' she said, forcing herself to stop thinking such dreamy thoughts about Gus. 'That's not strenuous. What do you think, Daisy?'

'Perfect,' Daisy said. She stood up – Beth could tell she was trying her best to seem strong and healthy, even though she was still pale and drawn – and shook Gus's hand. 'Thank you for looking after me.'

Beth gazed at Gus, proud as punch of him for being so good with Daisy. She'd never felt this proud of Paul, she thought rather unfairly. She didn't even know what he did at work all day.

'Beth!'

At first she thought she was imagining Paul's voice, but she turned and there he was, picking his way across the wet lawn towards them.

'Paul? What are you doing here?'

'Had to see a chap in Richmond about a munitions factory. Terribly dull.' Beth felt bad as she realised that Paul probably was doing important work after all, despite her dismissing his job. 'I thought I'd pop in and say hello.'

She smiled thinly. 'Hello.'

'You look so funny, Betsy. What are you wearing?'

'Overalls.'

'You're filthy.'

Beth looked down at her trousers which were thick with mud from kneeling next to Daisy when she fainted and decided not to answer.

Daisy was looking at Paul with curiosity. She stuck her hand out for him to shake and then pulled it away when she saw him glance at her dirty palms. She put her hand in her pocket instead. Beth felt ashamed of Paul being so fussy.

'This is Daisy,' she said. 'We work on the allotment together.'

'Paul Flint. Beth's boyfriend,' Paul said with a broad smile. 'I've heard a lot about you. You're the brains of the operation, I understand.'

It seemed he did listen to her after all. Beth was surprised. Daisy, who was still looking a bit peaky, smiled broadly. 'I'd be lost without Beth,' she said.

'Me too,' said Paul. 'Absolutely lost.'

'This is Will Potter , the head gardener,' Beth said, feeling self-conscious. 'And Dr Gus Campbell. He's on the drugs committee and he works at St Catherine's too.'

Paul turned to greet Will and Gus and practically drew back in shock as he took in Gus's appearance. Beth felt her cheeks flame.

'I won't shake your hand,' said Will jovially enough but Beth couldn't help thinking there was an edge to his tone.

'No,' Paul said, with a loud chuckle. Beth noticed he didn't offer to shake Gus's hand, which was – obviously – clean as a whistle.

'Shall we go, then?' Paul said.

'Go where?' Beth was genuinely confused.

'Home.'

'I'm not finished.'

'Yes, but I'm here now.'

'Do you want to plant out those sprouts?'

Paul stared at her. He looked a bit hurt and Beth felt guilty. 'I'm busy,' she said, more gently.

'You're always busy,' he said in a low tone. 'I miss you.'

'I'm not at the hospital until tomorrow. Maybe we could go to the pictures in town this evening? I can come straight there when we're done with these veg.' Paul looked much less pleased than Beth had expected. 'Or not?' she said.

'Will you get changed first?'

'You don't like the overalls?'

'You always look beautiful,' he said hurriedly. 'But they are quite mucky.'

Beth laughed. 'Of course I'll change first.'

'Then I will see you outside the Odeon,' Paul said. 'Seven o'clock?'

'Perfect.'

Paul turned to Daisy and the others, the perfect gentleman in his suit and overcoat, hat in hand. 'Lovely to meet you,' he said. He didn't sound like he thought it had been lovely. Or perhaps Beth was being unkind again.

He went off towards the path, picking his way across the lawn in his shiny shoes.

'Let's get on, shall we?' said Beth.

Gus was watching Paul leave. He glanced at Beth, his eyes resting on her for a split second, and then he turned to Daisy. 'Remember what I said?'

'I will. Don't worry. I'll be fine.'

'Cheerio, then.' Gus nodded to Beth and walked off, full of purpose, towards the main building.

Will grinned at Beth. 'Best not tell the Pathé people that you've got a sweetheart,' he said with a wink. 'I think they want you to be a pin-up girl for the Dig for Victory campaign.'

'Don't,' Beth said, but she wasn't sure if it was the mention of being a pin-up that had made her feel uncomfortable, or him calling Paul her sweetheart.

Daisy gave Beth an odd look. 'Let's get on, then, shall we? You need to finish if you're going to make it to the pictures.' She glanced over to where Paul was vanishing through the large iron gates. 'With your sweetheart.' She said 'sweetheart' as though it was a word she didn't understand. Once more, Beth felt like she'd done something wrong, but she didn't know what it was. So she simply picked up her spade and started digging.

Chapter Twenty-Six

Dear Rex,

No one knows. I keep thinking I'll tell Mum. Sit her down one evening and tell her what the doctor told me. In normal times, she'd have noticed. She'd have spotted that I'm raiding Archie's drawers for jumpers and living in my overalls from work most of the time. She'd have seen that I'm often light-headed and that I'm ravenous in the mornings. And Dad would have realised that my patch in the garden is overgrown and full of weeds because I'm so very, very tired when I get home from Kew that I can't possibly think about doing any more work.

But they haven't said a thing. They didn't even notice I'd left the shelter that night when the doctor told me about the baby. Mum saw I wasn't there when she woke up, of course, but she believed me when I told her I'd just popped out for some air after the all-clear went. And Dad wasn't there, so he didn't know how foolish I'd been, going out in the middle of all the bombs. I've not done it again, though sometimes I think about it. Waiting until the planes are right overhead, then just standing outside and letting it happen. But perhaps I am too cowardly. Not like you, Rex.

The raids are still happening every night and Dad is out in the streets, directing people to shelters and helping with recovery when houses collapse. He only has a tin hat to keep him safe. It's no protection at all.

And Mum's at the shelter most days. There are families with nothing, Rex. Just the clothes they stand up in. Sometimes not even that. Mum and the other women look after them, give them food and clothes and somewhere to go. And there's a pub, down by the tube station, where they're staying open all day and all night in case soldiers come home and don't know where their families are. The landlady has covered one wall in messages and photos and she knows everything and everyone and she's helping people find one another. You should see it, Rex.

Daisy paused in her scribbling and took a deep breath. Tears, never far away now, pricked her eyelids. Because Rex wouldn't see it, would he? He'd never see it. She shifted on the armchair where she sat and in her belly felt a swooshing and fluttering as her baby moved inside her, reminding her of what else Rex would never see. She pulled a cushion out from behind her back and put it over her abdomen, and then rested her notepad on top. She didn't want to think about that.

She put her pen back on the paper.

When I got the telegram, I felt like all the happiness was sucked out of the world. Things I used to enjoy, like going to the pictures, or having a gossip with the girls over a cup of tea, seem pointless now. The only thing that keeps me going is Kew Gardens. Putting my hands in the earth, watching the vegetables in our allotment growing, is giving me a reason to get up every day.

The Pathé people are coming to film us for the newsreel. Huw is delighted. Poppy's green with envy because she has decided she wants to be a war correspondent. I am trying to muster up some enthusiasm for the whole thing but I find smiling much more difficult than it used to be.

Luckily, I'm sure Beth will be the focus of all the attention because she is so pretty. Her hair is always glossy and she looks like she is wearing kohl round her eyes even when she is barefaced.

It's maddening because all she cares about is becoming a doctor. She doesn't even seem to be that bothered about her fella. Paul, his name is. He does seem a bit stuffy, but nice enough. And he's here, Rex. Here in London, safe behind a desk. I'm so jealous I could scream.

When I wake up, my first thought is of you, and my second is of our parsnips or our cabbages, or of Kew Gardens itself, and how it'll be looking today. And that's another reason why I've not told anyone. Because I'm scared they'll stop me working. Will wanted me to go home when I fainted, but I talked him out of it. If he knew the truth, I'm positive he'd not let me work. And if they take this away from me too, then I won't have any reason to get up in the morning. No reason at all.

She wiped her eyes. She felt a little bit better after putting her feelings down on paper. A little bit.

Nothing seems to matter now you're not here, she wrote finally. I miss you every minute of every day.

She turned the page over and with a deep breath she added:

I do not want to have your baby if you are not here with me. I do not want to be a mother without you by my side to be a father. I would swap this child to have you back safely. I do not want it. I do not want this life.

Shocked at how candid she'd been, and almost disgusted by her own feelings, she tore the page from her pad and crumpled it up in her fist. Then she uncurled her legs from underneath her, slowly, because she had learned that if she stood up too fast then she was bound to faint. She went through the kitchen and out of the backdoor to where her father stood, burning some rubbish at the side of the frosty garden.

'Hello, girl,' he said, looking pleased to see her. Daisy gave him a thin smile, thinking that he wouldn't be so happy if he knew what she was thinking. If he knew the awful, horrible things that were swirling around her head and which she'd put down on the paper she held in her hand. 'Fancy a cup of tea?'

Daisy nodded. She knew he was angling for her to offer to make it, but she didn't. Instead, she pretended to be distracted by a crop of pretty-looking mushrooms that had sprouted up at the foot of the small tree at the bottom of the garden. Out of the corner of her eye, she saw her father glance in her direction, then take off his gardening gloves and go inside. As soon as he was gone, Daisy went to the bonfire and dropped the letter onto the flames. It caught immediately. She picked up a stick and poked it down more firmly, not wanting it to blow away in the wintery wind that was whistling through the garden. She stood watching it vanish into ash for a few moments, her arms wrapped around herself against the cold. Then she went back inside where Jim was filling the kettle.

'I'll do that, Dad,' she said. 'You go and have a sit down.'

He gave her a quick hug. 'Sounds like a plan,' he said. He looked at her closely. 'Are you all right, Daisy?'

'I'm absolutely fine,' she lied. But she wasn't. And, deep down, she thought she would never really be fine ever again.

Chapter Twenty-Seven

Daisy woke up on the morning of the newsreel filming feeling worse than she had for weeks. It was really early, still dark outside, though everything was quiet and she knew it was safe to leave the shelter. Carefully, because her whole body ached and because she didn't want to stand up too suddenly in case she fainted, she eased herself off her narrow bunk and slid out of the door. The morning air was cold on her warm cheeks and she took a sharp breath, pulling her dressing gown round her more tightly.

Putting one foot in front of the other was an effort but she got to the kitchen where she made herself a cup of tea and began to feel slightly better. She absolutely had to go to work today – there was no way Beth could do the filming by herself. That wasn't fair. So instead, she heated the water for a bath and as the warmth soothed her aching legs, she let herself doze for a few minutes, and allowed herself to think about Rex – just for a moment or two – remembering the way his hand felt in hers, how safe she felt when she was wrapped in his arms. The times they'd laughed so much she thought she might be sick, or when he took her to see *Gone With the Wind* and he'd been so swept up in Scarlett's story that he'd definitely had tears in his eyes, even though he pretended he hadn't.

Beth had been reading books about how the brain worked, because she needed to fill what little spare time she had with studying. She said she wanted to understand how the mind helped people recover from injury. It sounded like gobbledygook to Daisy but Beth was adamant it made a difference. She'd said that Daisy should let herself be sad about Rex, so she'd taken to doing this. She would give herself a few minutes every day to remember, and then, like turning off a tap, she'd pack her memories away again and get on with her life. She didn't want to be sad all the time because she was scared that if she let it all out, she'd never stop crying. She'd hoped allowing herself a little time to wallow would help her feel better, but so far it hadn't worked. Perhaps today – when she really had to be fit and well – it would do the trick.

She let herself remember those things and cried into the bath water for a little while. She only had a couple of inches of water in the tub and her swollen belly rose up in front of her. She washed quickly, knowing that if anyone happened to come in while she was bathing, her secret would be out.

'Come on, Daisy,' she said out aloud, hauling herself out of the bath. 'Let's go.'

To her relief she was feeling better. The physical aches seemed to have lessened and her sadness was under control for a while. She got dressed in clean overalls and tied a scarf around her hair so the newsreel people could tease it into victory rolls later. She even put on some make-up. She rubbed rouge on her cheeks so that she didn't look so pale, smudged some kohl pencil on her eyes, and painted her lips with the lipstick she hadn't worn since her wedding day, then she dropped the tube into her bag so she could touch it up later.

When she went back downstairs, her family were sitting at the kitchen table, arguing about whose turn it was to refill the teapot. Jim was home, looking exhausted after another nightshift.

'All right, sweetheart?' Ivy said, her eyes taking in every inch of Daisy.

'I'm fine. Big day today.'

'Of course, it's the filming,' Jim said. He gave her a proud look. 'Imagine you being on the big screen like a film star.'

Daisy made a face. 'It's not really my thing.'

'Are you absolutely sure I can't come and help?' said Poppy, pushing the teapot across the table towards Daisy. 'I might want to be a reporter for Pathé one day. I think I'd be a natural. I'm very good on screen.'

'How on earth would you know?' Ivy rolled her eyes.

'I've wanted to be a news reporter my whole life,' Poppy told her, her expression earnest.

'And yet, you've never mentioned it before this morning?'

'I've mentioned it loads of times.' Poppy looked outraged. 'Haven't I, Daisy?'

Feeling a little disloyal, Daisy shrugged. 'Perhaps.'

Poppy looked triumphant and Ivy chuckled. 'Unfortunately, you need to go to school, not to Kew. Jim, I know you need to sleep, but could you go to the market garden first thing and sort those deliveries?'

'It wasn't too bad last night, so we got a bit of kip before things got busy,' Jim said good-naturedly. 'And I'm off tonight anyway.'

Ivy shot him a grateful glance and then she looked up at Daisy again. 'I thought I'd come with you today,' she said. 'If that's all right?'

Daisy went weak with relief. 'Oh Mum, it's more than all right. I would love you to be there.' She smiled – it felt like the first time she'd smiled for weeks and her lips felt odd as she moved them. 'I bet they would film you too, you know? If they knew you'd worked at Kew during the last war. They'd love that.'

Poppy's howls of outrage followed them all the way down the front path.

There was a buzz of excitement at Kew that morning. Everyone in the staffroom was talking about it when Daisy and Ivy arrived. They all wanted to get involved with the filming.

'I'm going to saunter past, just when they turn on the camera,' said one gardener – a young woman called Hetty, who was very sure of herself. 'Then when it's shown, some big shot Hollywood film director will see me in the background, and he'll say, "That's the girl I want in my next picture".' She adopted a remarkably good American accent and pretended to be smoking a cigar. 'I'll be a film star by next Christmas.'

Beth was lacing up her boots, looking nervous. 'Gosh, I wish you could do it instead of me,' she told Hetty. 'I'm so worried about looking like a fool.'

Hetty gave Beth an appraising look. 'I think they knew what they were doing when they chose you and Daisy for the model allotment,' she said. 'You've proved that already.'

Beth made a face but then she saw Daisy and Ivy loitering by the door. 'Oh you're here, and you brought your mum,' she said in delight. 'We should tell the news people about you, Ivy. They'd love that.'

'That's what I said.' Daisy tried to smile again and found it was easier this time. 'Are you ready? We should get everything set up before they arrive.'

They walked across the gardens to the allotment together, running through their patter and trying to calm each other's nerves.

'How are you feeling?' Beth asked Daisy.

'Fine,' she lied. In actual fact, she was still feeling exhausted, totally drained of energy, and her legs were starting to ache again. Plus she felt queasy, as though the ground was moving beneath her. But she was determined to get through it and not leave Beth in the lurch.

'You've done the most amazing job,' Ivy said in admiration as they arrived at the allotment. 'Those parsnips look great, too. I thought they'd be all right.'

Daisy nodded, pleased that her mother was impressed. 'We've worked really hard, and this is only the beginning. I think in the spring we'll need some of the other gardeners to help.'

'Oh heavens, they're here,' said Beth in horror, looking at a group of approaching people. 'They're here, Daisy.'

Daisy took a deep breath. 'It's fine. We know what we're doing,' she said, wishing she didn't feel so odd. 'Slap on a smile, Beth. Let's show them what the Kew Gardens girls are made of.'

'Here they are,' Huw was leading the Pathé people along the path towards them, 'my Dig for Victory girls.'

There were two men carrying what Daisy assumed was camera equipment, as well as another man – handsome and well-dressed – who, presumably, was the reporter. And hurrying along behind was a young woman, a large bag slung over her shoulder.

'Ladies,' called Huw, beaming like a proud father. 'Let me introduce you. This is the news reporter, Jonathan Buxton. Jonathan, this is Daisy Cooper and Beth Sanderson.'

Daisy and Beth shook hands with the handsome man.

'This is marvellous,' he said. 'It's really something. Let's get everything set up and we can get cracking.'

The woman with the bag checked Beth's and Daisy's make-up, brushed their hair and twisted it into neat victory rolls with such dexterity that Daisy wished they could film that instead so she could watch how it was done.

'This is my mother, Ivy,' she told Jonathan, as she waited for Beth's hair to be finished. 'She worked at Kew Gardens during the last war. She's helped us get the allotment set up.'

Jonathan's eyes lit up, as Daisy had known they would, and soon Ivy was having her hair done too. Taking advantage of the general business around her, Daisy nipped into the Anderson shelter while everyone was distracted. She sat down for a second and took a few deep breaths.

'Come on, Daisy,' she said aloud. 'Just get through today and then you'll be all right.'

Her legs were aching terribly now and she had stomach pains too. She hoped she wouldn't be sick while they were being filmed.

She poured herself a cup of water and drank it in one gulp. 'Come on,' she said again.

Daisy suspected it was just sheer bloody-mindedness that got her through the next few hours. She ignored the aching in her legs, and the cramps in her stomach, slapped on a smile and kept going. Fortunately, she and Beth had rehearsed their Christmas dinner routine so many times that it went like clockwork, the audience that had gathered – far bigger than normal because the cameras were attracting attention – asked useful and interesting questions and she found she could just follow Beth's lead.

When it came to the individual interviews, Beth saw Daisy was flagging and so she took charge. Jonathan didn't seem sorry. Beth pulled him aside and Daisy saw her speak into his ear. She assumed she was telling him about Rex and asking him not to speak to her individually, and she thought she'd never been so grateful to have Beth as her friend. Jonathan nodded thoughtfully, then whisked Beth away to talk about the allotment. One of the cameramen gestured to Ivy that she would be needed too and Daisy fled to the sanctuary of the Anderson shelter for some private time.

She slumped down into one of the deckchairs and took some deep breaths. She was feeling very odd now. Her legs were aching so much and her stomach was agony. 'Oh no,' she whispered. 'Oh no, not now.'

She was shaking with fear and the pain was getting worse. Quite quickly she discovered that sitting down made it more severe. She needed to be upright. She stood up on legs that were very wobbly and, taking another deep gulp of air, she hung on to the back of the chair as pain gripped her again. She wanted to call out for Beth, or for her mother, but she couldn't catch her breath. She was crying now – silent tears, because she couldn't seem to make a sound. Oh heavens, there was the pain again. It was coming regularly now, squeezing and tightening across her abdomen.

There was no doubting what this was, she thought with shock and something close to terror. No doubting whatsoever.

'Oh bloody Nora,' she whispered. 'Oh lord.'

The pain gripped her again, and she breathed deeply, in through her nose and out through her mouth. She thought she'd never missed Rex as much as she did at that very moment. Why did he have to die? Why was this happening?

'I don't want this,' she muttered under her breath as the pain subsided again. 'I don't want any of this.' If someone came to her now and offered her the choice of dying and going to be with Rex, or being here, feeling the way she did now, with this awful pain, she knew which decision she'd make.

And then the door to the shelter opened and a figure appeared, framed in the doorway with the light behind shining like a halo. Almost delirious with fright and pain, Daisy thought wildly for a moment that this was an angel come to take her away to be with Rex and she was glad. So very, very glad.

But the angel spoke. 'Daisy, oh my God.' It was Beth, of course it was.

Daisy tried to speak but another pain came and she could only moan.

Beth was by her side immediately. 'I'll get help,' she said. 'You need an ambulance. I'll get Ivy.'

Daisy grabbed her arm. 'Stay. Here,' she gasped.

Beth looked alarmed. 'You need help. You're ill.'

Shaking her head, Daisy took a deep breath. 'I'm not ill,' she said desperately, still holding Beth's arm. 'I'm having a baby.'

Chapter Twenty-Eight

Beth's expression went from confused, to shocked, and then to concern.

'What on earth . . .?' She sounded cross. 'Did you know?'

'Yes,' wailed Daisy as another wave of pain came. 'I just didn't tell anyone.'

Beth adjusted Daisy's grip on her arm so they were holding hands instead, and to Daisy's horror, she edged towards the door of the shelter.

'Don't. You. Dare,' Daisy hissed. 'I need you.'

Beth ignored her. Still clutching her hand, she pushed open the door, just enough to stick her head out, and called: 'Ivy, could I just borrow you for a second?'

There was a pause and then the door opened properly and there was Ivy.

'What's the matter?' she said, then she saw Daisy and her eyes widened in worry. 'What's going on?'

Daisy was crying now, big fat tears rolling down her cheeks, and she found she couldn't explain, couldn't find the words to tell her mother that all this time she'd been expecting a baby. Her baby. Rex's baby.

'It shouldn't be happening like this,' she cried. 'Not like this.'

Ivy was by her side in an instant. 'What's wrong, sweetheart? What's happening?'

'She's pregnant,' Beth said quietly. 'And the baby's coming now.'

Daisy expected her mother to be shocked but actually she was very calm. Wildly, Daisy wondered if Ivy had known all along. But how could she have known when Daisy had tried so hard to keep it a secret? She put her arm around Daisy's shoulders and Daisy sank back against her mum's strong embrace. 'All right,' she said. 'Let's do this.'

Beth stroked Daisy's arm. 'I think we've got a little while to go, but not long enough to move you,' she said. 'But that's fine. I just need to get a few bits. Ivy's going to stay here with you. It's all going to be all right.'

Soothed by her friend's calm words, Daisy nodded. 'Hurry,' she said.

Beth let go of her hand and went out of the door. Daisy slumped against her mother.

'Are you all right standing?' Ivy said. 'I know when I had Poppy I wanted to be on the move the whole time.'

Daisy nodded. 'I tried to sit down but it was worse.'

'Let's make some room, then, shall we?'

Because the shelter wasn't used as it was intended to be, there were no bunks inside. There was just a small folding table, a stand to hang their coats on, the two deckchairs and a few of the tools they used for the allotment. Now Ivy picked up the table and coat stand and slung them out of the door. The chairs followed.

'What about the newsreel people?' Daisy gasped, worried they would film the furniture being thrown across the allotment.

'They're gone, sweetheart. It's just us.'

Another pain tightened across Daisy's belly and Ivy took her in her arms, letting her use her for support until it lessened again.

'Well done,' Ivy said. 'Relax now, and get ready for the next one.'

'I can't,' said Daisy, panicking at the thought. 'I can't do it.'

'You can. You've done it so far.'

'I don't know what to do,' Daisy whimpered. 'I don't want this.'

'Your body knows what to do. Just listen to it and soon your baby will be in your arms. You'll be a mother.'

Daisy couldn't believe she was really going to have a baby. She'd been trying so hard not to think about this happening and now that it was, she felt oddly like she was watching herself from far away; as though all this was happening to someone else. Perhaps it was a bad dream. Soon she'd wake up and Rex would still be alive and maybe, one day, when the war was over and things were back to normal, they could have a baby.

Beth stuck her head round the door. 'I've spoken to Will and he's got some of the other gardeners to put up a temporary fence, so no visitors will be walking by,' she said. 'And Gus is here, if we need him.'

Daisy shook her head. 'I just want you,' she said. 'Please.'

'That's absolutely fine,' Beth said cheerfully and for the first time that day, Daisy felt as though someone was in control. 'Let's get you comfortable, shall we?'

After that, it was all a bit of a blur for Daisy. The pain was terrible but Beth kept talking to her, and Ivy mopped her brow with a sponge that Beth had brought from the staffroom. Gently, Beth had a look to see what was happening and said she thought it wouldn't be long. At one point, there was a trickle that made Daisy fear she'd wet herself. But Beth said her waters had broken and after that the pain – which had been unbearable before – got even worse.

Daisy felt herself drawing inward with every cramp, as though she was shrinking into the hurt and the fear, and listening to Beth and Ivy talking from far away.

'She's been so sad,' Beth was saying. 'It was a lot for her to deal with all at once.'

'I can't believe she didn't tell me.' Ivy sounded upset and Daisy felt a wave of guilt for worrying her.

'Maybe she was trying to pretend it wasn't happening. I asked her if she could be pregnant and she said no.'

'I'm ashamed of myself for being so busy that I didn't notice.'

'Don't feel bad,' Beth said. 'I'm a nurse and I didn't know. I just took her word for it.'

Daisy breathed deeply and let herself go further down, down into herself. She couldn't hear them talking now. All she could hear was her breathing. Everything else – her mother, Beth, the shelter – had vanished and she was all alone.

She wasn't sure how long it went on, the relentless, cramping pain, but suddenly she knew that if she wanted it to end, she had to push. She was still standing – had been all along because being still was agony – but now, slowly, she shuffled round so she could hold on to Ivy again.

'Daisy?' Beth said. 'Are you ready to push?'

Daisy didn't speak. She just held on to her mum and when the next pain came, she let her body do what it wanted.

Beth was crouched on the ground behind Daisy. 'I can see the baby's head,' she said. 'Daisy, you're doing so well. Your baby will be here soon.'

Daisy opened her mouth to say that she didn't want this baby, but instead all that came out was a kind of inhuman groan. There was a feeling of release and a slippery sensation and there was a small gasp from Beth.

'It's a girl,' she cried. 'A beautiful baby girl.'

Daisy's legs were trembling violently, and she was crying again as her daughter's wails filled the tiny shelter.

'Oh, Daisy,' Ivy said. 'A little girl.'

She helped Daisy sit on the floor, in a sort of nest of blankets Beth had made, while Beth wrapped the baby up.

'Here you are,' Beth said. 'Here's your baby girl.'

She carefully handed Daisy the bundle and Daisy cradled her newborn daughter. She gazed down at her face. She had the same dark red hair as Daisy, and she was pursing her pink lips. As Daisy looked at her, the tiny girl opened her eyes and looked at her mother, and Daisy's heart twisted as she saw Rex in her daughter's expression. She was perfect, this little person. She had perfect fingers and perfect toes and a perfect tiny nose, and Daisy looked down at this perfect girl and felt absolutely nothing.

'The baby was back to back,' she heard Beth saying to someone outside the shelter – Gus, presumably. 'That explains why she had cramps in her legs and why it was so painful.'

Gus put his head round the door, smiling broadly. 'Congratulations,' he said. 'I waited to see if I'd be needed but it seems Beth did a good job by herself.'

'How many babies have you delivered now?' Ivy asked. She was hovering by Daisy and the baby, obviously smitten with her new granddaughter already. She couldn't tear her eyes from the little girl, even though she was talking to Beth.

Beth giggled. 'How many including this little one?'

'Yes, how many altogether?'

'One.'

Ivy laughed and Beth joined in, and Gus laughed heartily too. Daisy felt as though her heart had been pulled from her body and ripped into tiny pieces.

'I think Baby is hungry,' Ivy said. Daisy looked down and, sure enough, the baby was nuzzling into her chest. At some point, Daisy had pulled her overalls off, so she was just wearing her shirt now with a blanket over her. Ivy rearranged things so the baby could latch on and with no trouble at all the little one began suckling.

'Look at that, what a clever thing she is,' Ivy said proudly.

'What are you going to call her?' Beth asked. 'She needs a name.'

Ivy stroked Daisy's hair. 'Did you and Rex ever talk about having children? Did you talk about names?'

Daisy remembered lying on the grass on Hackney Marshes, one warm summer day, telling Rex that any children they had would have to be named after plants.

'It's a tradition in our family,' she'd said. 'Ivy, Daisy, Poppy—'

'Archie,' Rex had joked.

Daisy had thumped him on the arm. 'Archie's named after Aunt Win's late husband, as you well know.'

'What if it's a boy?' Rex had said. 'Boys don't have flower names.'

'Doesn't have to be a flower. Could just be any plant.' Daisy had thought for a moment. 'Basil.'

'Urgh, no.'

'Ash?'

'Better.' Rex had rolled over onto his front. 'Grass,' he said, looking around for inspiration. 'Oak. Birch.'

'Now you're being silly.'

'What about for a girl?'

'I like Marigold,' Daisy had said. 'Because it means joy and happiness.'

'Marigold,' Rex said. 'I like it too.'

Now Daisy looked at her little girl and thought that giving her a name that meant joy would be a very odd thing to do.

'Daisy,' said Ivy gently. 'Do you have a name in mind? What about Holly? That's pretty and Christmas is just around the corner.'

Daisy shook her head. 'Not Holly.'

'What then?'

'Willow.'

'Lovely,' said Beth.

But Ivy frowned. 'Willow? Are you sure?' She gave her granddaughter a fond look. 'She's such a precious little thing and Willow means – well, it means sadness.'

'She's called Willow.' Daisy was firm. 'Willow Cooper.'

Once more she looked down at the baby in her arms, wondering if she'd feel differently now her daughter had a name. But though Willow slept peacefully, making little snuffling noises and looking beautifully serene wrapped in the blanket Beth had put her in, Daisy still felt nothing at all.

Chapter Twenty-Nine

Beth should have been exhausted. She'd worked at the hospital yesterday and obviously stayed on long after her shift had ended because everything was so busy. Then there had been the newsreel filming, and now Daisy's surprise arrival. She should have been drooping with tiredness but she felt exhilarated.

They'd helped Daisy to move from the shelter on the allotment into the staffroom, where she could settle down on a comfy sofa and wait for her dad to come in the ARP van and take them home. Little Willow was still wrapped in a blanket, fast asleep in her grandmother's arms. Ivy had taken today's drama in her stride and seemed thrilled to bits with the new baby.

Daisy, by contrast, was very quiet and she seemed subdued, but Beth wasn't surprised at all. She couldn't imagine how it would feel to get up in the morning, not accepting you were pregnant, and be a mother by teatime.

'How are you doing?' she asked, checking Daisy's temperature with an expert touch with the back of her hand. She didn't want her to get an infection and have to go to hospital. Beth sensed that Daisy just needed to be at home where she could come to terms with everything that had happened.

'I'm fine,' Daisy said, though her teary voice suggested she was anything but fine. Beth felt a stab of concern.

'Really?'

'I don't have anything, Beth,' she whispered. 'I've not done anything to get ready for this. I don't even know what babies need. I don't have any nappies or a cot or any clothes.'

'We'll get you what you need,' Beth said.

'Can I come and say hello?' Will put his head round the staffroom door. 'Everyone wants to meet the little one.'

Daisy raised her head and, with what seemed to Beth to be an enormous effort, she smiled. 'Come in.'

Cautiously, Will crept into the room.

'You gave us all a bit of a surprise,' he said, beaming at Daisy. 'Congratulations.'

'Thank you,' Daisy whispered.

'I told Huw and he's delighted.' He swallowed. 'He asked me to get Jonathan and the rest of the newsreel team back but I thought you wouldn't want that. I remember what my missus was like after ours were born.'

'Daisy needs to rest,' Beth agreed quickly.

'We compromised on a quick photo,' Will said, showing Beth the camera he was holding. 'Daisy, the little one, and you, Beth.'

Beth looked at Daisy. She closed her eyes briefly but she didn't argue, so Beth nodded. 'Just one photo,' she warned. 'What about Ivy?'

'Oh yes, her too. Three generations of Kew Gardens girls,' Will said.

Still holding Willow, Ivy came over and sat next to Daisy on the sofa. Beth stood behind them.

'Say cheese,' said Will. The flash blinded Beth momentarily.

'All done. I'll get this over to Jonathan as soon as possible.' He looked at Daisy. 'Huw said to tell you he's having a cot and a pram sent to your house. He thought you might need them.'

'There you go, Daisy,' said Beth.

'Thank you.' Daisy's voice was small and quiet, and as Will left the room, she turned her face into the back of the sofa.

Ivy looked down at Willow and then at Beth, giving her a questioning glance. Beth shrugged. She hoped Daisy was just a little overwhelmed by the events of the day.

'Knock, knock,' said a voice and Hetty came in.

'Ohhhh,' she breathed, seeing Willow in her grandmother's arms. 'What a precious little thing she is.'

'Isn't she just,' said Ivy proudly.

'Daisy,' Hetty said. Daisy slowly turned her head to look at her visitor. 'Some of the girls were worried that you wouldn't have anything for this little one, seeing as you didn't know you were expecting. So those of us with kids already, not me, of course, but some of the older girls, they all went home and got you a few bits theirs have grown out of.'

Beth grinned at Hetty, making it clear she didn't consider herself old enough to be a mother, but it was such a lovely thought. Daisy's eyes widened as Hetty produced a bag full of baby clothes, bootees, tiny cardigans and hats, and a pile of nappies.

'It's not new,' Hetty said. 'But it's clean. Oh and here . . .' She dug into the pocket of her overalls. 'Some nappy pins.'

Ivy looked delighted. 'This is what my friends did for me when you were born, Daisy.'

Daisy wiped away a tear. 'Thank you,' she said again. Beth watched her carefully. It seemed everyone was thrilled about Willow's unexpected arrival, from Huw and Will to the other gardeners, and Ivy of course. But not Daisy.

Out of the window of the staffroom, Beth saw Jim approaching and, relieved, she turned to Daisy. 'Here's your dad,' she said. 'You can go home now.'

Daisy wiped away another tear, and nodded.

'We'll leave you to it,' said Hetty. Beth took her hand as she turned to go and squeezed it. 'Daisy's a bit overwhelmed,' she said quietly. 'But I know she's grateful for all your help. It was a really kind thing to do.'

Hetty grinned and gave them all a jaunty wave goodbye.

Beth watched as Ivy deftly put a nappy onto a compliant Willow, showing Daisy what she was doing as she folded the square of fabric. 'You remember from when Poppy was born, Daisy?'

Daisy nodded half-heartedly.

'Do you want to dress her?' Ivy asked.

'You'll be quicker.'

Ivy gave Beth that questioning look again, but she didn't argue. She dressed Willow in a tiny romper suit donated by the gardeners, and Beth helped Daisy to her feet.

'You're going to feel a bit battered for a few days,' she said. 'Go easy.'

Daisy gathered Beth into a hug. 'Thank you for helping me,' she said. 'I was so scared and I don't know what would have happened if you hadn't been there.'

'I'm glad I was there.' Beth smiled. 'Can I come and visit you tomorrow?'

'Yes please,' Daisy said urgently. 'Please.'

When Ivy, Jim, Daisy, Willow and the bag of clothes and nappies, had all gone off to Jim's van, Beth sat down on the sofa. She felt full of nervous energy. She was thrilled to bits that Daisy and her baby were safe, that she had helped her friend when she needed her most, and that there was a new addition to the Kew Gardens girls.

'Just wanted to see how you were.' Gus came into the room. 'Has Daisy gone?'

'Yes, she's off home with little Willow.'

'Are you exhausted? You did well today.'

Beth stood up. 'Actually no,' she said, feeling a bubble of glee rise up inside her. 'I'm giddy as a schoolgirl and full of energy. I want to celebrate.'

'All right,' Gus said, drawling the words in a playful way. 'I like the sound of this. How do you want to celebrate?'

Beth took both his hands in hers and shook them. 'Let's go dancing,' she said.

Chapter Thirty

They went to the Café de Paris because Beth liked it there and Gus had been several times too, because they welcomed everyone and he didn't have to worry that he would be turned away. Plus, it was underground so they knew it would be safe and they wouldn't have to listen to the thudding of bombs if a raid happened.

'I'd almost forgotten what fun feels like,' said Beth as they got off the tube at Piccadilly Circus. She'd swapped her overalls for the dress she'd travelled to Kew in that morning – which seemed like a lifetime ago – and, fortunately, her hair and make-up from the filming was still intact. She'd blinked in surprise when she'd checked her appearance in the mirror in the staffroom, expecting to look a lot more tired and haggard than she actually did. Instead her eyes were shining and her cheeks were rosy. She looked happy, she thought. Happy and ready to dance.

'I know,' Gus said with a groan. 'It feels like it's just hospital, Kew, hospital, Kew, at the moment.'

Beth gazed at him, thinking how lucky she was to have a friend who understood her so completely. Gus was looking very handsome, not that she could see him clearly in the dim evening light of the blackout. He'd left his suit jacket in his locker at Kew and was just wearing a tweed waistcoat over his shirt. He'd taken off his tie but kept his trademark hat tilted down over his face. Beth could just see his bright smile under the rim.

'I'm going to have an enormous gin to toast little Willow's arrival,' she announced, taking Gus's arm as they walked down the stairs into the club. 'And then I'm going to dance the night away.'

Beth had been out dancing when she was a student nurse, but she hadn't been anywhere fun for an age. Paul wasn't fond of places like the Café de Paris. He said he couldn't hear himself think over the music. Beth had known him her whole life and she'd never seen him dance and here was Gus, whom she'd only known a few months, accompanying her to a nightclub. She wondered what Daisy would think and knew without a shadow of a doubt that she wouldn't approve. But it had been a difficult day and Beth wanted this, no matter what her friend would think.

There was a band playing already and people jiving and jitter-bugging. Beth felt her heart lift. This was exactly what she needed. 'It's marvellous, isn't it?'

She felt herself moving in time to the music even though they weren't on the dance floor. Gus was doing it too, swaying his hips. Beth thought he would be a marvellous dancer and couldn't wait to see him. She felt a little tingle in her bones as she thought about taking his hand and leading him onto the floor, getting closer as they moved to the music.

'Beth?' She blinked. Gus was leaning on the bar looking at her. 'Gin?'

'Yes please,' she shouted over the music.

Gus paid the barman, who didn't bat an eyelid at the colour of his skin. Beth noticed that several members of the band on stage and a couple of the cabaret dancers had dark colouring too. She understood why Gus felt so welcome here. They took their drinks to a table at the side of the room and sat, their chairs almost touching because they couldn't hear each other if they were too far away.

'When I first came to London, I missed music so badly,' said Gus. 'There's music everywhere at home. In the streets and in every house.'

'It sounds wonderful.' Beth sipped her gin through a straw and felt terribly sophisticated. She'd always felt very glamorous at the Café de Paris, even though she had really only ever been here with a gaggle of girls to celebrate birthdays when she was doing her nursing training. Once more she tried to imagine Paul here in his shiny shoes and buttoned-up collar and found she couldn't. Paul liked restaurants and the bars of fancy hotels where he could call the staff 'my man' and bump into people he knew from school.

'There's music here, too,' said Gus. 'You just have to know where to find it.'

'Is there?' Beth was genuinely surprised. 'Where do you go?'

'Denmark Street. Or there's a place in Soho Square I like. And a Spanish bar near Tottenham Court Road.'

'Spanish?' Beth had never been to Spain.

'Flamenco.' Gus raised his hands above his head and snapped his fingers together like a crab. Beth giggled in joy. She was having the most wonderful time.

'Let's dance,' she said, pushing her chair back. 'Come on.'

She took Gus by the hand and pulled him upright and then together they went to the dance floor where her confidence deserted her. The band was playing an energetic song, and Beth – who'd found dance lessons terribly boring at school – had no idea what her legs should be doing. She looked round at the other couples flinging themselves around all over the place and gave Gus a startled look. He laughed his lovely laugh and took her hands and wrapped his arm around her back. 'We can muddle through,' he said.

It wasn't pretty but they had a go. Beth was laughing so hard her stomach ached, and Gus was throwing his head back and chuckling and it was really the most fun Beth had had for months. Years, perhaps. She felt alive. Some of it was the atmosphere and the gin and the music and some of it was the adrenalin from delivering Daisy's baby and being filmed by a Pathé newsreel team, but, if she was completely honest, most of it was being so close to

Gus and feeling his body against hers, his fingers twisted around hers and his breath on her neck.

The music changed to a slower beat and suddenly the couples around them on the floor all twined around each other like fronds of ivy around a trellis, and Beth felt self-conscious for a second. She stopped dancing, her hands still in Gus's but their arms out-stretched so they were quite some distance from each other. But then he tugged gently and brought her closer and wound his arms right around her. Beth rested her head on his chest and shut her eyes and lost herself in the music and the moment and thought she'd never really been as happy – no, not happy, contented – as she was right at that very moment.

When the music changed again, she opened her eyes and looked up to see Gus looking down at her. The air between them felt charged, like the summer sky before a storm. Gus's expression was unreadable, his face not smiling but not unhappy either. His dark eyes were narrowed, as though he was reading her very carefully. Beth's arms had been clasped around his torso, but now – feeling bold – she snaked them up to his neck. She could feel his short hair under her fingers and stroked it. And then, shocked at her own actions, she very gently pulled his head down towards her and touched his lips with her own.

Gus's eyes widened but he didn't pull away. Feeling more con-fident, Beth leaned in again and this time he kissed her back, his lips opening against hers.

Beth had never been kissed like this before. Paul had kissed her, of course, but his kisses didn't make her feel this way. It always felt a little bit strange when he touched his lips to hers. They'd known each other for so long that Beth felt more like his sister than his girlfriend. Sometimes she thought Paul saw her the same way. But this kiss was different. Beth's whole body was touching Gus. They were pressed up against each other and every nerve in her body was zinging and tingling. She couldn't think of anything else, just him and the blood pulsing in her veins. She felt weak and stronger than she'd ever felt before all at the same time.

And then Gus pulled away. 'Beth,' he said.

She smiled dreamily, feeling almost drunk with the joy of it all. 'Yes?'

But Gus shook his head. 'No.'

Beth stepped backwards in shock. What did he mean, no?

Gus put his hand to his mouth. 'No,' he said again.

And then – to Beth's absolute horror and embarrassment – he left her standing there, in the middle of the dance floor at the Café de Paris, surrounding by smooching couples. He walked across the room without looking back, walked up the stairs, then disappeared out into the night.

Chapter Thirty-One

Beth felt like a fool. A silly fool. She didn't understand what had happened.

As Gus walked away, Beth stood there in the middle of the dance floor for a minute, wondering if he'd come back. But he didn't. So she scurried across the room and up the stairs into the street and looked both ways to see if there was any sign of him. It was impossible to see far, though, because it was dark now and the blackout had draped itself around the roads and pavements of the West End.

'Gus?' she called into the darkness. But he had gone. Despondent and humiliated, Beth gave up and hailed a taxi to take her home.

She tossed and turned all night in her makeshift bed in their basement air-raid shelter and was up and dressed before the house was properly stirring.

When she went downstairs in search of a cup of tea, her mother was in the dining room, eating toast. She called to Beth and after a moment's pause, Beth pushed open the door and went inside.

'Join me?' Agatha said.

Beth sat down, because she couldn't think of a reason not to, and poured herself a cup of tea.

They sat in silence for a little while, and then, out of the blue, Agatha said: 'Are you unhappy, darling?'

Beth stared at her mother in shock. 'Pardon?'

'You don't seem very happy.' Agatha put the crust of her toast onto her plate and pushed it away. 'You should be happy – you are nursing, just as you wanted, you are spending a lot of time at Kew Gardens, which is something else you wanted, and you have Paul by your side – but you don't seem to be.'

Beth swallowed. 'I'm not unhappy,' she said, choosing her words carefully because she loved her mother and didn't want to upset her. 'But I feel like life is happening to me, instead of being something I choose.'

Her mother nodded. 'Is this to do with your determination to study medicine?'

'Partly.'

Agatha poured herself more tea. 'And Paul?'

Beth thought about lying, but there seemed to be little point. She nodded.

Her mother added milk to her cup. 'I was engaged, you know, before I met your father?'

Beth was genuinely surprised. 'Engaged?' she said. 'Really?'

'I was a debutante,' Agatha said dreamily.

Beth raised an eyebrow. She hadn't known any of this.

'I was quite the belle of the ball.' Agatha looked at Beth over the top of her cup, her eyes wide with mischief. 'I had a reputation for being rather wild and daring.'

'You did?' Beth said.

'Indeed. And I caught the eye of a handsome young chap called Henry.'

Beth almost fell off her chair, she was so surprised. 'What was he like?'

'Oh, so handsome,' said Agatha. 'And funny. Spontaneous. He would turn up on my doorstep and say "Let's climb a mountain" or "Have you ever been in a hot air balloon?" and whisk me off somewhere.'

'A daredevil.'

'Exactly.'

Agatha got up from her seat, went over to her writing desk in the corner of the room, and took out a small, framed photograph. 'This is him.'

Beth took the photo. It showed an impossibly young man in an army uniform. His expression was serious but there was a glint of fun in his eye.

'We got engaged,' Agatha said. 'And I was so happy. And then the war happened.'

Beth looked at the photograph again. 'I'm sorry,' she said, feeling desperately sad for her mother.

'He was killed at the Somme.' Agatha added sounded remarkably matter-of-fact. She held her hand out for the photo and Beth gave it to her. Her mother dropped it back into the drawer and shut it.

'I didn't know this,' Beth said, bewildered. 'Does Father know?'

'Of course.'

'Why haven't you ever told me?'

'It's all in the past, darling. I lost Henry and I was terribly sad and then I moved on.'

Beth wasn't sure that was the best thing to do, but she gave her mother a small, reassuring smile. 'With Father.'

'We met a couple of years later,' Agatha said. 'He was older than me; he was kind and careful. A steady hand on the tiller, as it were. I felt like everything was being taken care of.'

'Like Paul,' Beth said.

'Like Paul.'

Agatha gave Beth a long knowing look. 'I loved Henry and I love your father,' she said. 'Geoffrey wasn't at all the man I thought I'd end up with, but that's not necessarily a negative.' She smiled. 'All I'm saying is, love is the most important thing.'

Beth had absolutely no doubt that her mother had intended to tell her that she could be happy with Paul. But that wasn't what she took from their unexpected heart-to-heart at the breakfast table. Instead, she realised that Paul had been the man she thought she'd end up with. After all, they'd been pushed together since they were children. But now she had met someone else. Someone different.

She was working the night shift at the hospital and wasn't due at Kew at all that day, but she knew she wouldn't be able to concentrate until she'd seen Gus and spoken to him about what had happened. So, after her chat with Agatha, she went straight to the gardens.

Gus worked with the committee almost every day now, so Beth knew there was a good chance he'd be at Kew. She marched through the gardens, past the allotment where no one was working today, briefly wondering how Daisy's first night with baby Willow had gone. She had planned to go and visit her friend today and felt guilty that, instead, she was on the opposite side of London, chasing after a man. But she knew she had to make sense of what had happened. It was freezing today, and the frosty grass crunched beneath her feet as she walked, but she felt a flush of warmth remembering the feeling of Gus's lips on hers and his firm body pressed up against hers.

Full of purpose, she went into the building where the committee met, along the corridor and into the lab. And there was Gus. He didn't see her at first, because he was reading some notes and discussing them with another man in a white coat whom Beth didn't recognise. She stood by the door, watching him for a second. The way his brow furrowed when he was concentrating, and the habit he had of rubbing his short hair with the palm of his hand. She ached to go to him and throw her arms around him and kiss him and she steadied herself on the doorframe. 'Oh heavens,' she muttered to herself. 'Oh heavens.'

It was clear to her – more clear than anything else in her whole life – that she had fallen hopelessly in love with Gus Campbell. And she was very worried that he didn't share those feelings and that's why he'd run away last night.

What on earth was she doing? Lurking here, watching him like a lovesick schoolgirl. She would go, she decided. She would turn around and leave, and go and see Daisy like she should have in the first place. And then she would go to work at the hospital and keep busy and pretend this whole thing had never happened.

'Beth!' To her horror, Gus had spotted her. He looked pleased to see her and then slightly sheepish. Beth wanted to cry with the embarrassment of it all, but instead she fixed a bright smile to her face.

'Could I just have a word?' she said, gesturing outside with her head. 'Bit of a query about a patient.'

Gus looked confused, as well he might, seeing as there were no patients, but then realisation dawned and he nodded. He put down his clipboard and followed her outside. Beth didn't want to be where the committee members would be wandering past so she went round to the car park at the side of the building, away from the main entrance, and leaned against the wall because her legs were shaky and she needed the support.

'Beth,' Gus said as he approached. 'I wanted to say—'

'I'm sorry,' she blurted out at the same time.

They both stopped talking and Beth waved a hand. 'You first.'

Gus reached out and took her fingers in his. Beth felt a tiny flare of hope. 'I like you, Beth,' he said. 'You're clever and brave and so very beautiful.'

She gazed at him, almost dizzy with relief. He shared her feelings. It was all going to be all right.

'At least that's what I thought,' Gus said.

'What?'

'Since the moment I met you on the hospital roof, I've been staggered by how bold you are.' He gazed at her, his brow furrowed, as though he was seeing her for the first time. 'But now I realise that you aren't the woman I thought you were.'

Beth stepped towards him, holding her hands up like a shield so she could fend off his horrible words.

'No,' she said. 'No.'

'You have a boyfriend,' Gus said.

Beth felt awful. 'I do. But—'

'You're not free to do as you wish.' He looked sad and defeated. 'I knew there was something between us and I shouldn't have taken you dancing. And you shouldn't have kissed me.'

She couldn't argue with that. She leaned her head back against the wall and looked up at the sky. 'I know you think I'm an awful person, but could I explain?'

She thought Gus might walk away, but to her relief he simply nodded.

'Paul and I have known each other since we were children, because our parents were friends,' she began. 'He never asked me out. It was like one minute we were running around the park together, and then suddenly our mothers were talking about us getting married one day.'

She felt a flush of anger. 'No one ever asked me what I thought.'

'No one asked you or you just didn't tell them?' Gus said. The cold tone of his voice made Beth feel wretched. 'You have all these problems in your life, Beth. Your boyfriend and your father. And instead of facing them head-on, you sneak around hoping you can just get away with doing what you want as long as you avoid talking about your feelings.'

'That's not true—' Beth began but then she stopped talking because it was true.

'I will not be another one of your lies.'

Beth thought about her parents' reaction if she broke things off with Paul. Of how awkward family parties would be with his mother and father. And then she tried to imagine Gus at those events instead of Paul. And found she couldn't. She stared at Gus in despair and he gave her a look that made her think she had let him down. Which, she supposed, she had.

'I have to go back to work,' he said.

She reached out and touched his arm and he shook her off,

as though she was a fly or a bit of dust. Then – once again – he turned and walked away from her without looking back.

'Beth?'

She turned, tears pricking her eyes, and to her surprise and horror saw her father standing in the car park, staring at her. 'What's going on?'

'I was just checking something,' she stammered. 'With Gus. Erm, Dr Campbell. What are you doing here?'

Geoffrey frowned. 'Checking what?'

'Committee business,' Beth said, realising that she had just done exactly as Gus had said she would – lied about him. 'You know that I help out every now and then. With the VDC.'

'I'm here to speak to the VDC.' Geoffrey looked quite pleased with himself. 'They want to run some drugs trials at St Catherine's.'

Beth, who'd suggested that very thing the week before, nodded. 'Sounds like a good idea. You're already monitoring your patients and these drugs need to be tested.'

Geoffrey looked at her curiously. 'You know a lot about it.'

'I don't just help out every now and then,' Beth admitted. 'I work there every week.' Feeling bolshie, she added: 'I thought it would help my applications to medical school.'

Her father raised an eyebrow but he didn't speak. Instead, he looked at his watch. 'I have to go,' he said. 'Are you at the hospital later?'

'Night shift.'

'Come and see me in my office, would you? When you arrive?'

Beth felt a glimmer of unease. She didn't like it when she was summoned to see her father formally. Those conversations never ended well. 'I will,' she said.

By the time she sat opposite her father later, her unease was full-blown discomfort. She hadn't been to visit Daisy in the end, because she'd decided to get some of her frustration out by digging the cabbage patch on the allotment. She put some netting over the broccoli so the hungry birds didn't attack it and put some old sacking over the lettuces to protect them from frost. Then she'd been 'borrowed' by Hetty and the team who were digging the empty borders and putting manure on top. Beth would normally have said no to doing anything so smelly – especially when it was supposed to be her day off – but she just wanted to keep busy, so she spent the day shovelling and digging and listening to the gardeners' chatter about Daisy and her dramatic birth, and her keeping her pregnancy secret, and how sad it was that Rex wasn't there to meet his baby girl. She told herself sternly that however glum she was feeling now it wasn't nearly as bad as how Daisy must be feeling.

She usually had a nap in the afternoon before a night shift, but she'd not had one today, so she was feeling tetchy and tired when she sat down in Geoffrey's office.

'Beth,' he began. He rested his elbows on the desk and tapped his chin with his fingertips. 'I can't lie that I was concerned when you came up with this hare-brained idea about working at Kew Gardens,' he said. 'But Dr Bloomberg told me the drug trial was your idea. He's pleased with the work you're doing there. I was impressed.'

Beth wanted to point out that she'd told her father that weeks ago, and he hadn't listened, but she didn't. Instead she basked in his rare praise.

'But this is a lot of work for you,' Geoffrey continued. 'Pressure. And I have to say, I'm not overly comfortable with you having to work so closely with Campbell. It's not appropriate.'

Beth sighed. 'It's fine,' she said.

'You seem to be spending a lot of time together.'

'We both work at the hospital and we both work at Kew.'

'I saw you talking at Kew today and he was very close to you. He's not the sort of person you should be friends with, Elizabeth. You need to remember that.'

'We're not friends,' said Beth, feeling sick as she thought of

Gus shaking off her hand. 'So you don't need to worry.'

'Hmm,' said Geoffrey. 'Anyway, I don't want you to burn out, darling. So I've spoken to Matron and asked her to reduce your shifts. To give you time to have some fun. This war is bloody bleak, and you need to take your rewards where you can find them.'

'Daddy,' said Beth, feeling helpless and furious all together, just as she had when he'd refused to sign her university application. She knew this wasn't to do with her being tired, or needing to have some fun. It was to do with her father wanting to control her. 'No. I'm needed on the ward, you know that. Please don't do this.'

'It's done,' he said. 'And I've swapped your shift this evening too. You're working first thing in the morning and Paul's picking you up for dinner.' He checked the clock on the wall. 'In about ten minutes. Have a lovely time, darling.'

Beth stared at him, speechless. She didn't argue. She didn't have the right words.

Chapter Thirty-Two

January 1941

Daisy looked at the cover of the *Picture Post* with awe and something that felt a little bit like envy. The photograph on the front was of Beth, her hair shining in its victory rolls, her skin glowing and her smile beaming, as she crouched down among the plants on the allotment. Her happiness shone out from the page and made Daisy want to cry. It wasn't that she envied Beth her beauty – though she did a bit – or that she wanted to be a cover girl on the *Picture Post*. It was more that seeing the picture made Daisy ache for the life she'd once had , and which now felt so far away.

In her crib in the corner of the room Willow made the little snuffly noise that meant she was about to wake up. Daisy's heart sank. The endless rotation of feeding, winding and changing was about to begin again. Holding her breath so she didn't make a sound, she peered over into the crib, but to her relief, Willow was quiet and Daisy relaxed a tiny bit. She regarded her daughter for a second. She had been a scrawny little scrunched-up thing when she'd burst into the world, but she'd filled out and lost the yellow tinge she'd had. She looked better, there was no mistake. More like babies were supposed to look. Poppy was absolutely smitten with her niece and spent hours gazing at her. 'I just think she's so beautiful,' she would breathe. 'Don't you think she's beautiful, Daisy?'

Ivy was the same – head over heels in love with her new grand-daughter. And Rex's mother, Judith, had been so overwhelmed when she'd seen Willow for the first time that she'd been unable to speak for almost half an hour.

'She looks just like Rex,' she whispered eventually. 'She's the spit of him, isn't she, Daisy?'

Daisy would always agree with their gushing compliments, but if she was to be perfectly honest, what she really felt when she looked at Willow was – nothing. She felt no connection to this tiny human. Nothing at all. When she looked down at her as she nursed, she always felt odd, as though there was a stranger cradled in her arms. She didn't think Willow was beautiful. She just thought she looked like any other baby she might have passed in the street. She remembered hearing stories about changelings when she was a little girl. She had been fascinated by the tales of babies that the fairies had taken away and replaced with one of their own. She felt that Willow was one of those creatures – except that she hadn't replaced a human baby, she'd just been dropped into Daisy's life and had turned it upside down.

She peered into the crib again. Willow was definitely stirring now. A huge wave of darkness swept over Daisy and she threw herself onto her bed and buried herself under the blanket. She couldn't do it. She couldn't do another day of caring for this child, pretending to be her mother, muddling through.

Willow made a small squawk. Daisy put the pillow over her head, trying to block out the sound. That poor little girl was relying on her for everything and she couldn't cope with the re-sponsibility. Not like this. In another world, Daisy and Rex would have been adoring parents, doting on Willow, but not now. Not in this world where Daisy was stuck alone with her grief and this tiny baby. Poor Willow. Poor baby girl to be born into this awful life instead of the one she deserved.

Daisy stifled a sob with her pillow. She felt awful. Although, oddly, she welcomed the feeling because it was better than this unrelenting numbness. Cautiously she took her head out from under the bedding. Willow was definitely working up to proper screeching now. Daisy slid off the bed and picked up her daughter. The baby gazed at her with large dark-blue eyes and Daisy looked away. It was ridiculous, but she really felt as though Willow knew how she was feeling. That she knew Daisy wasn't good enough to be her mother.

She sat down in the chair by the window and put Willow to her breast, bracing herself for more cries. Sometimes the baby latched on and fed perfectly. Other days, Willow would arch her back and howl, her little red face growing purple with frustration. Those days were terrible. She didn't understand why they happened or how to put them right and each time Willow had a bad feed, Daisy felt a little bit more broken.

Today, though, Willow was feeding beautifully. And somehow that also made Daisy feel broken. It was like Willow was leading her down this bewildering road of motherhood, rather than herself. And that, she thought firmly, staring out into the street which was still dusty after last night's raid, was not the way things were supposed to be.

A knock on her bedroom door made her jump, but then Beth put her head round and Daisy felt a rush of relief at seeing it was her friend.

'Beth, it's so good to see you,' she said.

'I'm not working today so I thought I'd come and say hello.' Beth came into the room, making Daisy feel as though a light had been switched on. 'How are you?'

'Fine,' Daisy said. It was what she always said when someone asked. 'Fine.'

'And Willow?' Beth looked down at the nursing baby, running her eyes over her approvingly. 'She looks well.'

Daisy let out her breath – she hadn't even realised she'd been holding it, waiting for Beth to give her verdict, for her nurse's eye to spot that things weren't quite right. But she simply stroked the top of the baby's head, and then sat down on the bed.

Awkwardly, because Willow was still at her breast, Daisy reached over, picked up the copy of the *Picture Post* and waved it at Beth.

'Look at you,' she said.

Beth groaned. 'It's all gone slightly crazy.'

'Tell me everything.' Daisy was hungry for news of life outside the suffocating world of babies. 'From the beginning – from the newsreel.'

'You know everything,' Beth pointed out. She'd been to visit several times since Willow was born and had kept Daisy up to date on everything that had been happening.

Daisy shook her head. 'I know, but tell me again anyway. The newsreel went out . . .'

'We all went to the pictures to see it.'

Daisy bit down the resentment she had that she'd missed it because she'd been stuck indoors with Willow and instead forced a smile. 'Who's we?'

'Me, some of the gardeners, Will—'

'Gus?'

Beth flushed. 'No. I've not seen much of him, actually.'

'And what was it like?'

'It was so strange to see us on that enormous screen,' Beth said, grinning. 'Honestly, Daisy, it was like being in a dream. They showed the allotment and lots of us talking about Dig for Victory. And they said your mum had worked at Kew during the last war, and they had a picture of Ivy in her wedding dress with her friends.'

'Louisa,' Daisy said, even though Beth knew who they were. 'And Aunt Win.'

'And right at the end, they did a little bit about you and Willow, and said she was the newest addition to the Kew Gardens girls and everyone in the seats clapped.'

'Amazing,' breathed Daisy. 'And then what?'

'And then it all got even stranger,' Beth said. 'Someone from the *Daily Mirror* wrote about us, and they came to take some photographs. There was a piece in the *Sunday Express*, too, and they want us to do a bit every month telling everyone what they should be planting. And then the chap from the *Picture Post* came.'

'And you're on the cover,' said Daisy with glee.

'I never dreamed I'd be the cover girl.'

'Oh get off, you're the perfect cover girl, with your shiny hair and your lovely smile and your neat waist.'

Beth looked uncomfortable. 'It's not what I'd have chosen but if it helps, then I'm happy.'

Daisy wondered if there was anyone else in the whole world as sweet-natured as Beth. She doubted it.

'What do your parents think?' she asked. 'Are they pleased with you for once?'

Beth winced. 'They don't know.'

'What?' Daisy was surprised. 'But you're famous. You're in all the papers and everything.'

'My parents never go to the pictures, and my father reads the *Telegraph*, not the *Daily Mirror* and certainly not the *Picture Post*.' Beth's expression had darkened. 'You know me, Daisy. Always sneaking around, refusing to face my problems head-on.'

Daisy wasn't sure what to say. Instead she just frowned. 'They really don't know?'

'No.'

'Maybe your father should read the *Picture Post* more often,' Daisy said, astonished that Beth hadn't told her parents what she was up to. 'Might learn something.'

Willow had stopped feeding and was slumbering in her arms. Daisy started to put her back in the crib and Beth held her hands out.

'Can I have a cuddle first? I promise not to wake her.'

Gladly, Daisy handed over the child and watched as Beth

cradled her expertly and cooed at her. For one wild moment she thought about telling Beth to keep her. To take the baby and look after her better than Daisy ever could.

'Daisy?' Beth jolted her out of her silly thoughts. 'Are you all right? Tired?'

Daisy blinked. 'Sorry,' she said. 'Yes, a bit tired.'

'I should let you rest.'

'No,' Daisy almost shouted. 'Please stay. How is it at Kew since the newsreel and all the articles?'

Beth made a face. 'Terribly busy. We're rushed off our feet. Hetty's helping on the allotment and the other gardeners too, when they can. There's an endless stream of people asking questions and wanting advice. I do my best, but I'm not as knowledgeable as you are. I'm always worrying that I'm going to say the wrong thing or tell them to plant sprouts when they should be planting lettuces.'

'And you working at the hospital, too,' Daisy said.

'Well, I'm not working as many shifts as I was.' Beth looked cross and Daisy was going to ask why, but her friend hadn't finished. 'I wish you were at Kew to help with the allotment.'

Suddenly Daisy saw an escape route. It was like a door being unlocked and light flooding in.

'I could come back,' she said.

'Oh gosh, that's not what I meant at all,' Beth said, looking horrified. 'You've got this little one to worry about.' She gazed down at Willow adoringly and once more Daisy felt that urge to persuade her to take the baby away.

'Mum can look after Willow,' she said. 'She won't mind at all. She can take her to the centre with her while I'm at Kew. Or I'll bring her with me.'

'I'm not sure it's a good idea.' Beth frowned at Daisy. 'It was a difficult birth. How's your recovery?'

Some days Daisy felt as though she'd been run over because she was so bruised and battered from Willow's arrival, but the very thought of going back to Kew made her less aware of the pain.

'I'm fine,' she said. 'Absolutely fine. I can always take it a bit easy when it comes to the more physical stuff. For a while at least.'

'I can't deny we need you, but it doesn't seem right . . .'

'Please,' Daisy said. 'Please.'

The urgency in her voice made Beth look startled. 'All right,' she said. 'I'll speak to Will. But you should check with Ivy first.'

'We'll ask her now,' Daisy said. She jumped to her feet, more energetic than she'd been for weeks, and ran downstairs, followed by Beth with Willow.

'Mum,' she called. 'Mum?'

'In here, where's the fire?' grumbled Ivy, appearing from the back room. Her face softened as she saw Willow in Beth's arms. 'Has she had her feed? Did she take much?'

Distracted, Daisy just nodded. Ivy took the baby – who'd woken up again and who was contentedly waving her arms in the air – and clucked at her. 'Are you my best greedy girl?' she said. 'Are you Nanny's best girl?'

'They need me to go back to Kew,' Daisy said. 'They're rushed off their feet. Beth can't cope.'

Beth looked as though she was going to argue, but Daisy glared at her and Beth didn't speak. 'Mum?' Daisy said. 'Did you hear?'

Ivy dragged her eyes away from Willow's face. 'What's that?'

'I need to go back to Kew.'

'Oh, Daisy, really? Surely they can manage without you?'

Daisy arranged her face into what she hoped was a resigned, reluctant expression. 'I thought so, too, but Beth says it's gone crazy since the newsreel and all the stuff in the papers. They need me working on the allotment, Mum.'

'What about Willow?' Ivy looked at the baby and started her clucking again. 'Someone's got to look after you, haven't they?'

Daisy wanted to scream with frustration, but instead she swallowed. 'I thought maybe you could take her to the centre with you? There are lots of children there, and someone will always be around to give her a cuddle.' She took a breath. 'Or a bottle.'

'A bottle?' Ivy looked disapproving. 'Daisy—'

'I can still feed her when I'm here,' Daisy jumped in quickly, even though she thought it would be much easier to use bottles all the time. 'It'll just be during the day that she needs a bottle. And she won't miss me at all, will she? Because she'll be with her nanna. And she loves you, Mum. Look at her staring at you.'

Right enough, Willow was gazing up at Ivy with wide eyes. Ivy's expression softened and Daisy felt a tiny glimmer of hope. 'What do you say?'

'They really need you at Kew?'

Daisy nodded. 'Beth says they're frantic.' She looked over at Beth, who was wearing a slightly wretched expression. 'Aren't you, Beth?'

'We are really busy,' Beth admitted. 'And I don't know nearly enough about the veg to answer everyone's questions. Daisy's the one with all the knowledge.'

There was a pause. Daisy could feel her heart pounding in her chest. Suddenly, it seemed that her whole future rested on what Ivy was about to say. If she said she would look after Willow, then Daisy could go back to Kew and keep busy and forget about Rex. And Ivy was a wonderful mother. She'd done a great job with Archie and Poppy – and Daisy – and she would do the same with Willow. She was much better for the little girl than Daisy was. There was no doubt about that. She looked at her mother, holding her breath.

'What do you say?'

Ivy dropped a kiss on the baby's forehead. 'All right,' she said. 'But if it gets too difficult, Daisy, or you're missing her too much, you need to tell them you can't work.'

Daisy's legs went weak with relief. 'Good,' she said. 'Great.'

She felt her mother's eyes on her and avoided her gaze. 'Beth, I'll be there in the morning.'

Beth gave her a small smile. 'I won't be there first thing,' she said.

Daisy shrugged. 'Then I'll get everything started.'

Feeling lighter already, she grinned at her friend. Perhaps everything was going to be all right after all.

Chapter Thirty-Three

Beth had been a little naïve thinking her family wouldn't see the *Picture Post*. It was everywhere. She saw her own picture staring out from news stands on every corner. She had even, on one bewildering occasion, been recognised by two schoolgirls who'd asked if she was 'the lady from Kew Gardens' and then when she'd admitted that she was, they'd simply sighed in wonder.

But even so, she was surprised when she arrived home from Daisy's house to find her parents and Paul sitting in the lounge and a copy of the *Post* on the coffee table in front of them.

They all looked up at her as she entered. Paul looked furious. Beth was quite pleased because generally he always wore the same jovial expression. Her parents' faces were unreadable.

'Ah,' she said. 'You've seen it.'

Paul nodded.

'And the *Daily Mirror*,' added her mother. Beth glanced at her. Was Agatha smiling? She couldn't tell.

'And what did you think?' she asked, not sure if she wanted to know what they thought.

Paul sighed dramatically. 'Betsy, I'm really proud of you for doing your bit, you know that. But this isn't right.'

'Which bit isn't right?'

Paul picked up the magazine and pointed at Beth's face smiling out at them. 'This. You on the front cover. Men are looking at you,' he said. 'Gawping. I heard two chaps at work saying you were pretty.'

'I didn't want to be on the cover,' Beth said. 'They didn't ask me.'

'I think you look lovely, darling,' Agatha said. 'Paul's just surprised, that's all.'

Paul shot her mother a furious look that made Beth bristle with annoyance.

Did you read the article?' she asked, her voice cold.

'Pardon me?'

'Did you read the words? Or just look at the pictures?'

'Beth.' Her father's tone held a warning but Beth didn't even look at him. She just carried on staring at Paul. 'Did you read it?' she asked again.

'Well, no, not all of it.'

'Maybe you should.'

'I do not want to,' Paul growled.

He and Beth stared at one another. Beth had the sudden, ridiculous thought that this was the most passionate she'd ever seen Paul.

'Shall we go into the garden?' she said. She didn't want an audience. 'I think we should talk.'

Paul glared at her, but he didn't argue. He stood up and followed her out of the front door and across the road to the garden in the middle of the square. He strode ahead, as if to make Beth understand that he was calling the shots.

They reached a bench in the middle of the garden and Paul sat down, then he looked up at Bet

'Go on, then.'

'What?'

'Explain.'

Beth felt a little spark of anger ignite within her.

'Do you know what this plant is?' she said suddenly, bending down to a little crop of weeds next to the bench.

Paul, looking startled, said: 'It's a stinging nettle, Beth.'

'And do you know what it can do?'

'Sting you.'

'It reduces inflammation,' Beth said. 'It's very useful for wound care.'

'And I suppose you learned all this at Kew Gardens, did you?'

'I did. Not that you've ever been interested enough to ask.'

Paul's face went a bit red. 'That's not fair, Beth.'

'Isn't it? You never ask me anything about myself or my job,' Beth said. 'You don't know anything about me.'

Paul sighed. 'It sounds like you're doing a marvellous job. But all this publicity,' he said, shaking his head. 'It makes me very uncomfortable. I don't like the—'

'Gawping?' Beth said. 'Yes, you made that perfectly clear.'

'I'm not happy about it.'

'But do you know what?' Beth snapped. 'I don't much care. It's got absolutely nothing to do with you.'

Paul's jaw dropped. 'Well, if we're getting married, I rather think it does have something to do with me,' he said.

'Are we getting married?'

The question hung between them heavily.

Paul lifted his chin. 'What about me?'

'What?'

'Do you even know what I do all day?'

'Well, yes,' Beth blustered. 'You work at the War Office.'

'But what do I do?'

At a loss, Beth looked at her feet.

'What are my dreams? What do I want from life?'

Again Beth was blank. She shook her head.

'Because you've never asked,' said Paul.

Beth opened and closed her mouth, but no words came out.

'You're not the only person with ambition,' Paul said. He took a breath. 'I'd like to be an MP someday.'

It was so completely perfect for him that Beth almost gasped. 'Of course,' she said.

'But if I'm going to do that, then I need a supportive family,' Paul said. 'A supportive wife.' He looked at her, and all she could see in his face was disgust. 'One who will not put her own ambitions ahead of mine. One who will not offer herself up to the tabloid press to be primped and preened and pictured.'

It was so unfair that Beth wanted to scream but she clenched her hands into fists behind her back instead and stared at Paul.

'What exactly are you saying?' she asked, spitting each word out because she was so angry.

'I'm afraid this is the end of the road for us, Beth.'

Beth's anger subsided as quickly as it had arrived. Now all she felt was relief. 'I never meant to cause you so much trouble,' she said, honestly. 'You're a nice man.'

He stared back at her, unsmiling. 'Please say goodbye to your parents for me. I think I should go straight home, don't you?'

Beth nodded and without another word, Paul got up from the bench and walked out of the garden.

She stood there for a second, not wanting to catch him up, and then when he was safely down the street, she left too, hauling herself up the steps to the front door as though they were Mount Snowdon.

Her parents were sitting on the sofa where they'd been when she'd left. Agatha raised an eyebrow and Beth, much to her surprise, burst into tears.

'Oh darling,' said her mother. 'Come here.' She pulled Beth down onto the sofa next to her.

'Was Paul very cross?'

Beth wiped her eyes. 'He was. And he said some horrible things and the worst thing is they're all true.'

'And did he –?'

'We've broken up,' Beth said. 'I'm sorry.'

Geoffrey had been sitting quietly but now he snorted.

'It's a bit late to say sorry, Elizabeth.'

Beth winced.

'Your insistence on doing exactly what you want with no regard to the consequences has finally made everything fall apart,' he said. He was speaking calmly but Beth knew just how angry he was because there was a vein pumping in his temple. 'You have been very selfish, but perhaps if we act quickly enough we can persuade Paul that this was all just a silly mistake.'

'It wasn't a mistake,' Beth said. 'None of this has been a mistake.'

Geoffrey's eyes bulged in fury. 'What do you mean?'

'I love working at Kew Gardens,' Beth said. 'And I'm proud that they chose me to be the face of the Dig for Victory campaign. It's not a mistake.'

Agatha, always the peacekeeper, patted Geoffrey's arm. 'Maybe if Beth explains a little about what she's doing at Kew, it will make more sense?'

Beth picked up the *Picture Post*. 'It's all in here,' she said. 'Did you read it?'

Her father looked uncomfortable but Agatha, much to Beth's surprise, nodded. 'I did, actually.' She put her hand down the side of the sofa cushion and pulled out another copy of the *Post*. 'I bought one to show the girls at bridge,' she said with a grin. 'They'll adore it. You're very clever, darling. I knew you were running about here, there and everywhere, but I didn't for one minute think you were doing all this.' She looked down at her knees. 'I wish you'd told me about it.'

Beth was pleased and touched by her mother's support, and a little guilty that she'd not been more honest. 'Daddy?' she asked.

Agatha held out the copy she had in her hand to her husband. 'Have a look,' she said.

'No,' he said.

'Geoffrey.' Agatha's tone was sharp. 'Read it.'

Beth watched as her father reluctantly took the magazine. He turned the pages until he found the article and then he was quiet again for a long time. Beth got to her feet, pacing the floor in the lounge and feeling her palms sweating.

'Good lord,' Geoffrey said eventually. 'I see the hospital gets a mention.'

'Well, they discovered I was a nurse.'

'Because of the baby?'

'Because of the baby.' Beth nodded. 'It was rather a surprise.'

'You delivered a baby on an allotment?'

'I did.'

Her father stared at her. 'Normal delivery?'

'Back to back.'

His eyebrows lifted. 'Back to back?'

Beth swallowed. 'None of us knew Daisy was expecting. She'd lost her husband – he was RAF – and she'd been pretending it wasn't happening.'

Her father's eyebrows were so far up his forehead they'd almost disappeared into his hairline.

'Good lord.'

'How is Daisy?' Agatha asked.

Beth shrugged. 'She wants to come back to work. I'm not sure she's coping very well with her baby.' She glanced at her father, whose anger seemed to be easing. 'I've been reading about nervous exhaustion in new mothers. I want to help her.'

Geoffrey nodded and, heartened that he didn't seem to be lashing out anymore, Beth took a chance.

'Perhaps I could go back to my old shift pattern at the hospital?' she said. 'Now that Paul and I are – now that I'll have more time.'

Again Geoffrey nodded without speaking.

'I need to get ready for my night shift.' Beth looked at her parents. 'I really am sorry about the trouble I've caused.'

Agatha smiled. 'Be happy, darling,' she said.

Beth looked at her father. He wasn't smiling but the vein wasn't pulsing anymore either. 'You did well,' he said. 'Delivering that baby. Can't have been easy.'

'It wasn't,' Beth said. 'I was scared.'

'The day you stop being scared is the day you should give up nursing,' Geoffrey said gruffly.

Beth grinned. 'I'll remember that,' she said.

Chapter Thirty-Four

With her worries about Paul and her parents seeing the *Picture Post* article having been dealt with, Beth should have been feeling happier. But she was fretting about Daisy. She'd been reading every book she could get her hands on about nervous exhaustion in new mothers, though there hadn't been much written about it, and Daisy seemed to be suffering badly, as far as Beth could see. But she refused to talk about anything personal. She wouldn't talk about Rex, or Willow. Instead, she was focused on coming back to work at Kew. Beth was worried that if it didn't happen for some reason, Daisy would be devastated.

She didn't really know the best way to help her friend, and so she'd come to the centre in Hackney where Ivy volunteered because she wanted to speak to her. As her bus drew nearer to the East End, Beth realised she might have made a mistake. Last night's raid had been a bad one. It had started early and gone on and on. At one point, Beth had wondered if she'd slept through the all-clear because it had been hours since the first bombs had dropped – but then she heard another crash and realised there were still planes overhead.

'They're taking advantage of the darkness,' her father had muttered from his bunk on the other side of the basement. 'Long winter nights and clear, cold skies are perfect for the Luftwaffe.'

So Beth had started her day ragged with lack of sleep, though, to their relief, their road had escaped the worst of the damage. The East End, though, once again had borne the brunt of the bombs.

'Oh my,' Beth breathed as the bus trundled towards Hackney. 'Oh my goodness.'

Everywhere there were piles of rubble. For a moment, Beth couldn't get her bearings because there was no landmark to navigate from and then she realised the pub she was looking for, on the corner of the road, had gone. Reduced to a pile of bricks. The bus stopped at traffic lights and Beth gazed out of the dirty window, seeing people being dragged from underneath the fallen building. They were all covered in reddish grey dust, their eyes wide and shocked in their pale faces. A little girl emerged, in her nightie, holding a doll and Beth felt a flood of relief. But as the bus started moving again, she saw a lifeless woman on a stretcher, a blanket being pulled over her head by the ambulance crew. Was it the little girl's mother? She'd never know.

When the bus got to her stop, Beth got out and immediately started coughing as the smell of smoke and burning wood caught her throat. There was a strange orange glow in the air, from far-away fires still burning. All around her people were running and shouting, and fire engines were wailing. The heavy-rescue ARP wardens were propping up houses, turning off the gas supply and dealing with leaking water pipes.

She paused for a moment. She was a nurse, after all. Should she go and help? She could see injured people around her, though the ambulance crews were all there and doing their job. Perhaps she'd just get in the way.

'Beth!' A shout made her look round and there was Ivy, by the door of the church hall that was used as the centre, holding up a woman who was as naked as the day she was born. The woman was staggering, her head was bleeding and she looked dazed. 'Beth! Over here!'

Beth dashed over and took the shivering woman's arm so that

Ivy could drape her with a blanket and together they helped her into the shelter.

'Clothes blown clean off,' Ivy muttered as they sat her down. 'Happens a lot. I'll find a nightgown for her, if you can have a look at her head? First aid kit's over there.'

Slightly overwhelmed to have been thrust into the action without expecting to be, Beth found the first aid kit and gently cleaned the woman's wound. It was quite deep and there was a large lump there too. The woman didn't know her name or where she was, so as Ivy came back and carefully helped the woman into a nightie and a too-big cardigan, and put some socks on her freezing cold feet, Beth turned to her. 'She needs to go to hospital,' she said in a low voice. 'She's in a bad way.'

Ivy nodded. 'I'll fetch an ambulance crew.'

Beth sat with the woman, who still wasn't talking, until Ivy came back with the crew and they took over. They took the woman outside and Beth and Ivy watched her climb into the ambulance, still looking as though she didn't understand what had happened.

'Poor sod,' Ivy said. Her voice cracked. 'She lives a couple of streets along. Got four kids. Lord knows where they are.'

Beth felt tears pricking her own eyes. This was awful. And she knew it was awful because she dealt with the aftermath at the hospital all the time. But to see it in people's homes, to see belongings scattered across streets and personal possessions being blown around by the January winds, seemed so cruel. How were people dealing with such destruction, day after day, after day? The resilience of human beings never failed to impress her. She patted Ivy on the shoulder. 'You're doing a good job.'

Ivy looked at Beth properly for the first time since she'd arrived. 'Why are you here?'

'I wanted to speak to you about Daisy.'

'Thought that might be it.' Ivy looked round. 'Things are calming down a bit. Shall we have a cuppa and a quick chat?'

She led Beth through the centre where a long queue of people was standing waiting for their vouchers which would pay for them to get a new set of clothes. Beth marvelled at the organisation and the systems that had been set up so quickly, in such strange and frightening circumstances.

'This is very impressive,' she said to Ivy as she led the way into a side room. 'Thank goodness you're all here to help.'

'East End pulls together in a crisis,' said Ivy, shrugging as though it was nothing special. 'We help each other out.'

The centre was in a large church hall and had spilled over into the church itself. Ivy had taken Beth into an office, which obviously belonged to the vicar – a cassock was hanging on a hook on the door, and a bible was open on the desk. There was a table at one side with mugs, and a small gas stove and a kettle, as well as a bottle of milk.

'How do you think Daisy is?' Beth asked.

Ivy poured water into the teapot and swirled it round, then she turned to look at Beth. The younger woman was shocked to see her eyes brimming with tears. 'Honestly?' Ivy said. 'I think she's falling apart.'

'Baby blues?'

Ivy shook her head. 'I think it's worse than that.'

Beth closed her eyes briefly, relieved that Ivy had seen it too, but feeling desperately sad for her friend. 'I think so too.'

Ivy wiped her eyes and gave Beth a small smile. 'Are you speaking as a friend or a nurse?'

'Both,' said Beth. She took a breath. 'I think Daisy has nervous exhaustion. It happens to some new mothers. She's had the shock of losing Rex, and then the drama of Willow's arrival. It's no wonder she's struggling.'

Ivy pinched her lips together. 'What do you suggest we do?'

'I could speak to someone at the hospital—' Beth began. But Ivy stopped her by holding up a hand.

'Absolutely not.'

'Oh Ivy, I think she needs help. And I'm trying to learn but I think a doctor might know better than I do. My father perhaps?'

'No,' Ivy spat. 'I know what happens to mothers who ask for help. I've seen it too many times. They get carted off to a sanatorium or, worse, to an asylum, and they never get better. Separated from their littl'uns, tarred as unfit mothers. Happened to Marge Hobbs down our street. She couldn't stop crying when she had her twins. Just sobbed the whole time, and then she tried to jump into the canal.'

'That's awful.'

'It was, but they took her off to some hospital and she never came home again. Last I heard, her husband had taken up with Rosalie from the King's Head and the twins call her mum now.'

It was clear Ivy was agitated about the idea of calling the doctor. 'I just think speaking to someone who knows what they're doing would help,' Beth said.

'No.' Ivy was firm. 'Daisy's having a difficult time, there's no question about that. But the best thing for her is to talk about it. I'll help with Willow for now, and we'll keep an eye on her, and just be kind. Take it slow.'

Beth wasn't sure. She had a lot of faith in doctors and medicine and her instinct was always to go to the experts for help, but Ivy was looking bullish and Beth had a sudden glimpse of the determination that had got her through the last war and the Suffragettes' fight. 'You really think that's best?'

'For now,' Ivy said. 'I won't see my daughter locked away in some asylum and Willow left with no parents.'

Beth could see there was no persuading her so she nodded slowly. 'All right,' she said. 'But I've got some conditions.'

Ivy poured the tea into two mugs and added the milk before she spoke. 'What are the conditions?' she asked, handing a mug to Beth.

'We keep talking to her, encouraging her to open up about how she's feeling.'

'Fine.'

'And we check in with each other regularly. You know her better than I do, but she might talk to me too.'

'Good idea.'

'But—' Beth looked down at her tea. 'I really think a doctor might be able to help. Perhaps I could speak to someone in confidence – just to see what they think?'

'I'm not sure,' Ivy said.

'How about if it was someone you trust? Your family doctor, perhaps? Or someone from the centre?'

Ivy shook her head. 'Too close.' She looked thoughtful. 'How about Gus?'

Beth blinked at her. She hadn't seen Gus at all since their horrible talk outside the committee room at Kew, and she suspected he'd changed his shifts specifically to avoid her.

'Oh, I'm not sure he'd know much. He's a cardiologist. A heart specialist.'

'But he knows Daisy,' Ivy pointed out. 'At least, he's met her.'

Beth nodded. She was nervous about speaking to Gus but she was also quite pleased to have a reason to see him. Perhaps she could help Daisy and repair her friendship with Gus too.

'You'd let me speak to Gus?' she asked Ivy.

The older woman sighed. 'I'd really rather you didn't speak to anyone, but if you have to, then Gus is the one. But if he suggests a sanatorium, the answer's no.'

Beth took a gulp of tea. 'All right,' she said.

Beth wasn't working at the hospital that day, and because she was only working the afternoon at Kew Gardens, having arranged the morning off to speak to Ivy, she had time to pop in to the committee and speak to Gus about Daisy. She was nervous about seeing him. She'd kept herself to herself when she was working at the lab, not crossing paths with him if she could help it. But now she had a proper reason to speak to him and she hoped it might break the ice after their last horrible conversation.

It was lunchtime when she arrived at the gardens and the lab was quiet, but Gus was there, sitting at a desk in the corner of the room, reading a textbook. He looked up as she entered the room and smiled. He shut the book and placed it carefully on top of a pile of papers on his desk. Beth, who'd been very worried about how he'd react when he saw her, relaxed a little bit.

'Hello,' she said.

'Hello.'

'Are you busy?'

Gus made a face. 'So, so.'

'I wondered if we could have a chat?'

Gus looked reluctant, which made Beth's heart twist in sadness. 'It's about Daisy,' she added hurriedly. 'I need some advice.'

'Have a seat,' he said. 'What's up?'

'I'm worried about Daisy,' Beth began. Briefly she outlined everything that was playing on her mind. Daisy's dull eyes, her forced smiles, her lack of interest in Willow, the way Beth felt that every time she left, Daisy would burst into tears. 'I know it all sounds vague but I've spoken to Ivy and she feels the same. I've done some reading and I think she has a sort of nervous exhaustion. She just can't see the good in anything. It's like her mind is bruised in a way, and she needs it to heal.'

'You probably know more than I do, if you've been reading up,' Gus said. 'But I do know that it's common in new mothers. More common than we realise, I suspect.'

'What can we do about it? Is there any medicine she can take?' Beth asked. 'Anything you know of from working at the pharmacy?'

Gus looked at a loss. 'Not that I've heard about, but I can ask around.'

'That would be helpful,' Beth said. 'Thank you.' She paused.

'I've done a lot of reading about shell-shock, because there's rather more written about that than nervous exhaustion. I was wondering about electric shock therapy?'

Gus made a face. 'Not for this,' he said. 'And I have my reservations about it.'

'Me too,' Beth admitted, feeling rather relieved. 'I feel like she needs more gentle care. So you think there's nothing we can do at the moment?'

'Not nothing; she has a strong family, and good friends. She'll have support. Gentle care is definitely what she needs.'

'Ivy said she just needs to talk.' Beth made a face. 'But I don't see how that can help.' She looked around the lab. 'Can't we discover a drug that can mend her? Talking seems such a small thing compared to how badly she's suffering.'

Gus nudged her gently. 'Come on, Beth,' he said. 'Surely that's what nursing is all about? You know very well that sometimes a listening ear is more effective than a pill.'

He was right. Beth felt mildly ashamed of herself. She nodded. 'I'll do everything I can to help her.'

'And I will support you in every way I can.'

Beth reached out to touch his arm, then thought better of it. 'You're a good friend.'

Gus pinched his lips together. He took a deep breath and Beth felt a lurch of nerves. What was he going to say?

'Beth, listen. You can't fix everyone. Sometimes you have to look at fixing your own problems before you mend everyone else. I think that if you put your own affairs in order, you'll be in a better position to help Daisy.'

Beth looked down at the desk. 'Paul and I broke up,' she muttered into her chest.

'Pardon?'

'We broke up,' she said, more loudly this time.

Gus looked straight at her and she felt her heart almost flip over. But he didn't speak. He just nodded.

'I should go,' Beth said. 'I need to get changed into my overalls before Will realises I'm late.'

'I hope I was helpful.'

'You were, thank you.' She smiled at him. 'It was good to see you.'

'And you.'

Beth walked away, feeling happier than she'd felt for weeks, because she'd seen that underneath Gus's textbook, on his desk, was a copy of the *Picture Post* with her face smiling out from it.

Chapter Thirty-Five

Daisy was in a world of her own as she marched along the road towards Kew Gardens. She was exhausted. Last night's raid had been a bad one and she'd barely slept. Willow, though, only woke twice to feed and she'd dozed off again almost straight away. Ivy had said, in wonder, that she'd been born into the sound of bombs dropping and knew nothing else.

'Probably, when the war's over, she'll not be able to sleep because it'll be too quiet,' she'd joked as she gazed into the tiny crib they'd squeezed into the shelter. Poppy and Willow slept well, like babies. Ivy and Daisy usually tossed and turned or sat up listening to the bombs falling.

But tired as Daisy was, she was pleased to be going back to Kew. Pleased and nervous and scared. She'd written to Will, asking if she could talk to him about her working on the allotment again. He'd written back almost immediately, asking her to come for a meeting. Daisy was chuffed to bits. She was obviously needed there, and she knew Will would want her to start as soon as possible after their meeting. She was really hoping that getting back to work would help her feel more normal again. More herself. She felt so odd all the time. As though the emotions she knew she should be feeling were just out of reach. She should be sad about Rex, happy to have Willow, worried about leaving her all day, excited about returning to the allotment, and yet, mostly, she felt numb.

She turned the corner from the bridge to head to the entrance to the gardens alongside Kew Green and gasped. While most of the bombing raids had left West London alone, it was clear that last night's had spread this far. There was a small terrace of houses that ran along the edge of the green and, slap bang in the centre, was a pile of rubble. Daisy stopped walking, shocked to see such destruction on this side of town. Where the house had been, there were simply bricks and scorched timbers; but the houses on either side, which had once been attached to those that had been bombed, stood steady. At least, parts of them did. Daisy could see the jagged edge where the bomb had torn through the brickwork, exposing half of a bedroom, where – unbelievably – a dressing table still stood with an unbroken mirror. She could see a lounge where a couch smouldered with acrid smoke and, on the other side, part of a kitchen where water was spurting from a burst pipe.

'Oh lord,' she whispered. She felt sick suddenly. Kew was a place of safety in her eyes. Far from the horrors of the bombed-out East End and away from the chaos of Central London. But the poisonous tendrils of the war had come here too.

The way into the gardens was busy with rescue crews and blocked by debris, so Daisy changed course and walked across Kew Green. St Anne's church – where her parents had got married – sat squarely on the other edge of the grass looking pretty in the frosty morning light and there was a bench nearby. Daisy headed for that and sat down for a second to gather her thoughts, still feeling shaken that there had been a bomb here in Kew. She was very early for her meeting with Will, so she had lots of time to spare to collect herself. She closed her eyes and took some deep breaths. She just needed a moment and then she'd go into the gardens, speak to Will and start work, and everything would be like it was. Before Willow arrived. Before Rex was killed. She breathed out slowly and unevenly. Except that it wouldn't be like it was. Because Rex was dead and Willow was here and no matter how many hours Daisy put in at the allotment, she couldn't change that. She swallowed a sob.

'Can I help?' a voice said, making her jump. She opened her eyes to see a clergyman standing beside the bench.

'No,' Daisy snapped, her surprise making her ruder than she would normally be. She swallowed. 'Thank you.'

'You looked upset.' The clergyman sat down on the bench next to her, without asking if she minded. 'Do you live here?' He nodded towards the bombed-out houses.

'No,' Daisy said. She wanted him to go away and leave her alone.

'The destruction is dreadful,' he said, undeterred by her lack of responses. 'Horrifying. And yet people carry on.' He looked at Daisy. 'It is shocking, though, to see it up close.'

'I live in Hackney.'

'So you're living with this every day?'

'Pretty much.'

'Then you know better than I do. I apologise.'

Daisy felt sorry for him. He was just trying to be nice. With a big effort, she turned to him and smiled. It made her lips feel strange. 'I work at the gardens – or, at least, I did work there last year,' she said. 'Kew has felt very safe and now it doesn't.'

'I can understand that.'

'I've been—' Daisy paused. 'Away for a while. I've come to talk about starting work again. I thought it would be as it was before. I wasn't expecting this.'

The clergyman nodded. He didn't say anything else, but he didn't leave either. He sat with Daisy for a short while and they watched the rescue teams working on the bombsite. Daisy felt herself growing calmer as they sat still, thinking about everything that had happened.

'My husband died,' she said suddenly. 'He was in the RAF and he died.'

'I'm very sorry.'

'And I had a baby.' She started to cry. 'He'll never meet her.'

The clergyman reached under his cassock and pulled out a handkerchief, which he handed to Daisy. She took it. It smelled nice and it was neatly darned. She wiped her eyes with it and blew her nose. 'Thank you.'

Much to her surprise, she felt ever so slightly better. Less numb. 'I have to go to work,' she said. She held the hanky out to him and then changed her mind as she remembered she'd blown her nose. 'I'll wash it and return it.'

'Keep it,' he said.

She smiled – a genuine smile this time. 'Thank you.'

'These are difficult times,' the man said. 'If you ever want to chat, or just sit quietly and think, feel free to pop into St Anne's. I'm Reverend King.'

Daisy had never been much interested in religion, but the idea of sitting in a still, silent church felt very appealing all of a sudden. 'I think I will,' she said.

With her spirits raised the tiniest amount, Daisy set off towards Kew feeling more positive than she had since she'd walked through the black iron gates with Willow in her arms over a month ago.

But her positivity didn't last long. Almost as soon as she got into the gardens, she became aware of a hubbub of activity, of people rushing purposefully in the same direction. There was a smell of smoke and she felt dust on her face.

'Oh no,' she said aloud. 'Oh no.'

Following the gardeners and other staff members who were all dashing towards the centre of Kew, she felt glass crunching beneath her feet. Around her were scorched bushes and skeletal trees reaching into the steely grey winter sky. And there was the Palm House, the very heart of Kew Gardens, its windows shattered.

Daisy stopped walking with a gasp and stared up at the damage.

'All right, Daisy?' Hetty appeared at her side, her hair tied up in a scarf and a smear of dust across her cheek, greeting Daisy as though she'd only seen her the day before, not weeks ago with a newborn baby in her arms. 'Rotten isn't it?'

'How bad is it?' Daisy felt a twist of sadness, which was silly because it was just a glass building full of plants. There would have been no people in there overnight. No one hurt. It simply felt as though her heart had shattered along with the windows.

'Not as bad as it looks,' Hetty said cheerfully. 'It wasn't a direct hit and it's only on one side where the windows are smashed. Just a lot of mess to clean up and a right massive crater in the lawn. Come and see.'

She tugged Daisy's sleeve and, silently, Daisy followed her across the grass to where there was, indeed, an enormous hole in the ground. They stood on the edge peering in.

'Makes you think, don't it? That was just one bomb,' Hetty said, her usual good-nature subdued.

'Why would they bomb Kew Gardens?' Daisy wondered aloud. 'Why here?'

'They reckon they were aiming for the pagoda, but they missed.' Hetty grinned at Daisy. 'All them rumours must be true.'

Daisy remembered – vaguely – hearing talk that the army had dug a huge pit under the pagoda and were using it to test their own bombs. It had sounded outlandish to her at the time, but it seemed that anything could happen now.

Hetty was still talking. 'Good to have you back, by the way. How's the littl'un? Is she doing all right?'

Daisy found she couldn't answer. She looked down into the crater, wondering what would happen if she let herself topple forwards. How would it feel to sink down into its muddy depths and feel the soil falling over her head, covering her like a blanket?

'Daisy?' Hetty was saying, jolting her back to reality. 'We need to go and help.'

'Oh, sorry,' she stammered, shocked by how dark her daydreams had been. 'Of course.'

She and Hetty crunched back across the scattered glass

253

fragments, someone handed her a broom and soon she was so busy, she didn't get a chance to think about her own problems. Which was a blessed relief.

They swept up glass, boarded broken windows and moved plants. Daisy's back was aching after a couple of hours and she felt more than a little light-headed. Hetty looked at her. 'Feeling it?'

'A bit.'

'I don't think you should be working so hard when you've just had a baby.' She raised her voice and shouted at one of the senior gardeners who was co-ordinating the clean-up. 'We're done here!'

Daisy marvelled at Hetty's confidence and self-assuredness. She thought she herself might have been like that once upon a time. But it seemed like a very long time ago. She let Hetty take the broom from her.

'Why don't we go over to the allotment?' Hetty said. 'I'll show you what we've been doing.'

'Have you been working there a lot?' asked Daisy. It was funny, she thought, that Hetty had been so desperate to be a part of the allotment when the film crew were there, and now she'd taken Daisy's place and Daisy was the one feeling envious.

'Here and there,' Hetty said cheerfully. 'I don't know as much as you, though. Come and see.'

'I'm meant to be meeting Will,' Daisy said with real regret because she did want to see the allotment. Daisy was no bighead, but she felt happy that Hetty had acknowledged her gardening skills. 'Is he here?'

'Over the other side of the Palm House, I think. I'll walk with you.'

They started to walk across the gardens – quiet today because they were closed to visitors due to the bombs that had fallen – with Hetty chattering all the time. Daisy liked hearing her talk. The words flowed over her and Hetty never waited for her to answer so it didn't matter that Daisy couldn't think what to say.

'Like I said, it's been so busy at the allotment, I've been helping them out. I know it's your thing really, yours and Beth's, but she was rushed off her feet and she's not always here, is she? With her nursing and that.'

Daisy nodded and Hetty carried on. 'Did Beth tell you how crazy it's been? The newsreel and the stuff in the papers has made her famous. Someone asked for her autograph the other day. They wanted her to sign their copy of the *Picture Post*.'

'She didn't tell me that,' Daisy said.

'Nah, she wouldn't,' Hetty said, slowing down as she turned the corner. 'She's too modest for her own good, is Beth. There he is. Will!'

Will was looking up at the Palm House, talking to another man in a suit and shaking his head. He waved to Daisy and she waved back.

'Come and find me before you go,' Hetty said, wandering off. 'Nice to have you back.'

'Nice to be back,' Daisy said honestly.

'Hello, hello,' Will said jovially, arriving at Daisy's side. 'Heard you were helping with the clean-up? Thanks for that.'

Daisy shrugged. 'All part of the job, isn't it?'

'Ah,' said Will. 'Ah.'

Daisy felt sick suddenly. What did he mean by 'ah'?

'Let's go up to the office,' he said.

'No,' Daisy said. 'Tell me now.'

'I'm afraid we can't have you back at Kew Gardens,' said Will stiffly. 'There is no job here for you now.'

'But you wrote to me. You asked me to come in today.' Daisy heard her voice tremble. 'I thought you were going to ask me to come back. I thought you needed me.'

Will closed his eyes briefly.

'I'm sorry, Daisy. This is out of my hands.'

'What is?'

'Married women is fine, but mothers? I'm afraid the powers

that be won't allow it. So, much as I'd love to have you back – and goodness knows we could do with your skills now we're so bloody busy – I'm afraid it's a no.'

'I wouldn't bring her with me. She's being looked after.'

'I know that. But you know what the men at the top are like. Stuck in their ways. I tried to argue your case, but they think if they allow you to come back, then there will be a queue of women wanting to work here, and soon Kew will be more like a primary school than gardens.'

'That's ridiculous.'

Will shrugged. 'It's the way they see it.'

'But Sir Edward's nice, Louisa told me.'

'He is nice. But that doesn't change anything.'

Helpless, Daisy stared at him. 'So I can't come back to work?'

'I'm afraid not.'

Daisy, who had felt the tiniest glimmer of hope like a crocus sprouting through the frozen earth bringing signs of spring, now felt nothing but darkness. She nodded slowly, and tried to smile. She knew she should thank Will for fighting her corner, say a polite goodbye, but the words wouldn't come.

Instead, feeling Will's concerned gaze on her back, she simply turned and walked away through the gardens to the gate.

There was nothing to look forward to, she thought. Nothing in the future except more of this unrelenting misery. This never-ending gloom. She felt as though all the colour had drained out of the world. Of course, Kew was dusty and gritty, and the sky was grey, but it was more than the weather or the after-effects of the bombing raid, or Will stopping her returning to work. Daisy felt the problem was with her. She just felt sad. No, not sad. It was more than that. She felt wretched. Hopeless. She knew with absolute certainty that winter would pass, and then spring would arrive. And after that it would be summer. Time would go on and she would never, ever feel better. She would feel this way forever. This misery would never end. And she wasn't sure she could face it.

Chapter Thirty-Six

Daisy didn't tell anyone what Will had said. Instead, she lied to her mother when she got back home that afternoon.

'I'm going to do a couple of days a week,' she said. 'But I can't take Willow, so if you could look after her, it would be very helpful.'

'Of course,' said Ivy. 'Are you sure about this?'

'They really need my help.' Daisy wished that what she was saying was true, and she hoped her mother wouldn't ask too many questions. But Ivy was so busy at the shelter and with delivering fruit and vegetables from the market garden, as well as making sure Poppy was keeping up with her school work, and then worrying about Archie, who'd sounded rather glum in his last letter home and who'd had his leave cancelled again, that she simply nodded.

'Willow will be fine with me,' she said.

Daisy thought that Willow would be better than fine with her mother. She thought she would be much happier than she was with her, when she grizzled and grouched and made cross faces and waved her little fists in the air. Daisy couldn't blame her, really.

So, Daisy put on overalls and boots and got on the bus and went to Kew. It was only when she'd walked across the bridge that suddenly she wondered what she was going to do when she got there. She couldn't just go and start digging in the allotment. Will would find out almost immediately. And if Beth was there, she'd ask all sorts of awkward, nursey questions. And Hetty would quiz her about Willow. No, she couldn't do that. And she couldn't just go and wander around the gardens because someone would spot her. She knew all the gardeners now and news of her giving birth to Willow had spread around all the staff so that even the doctors, botanists and pharmacists on the committee knew who she was, and so too did the men in the suits who ran the gardens from their offices in the buildings by the gate. The men who'd stopped her going back to work. No, she couldn't go there. It wouldn't work at all.

She walked slowly along the road, past the pub next to Kew Green. And then she looked over to where St Anne's sat at the edge of the grass, overlooking the gardens. Perhaps she could go there, she thought. Just sit quietly by herself and gather her thoughts.

She trudged over the lawn and into the churchyard. The church was large but not imposing. It looked, thought Daisy, almost friendly. It was so familiar to her from her visits to Kew and the photographs she'd seen of her parents' wedding. It felt safe. And that was all she wanted right now.

She went in the open door and sat in a pew at the back. The church had a white arched ceiling and stone pillars. It seemed to welcome her and she was glad.

She sat there for ages. An hour or more. Lost in her thoughts for a while, and then not really thinking of anything. Just being.

Eventually, a door banged, startling her out of her quiet contemplation. She heard footsteps and someone began playing a piano somewhere. It was quite nice to hear the music but it wasn't as peaceful as it had been. She thought perhaps it was time to go.

'Hello,' a voice said behind her. She turned to see the vicar – Reverend King – standing there. He was smiling and he looked pleased to see her. 'You came back?'

'It's nice here,' said Daisy, feeling slightly like she'd been caught out. 'Peaceful.'

'I think a bit of quiet thought is very good for the head,' Reverend King said. 'Healing.'

Daisy nodded.

'How are you feeling?'

She shrugged. 'Some days are better than others.'

'A lot of my parishioners have lost loved ones and while I can't assume to know how you're feeling, I know they've all said that taking each day at a time helps.'

Daisy felt a shiver of shame. She was being rather self-indulgent, she thought, wallowing in misery when she was just one of many. Think of all the poor people in England who'd lost husbands, sons, fathers. So many deaths, so much grief. And she still had her family, and a house to live in, and food to eat. She was one of the lucky ones really.

She slid along the pew and stood up. 'I have to go,' she said.

'Will you come again?'

Daisy gave him a tiny smile. 'I still have your handkerchief,' she said. 'I'll bring it back.'

'No need.'

'No,' Daisy said. 'But I will.'

And so she fell into a bit of an odd routine. Two or three times a week she would announce she was going to Kew – it wasn't a lie as such, she told herself. She really was going to Kew. Just not to the gardens. Ivy would look after Willow and Daisy would set off on the tube across London. But when she arrived at Kew, she wouldn't go into the gardens, she would walk over to St Anne's and sit quietly for an hour or two.

Sometimes Reverend King would join her in her pew. Occasionally, he'd chat to her, but more often they just sat in companionable silence for a while. Daisy found she was relying more and more on the quiet peacefulness of St Anne's, where no one expected anything of her.

Daisy would sometimes wander around the churchyard, reading

the headstones on the graves. For every grave she wondered about the people left behind. The husbands and wives grieving their spouses. The parents who'd lost children. Or children without parents. Sometimes she even cried a little. Often she wished Rex had a grave for her to visit. Somewhere she could go to feel close to him. The war hadn't just torn him from her, it had also robbed her of a proper chance to say goodbye.

As spring began to emerge from the freezing wintery days, she began weeding some of the neglected plots. She didn't speak to Reverend King about it, but he knew what she was doing because she saw him watching her from the porch and when she caught his eye, he gave her a little nod. One day she put a trowel and a little garden fork in her bag and she set about clearing the churchyard properly. There were bulbs beginning to grow but they were choked with weeds, so she pulled out the other strands and let the crocuses and daffodils have some space. She wondered if, when the flowers bloomed, she would feel better. She didn't think she would, but it brought her a little comfort to have something to plan for.

She took some summer-flowering bulbs from her own garden and planted them along the path leading to the church door. They would look pretty, she thought, when the sun finally came out. She wondered if Beth had remembered that now was the time to get the broad beans in the soil at the allotment. Beth had been trying to arrange a visit. She wanted to see Willow, she kept saying, and to tell Daisy all about the allotment and her work at the hospital. But Daisy kept putting her off because if Beth and Ivy came face to face, they'd soon find out that Daisy wasn't working at Kew Gardens at all.

And then, one wild day in March when the wind was whistling around Kew and Daisy was huddled down in her coat, she saw Beth walking towards her. She was startled, because she knew Beth generally went into the gardens through the other gate, away from the church.

'Daisy!' her friend said. 'How lovely to see you. What are you doing here?'

'I came to see you,' Daisy lied. 'Of course.'

'Where's Willow?'

For a second, Daisy didn't even know. Then she said: 'With my mother.'

Beth looked disappointed. 'Maybe you could bring her next time.'

'Maybe.'

They both stood there, slightly awkward. Then Beth put her arm through Daisy's. 'Come and see the allotment,' she said.

Beth chattered at Daisy all the way, telling her about the vegetables she, Hetty and the others had been planting. She was so proud of how the allotment was looking, bursting with it, that Daisy felt like a little shrivelled-up ball of jealousy. She was so envious of Beth for doing the job she wanted to do. She didn't want to see the allotment blooming with life as it was. Flourishing, in fact.

'Ta-dah,' said Beth as they drew near, flinging her arms out. 'What do you think?'

Daisy thought it was astonishing. Really incredible. Every inch of the plot was covered in neat rows of vegetables. Some, like the leeks, were ready to be harvested; others, like the spring cabbage and – she frowned, trying to recognise the different leaves – swedes, were growing well and looking strong enough to pick in a couple of weeks. There were tomato plants under glass that looked like they would yield a bumper crop come summer. The Anderson shelter was covered in plants, and the daffodils they'd planted so very, very long ago, were waving gently in the breeze, bringing a bright sunshine-yellow to the greenery. It was very impressive.

Daisy hated it.

'What do you think?' asked Beth.

Daisy knew what she should say. She should congratulate Beth on working so hard. On juggling the pressures of working at the hospital with gardening at Kew. She should express surprise and pride that her friend had learned so much in such a short time. She should ask how her work on the Vegetable Drugs Committee was going. But she didn't. She didn't say anything at all.

'Daisy?' Beth said. 'What do you think?'

Daisy felt the little desiccated kernel of hate at her core swell and grow. 'I think it's awful,' she said.

'Really?' Beth looked surprised and more than a little annoyed. 'Awful?'

'I wouldn't have done it at all like this,' Daisy said. 'Those potatoes are in the wrong place. It wouldn't surprise me if they get terrible blight. And the cabbages are being eaten alive by slugs. What a waste. You've really messed this up, Beth.'

Beth's mouth opened and closed like a fish.

'And those parsnips need picking straight away or they're going to rot,' Daisy said. It wasn't true, but somehow she couldn't stop saying horrible things. It was as though being mean to Beth was making her feel better.

'Daisy,' Beth said softly. 'Don't.'

But that just made Daisy lash out more. 'You've obviously spent too much time signing autographs and not enough time thinking about what to plant where.'

'That is not true.' Beth sounded cross now. 'That's not fair, Daisy.'

'Fair?' said Daisy with a hollow laugh. 'Do you think it's fair that I'm not allowed to work here?'

'No.' Beth shook her head vigorously. 'I absolutely don't think that's fair and I've told Will that.'

'Do you think it's fair that my husband was killed?'

'Of course not.'

'Or that your boyfriend is safe behind a desk while you wish he was fighting.'

Beth's jaw dropped. Somehow that made Daisy angrier. It felt good to be so full of rage. Like she'd turned on a tap and now her anger was spilling out, uncontrollably. 'Don't look so shocked,' Daisy hissed. 'I know you've been making eyes at Gus and wishing Paul would enlist so he was out of your hair.'

'Stop this.' Beth turned away from Daisy but Daisy made a grab for her, clawing at her arm to get her to listen.

'You've probably been wishing Paul would die, haven't you? You've been wishing him dead.'

'That's an awful thing to say. And it's definitely not true. I'm not even with Paul anymore. How could you say those things?'

Daisy looked at her friend, who she – when she was thinking straight – thought was marvellous and one of the cleverest, kindest, most brilliant people she knew. And she scowled at her. 'Because it's true,' she said.

Beth's face had gone blotchy and her eyes were filled with tears. 'Why are you being like this?'

Daisy shrugged and Beth shook her head. 'I know that things have been really hard for you, Daisy. I know that you're missing Rex and struggling to cope with Willow, and I want to help you. But you're not making it easy.'

Daisy felt numb. She could hear the words she was saying and she knew they were awful, terrible things to say. But she couldn't quite bring herself to care. She looked straight at Beth.

'I don't need your help,' she said. 'Get away from me.'

She was crying as Beth walked away.

Chapter Thirty-Seven

May 1941

Sometimes, Daisy remembered how she'd felt that day at Kew Gardens when Will had told her she couldn't return, and marvelled that she'd been so insightful about how the next few months would be.

The bulbs she'd planted in the churchyard had grown and were about to flower. The daffodils had been dead-headed and tied off, and every gravestone was neatly tended and cared for, and still Daisy felt no better.

Willow had grown from a little scrap of a thing to a chubby, smiley baby who could sit up by herself and shout for attention and fight to hold her own bottle in her podgy fingers. And still Daisy felt no better.

Even when the nightly raids on London slowed down and stopped altogether, Daisy didn't feel happier. She wore her melancholy like a blanket, draped over her head, shutting out the world.

She missed Beth dreadfully but she knew she was a terrible person to have said all those awful things to her friend and she thought that even though she longed to apologise, Beth wouldn't want to hear it. And she couldn't blame her. Not one bit.

She did, she thought, hide it well. She still went to Kew

regularly. Gardening in the churchyard, or sitting in the pews, lost in thought.

Sometimes Ivy would ask Daisy if she was feeling all right, and Daisy would smile and nod and say she was 'on the mend, thank you for asking' and her mother would leave it for a few days before mentioning it again.

Willow was the sweetest, happiest little girl. She charmed everyone who met her. The volunteers at Ivy's centre were all smitten with her and fought over who got to cuddle her when Ivy was looking after her. Poppy couldn't do enough for her, endlessly picking up toys she dropped and not minding when Willow pulled her hair. Jim thought she was hilarious when she stole his glasses and waved them about. And Ivy simply adored her.

'I can hardly remember what life was like before Willow arrived,' Ivy would say in wonder.

It should have made things easier for Daisy, knowing that her family all loved her daughter as they did. But somehow it just made her feel worse. The hard kernel of sadness that had lodged in her chest when Rex died, and the feeling of confusion and chaos that arrived with Willow, just grew and grew. The numbness was all-consuming. She couldn't remember how to feel happy, or how to feel love. She felt nothing at all.

She cared for Willow but she knew she wasn't doing it right. It was Ivy the child reached for when she was tired or fussy. It was Jim she wanted to make her giggle. Poppy changed nappies and blew raspberries on Willow's little podgy tummy and did it all so efficiently that Daisy knew she herself couldn't do it better.

The end of the air raids meant that the family spent their nights back in their bedrooms again. Poppy had moved into Archie's room for the time being, leaving more space for Daisy and Willow. Daisy was grateful but she hated having Willow all to herself overnight. If the baby woke, fussing or crying, Daisy was always worried she wouldn't settle for her. She knew it was Ivy she wanted really, but she couldn't wake her mother up for help – she was supposed to know what to do and she didn't want Ivy to know how badly she was failing. She understood with a horrible clarity that she had let everyone down. Ivy. Willow. Even Rex, for not caring for his daughter as she should be cared for. He would be horrified, she often thought, if he were here to see how Daisy was coping.

Ivy still took Willow every day when Daisy went to Kew Gardens. And thank goodness she did.

But then, one morning, not long after the air raids had ended, when Londoners were emerging from the relentless bombing and trying to repair the awful damage that had been done, Ivy sat at the breakfast table and looked at Daisy.

'We're short-staffed at the centre,' she said.

Daisy wrapped her fingers round her mug of tea – she found she had no appetite these days and she never ate breakfast now – and looked at her mother. 'Do you need more volunteers?'

'We do, and there are new people signing up all the time but until they get to know how it all works, I'm going to have to spend more time there.'

Daisy shrugged. 'Whatever you need to do.'

'I can help,' said Poppy who was trying to get Willow to eat some sloppy porridge. 'If you need me.'

'That's really kind, but you've got school.' Ivy sighed and turned her attention back to Daisy. 'I'm afraid I won't be able to take Willow as much as I have been.'

Daisy gripped her mug tightly to stop her hands shaking. 'But she loves being at the centre with you.'

'I know.' Ivy blew her granddaughter a kiss. 'But I need to be able to pitch in properly. It's just for a few weeks. Perhaps you could cut your shifts at Kew for now?'

Panic rose up in Daisy. She wanted to say no, to tell her mother than she didn't know how to look after Willow properly. That she would do everything wrong. But instead she just nodded. 'I'll sort it out,' she mumbled. Not that there was anything to sort out, of course. She was living a lie and perhaps her mother had got wise to it.

She saw Ivy catch Jim's eye across the table and give him a tiny nod. Daisy wondered if they'd been talking about her. Probably they'd predicted she'd react this way. They obviously knew she didn't want to look after her own child. She had no doubt that they would be disgusted with her. Sickened by what a dreadful mother she was turning out to be.

'I have to go,' she said.

Her first few days alone with Willow weren't great. She couldn't get her to sleep, so she walked for ages around the park, even though the weather was drizzly and chilly for the time of year, but she forgot the rain cover for the pram and Willow ended up wide awake and damp to boot. The next day, she dropped her bottle on the kitchen floor and watched in horror as the milk spurted all over the tiles while Willow whimpered with hunger.

Another day, Willow struggled while Daisy was trying to put a cardigan on her, her arm bent backwards and the little girl went red in the face because she was screaming so much.

'I'm sorry,' Daisy kept saying. 'I'm sorry.' She felt as though all she was doing was apologising to her daughter, who didn't even understand.

She ached for Kew. Hackney was home, but Kew was a haven away from the dust and the noise of falling masonry as bombsites were cleared. The buses rumbling along the road, car horns tooting, children shouting, and even Willow's cries all made Daisy's nerves jangle. She longed to go to St Anne's and sit quietly by herself but she couldn't.

But every day when Ivy came home from the centre and asked how Daisy's day had been, she would smile and say 'not bad'.

And then things got worse.

The sun was out for the first time in weeks, and as Daisy looked out of her bedroom window across the rooftops of the East End, she realised that Willow would be too warm in the thick cardigan she'd dressed her in.

Her heart sank at the thought of getting the little girl changed. She always wriggled so much when Daisy did it. For a moment she considered staying inside instead of going out for a walk, but that really didn't appeal. So she put Willow on her bed and peeled off her woolly top layer.

Willow wriggled, grizzling because she always wanted to be upright now, watching what was going on around her. She kicked her little feet and squawked at Daisy.

'It's sunny,' she said to the baby. 'You need to wear something lighter.'

Willow watched Daisy silently and then, like she'd decided a noisy protest was the best course of action, she opened her mouth wide and wailed. Daisy's heart gave a lurch.

'Oh no, Willow, not now,' she begged. 'I just need to get you changed.'

Willow screamed louder, bashing her legs on the counterpane. Every cry was like a dagger in Daisy's head.

'Stop it,' she said. 'Please stop.'

Trying to be quick because this was just too much, Daisy pulled the cardigan off Willow's arm and dropped it on the bed, looking around for the romper suit she'd taken out for Willow to wear. Oh, there it was, on top of the chest of drawers.

'Oh for heaven's sake,' she hissed. Willow's sobs were filling the room, stopping Daisy from thinking straight.

Leaving Willow where she was writhing on the bed in fury, Daisy took the two – maybe three – steps across the room to the drawers. But as she turned away, there was a thump and then an even more heart-breaking wail. Daisy whirled round and saw Willow face-down on the floor next to the bed.

'Oh my goodness,' she cried. She scooped the baby up and tried to soothe her, while frantically checking that she wasn't bleeding. She seemed all right. Her cheek was red where she'd hit the rug, but there was no lump on her head, and no blood. But Willow was furious, crying real tears now, her little hands clenched in tiny fists as she roared.

'You got a fright,' Daisy sobbed. 'It was my fault. I didn't know you could roll over. I didn't know. I'm sorry, I'm sorry, I'm sorry.'

She didn't know how long she sat there, holding her wailing daughter in her arms. But eventually, thankfully, Willow fell asleep and Daisy knew absolutely what she had to do. It seemed obvious, now she thought of it. She almost couldn't understand why she hadn't thought of it before.

Carefully putting Willow into her crib, she pulled out the drawers where she kept the baby clothes and packed up some towelling nappies, a few pins, a couple of cardigans and rompers and some tiny socks. She darted downstairs and found bottles and teats. Then she put everything into a bag and stuffed it under the pram. She found a piece of paper and wrote 'Willow' on it and tucked it under the mattress. Then she took the sleeping baby and put her gently into the pram without waking her, then covered her with a blanket.

The pram was large and awkward, but thankfully she managed to get it onto a bus – not all conductors were welcoming but eventually she clambered on board a bus with a female conductor who cooed over Willow. It didn't go all the way, but far enough so that she could walk the rest.

She felt strangely calm, now she'd made her mind up. She walked along, looking at the little clouds in the blue sky, feeling the sun on her face. Today was a good day, she thought. A good day to say goodbye.

Walking purposefully, but not hurrying, she pushed the pram across Kew Bridge and down towards the green. Then, bumping it over the kerb and onto the grass, she headed to St Anne's.

It was quiet at the church, as usual. There was no sign of Reverend King. No one doing the flowers, or visiting a grave. Daisy left the pram in the porch and took Willow out, then she sat down in a pew at the back of the church, close to the font. She'd not had Willow christened, she realised. She'd never got round to it. Perhaps Reverend King could arrange something. Afterwards.

Willow sat on her lap, looking around with wide eyes.

'Willow,' Daisy said quietly. 'You are very precious. I can't tell you how much I wish you'd arrived in another lifetime. A lifetime where you had a daddy.' She stroked the little girl's cheek. 'He'd have loved you so much,' she said. 'He'd have been so proud of you.' She took a breath. 'You should have a daddy who adores you, and a mummy who can love you the way you deserve to be loved.' She was crying now, tears falling onto Willow's podgy arms. 'I'm so sorry, but that's not me. I'm not that mummy. I wish I was, but I'm not. I've let everyone down, but now I'm going to put it right.'

She gathered Willow into her arms and breathed in the smell of her little girl. Willow grabbed a piece of Daisy's hair and cooed softly and so sweetly that Daisy almost changed her mind. But no. She had to do this. It was best for everyone.

Clutching her baby, she went back into the porch and put her into the pram. She gave Willow her dummy so she wouldn't cry and tucked a blanket round her because though it was a warm day, there was a chill inside the church. She made sure the slip of paper saying Willow was still there, and then she kissed her daughter on the forehead.

'Goodbye,' she said.

Halfway across Kew Bridge, the pain of what she'd done hit Daisy with a force that made her stop walking and double over, gasping for air. She'd left her baby girl. Abandoned her. What if no one found her? What if she starved? Daisy's heart was thumping and her legs were weak. She had to go back. She had to find Willow before any harm came to her. But then what? How could she go on as she had been? Taking ragged, desperate breaths, she clung onto the wall at the side of the bridge and looked down into the murky waters of the Thames. The tide was high and the river was swirling beneath her. She watched a plank of wood spin round in the current and then vanish beneath the surface. Willow would be safe, she thought. She was in St Anne's and wasn't a church a place of sanctuary? Reverend King would find her, and he would care for her and find her a new mother who could love her properly.

Daisy nodded to herself. This was for the best. But the pain was still there, jabbing her heart like a shard of ice. She thought about the wood, sinking below the water and disappearing and thought how simple everything would be if she could do the same – simply vanish.

And then, as though her body was working on its own, independently from her mind and her heart, she looked over the side of the bridge again, watching as the water flowed and churned, and slowly, carefully, deliberately, she put one foot onto the bottom of the wall and climbed over.

Chapter Thirty-Eight

Ivy was speaking so fast and in such a panic that it took Beth a while to understand what she was saying or even who was speaking.

'Slow down,' she said into the telephone. She'd never had a call at work before so even that had been confusing – Matron holding out the receiver and saying it was for her. 'Ivy? What's wrong?'

'Daisy's gone,' Ivy sobbed. Beth could hear her panic even though she was on the other side of London. 'She's gone.'

'I don't understand,' Beth said, feeling her palm sweaty on the heavy telephone receiver. 'Gone where?'

Ivy paused, clearly gathering herself, and when she spoke again she sounded slightly calmer. 'I popped home from the centre, just to check on her,' she said. 'She's been finding it hard, having Willow on her own.'

'And she's not there?'

'No. Which isn't unusual. She goes out for a walk sometimes. But her room—' Ivy gave a little gasping sob. 'Her room looks like it's been ransacked. All the drawers are pulled out. And lots of Willow's clothes and nappies are missing.'

'Maybe she's had a clear out?'

'No,' said Ivy. 'Something's wrong. I know it. I can feel it. How do you think she's been recently? Has she seemed any better?'

Beth swallowed. 'I've not seen her, Ivy. Not for weeks.'

'Not at work?'

'Work?'

Ivy sounded frustrated. 'At Kew.'

'Daisy doesn't work at Kew,' Beth said, her head spinning. 'Will wasn't allowed to take her back.'

There was a stunned silence at the other end of the line.

'Ivy?'

'She told me she was working,' Ivy said, sounding small and quiet. 'She asked me to have Willow two or three times a week, sometimes more. And she went off in her overalls. Where has she been going?'

Beth sat down on the chair next to Matron's desk, gripping the receiver tightly. 'I have no idea,' she said.

'Perhaps she's been going to Kew Gardens anyway,' said Ivy. 'Have you seen her there?'

Beth opened her mouth to say no, then remembered that awful, horrible day when Daisy had said all those nasty things to her. 'I saw her once,' she said.

Ivy breathed out. 'I think she might be there now.'

Beth's hands were sweating. 'Then she'll be safe.'

Ivy whispered so softly that Beth had to strain to hear. 'I don't think so.'

'She wouldn't do anything – silly, would she?' Beth swapped hands on the receiver so she could wipe her palms on her apron. 'She wouldn't hurt herself. Or Willow?'

'No,' Ivy said. 'She wouldn't hurt Willow.'

'But herself?'

There was such a long pause that Beth thought the call had been cut off. 'Ivy? Would she hurt herself?'

'She might.'

Beth's stomach lurched and she tasted the toast she'd had for breakfast, hours ago. 'Oh God.'

'I'm at the post office and Jim's coming with the van, but it'll take us a while to get there. Can you go?'

'Of course.' Beth's voice was shaky. 'I'll go now.'

'Find her,' Ivy begged. 'Find my girl.'

Beth dropped the receiver back onto the cradle. Luckily Matron had heard most of her conversation and realised it was an emergency. 'Go,' she said, taking Beth's apron and cap from her. 'Go, now.'

Beth didn't need to be told twice. She raced out of the ward, her soft shoes squeaking on the floor, down the stairs and along the corridor towards the exit, where a shout made her look round.

'Beth!' It was Gus. He wasn't at the hospital very often these days, but here he was like an angel in a white coat. 'Beth, are you all right?'

She stopped, out of breath already. 'No,' she said. 'Daisy's gone missing. I have to find her. I'm scared, Gus—'

Gus didn't hesitate. 'I'll come with you.'

'Quickly,' Beth said.

Together, they raced out onto the street. Gus hailed a cab and, to Beth's huge relief, one pulled up immediately.

'Kew Gardens,' she told the driver. 'As fast as you can.'

As the taxi sped west, Beth found Gus's hand and held it tightly. He pulled her close and she thanked her lucky stars she'd bumped into him. He was always so controlled. She felt his calmness shining from him, making her feel less panicked. She knew what a wonderful doctor he was and thought for the hundredth time how stupid it was that he could only treat patients when things were desperate. All that skill going to waste because of people like her father being short-sighted and inward-looking.

'Tell me about Daisy,' Gus said.

'Ivy said she's not been eating properly, she's not sleeping, she barely talks,' she told Gus frantically. 'And she's been lying about working at Kew Gardens. She told Ivy she'd come back, but she hasn't. Will wasn't allowed to take her back. I saw her once, a few weeks ago, and she was horrible, Gus. She said some awful things.'

'That would have been her illness talking,' Gus said softly.

'I know.' Beth nodded. 'But I let her walk away and I've not been in touch since.' She clenched her fists. 'I'm so stupid.'

'This isn't your fault,' Gus said. He squeezed her hand.

'I've been reading some books about psychiatry,' Beth went on. 'Every book I can find.'

Gus smiled. 'Me too.'

'You have?' Beth was touched. 'Then you'll know there's not much in the way of treatments available. They all seem to involve Daisy being separated from Willow, just as Ivy feared.'

Gus nodded. 'I believe that's the standard response.'

Beth felt wretched. That seemed too cruel to consider. 'It really seems to me to be a physical condition that's affecting Daisy's moods. Like having Willow has made something go wrong and it needs to be fixed. Does that make sense? It makes me wonder if there could be a drug to help. But the only things I've read about are so strong that they seem to change the patient more than their illness does.'

Gus frowned. 'I know some doctors believe that's the case, definitely, but I've had a quiet word with some of the pharmacists at Kew. I think we can find something that will help Daisy.'

'No hospital?'

'No.'

Beth was astonished that Gus had been doing all this research quietly, in his own time. Doing it for Daisy. She sneaked a look at his profile as he stared out at the West London streets. His jaw was clenched and he looked worried. He really cares, she thought.

The traffic was light, and the cabbie knew every back street so, in no time at all, they were approaching Kew Bridge.

'Would she be at the allotment?' Gus asked, looking out of the window.

'It seems the obvious place to start.' Beth's heart was beating faster as they got closer. 'I just hope we get there in time, Gus.'

She looked over the taxi driver's shoulder and saw, up ahead on the bridge, a flash of red hair. She blinked and looked again and there was Daisy, doubled over as though she was in terrible pain.

'Stop!' Beth screeched. The taxi driver slammed on the brakes, making a bus behind hoot at him. 'She's there, Gus. Do you see?'

She threw open the door of the cab and ran along the bridge, dodging the traffic as she raced across the road towards her friend.

But as she got closer, she saw – with growing horror – Daisy gripping the wall at the edge of the bridge and then slowly climbing over onto the other side. There was nothing stopping her plunging into the grey water below. Beth didn't want to shout, or startle her, or do anything that might make Daisy tumble from the wall. She stopped short, a few feet from her. Daisy was balanced precariously on the ledge on the other side of the bridge, her back against the stone and her arms spread out. Beth could see her knuckles white as she held onto the ridge on the top of the wall. She was so thin and frail that Beth worried that a large gust of wind would blow her right off the bridge and into the water.

'Daisy,' she said, quietly. 'Daisy, my love.'

Daisy turned her head, the breeze blowing her red hair across her face. She looked like something from a painting, ethereal and unworldly. Beth saw she was crying.

'Daisy,' she said again.

'I left her,' Daisy said faintly. Beth took a step towards her. 'I left Willow.'

Beth looked over her shoulder. Gus was standing next to the parked taxi. As she looked he paid the driver and the cab moved off. Gus stayed where he was, watching from a distance. She was so relieved he was there.

'Where did you leave her?' Beth said, taking another step.

Daisy looked straight at Beth. 'I didn't know what else to do,' she said. 'I am not the right mother for her.'

'Tell me where she is,' Beth said. She didn't know what to say, how to make this better, but she knew she had to find Willow and somehow keep Daisy talking. She edged closer again. 'Where's Willow, Daisy?'

'She's going to have a real mother,' Daisy said. 'Someone who can love her properly. And a father who's there, not just a memory. She needs to be loved.'

'You're all she needs,' Beth said quietly. 'You and Ivy and Jim, and Rex's parents, and me. We all love her. That's enough.'

'It's not,' said Daisy fiercely. 'I've let her down. And I've let Rex down. And I can't bear to go on feeling like this. It needs to end.' She hung forward, her arms straining, and Beth let out a gasp. She was almost close enough to touch Daisy now. Just a little further and she could hold on to her.

'We're going to get you some help,' she said. 'We'll help you stop feeling sad, and we'll help you look after Willow. All of us together, Daisy.'

Daisy leaned back against the wall. 'Can you help me?' she asked Beth. Desperation shone in her swollen eyes. 'Please help me.'

'Of course I'll help you,' Beth took another step forward and put her hand on top of Daisy's. Her fingers were cold on the stone bridge. 'Of course I will. But you need to tell me where the baby is.'

Daisy turned her hand around so she was holding Beth's fingers and Beth clung on. *Please don't fall*, she thought. *Please don't fall.* Daisy wiped her face with the heel of her other hand, looking like a little girl. 'She's at St Anne's.' She breathed in a long, shuddering breath. 'But Reverend King wasn't there when I left her. There was no one there. What if no one comes?'

'Gus will go and fetch her,' Beth said softly. 'He can go now.'

There was an awful silence as Daisy thought about it and then, slowly, she nodded.

Hanging on to Daisy's fingers for dear life with one hand, Beth turned and frantically beckoned to Gus. He darted across the traffic, and as he got near, she could see how worried he looked. 'Willow's at St Anne's,' she said trying to sound calm when she felt anything but. 'Can you go and fetch her?'

Gus wasted no time on questions, to Beth's enormous relief.

Instead he just nodded and ran off towards the end of the bridge.

'She'll be safe now,' she reassured Daisy.

Daisy moved, stepping along the narrow ledge and making Beth's heart lurch with fear that she was going to fall. But instead, Daisy turned so she was facing Beth and threw her arms around her. Beth clutched her tightly, realising how thin she was. She could feel every rib and her shoulder blades stuck out like wings. 'I've got you.'

They stayed there for a while, Beth holding Daisy with the stone wall of the bridge between them. Beth felt Daisy's tears trickling down her neck.

'Can you climb over?' she said eventually. 'If I help you.'

Daisy let Beth half drag her over the wall and they both slumped onto the pavement.

'I'm so sorry,' said Daisy. 'I didn't mean for any of this to happen.'

Beth was still holding her hand. She didn't want to let go. Not yet.

'None of this is your fault.'

'I need my baby.'

'Gus has gone to the church,' Beth reminded her. Daisy was confused and vague, and Beth thought with a lurch of fear that perhaps Willow wasn't at St Anne's. Perhaps Daisy was getting muddled.

Daisy nodded.

'Do you want to go there too?' Beth asked.

Daisy nodded again so Beth got up and helped her to her feet. Her face was pale and she had dark smudges under both eyes. She would benefit from some proper sleep, Beth thought. Away from London and the bombs and the memories. If only there was somewhere she could go. Not an asylum but a safe place somewhere.

'Come on,' Daisy said, pulling Beth's hand. 'We need to hurry.'

Chapter Thirty-Nine

Daisy was off, racing along the street towards Kew Green. Beth – on legs that were still shaking from everything that had happened – dashed after her.

'Daisy, wait,' she panted, but Daisy was off – ignoring the curious glances from people they passed as she hurtled towards the church.

When they reached the corner of the green, Daisy darted across the road and onto the grass. Beth paused, resting her arms on her thighs and trying to catch her breath, as a van hurtled round the corner and screeched to a halt next to her. Ivy threw open the passenger door.

'Beth!' she called. 'Did you find her?'

Beth looked up, still gasping for air. 'Willow's at the church,' she panted. Ivy jumped down from the van, followed by Jim, who was in the driver's seat. 'Is she all right?' she said urgently. 'Is Daisy all right?'

Beth's breathing was easier now. She shook her head. 'She was on the bridge,' she said, her voice cracking. 'She was—'

Ivy went pale and Jim wrapped his arms round her, steadying her as she swayed with the shock.

'Is she?' Ivy muttered. 'Has she?'

Feeling awful that she'd not explained things properly – her mind was whirling and she was finding it hard to think straight

– Beth put her hand on Ivy's arm. 'She's safe,' she assured her. 'She's there, look.' She pointed to where Daisy was running across the green, her red hair glowing in the spring sunshine.

Ivy and Jim exchanged a look. 'What's she doing? Why is Willow at the church?'

'I'll explain as we go,' said Beth, desperate to be with Daisy. 'Come on.'

She followed Daisy across the grass, Ivy and Jim trailing after her. For a brief moment, Beth thought how farcical they must look – her in her nurse's uniform, Ivy in her WVS get-up and Jim in his gardener's overalls, running across Kew Green – but there was no time to worry about that now. She just wanted to find Daisy, and Willow, and Gus.

Daisy stopped running once she reached the door to the church and Beth caught up with her.

'What if she's not there?' she said to Beth, her eyes fixed on the imposing church entrance, with its stone pillars. 'What if someone's taken her?'

Beth took Daisy's hand and the women stood side by side for a second, both looking up at the cross on top of the church's clock tower. Beth closed her eyes briefly, praying that Willow would be safe, then she squeezed Daisy's fingers.

'Come on,' she said. 'Let's go and get your little girl.'

Together they pushed open the heavy door and went inside, taking a second for their eyes to adjust to the dim light.

And there, sitting in a pew at the back of the church, was Gus and in his arms was Willow, who was looking up at the sunlight streaming through the windows and seemed none the worse for her ordeal.

'Willow,' gasped Daisy. And then – to Beth's horror – she slumped to the floor in a faint, just as Jim and Ivy arrived at the door of the church.

'Daisy,' wailed Ivy.

Beth sprang into action. 'She's fainted,' she said. 'We just need to give her some air.' She bent down next to Daisy, who was pale but breathing. Her eyelids were flickering. 'Ivy, take Willow, please,' Beth said briskly. She felt more in control than she'd felt all day. She could deal with medical emergencies. Balancing on bridges was less easy. She felt a bit light-headed when she thought of it, and focused on Daisy instead.

'Jim, can you pass me some of those kneelers to put under her feet? We should raise them up, get the blood flowing back to her head.'

Obediently, Jim handed them over, looking worried. 'Is she all right?' he said. 'She's not been eating much, I know. She's so thin. I put some extra sandwiches in her bag every day but I don't think she eats them.'

Beth's heart ached at the idea of Jim looking out for his daughter that way. She couldn't imagine her father ever making her a sandwich.

Ivy had Willow in her arms, and Willow was babbling away at her grandmother, happy as Larry.

Gus dropped to his knees next to Beth and felt for Daisy's pulse.

'Are you all right?' he asked Beth, his eyes full of concern.

Tears sprang up in Beth's eyes. 'Fine,' she whispered. And the strange thing was, she really was fine now she was with Gus. She felt like she could cope with anything when he was by her side.

'Daisy,' she said softly, stroking her friend's forehead. 'Can you hear me? Willow's safe. She's here with your mum.'

Daisy opened her eyes. Beth was relieved to see she clearly knew where she was and what had been happening. 'Willow?'

'She's here.' Ivy knelt down next to Daisy, opposite Beth, still holding the baby. Daisy struggled to sit up and then threw her arms around her daughter. Ivy hugged Daisy and the three generations of women all sat together on the stone floor of the church. Beth and Gus, feeling a bit like they were intruding suddenly, got up and moved to the side, as Jim joined his family in their embrace.

'Oh heavens,' said Beth, wiping away a tear. She was so tired she thought her legs wouldn't hold her up for a second longer. 'I think I need to sit down.'

Gus guided her into a pew and Beth sank down onto the shiny wooden bench gratefully. 'What a day.'

Gus slid into the pew next to her and looked straight at her. Beth looked back. She couldn't read the expression in Gus's dark eyes, but she knew what her own face was showing. Exhaustion, of course, and relief. But also love. She had tried so hard to get over Gus. To tell herself there was no future in her feelings towards him, but there was no denying how hard she'd fallen for him. And now, weak with the emotions of the day, she couldn't disguise her love any longer. She gazed at him, finding she couldn't tear her eyes away, and Gus gazed back at her. 'You are extraordinary,' he said. 'You just saved Daisy's life, you know? And possibly Willow's too. I don't like to think what could have happened if you'd not been there.'

'She's my friend,' Beth said. She glanced over at where the whole family were still sitting on the floor, clutching each other and talking softly, Willow's little chuckles making them all smile. 'She'd have done the same for me.'

'I have never met anyone like you.' Gus sounded bewildered, almost. He shook his head. 'I've tried so hard to fight the way I feel, but I can't help it.' He smiled. 'I think I'm falling in love with you.'

Beth's head was spinning. At some point Gus seemed to have taken her hand, and now he was holding it tightly. She liked it.

She realised that Gus was suddenly very close to her. Had he moved, or had she? She didn't know, but she could feel his breath on her face. Their noses were almost touching and then Gus leaned forward, just a fraction, and tilted his head, and, ever so gently, he touched his lips to hers. Beth drew her breath in sharply and Gus pulled away.

'No,' she said firmly. 'Don't move.'

This time it was she who leaned in, and then they were kissing properly. There in the pew at St Anne's, with Daisy and her family on the floor next to them. But Beth wasn't thinking of any of that. All she cared about was being close to Gus, feeling the warmth of his body next to her and the way his hand felt on her back.

'Ahem.' Someone cleared their throat next to them and Beth and Gus sprang apart. Standing in the aisle, just in front of where Daisy and her family still sat on the floor, was a man in clerical dress. 'I don't want anyone to think they're not welcome here,' he said. 'But I wondered if someone could tell me what's going on.'

Beth felt her cheeks flame. Imagine kissing Gus in a church! Her mother would be horrified. But Gus's fingers were still entwined with hers and she didn't move them. Instead they shared a small, secret smile.

'Good lord,' the clergyman said. 'Daisy?'

Jim and Ivy got to their feet and Jim helped Daisy stand up, too. She was holding Willow tightly and her cheeks had more colour, Beth was pleased to see, though she still looked pale and weary.

'Reverend King,' Daisy said. She looked like she was going to try to explain, but her voice trailed off and she didn't say anything else. Instead, she just looked helplessly at her family, then she gave the ghost of a smile. 'This is Willow,' she said. 'My daughter.'

Reverend King reached out and took Willow's little hand in the tips of his fingers. 'Pleased to meet you, Willow,' he said, and Willow gave him a gummy smile.

'And my parents, Ivy and Jim,' Daisy said. 'And my friends, Beth and Gus.'

The vicar nodded at them all, still looking vaguely confused.

'Are you all right, Daisy?' he asked.

Daisy frowned, her forehead furrowing into lines like the vegetable patch at Kew. 'Not really,' she said. 'Actually, I've not been all right for a while now.'

'I understand,' Reverend King said. Beth thought he seemed

like a very kind man and it was clear he'd met Daisy several times before. 'What can I do to help?'

Daisy smiled at him and shifted Willow on her hip, so she was holding her even closer. 'You've already helped more than you can ever know,' she said. 'But perhaps I could keep coming to the church.'

'You are always welcome,' he said. He clasped his hands together and stood, rather awkwardly, looking at the strangers who had arrived on his doorstep.

'We should go,' Daisy said. 'I'll see you soon.'

Much to Beth's surprise, Daisy stood on tiptoe and kissed the vicar on his cheek. He looked startled and pleased at the same time. Daisy and her parents all trooped back to the church porch, where Willow's pram still stood. Gus followed, but Beth hung back.

'I'm sorry,' she said to Reverend King. 'About Gus and I, erm, you know.'

The vicar gave her a broad smile that made him look much younger. 'This is a house of love,' he said. 'But maybe save that for private next time.'

Flushing, Beth promised she would and hurried after her friends.

'Go home and get some sleep,' she urged Daisy. 'Can I visit tomorrow?'

'Please,' Daisy said, hugging her tightly. 'Beth, I can't thank you enough. I'm sorry about all those awful things I said.'

'Don't mention it,' Beth said. She didn't want her thanks. She was just pleased her friend was standing here on Kew Green, safe and sound, with her baby tucked up in the pram next to her. She screwed her nose up. 'I'll see you tomorrow,' she said.

She and Gus stood and watched as Daisy, Willow, Ivy and Jim all got into the van and headed off back to Hackney.

'She's got a long road ahead of her,' said Gus.

'Do you really think there are things that could help her?' Beth walked over to where there was a bench overlooking the green and sat down. She was drained of all energy and she honestly thought she could curl up right where she was and go to sleep. Especially if Gus was there for her to cuddle up with. 'I've read about a chap who helped soldiers with shell-shock with hypnosis and talking therapy. It sounded much more helpful than strong drugs and electric shocks.'

'I'll make some enquiries,' Gus said. He didn't sit down but hovered close by where Beth sat. 'We'll get the best doctors and the best medicines and we'll make sure she's looked after.'

He walked a few paces one way, then turned and walked the other way. 'Beth—'

'Gus—' Beth said at the same time.

He turned to her and she was shocked to see his face looked absolutely wretched. Despairing. Desolate.

'Beth,' he said again. 'We can't be together.'

'We can.' She felt desperate suddenly. 'I split up with Paul. It's fine. We can be together.'

'It's impossible.' He stepped forward and took both her hands in his. 'In another lifetime, perhaps. But not here. Not now. Not when everyone regards me with suspicion.'

'But—' Beth began, but Gus shushed her. 'They won't let me work,' he said, so matter-of-factly that Beth's heart broke for him. 'They want my knowledge, but they won't let me see patients. Cab drivers won't pick me up on the street. People cross the road when they see me coming.' He let go of Beth's hands and looked away. 'We were turned away from the shelter, remember.' He swallowed. 'We were in danger because of the colour of my skin.'

'Oh, Gus,' said Beth. Her voice shook. 'I know this. But I don't care. We can make it work.'

'Do you know why I live in hospital digs?' he went on.

She shook her head. 'I just assumed it was convenient.'

'I tried to find somewhere else but the flats that were available had always mysteriously just been rented when I met the agents.'

Beth felt sick. 'It's not right,' she said.

'No, it's not.'

'I'm a nurse, Gus. I know how the human body works. We both know better than anyone that underneath we're all the same. What difference does the colour of your skin make?'

'It makes no difference,' said Gus. Beth had never heard him sound so resigned before. Resigned and tightly, bitterly angry. 'And yet it makes all the difference in the world.'

Beth felt actual physical pain in her chest. Was this how it felt, then, when your heart broke?

'We can't be together,' Gus said.

'But I love you.' Beth was surprised by how easy the words came. 'I love you.'

'I want to love you.' Gus's face twisted in pain and Beth thought how awful to be the cause of that pain, and the only person who could make it better, and yet know that she couldn't do anything at all. 'I do. But it's because I feel that way that we can't be together.' He leaned down and kissed her cheek. Beth reached out and wrapped her arms round him and squeezed him tightly for a second, then she let go and Gus stood for a second looking at her.

'I'm so sorry,' he said. He turned and walked away quickly, in the direction of the tube station as Beth put her head in her hands and cried.

Chapter Forty

Louisa thought Ivy had aged ten years in the few months since she'd last seen her. Her forehead was etched with lines and there were grey strands around her temples and scattered through her fading red hair. But she wasn't surprised, given what Ivy had been through recently. Supporting Daisy through Rex's death and her unexpected new arrival had been tricky enough, and now this.

'I have nightmares where she's on the bridge and I can't get to her on time,' Ivy was saying. 'I didn't even see her there – it was Beth who talked her down – but every night when I close my eyes I can see her, balancing on the edge.'

'Has she spoken about it?' Louisa squinted into the sun to see if she could spot Daisy. She and Ivy were at Kew Gardens – they always met at Kew when Louisa was doing her VDC work – and across the grass she could see Beth talking to Daisy on the allotment. Daisy still wasn't allowed to work at Kew, but Ivy thought that was no bad thing really. She needed time to heal.

'Not much to me or Jim. Beth says she told her she didn't want to—' Ivy's voice broke and Louisa reached out and took her friend's hand. 'She said she didn't want to die. She just couldn't cope with feeling so awful.'

'Oh that poor girl,' Louisa said. She hated seeing her friends suffer in this way.

'She's better now she's talking,' Ivy went on. She was watching Daisy across the garden too, Louisa noticed. Her eyes were always fixed on her daughter as they talked, checking she was all right. 'She's being more honest about how she's feeling. Telling us when it gets too much and asking for help when she needs it.' Ivy took a breath. 'I felt as though it was my fault, you know.'

'No.' Louisa was firm. 'None of this was your fault.'

'Beth wanted to get her to a doctor months ago and I said no.' Ivy sounded wretched. 'And then I stopped taking Willow to the centre with me, so she had to look after her. I pushed her too hard and too fast.'

'You did what you thought was best.'

'And I nearly lost her.' Ivy wiped a tear from her cheek with her fingertips. 'I just want her to be all right.'

'She's had enough heartbreak for a lifetime, two lifetimes,' Louisa said. 'But she's got you and Jim, and the other kids, and Beth is a treasure. She'll get through this.'

'I hope so,' Ivy whispered.

They sat for a while, enjoying the sunshine on their faces and the smell of the flowers. Louisa loved her life in Kent. She adored Teddy and enjoyed being close to her family, but she thought she never felt quite so contented as when she was at Kew.

'Tell me about the County Herb Committees,' Ivy said. 'I could do with the distraction.'

Louisa sighed happily. 'It's more successful than I could ever have dreamed.'

'Beth is enjoying being involved with the committee, I know that.'

'She's come up with some excellent ideas, so I've heard. I think there's a plan to get more nurses involved because Beth's been so useful.'

'So how does it work? The experts here at Kew tell you what to grow?'

'Pretty much,' said Louisa. 'At first it was just small quantities

288

of a few plants, but it expanded fast. Now we've got WIs growing tons of flowers and herbs across the whole country.'

Ivy looked impressed. 'And you're co-ordinating it all?'

Louisa tried to appear modest but the truth was she was extremely proud of what she'd achieved so far. 'At first, I did it all in my front room,' she said. 'I had maps pinned to the wall and plans of who was growing what, where. But Teddy got fed up with not being able to sit in his chair to listen to the wireless. So I decamped into the old doctor's surgery – the doctor's got a fancy new office at the edge of the village and it was empty. Teddy's got a desk there too now and we sit together while he does his evacuee organisation and I do my work.' She smiled thinking about Teddy sitting calmly in the corner of the room, finding billets for children and checking they were all OK, while she dashed about like a mad thing, making telephone calls, sending telegrams, writing letters and trying to find enough places to store all the herbs they were growing. 'And Christopher's been helping, but I have to be honest, he's often more of a hindrance.'

Ivy smiled. 'I remember when he was a little boy; he'd trip over his own feet.'

'He means well, bless him, but he's much better outside in the fields than in an office.' Louisa sighed. 'I'm so relieved to have him home, though, that I just go along with whatever he says.'

'I can understand that.' Ivy nodded, looking over at Daisy once more.

'But it's going very well,' Louisa went on. 'Almost too well.'

'Who's going to pick everything?' Ivy said, frowning. 'If you're growing so much, who will pick it?'

'My WIs, obviously, but also Brownies, Cubs, retired people, schoolkids. Everyone's pitching in.'

'Goodness gracious. You've really thought of everything.'

Louisa beamed at her. 'I was feeling like a spare part,' she admitted. 'Old and useless.'

'You're not old and useless,' Ivy protested, but Louisa shrugged.

'That's how I felt. You were into your WVS work straight away but there was no call for that in the village, and even if there had been, I'm not as young as I was. I missed Kew so badly, and the thrill of being a Suffragette.'

'They were good times,' said Ivy. 'Even though there was sadness there too.'

'And I really felt we were doing something useful back then,' Louisa said. 'I wanted to do the same again. Teddy said I needed an outlet for my zeal.'

'You've certainly done that.' Ivy grinned, looking more like the young woman Louisa had met in the last war and not the worried grandmother she actually was.

'It's wonderful that it's been so successful—' Louisa paused, wondering for a moment if she should burden Ivy with her troubles. But she saw Ivy's sharp eyes watching her and realised she couldn't pretend everything was fine when it wasn't. She sighed. 'But, as I said, it's almost too successful and I'm not sure I'm coping.'

'I knew you were worrying about something,' Ivy said. 'What do you mean, too successful?'

'I'm rushed off my feet.' Louisa felt slightly foolish after her earlier boasting. 'I've got County Herb Committees all over the country, and although we have a hierarchy, it's me who's ultimately calling the shots.'

'Which you love doing.'

'Oh God, I really love it,' Louisa said with a smile. 'But it's just too much for me to handle on my own. I'm drowning in the paperwork, I have to let the phone ring out because I don't have time to answer it and Christopher's so dreamy he just ignores it. He gets distracted by a bug crawling on the wall or absorbed in a book and doesn't do the jobs I asked him to do, or he'll do one job so brilliantly that it takes him all day.' She laughed fondly but then frowned again, remembering. 'I work all hours, and, I have to admit, Ivy, I'm exhausted. Teddy worries about me, then gets cross when I just keep working anyway, so we're bickering the whole time.'

Suddenly, and quite ridiculously, given what Ivy was going through, Louisa felt close to tears. 'I'm just really tired and perhaps I need to accept that I'm not as young as I was.'

Ivy was watching Daisy again. 'You need an assistant,' she said. 'Someone to answer the phone and do your paperwork for you. Do you think Daisy's all right?'

Louisa strained to see Daisy's face. 'She looks content enough,' she said. 'Pale, though. And very thin.'

'She's eating better but she's still not herself.' Ivy ran her fingers through her hair. 'I worry about her constantly.'

'You'll make yourself ill, if you keep on like that.' Louisa stared at her friend as something occurred to her. 'What did you say?'

Ivy widened her eyes. 'I said I worried about Daisy constantly?'

'No, before that. What did you say about my paperwork?'

'That you need someone to do it for you.'

'Yes!' Louisa pointed at Ivy, making her jump. 'That's it. I need an assistant. I need Daisy.'

'In Kent?'

'Of course in Kent. Away from the memories of Rex. Lots of fresh air. New people to meet.'

'With Willow?'

'Absolutely with Willow. They come as a package, I presume.'

Ivy smiled at the mention of her beloved granddaughter. 'They do.'

Louisa's mind was whirling, as she tried to work out how to organise things. 'I would ask them to stay with us, but we simply don't have room,' she murmured almost to herself. 'I'm sure we could find somewhere, though. Teddy knows all the billets, of course. Perhaps one of the farms—' She gripped Ivy's arm, and squeezed it. 'Or, upstairs from the surgery.'

'I have no idea what you're talking about,' said Ivy.

Louisa chuckled. 'There's a flat upstairs at the old surgery. The doctor lived there with his wife when they were first married, I believe. Daisy could stay there with Willow. It's right across the road from our cottage so I can keep an eye on her, but she'd have her independence.'

She was very pleased with herself, but Ivy frowned. 'Oh Louisa, I don't know if we could stretch to paying rent somewhere on top of our normal bills. I'm barely working at the market garden now, and Poppy wants to stay on at school.'

Louisa held her hand out to stop her. 'There would be no rent to pay,' she said. That wasn't completely true, but she would make sure Ivy and Jim weren't out of pocket. 'And anyway, Daisy would be earning a salary. I'll speak to the VDC and make sure they offer her a proper wage.'

Ivy was staring at Louisa in a way that made her feel slightly uncomfortable. 'Ivy?' she said.

'Ohh,' breathed Ivy. 'Oh, you are a clever old stick, Lou.'

'Less of the old,' said Louisa frostily. 'Do you think Daisy would like to come and work with me for a while?'

'I think she would,' Ivy said. 'But I also think she would want to think it was all her idea.'

She jumped to her feet and held her hand out to Louisa to help her up too. 'Why don't we ask her? But let me do the talking.'

She dragged Louisa across the grass to where Daisy and Beth were sitting having a cup of tea in the deckchairs.

'Daisy,' Ivy called as they approached. Daisy looked up and Louisa was shocked to see how pale and drawn she was. Some country air would do her the world of good, she thought.

'Louisa's got a problem and she thought you could help.'

Daisy struggled to her feet and came over to give Lou a kiss. 'Hello, Auntie Louisa,' she said. Louisa looked at her critically. There was no light in her eyes, and no happiness in the smile she pasted on her face. Beth said hello too and then Ivy spoke.

'Lou's in need of an assistant,' she said. 'Someone to do

292

paperwork, answer the telephone, give support to the County Herb Committees.'

Daisy nodded. 'What's that got to do with me?'

'I thought you might know someone. Perhaps one of the girls you worked with at the Home Office would fancy getting out of London for a while.'

Daisy looked at Louisa. 'It would be in Kent?'

'Afraid so,' Lou said cheerily. 'They'd have to work quite closely with me. I can sort out accommodation, though I've not confirmed the salary yet.' She crossed her fingers behind her back and hoped that the VDC would approve her request for an assistant. 'Can you think of anyone?'

Daisy glanced at Beth and her friend gave a tiny nod. Louisa was reminded of her friendship with Ivy when they were working at Kew. How they relied on one another.

'What about me?' Daisy said in a small voice. 'Would it be something I could do?'

'Almost certainly,' said Louisa. 'Would you want to come and stay in Kent?'

Daisy took a step towards Louisa. 'Yes,' she said urgently. 'More than anything.' She looked worried for a second. 'Could I bring Willow?'

'Of course you could,' Lou said. 'She could come to work with you every day.'

Daisy glanced at her mother. 'Could I, do you think? Could I do it?'

'You could.' Ivy nodded vigorously.

'But you wouldn't be there to help. Willow would miss you.'

'We'd come and visit all the time.'

'What if I can't cope? I'm not as good with her as you are.'

Ivy went to her daughter and took her face in her hands. 'You're her mother, and she loves you and that's all that matters.'

Daisy opened her mouth to argue but Ivy shushed her. 'Louisa will be there to help, if you need her. And Teddy.'

'And the WI will be fighting over who gets to give Willow a cuddle,' Louisa added.

Daisy looked like she might cry. Or throw up. Louisa wasn't sure which.

'I'll miss London,' she said. 'Oh, and I'll miss Kew Gardens, so much.' But then she took a deep breath. 'But I have to get away from all these memories.'

Louisa smiled. 'Why not come for a fortnight and see what you think? If you like it, you can stay, and if not, you can come home.'

'That is a good idea,' Beth said. 'I think you should do it, Daisy.'

Daisy looked at Beth, then at Ivy and, finally, at Louisa. Then she nodded.

'Is that a yes?' Louisa said.

Daisy smiled – more genuinely this time. 'It's a yes.'

Chapter Forty-One

July 1941

Daisy had asked Beth to go with her to Kent. Just for the day – to help with her bags and Willow's pram and all the ridiculous amount of luggage babies seemed to need. To her relief, Beth had said yes straight away. 'I could do with some time off,' she'd said. 'It's been hard work recently.'

They were at Charing Cross station and it was crowded with people. There were soldiers milling around in groups and sweethearts saying goodbye. Daisy averted her eyes from them all, trying not to think about the last time she'd seen Rex. Beth was quiet and Daisy looked at her friend curiously. Because she had been visiting Kew regularly, she knew that the allotment was flourishing. Beth and the team were harvesting all sorts of wonderful vegetables and showing an ever-increasing number of visitors how to rotate the beds so that everything grew well, or how to crop lettuces so they grew back again and provided salad the whole summer long, but, generally speaking, things felt calmer. Now the garden was established, the gardeners were really just overseeing it and keeping it all ticking along. Plus, with the bombing raids no longer happening every night, there were fewer emergencies to deal with at the hospital, giving the nurses some much-needed rest. Beth had barely been doing her weekly VDC shifts, always claiming she wasn't needed.

'Are you all right, Beth?' Daisy asked, thinking that it would be a rum deal if, just as she started to recover, Beth wasn't well.

'I'm fine,' Beth said. She sounded sharper than Daisy was used to. 'Why do you ask?'

'You just seem a bit gloomy, that's all.'

'Must be the weather,' Beth said and, sure enough, it was a particularly rainy summer. Daisy dropped the subject.

'It's platform four,' she said.

'Ready?' said Beth gently.

'Ready.'

Together they went onto the platform where the train was waiting. Daisy put Willow's pram into the guard's compartment, and with the little girl in her arms she went back to where Beth was standing with the luggage.

'You do think I'm doing the right thing?' She felt nervous suddenly, as though travelling the twenty or so miles to Louisa's village was a treacherous voyage.

'I think it's worth a shot,' said Beth. She looked at Daisy in a way that made Daisy feel like Beth was seeing every part of her. 'You've been very poorly, Daisy. And I know you're better than you were but you're still not right.'

Daisy bit her lip and hugged Willow closer. She hated being reminded of that day on the bridge. 'The medicine that Gus recommended is helping.'

A shadow crossed Beth's face, but Daisy didn't really know why. 'Good,' she said. 'That's a great start.'

Daisy looked at the train, thoughtfully. 'If I don't get on there, I can come home. It's not far.'

'Of course you can.'

'And if Willow doesn't like it, we'll leave.'

'Any time you want.'

'What if I can't cope with Willow? I'm not a natural mother,

Beth. You know that. I'm so awkward and I forget things.' Daisy felt panic beginning to rise up inside her and she looked at Beth, frightened as her heart began to race and her chest got tight. 'Beth—'

Beth, bless her, knew what to do. She had been such a good friend to Daisy these last few weeks. Reading everything she could about nervous exhaustion and trying out new techniques that she'd heard about. Some of them sounded like something close to hocus pocus to Daisy, but she tried them all at Beth's insistence and, to her surprise, a lot of them worked. Now Beth put her hands on Daisy's shoulders and looked straight at her.

'Copy my breathing,' she said firmly, as she'd done many times before. 'Come on, Daisy. In and out, that's it. In and out.'

Daisy did as instructed, keeping her eyes fixed on Beth's and trying to breathe deeply and slowly. She felt the surge of anxiety begin to subside.

'All right?' said Beth. 'Better?'

Daisy nodded. 'Better.'

'Shall we get on board?'

Daisy wasn't sure how she'd manage without Beth by her side. Talking her through these surges of panic that overtook her and making sure she was eating properly. 'Will you come and visit?'

'You'll be sick of the sight of me.'

Trying to ignore the butterflies in her stomach, Daisy nodded. 'Let's go.'

She climbed the step to the carriage and Beth handed some bags up to her before climbing aboard herself, clutching the rest.

'I think it'll be good,' Daisy said firmly as they looked for a compartment to sit in. 'Being somewhere new will really help.'

'Here's an empty one,' Beth said, opening a door. 'Maybe we'll have it to ourselves all the way to Kent.'

Daisy put Willow onto the seat and, standing in front of her so she couldn't tip off – she'd learned her lesson about that – she helped Beth put their bags up on the luggage rack.

'I love London and I love Hackney, but everywhere I go there's a memory,' she said with a sigh, sitting down with Willow on her lap and gazing out of the window at the busy station. 'My head is buzzing with memories all the time, like constant background noise.'

'I understand,' said Beth.

'I'm hoping Kent will be—' Daisy paused, trying to think of the best way to describe the constant sounds in her head. Her own voice telling her she was doing everything wrong, making her doubt herself. Or memories of laughing with Rex, or the last time she saw him. 'Quiet,' she said eventually. 'I just want it to be quiet.'

Beth reached out and took her hand and they sat without speaking as the guard's whistle blew and they puffed off across the river and headed towards Kent.

Teddy collected them from the station and did a good job of hiding his dismay at how much luggage they had.

'Good lord,' he said, as the guard took Willow's pram from his compartment. 'Good lord.'

He strapped Daisy's suitcases onto the rack on the back of the car, but after much scratching of his head, and two porters trying to make the pram fit somewhere, they gave up. Daisy looked at the pram standing on the pavement outside the station, and felt the weight of Willow in her arms, and thought she wouldn't be able to do much, or be of any use to Louisa at all, if she had no pram. She felt her pulse quicken and her chest tighten, and Beth looked at her in concern. But then one of the porters said Louisa's house was on the way home and he'd push it there himself later, and Teddy gave him some money and said thank you, and before she knew it, Daisy was in the back seat of the car, Willow on her lap, feeling slightly stunned by how straightforward that had been.

Beth, who was sitting in the passenger seat, turned around and smiled at Daisy over her shoulder. 'Quiet?' she said.

'I think it will be.'

Daisy had been to Louisa's cottage before, of course, and had seen the village that she'd made her home, but today she saw it with new eyes. There was a duck pond where she could take Willow, and lots of space for walking. The air smelled clean and fresh – no dust, no scorched wood. Deep down inside her she felt something that might have been hope.

Louisa was standing outside the cottage as they pulled up, eager to see them. As soon as Daisy and Willow were out of the car, she bundled them into her arms and squeezed them tightly.

'I am so glad you're here,' she said.

'Me too,' said Daisy, realising she meant it.

And then it was a bit of a whirlwind as Louisa made them all tea and fussed over Willow. Finally, when an exhausted Willow fell asleep and Teddy said he'd keep an eye on her, Louisa took the younger women over the road to the former doctor's surgery that was her office – and Daisy's new home.

Inside the main entrance was a large space that had obviously once been the waiting room and reception area. There was still a sliding window where the receptionist would have sat. Round the grubby walls, at head height, were marks from where men had leaned against the wall and their hair oil had rubbed off. Daisy made a face.

'I know,' said Louisa. 'But this bit is nicer.'

She showed Daisy and Beth along a short hallway that led to the former doctor's office and threw open the door. It was a big, airy room with a large desk at one end, and a smaller desk tucked under the window. One wall was covered in maps of various parts of England, while another had pictures of herbs and flowers tacked up. There was even a blackboard on an easel that had lists of counties scrawled on it. There was a cabinet and a bookshelf which were both groaning with piles of papers and folders.

'It's a lovely room,' said Daisy, beginning to feel overwhelmed.

'It's absolute bloody chaos,' said Louisa cheerfully. 'But here's what I thought. Today's Saturday, so we'll have tomorrow to get you settled in. Maybe come to church? It's the best way to meet everyone.'

Daisy looked at Beth who grinned at her. Daisy relaxed slightly. 'Church, yes,' she said.

'Then we'll devote Monday and Tuesday to organising. Teddy's been using this desk, but I thought we'd turf him out into the waiting room and you can have his desk?'

'Sounds good,' said Daisy faintly.

'We can make space for Willow – there's room for a playpen and toys. And she can have her nap in the little nurse's room next door.'

'It's perfect.' Daisy was astonished – not for the first time in her life – at how Louisa made things happen.

Beth squeezed Daisy's arm. 'What do you think?'

'It's a lot of work,' Daisy said. She glanced out of the large window that overlooked the village green. 'And it's indoors.'

'There are plenty of opportunities to get out and about,' said Louisa briskly. 'Do you drive, Daisy? I've forgotten.'

'No, I've never learned.'

Louisa waved her hand dismissively. 'Teddy will teach you in no time. It'll be handy if you know how to.'

Daisy looked around her again. 'Can I move my desk so I can see out of the window?'

'Whatever you want.'

She nodded. She felt very nervous about this new job, and this new place, but there was that feeling again, like a green shoot bursting through the bare soil after winter. Hope. A tiny, unfurling stem of hope.

'Could I see where Willow and I will be living?'

And that was the best bit, as it turned out. Upstairs was a small but clean and well-looked-after flat. It had one large bedroom and one tiny box room, a small kitchen, an even smaller bathroom, and a fairly big sitting room. There was a saggy but comfortable couch and a bookcase in the sitting room, a double bed already made up with a pretty patchwork quilt in the bedroom, and a cot in the little box room.

'Where did this come from?' Daisy said in delight.

'One of the WI ladies had it in her garage,' Louisa said with a smile. 'And Teddy put it together.'

Daisy noticed that there was a photograph on the bookshelf in a frame. She went over and picked it up.

'Louisa,' she said with a smile. It was the photograph of her mother on her wedding day, pregnant to bursting with Daisy, and flanked on either side by Louisa and Aunt Win. 'I love this picture.'

'Thought it might make you feel more at home.'

Daisy gave her a hug. 'Thank you.'

Louisa hugged her back and then picked up another frame that had been placed face down on the shelf. Daisy hadn't noticed it before now.

'I wasn't sure if you'd want this one,' she said. 'Your mum sent it to me. I wanted to see how you felt before I put it on display.'

She turned the frame round and there was a photograph of Daisy and Rex on their impromptu wedding day.

Daisy couldn't speak for a second. She gazed at the picture of herself and the husband she'd loved so much, and her heart twisted with sadness, but also – and for the first time since Rex was killed – with happiness that she'd had that day at all.

'Daisy?' said Beth, obviously concerned as Daisy clutched the photograph to her chest. 'All right, Daisy?'

Still unable to talk, Daisy tried to smile, but couldn't quite manage it. Instead, she just nodded.

Louisa gave her another hug.

'Now, I believe there's tea in the cupboard, and milk in the fridge,' she said. 'How about a cup of tea before Willow wakes up?'

Chapter Forty-Two

Beth was feeling miserable, but that was nothing new. Since her kiss with Gus in the church, she'd felt miserable whenever she thought of him. Because she'd barely seen him. He'd done exactly as he'd done last time they'd kissed and had changed his timetable so that he was doing extra shifts in the pharmacy when she was at Kew, and when she was on the ward, he was nowhere to be seen. His work at the VDC had apparently changed so now he was never there when Beth was doing her Friday-afternoon shift.

She stood by the window in Daisy's cosy new home and felt rather sorry for herself. She'd lost Gus and now Daisy was here in Kent. Beth felt very alone.

'The war seems further away here, doesn't it?' Daisy said, coming to stand next to her as she gazed out at the village.

Beth thought about the destruction in London that they lived with every day. The piles of rubble, the trees that were bare of leaves because the bombs had blown them to twigs, the dust that still blanketed every surface and made your eyes feel gritty. She thought about the air-raid sirens blasting through the evening twilight and the sensation of always being a little bit afraid. Then she looked at the quiet village. There was no bomb damage here and the trees were sprouting bright green leaves. As she watched, a man emerged from a nearby house and walked off down the road, his long skinny legs making him look like a funny sort of insect. He waved as he passed Louisa's house and Beth saw a figure in the window – Teddy presumably – wave back. It was just how she'd always imagined a village to be. Stone cottages, the duck pond, everyone knowing everyone else.

'I can barely remember there's a war on now we're here,' she said in wonder.

But Louisa, who was standing behind them, scoffed. 'Down that way is an RAF base,' she said, pointing out of the window and down to her left. 'We had planes going over constantly last summer, and then when the raids started, there was all sorts going on. We got off lightly compared to London, of course, I grant you that. But we still had the odd stray bomb dropped. We had a Spitfire shot down in that field over there.' She pointed again, this time in the other direction. 'Teddy and I and Mr Farthing, the farmer who owns the field, rescued the pilot. Teddy and I dragged him from the burning plane just in the nick of time. The pilot survived, but Mr Farthing was in the trenches last time round and it brought back some bad memories. He's not been right, since.' She sighed. 'I can't deny that it's less of a struggle here, but it's still a struggle. The war's everywhere.'

Beth felt rather like she'd been told off. 'Sorry,' she muttered.

Louisa grinned. 'Don't be silly. Now come and sit down and we'll have tea and you can tell me all about the VDC.'

To Beth's absolute embarrassment and, judging by the looks on their faces, Louisa's absolute horror and Daisy's absolute confusion, Beth burst into tears.

'Beth,' said Daisy. 'What's wrong?'

Beth slumped down on the sofa, and tried to explain between sobs. 'Gus,' she managed to say, gulping for air. 'At the church . . . changed his shifts.' She saw Daisy and Louisa exchange puzzled glances and took a breath, trying to gather herself. 'I miss him!' she wailed. 'I just really miss him.'

'Can you start at the beginning, do you think?' Daisy said, sitting down next to her. 'What happened to Gus at the church?'

With flushing cheeks, Beth explained how she and Gus had kissed, right there in the pew, while Daisy was reunited with Willow.

'You never did?' Daisy looked impressed. 'You're not as goodie-goodie as you look, are you?'

Beth gave her a shove and Daisy laughed, which made Beth feel happier – briefly.

'And we kissed before at the Café de Paris.'

Daisy looked annoyed. 'And you didn't think to tell me?'

'It was the day you had Willow,' Beth said. 'And it was awful because I was still with Paul then, and Gus knew it, and he ran away afterwards and it took me ages get to talking to him again because I was so embarrassed.'

'But now you've kissed again?'

Beth threw her head back in despair. 'Yes, and it was wonderful. But he said we couldn't be together because things are so hard for him. He's not given a fair shot because of his skin, and he thinks people won't accept us together.' She sniffed. 'Once we were going to Kew together and the man at the station asked if I needed help. He says no one would accept us as a couple. That it would be too hard for me. He says he loves me but because he loves me, he can't be with me.' She started crying again. 'But it's so hard not being with him.'

Daisy shuffled her bum along the saggy sofa so she was nearer Beth. 'I hate to say it, Beth, but he might have a point.'

'I know,' said Beth sadly. 'I just think he's worth it, that's all.'

'It's quite sweet that he's protecting you,' said Daisy. She winced as Louisa gave her a sharp prod. 'What?'

'Daisy Cooper, I thought you knew better than that.'

'Better than what?' Daisy looked outraged.

'Have a look at your friend Beth here,' Louisa said. She and Daisy both turned and stared at Beth, who felt quite uncomfortable under the weight of their gaze. 'She delivered your baby, or had you forgotten that? She saved your life, and she saved Willow's life. And then she saved your life again, that day on the bridge.'

Daisy dropped her eyes from Beth's face to her own hands and Beth felt bad for her. 'Of course I did,' she said to Louisa. 'I'm her friend.'

'My point, Beth, is that you are rather good in a crisis. You've proved that. You're resilient and quick-thinking and, I think, stubborn as a mule.'

Beth opened her mouth to protest but Louisa stopped her. 'I think that's a good way to be. Are you still studying medicine in your spare time?'

Beth nodded, but sadly, because she'd not been doing as much studying as she knew she should have been because it made her think of Gus.

'Beth's brilliant,' agreed Daisy. 'So?'

'So she doesn't need Gus to protect her.'

Beth sat up a little bit straighter. She thought the world of Louisa and having her say these lovely things about her was very nice indeed. 'It's funny,' she said thoughtfully, 'when the man at the station asked if I needed help, I wanted to argue on Gus's behalf. But he wouldn't let me. He said he didn't need me to fight his battles for him.'

'And yet he's fighting yours.'

'Oh my goodness,' Beth said, suddenly realising what she had to do. She stood up. 'Oh my goodness.'

'Where are you going?' Daisy asked. 'You haven't finished your tea.'

'I have to go and see Gus.'

'Now?'

'Yes. I have to tell him that he doesn't get to make this decision for me. He doesn't get to fight this battle for me.'

Louisa clapped her hands. 'That's the spirit,' she declared and Beth thought again that she must have really been something in her Suffragette get-up, waving placards and throwing potatoes at the Prime Minister.

'Is there a train?' she asked Louisa breathlessly. 'An earlier train than I was planning to get?'

Louisa looked at her watch and nodded. 'If you go now. You can make it, if you hurry. Just go left out of the front door. It's not far.'

Without even saying a proper goodbye, Beth blew them both a kiss, picked up her handbag and hurtled down the stairs. She ran along the lane that Teddy had driven down just a few hours earlier, and into the station and made the train with a minute or two to spare.

It was only when she was almost back in London that she started to doubt herself. Was she doing the right thing? Was she about to make an enormous fool of herself?

But no, she thought, as the train pulled into London Bridge Station. She had to do this. Gus had made his decision but he hadn't let her make her own. And he hadn't even given her a chance to speak. Not really. So even if this didn't go as she was hoping, even if Gus didn't change his mind, she knew she had to go and tell him how she felt.

Full of nervous energy, she almost threw herself from the train before it had even stopped properly, pushed past the people looking at the departures board and ran along the road to the hospital accommodation block. It was mostly nurses who lived at the hospital, but Gus and a few junior doctors stayed there too. Beth had never been to his room, but she knew which number it was and though it took her a while to find it, she bumped into a couple of nurses she knew who showed her where to go.

And then she was there, standing in front of his door.

I could go away, she thought to herself. I could leave now and he would never know I'd been here.

But then she thought about Louisa and how determined she was. And about Daisy and how brave she was. And she raised her hand and knocked quickly on the door before she could change her mind.

When Gus answered, he was wearing his trousers and a vest. He had a towel draped across his shoulders and his face was half covered in soapy lather.

'Beth,' he said, looking shocked. 'I'm sorry, I thought you'd be one of the doctors wanting to borrow some tea.' He wiped his face with the towel, spreading the lather over more of his face. 'I was just having a shave.'

'I can see that.' Beth tried not to look at his broad shoulders or the smooth, sculpted shape of his arms.

'Let me go and wash my face—' Gus began, but Beth stopped him.

'No,' she cried. 'Please. I just have to say this.'

Gus wiped his face again and nodded. 'Go ahead.'

Beth's nerve almost deserted her, but she took a deep breath and, focusing on the middle of Gus's forehead, she began to talk.

'When we were in the church,' she said, 'and afterwards, when you said you loved me, I was happier than I'd ever been in my life.'

'Beth—'

'Shush,' she said firmly. 'Let. Me. Talk.'

Gus leaned against the doorframe, looking chastened. 'Sorry. Go on.'

'I was happier than I'd ever been,' Beth said again. 'And then you said we couldn't be together and I understood. At least, I thought I did. But it hasn't been easy.'

Gus shook his head. 'It hasn't been easy at all.'

'I miss you every second of every day,' Beth went on. 'We belong together.'

Gus looked so sad, but Beth rushed on.

'And the thing is,' she said. 'You didn't ask me what I thought. You told me how hard things are for you – and I know that because I've seen it first-hand. But remember that day at the station? You told me I couldn't fight your battles for you?'

'I remember.'

'This is you, fighting mine for me.'

Gus straightened up. 'That's not what I meant to do.'

'I know. But I can fight my own battles, Gus. And I can fight them much better with you by my side.'

Gus's face was changing – at least the bit of his face that wasn't covered in soap was changing. He looked more like himself again. Happier. Encouraged, Beth carried on. 'I know being with you won't be easy. People will say some awful things. They might not want to be around us. But I think you're worth the pain. Because the pain of being without you will be worse.'

Gus looked at Beth and she looked back at him. 'You don't get to decide for me, Gus,' she said. 'You can walk away if you want, but I'm here to tell you that I know all the bad stuff, and I understand all the difficulties we could face. But we're a team. I can't fight your battles and you can't fight mine, but together we can fight them both.' She opened her arms wide. 'I'm in,' she declared. 'Sign me up.'

There was a long, agonising pause. Beth cringed. *Sign me up?* she thought. What on earth had possessed her to say that? She dropped her arms to her side, feeling sick. 'I'll go,' she said.

But as she turned to leave, head hanging and shoulders drooping, Gus reached out and grabbed her hand.

'No,' he said. 'Stay.'

Chapter Forty-Three

Daisy had only been in Kent for a week, but already it felt like home. She was, she had to admit, quite surprised about that. She'd been expecting to find it hard, being away from her parents and Poppy. Being away from Kew. But actually it was easier. Quieter. The constant noise in her head was already less intrusive.

She'd spent a couple of happy evenings pottering around her flat, making it her own. She hadn't brought many things with her, but she took out the few possessions she had packed – Willow's teddy bear and teething ring, the photograph of Rex she kept beside her bed and the letters he'd written her, a battered copy of *The Secret Garden* – and found places for them.

Working with Louisa was really hard. There was so much to do because the County Herb Committees had been more successful than anyone had dreamed they would be. Louisa was busy recruiting teams of Brownies and Cubs, WIs, retired gentlemen and anyone who was willing to pick the flowers that the committees had grown. She and Daisy had to ensure there were enough people to pick the crops, enough people to pack them all carefully and take them to be dried, and places to store the flowers, leaves and herbs. One of Daisy's jobs was putting together information sheets about what the teams had to pick, how to identify the plants and how to gather them correctly. It wasn't easy and took careful co-ordination. After just a week in the job, Daisy knew more about herbs than she ever had before.

It wasn't all plain sailing. She knew she wasn't her old self yet. She doubted herself constantly. She worried about Willow constantly. With considerable difficulty and a lot of huffing and puffing, Daisy had moved the cot into her bedroom so that she could see her daughter while she slept. She still had regular bouts of panic, rising up in her chest and making her gasp for breath, and the voice in her head – her own voice – telling her she was doing everything wrong was still there, but somehow it all felt more manageable while she was here.

Gus had suggested that it might help to write down her feelings. Daisy wasn't really one for keeping a diary but instead she'd started writing to Rex again. She knew he would never read the letters – it wasn't about that. It was for herself and for Willow. She wrote about their new house, and all the things Willow was learning to do.

> *She is so fast now she's crawling,* she wrote. *She can whizz around any room in the blink of an eye. Louisa and I have learned not to leave the door open when we're in the office because Willow will be out of it before we even know she's gone.*

Daisy paused, tapping her pencil against the page. She was sitting up in bed writing. Willow was fast asleep in her cot, her little hands like starfishes on the blanket.

> *When she sleeps, she looks like you,* she carried on. *She looks more like you than I first thought, actually. She has my colouring and my red hair, but she has a little frown when she's concentrating that reminds me of you. And her laugh is definitely all yours.*

She smiled, even though she felt tears in her eyes. They were never far away when she was thinking of Rex.

And as for me, well, I'm going to learn to drive! Teddy has a car and he has an extra petrol ration because of doing his work with the evacuees, so he is going to teach me. My first lesson is tomorrow. I'm worried I'm going to be awful but he has promised me I can't get into any trouble. We'll see.

With her eyes beginning to droop, Daisy set aside her pencil and paper and snuggled down under the blanket. She was nervous about her lesson but looking forward to it, too. She hadn't looked forward to anything for what seemed like a very long time.

At first the lesson went swimmingly. Daisy had picked up enough from doing deliveries in the van with Jim and Ivy that she knew the basics. She even started to enjoy herself and Teddy was pleased. It was late afternoon on a Saturday and the village was quiet. They were on a side road quite close to the office and Daisy's flat, and they had been driving up and down for a while. Daisy would drive one way along the road, then Teddy would swap places with her and turn the car around, then Daisy would drive it back again. Teddy was a very good teacher, patient and encouraging. She was getting more confident at changing gears and the car wasn't doing that awful jumping thing it had been doing at the start.

'I think we've done enough for today,' Teddy said eventually. 'How about we try going backwards, just before we finish?'

'Really?' Daisy was doubtful. 'I don't want to push my luck.'

'Only a couple of feet. We'll take it slowly.'

'All right.'

Teddy showed her how to put the car into reverse and reminded her to use her mirror and turn round in her seat when she was going backwards.

'Ready?'

Daisy nodded. Teddy turned round in the passenger seat, looking out of the back window, and Daisy followed, shifting so she was looking behind her. But she was nervous and she lifted her foot off the clutch too fast. With a big jolt, the car leapt forward. Forward! Daisy had forgotten to put it into reverse. She let out a little shocked gasp – so did Teddy, in fact – and slammed her foot onto the brake in alarm. Except that it wasn't the brake, it was the accelerator. The car shot forwards and hit a tall, gangly man who was crossing the road with his nose in a book.

Daisy shrieked and, stamping her foot on the brake this time, she finally managed to stop. Teddy was out of the car in an instant, running round to where the man sat on the road, blinking in surprise.

He was, Daisy was thoroughly relieved to see, still alive. But he had ripped his trousers when he fell and his hands were grazed where he'd put them out to break his fall. The book he'd been reading was face down in the gutter.

'Oh my goodness, oh my goodness,' Daisy said, rushing over to him. 'I am so sorry, I forgot to put it in reverse. I'm just learning.'

She felt completely awful. This was proof, surely, that she wasn't up to the task. Imagine if she'd been driving faster, or if the man had been closer to the car? She could have killed him. Her chest tightened and her throat felt scratchy with tears. 'I'm sorry,' she muttered again.

Teddy was crouching down beside the man. 'For heaven's sake, Christopher. Are you all right?' he said in concern.

The man looked about Daisy's age. He had dark blond hair and he was tall and thin. His legs were folded up in front of him like a concertina and his hands were huge. He turned to Teddy and grinned. 'Oh Lord,' he said cheerfully. 'I can't believe I've been run over again.'

Daisy was so surprised – and relieved – that she let out a bark of laughter. The man looked up at her and grinned again. 'Hello, Daisy,' he said. 'Goodness, you look different.'

Daisy could only wave, because she was still thoroughly confused by what had happened and couldn't seem to speak.

'I thought you'd have grown out of this by now,' Teddy said, helping the man to his feet. 'Daisy, you remember my nephew? Christopher Hall.'

'I do, though we've not seen each other for years,' Daisy said, finding her voice.

'Sorry for running you over.'

'Don't mention it. It was totally my fault. I was reading, which is really a very stupid thing to do when you're crossing the road.'

Teddy picked up the book and handed it to him but Christopher shook his head and held his palms upwards showing Daisy and Teddy that he was injured. 'I'm bleeding, could you hang on to that for a minute?'

Daisy saw a chance to make amends. 'Let me help,' she said. 'I only live round the corner and there are lots of leftover medical supplies in the office. I can get you cleaned up a bit. I could darn your trousers, too, if we can find you something else to put on.'

Christopher grinned again. 'That's very kind,' he said.

Daisy chuckled, marvelling at the turn the day had taken. 'Come on, then,' she said.

She led Christopher round the corner to the doctor's surgery, while Teddy parked the car and then went over to tell Louisa what had happened.

'It's nice to see you again, Daisy,' Christopher said as Daisy showed him inside. 'Goodness, you've done lots to the office. I was helping Louisa for a while, but I'm better outdoors really.'

Daisy glanced at him. 'I heard,' she said with a small smile. 'I thought you'd enlisted.'

She felt prickly because Christopher was a strong, healthy man, and he could have been fighting – like Rex had been – but he wasn't. It made her feel unsettled.

'I did,' Christopher said cheerfully. 'But I got shot.'

'Oh Lord.' Daisy put her hand to her mouth. 'How awful.'

Christopher made a face. 'Louisa didn't tell you what happened?'

Daisy cast her mind back to hearing about Christopher signing up and realised it must have been shortly before Rex was killed. She shrugged. 'I had a lot on.'

Christopher's face reddened. His hair was so fair that his blush spread right up to his scalp. 'One of the chaps from my battalion shot me.'

'Deliberately?' Daisy straightened up, clenching her fists. She felt a surge of anger. 'So you would be sent home?'

'Goodness, no.' Christopher looked even more embarrassed. 'There was a bit of an investigation but they soon realised it was a genuine mistake. Timmins was having a bit of a time of it, poor sod.'

'Were you hurt?'

'Lost three toes.'

'Oh God.'

Christopher grinned. 'Honestly, it's for the best. I'm much better off back on the farm. I'm growing valerian and chamomile, actually, for the WI to pick.'

'You are?' Daisy was thrilled – those plants had been added to the list thanks to Beth's idea about helping wounded soldiers sleep. 'You're a farmer?'

'Well, I work on a farm. I'm hoping to have my own farm one day, though.'

Daisy almost laughed. She'd never really met anyone who seemed less like a farmer. Mind you, she didn't meet a lot of farmers in Hackney. Perhaps it was she who was wrong, not Christopher.

She found some cotton wool in a cupboard and an unopened bottle of iodine. That would do, she thought. She filled a mug with water, because they had no bowls, and then crouched down in front of Christopher. He held out his enormous hands for her and she gently dabbed them with damp cotton wool, taking out all the gravel that had stuck to the blood. The cuts weren't deep but his hands were badly grazed and it would sting for a few days.

'I'm really sorry,' she said again as she cleaned the wounds with iodine and he winced. 'I feel awful.'

'Honestly, there's no need,' Christopher said. 'It's happened so many times – and, like I say, I shouldn't have been reading. When I'm focusing on something I don't see what's going on around me. It's a blessing and a curse.'

'I'm sure it is.' Daisy wasn't sure what to make of the funny, good-natured giant of a man she'd not seen since they were both children. 'What were you reading that had you so gripped?'

'It was a book about growing vegetables,' Christopher said, looking slightly embarrassed but Daisy was thrilled.

'Really?'

'It's ever so good,' Christopher went on, looking eager. 'It's given me all sorts of ideas for the farm. I thought perhaps we could use the lower field, where the sheep were, for potatoes. We're supposed to be growing more potatoes.'

'We need the food,' Daisy agreed. She'd read about the farmers who were 'fighting the war in the fields', according to Mr Churchill.

'But I also want to make a kitchen garden, just for us,' Christopher was saying. He was looking out into the middle distance, over Daisy's shoulder somewhere, as if he could picture exactly what he was talking about. 'There's a small space just to the side of the house that I think would be perfect because of the sun it gets, but it's really not very big.'

Even though she was fairly sure Christopher wasn't talking to her anymore, Daisy laughed in delight. 'Now that I can help you with.'

Jolted out of his daydream, Christopher blinked at her. 'You can?'

'I worked at Kew Gardens on the model allotment,' Daisy said. 'Dig for Victory?'

'I read about that in the *Picture Post*.' Christopher looked triumphant. 'I saw your photograph.'

'Well, that wasn't me,' Daisy said, wondering how on earth he could get mixed up between her and Beth. 'It was my friend.'

'Could you come up to the farm and tell us what to plant?'

'I'd like that,' Daisy said.

'Daisy?' Louisa called from the waiting room.

'In here.'

Louisa, Teddy and Willow all appeared in the door.

'Oh Christopher,' said Louisa, giving Willow to Daisy, who smothered her in kisses and made her giggle. 'I can't believe you were run over again.'

'Don't tell my mother, will you?' he said. 'She's still cross about the shooting thing.'

'Here's your book.' Teddy handed it over. 'You ought to speak to Daisy if you want to grow veg.'

'Already done it.' Christopher looked pleased with himself. 'She's going to come up to Beech Tree and give us some advice.'

Louisa gave Daisy an approving look and Daisy smiled back. She felt like she'd achieved something really important today – she'd made a new friend.

Chapter Forty-Four

And so, a few days later, Daisy headed out of the village on a bicycle she'd borrowed from Louisa, along the lanes to Beech Tree Farm.

She was nervous about venturing out of the village, and worried that she'd forgotten everything she knew about growing vegetables. But Louisa had gently shown her the articles she'd saved all about the Kew Gardens girls and had reminded her that she did know about growing veg, and had known since she was a little girl.

'And I think you should go and have a cup of tea and a chat with him,' she had said. 'It's good for you to make some friends your own age while you're here.'

'He seems a bit odd,' Daisy replied. 'I remember him being a bit quirky as a little boy, actually. Sweet, though.'

Louisa laughed. 'He ploughs his own furrow, that's true. Christopher has his head in the clouds half the time. He's either thinking about one thing so much that he can't concentrate on anything else, or thinking of a million things at once, and it's hard to keep up.' She smiled. 'But he's a nice man. Very kind. I think he'd be a good friend.'

'I've got Willow to look after.'

'I'll take her for a couple of hours after lunch. She'll be napping then anyway, and I'll go through some of the post.'

'All right,' said Daisy, all out of excuses and mildly disappointed that Louisa hadn't offered to visit Beech Tree with her.

And so here she was, wobbling along the lane. Despite her nerves, she had to admit it was rather nice, bicycling in the sunshine, hearing the birds singing and watching a tractor chugging across a field in the distance.

Beech Tree was a small farm just outside Cassingham, not far from the farm where Louisa had grown up, which her nephew now ran. Louisa had told Daisy that Christopher wasn't from a farming family – his father had been a school teacher. But Christopher had been fascinated by nature and loved working for Mr and Mrs Oliver. They had no children of their own, so he was like a son to them.

Daisy wobbled more as she felt a wave of sadness for Rex's parents who'd lost their only child, and breathed in deeply, forcing herself to focus on her bike ride, as she turned into the farmyard.

A woman was in the yard with her back to Daisy. She was crouching, putting some food down for a cat and her kittens which were rolling around on the sun-warmed stones. That must be Mrs Oliver, Daisy thought.

'Hello,' she called cautiously. The woman stood up and looked round. She was in her fifties, Daisy thought, with fading blonde hair and a wide smile.

'Daisy?' the woman said.

'That's me.' Daisy got off her bicycle in a not-very-elegant fashion, and held her hand out for Mrs Oliver to shake.

Mrs Oliver, though, ignored Daisy's hand and instead pulled her into a hug. 'Lovely to meet you,' she said.

'And you,' Daisy muttered into the woman's shoulder. 'I came to see Christopher,' she added as Mrs Oliver let her go. 'He wanted some advice about growing vegetables.'

'He's round the back, I'll give him a shout,' the older woman said. 'By the way, I wanted to thank you for patching him up the other day.'

'He told you what I did?'

'You mustn't feel bad,' Mrs Oliver said earnestly. 'He's been run over so many times it's like his hobby. I've even done it myself once or twice.' Mrs Oliver rolled her eyes. 'Christopher!' She headed off round the side of the house, bellowing, leaving Daisy in the yard with the kittens.

She bent down and stroked one of the little cats. They were very sweet – half tabby and half black – with little pink noses.

'You can have one, if you like,' Christopher said, appearing next to her. He was very light-footed for such a big man. 'They're ready to leave their mother.'

'Really?' Daisy was delighted, but then she frowned. 'I've never had a pet before. I wouldn't know what to do with it.'

Christopher looked straight at her. 'You do that a lot.'

'What?'

'Doubt yourself.'

Daisy was embarrassed. She bent down and fussed the cats to hide the flush in her cheeks.

'Sorry,' Christopher said. 'I'm too direct sometimes. I didn't mean to upset you.'

'You didn't,' Daisy lied. She stood up and forced herself to look at him. 'Show me your vegetable patch.'

It was an awkward start but once Daisy saw the space they had, she was away. It felt like being back on the allotment at Kew as she bounded around, showing Christopher what he could do with the vegetable patch.

Christopher darted about too, throwing in suggestions which were half inspired and half totally off the wall. But the ones that were good were so good that Daisy thought she might pass them on to her parents and Beth.

'You've given me so many wonderful ideas,' Christopher said in awe as Daisy finished explaining how he could grow carrots and sprouts together to make the most of the space. 'Could we really grow all that?'

'And then some,' Daisy told him. 'There are some leaflets. I'll ask my friend Beth to send them. You just have to be clever about rotating the crops.' She looked around. 'And you should get a beehive. It really helps the plants to grow. My parents have a few in their market garden and my father swears it makes all the difference.'

'You know so much.'

Daisy felt a flush of pride. She did know what she was talking about, she realised. She honestly did. She made a little note to remember that more often.

Christopher sat down on the garden bench and looked out over the fields. 'I know a lot about farming, but growing fruit and veg like this is a different skill.'

'My dad always says food tastes better when you've grown it yourself.' Daisy sat down next to him. She felt very comfortable with Christopher, despite the unconventional way they'd been reintroduced. She liked how his mind worked – jumping from idea to idea and back again. He reminded her of her brother Archie, who always had a scheme up his sleeve or a new passion to explore.

'I think he's right.' Christopher sighed contentedly. He sat back against the bench and looked over the fields. Daisy could almost see the cogs whirring in his head as his eyes took in the scenery. He even pulled a scrap of paper and a pencil from his pocket and jotted down something – an idea or a reminder, perhaps – as he sat there.

'You really love this, don't you?' Daisy said.

'Farming? I can't imagine doing anything else.'

'That's nice. You're lucky to know what you want to do.'

'You don't?'

'I thought I did but then everything changed.'

'The war?'

Daisy pinched her lips together and nodded. 'My husband was killed,' she said. She'd only ever said those words a few times, because everyone in London knew what had happened – she never had to explain. 'And then I had Willow.'

'Your baby?'

Daisy smiled. 'Yes.' She let out her breath slowly.

Christopher turned to look at her. 'Is that why you came here?'

Goodness, he really was direct. This time, though, she didn't mind as much. 'It was hard at home,' she said slowly. 'I wasn't very well for a time.' She tried to give him a smile but couldn't quite manage it. 'It's good to get away.'

'I'm sorry I said that earlier, about you doubting yourself.'

Daisy looked away, over the farmland. 'I do doubt myself,' she said. 'It's one of the things that happened when I was – when I wasn't well.'

She glanced at Christopher, wondering if he'd think she should be locked up in asylum, but he simply smiled. 'Everyone approaches life in a different way,' he said. 'Sometimes it works and sometimes it doesn't, and sometimes we find things hard that other people find easy.'

Daisy was surprised. 'That's it exactly,' she said. 'I was finding existing too hard to cope with. I couldn't understand why everyone else could do it when I couldn't.'

'When I was at school, I couldn't stay in my seat for more than five minutes,' Christopher said. 'My knuckles were red and swollen from being rapped with the teacher's cane.'

'That's awful.'

He smiled. 'My father, though, realised I learned in a different way from other children. He gave me lots of breaks to run around, made sure I got lots of fresh air, and encouraged me to focus on the things I loved. Because of him I passed my exams.'

'What a wonderful man,' Daisy breathed.

It was Christopher's turn to bite his lip. 'He passed away just before the war broke out,' he said. Daisy nodded. She understood grief. 'We miss him,' Christopher said after a long pause. 'But what I wanted to tell you was that he would always say that I

321

should be proud of doing things that were difficult for me, even if they didn't always work out.' He grinned at Daisy, and she had a sudden memory of the little boy he'd once been, fidgeting in his seat and longing to be outdoors. 'I think you should be really proud of coming here.'

Daisy felt a bit tearful. 'Thank you,' she said. She got to her feet. 'I should really go home. Louisa's got Willow and I don't like to take advantage.'

Together, they walked round the house to where Daisy had left her bicycle leaning against the wall.

'Pop into the office if you're passing,' she said. 'We can have a cup of tea and a chat any time.'

'I'm going to say that I definitely want to do that,' Christopher said. 'But I'm also going to warn you that I'll almost certainly forget and you're not to take it personally.'

Daisy laughed. He was so funny and self-aware. She liked his honesty. She put her foot over the crossbar and made to cycle away but Christopher stopped her.

'Wait,' he said. He darted over to where the kittens lay snoozing in the sunshine. 'Which one do you want?'

'Really?'

'Really.' He picked up a drowsy tabby. 'This is a boy,' he said, peering underneath the kitten. 'And this one is a girl.' He picked up a little smoky black cat with the faintest hint of the tabby markings her brother and sisters had.

'That one.' Daisy pointed at the girl. 'Are you sure I'm the right person to look after her?'

Christopher didn't answer because he was pulling off his shirt. Daisy widened her eyes. What on earth was he doing? She averted her gaze from his broad chest and focused on the tiny kitten as he stuffed the shirt into her bicycle basket and tucked the kitten inside. She immediately snuggled down looking safe and cosy.

'She'll be all right in there, as long as you don't cycle too fast,' he said. 'Bye, then.'

He turned and, with a quick wave, headed into the farmhouse – to find a new shirt, Daisy assumed.

'Right, then,' she said to the kitten. 'Let's go home.'

Chapter Forty-Five

Beth was going to the pictures with Gus. She had been to the pictures a lot in her life, and she had spent plenty of time with Gus, but somehow these two things happening together made her extremely nervous. And she didn't even have Daisy here to share her worries with.

She spent ages deciding what to wear. Gus was used to seeing her in overalls or in her nurse's uniform and she wanted to look nice for their night out. In the end she chose a pink dress covered with deep red rosebuds. She'd had it since she was at school. Her mother had bought it for her going to a birthday party. The very idea of buying a new dress just for one afternoon seemed so odd now. Beth wondered if, when the war was over, she would stick to making do and mending or go wild, buying new dresses for every occasion. She had a feeling she might be darning stockings and unpicking holey jumpers for the rest of her life, while Daisy would be first in the queue for a new frock. At least, the old Daisy would have been. And hopefully she would be again.

Beth shook her head. She didn't have time to think about Daisy now. She was doing well down in Kent and Beth was visiting in a few days. She hoped she'd have lots to tell her friend about tonight's big adventure. She couldn't believe she was going out with Gus. Like a proper couple.

After she'd gone to his digs and declared her love for him, he'd gathered her into his arms – right there on the doorstep – and kissed her so thoroughly that she'd ended up covered in his shaving soap, giggling wildly.

But from that unconventional beginning, Gus had decided that they had to do things properly.

'I will take you out,' he said. 'Where would you like to go?'

Beth had thought for a moment. She wasn't sure going dancing was a good idea, not after their trip to the Café de Paris. And she wasn't sure about which restaurants would welcome Gus. She had an inkling the hotel bars she often visited with Paul wouldn't be the sort of place to open their arms to her new beau. So, instead, she'd said she wanted to see the new Olivier film and perhaps they could go to see it in the fancy place on Leicester Square. The brief look of relief that swept across Gus's face had told her she'd done the right thing.

'I should come and pick you up,' Gus said. 'Say hello to your parents.'

'No,' Beth said, thinking about the awful things her father had said about Gus in the past. 'I'll meet you there. Much easier.'

So now she was hurrying through Leicester Square in her rosebud dress. Up ahead she saw Gus waiting for her and her stomach did that little flip. She looked at him in his bright white shirt, his hat tipped over his face, Cary Grant style. He was so handsome. She was so proud that she would be on his arm.

'You look beautiful,' he said as she approached.

Beth gave him a twirl. 'Anything's an improvement on overalls,' she pointed out, but she was pleased he'd noticed the effort she'd made. 'You look good too.' She leaned over and kissed him on the cheek. The smell of his shaving soap made her head spin with the memory of their doorstep kiss and his hand was warm on her back. 'Shall we go in?'

It was a lovely film and just being together made it even more special. About halfway through, Gus took Beth's hand and she leaned her head on his shoulder and they stayed that way until the credits rolled at the end, not even moving when everyone else started getting up to go.

Eventually, the film flickered showing the reel was almost at an end and, reluctantly, Beth sat upright.

'Shall we go for a drink?' she said, not wanting the evening to end.

'Good idea. There's a little place just off Denmark Street I think you'll love. It's a basement bar with live jazz.'

Beth thought that sounded fabulous. 'Let's go.'

As they went to get up, a woman stopped them. 'I was sitting behind you,' she said. She was an older woman – older than Beth's parents. 'I just wanted to say what a sweet couple you are. Reminded me of me and my husband when we were courting.'

'That's such a lovely thing to say.' Beth was touched. 'Thank you.' She gave Gus a gentle nudge, as if to say, 'See, it's not as bad as you thought it would be'.

'Very kind,' said Gus politely.

'I wish you many years of happiness together,' the woman said. As she spoke, the house lights went on, and they all blinked in the sudden brightness. 'Oh,' she said as she saw Gus. 'Oh, that ain't right.'

Beth raised her chin. 'What isn't right?'

'Well, you and him.' The woman leaned towards Beth and lowered her voice. 'When you're one thing and he's another.'

Gus turned and began walking away without saying a word. Beth glared at the woman. 'Bugger off,' she hissed. She span on her heel and followed, swishing her rosebud dress and leaving the woman opening and closing her mouth like a goldfish.

She caught up with Gus outside, as he marched towards the tube.

'Wait,' she said, grabbing his arm. 'I thought we were going for a drink?'

'Do you still want to?' He didn't stop walking and Beth had to trot along beside him.

'Of course.'

'But that woman—'

'Was one person.'

Gus stopped, thankfully. 'There will be more like her.'

'And I'll tell them to bugger off, like I did her.'

'You didn't?'

'I did.' She grinned. 'You're worth it.'

Gus pulled her close to him and kissed her. Two men in army uniform who happened to be walking past cheered.

'Treat her right,' one of them said to Gus as he and Beth drew apart. 'I didn't treat my girl right and now she's married to someone else.'

'I will,' Gus said. 'She's worth it.'

The jazz club was just as Beth had imagined. Dimly lit, smoky, sophisticated. Gus knew lots of people there and she loved seeing him so relaxed and happy, chatting with the barman and laughing with his friends.

'Let's come here every day,' she said, only half joking. 'Everyone's so nice.'

There were some other Jamaican men in the bar and two of them stopped by their table and they all talked to each other so fast that Beth could only understand a few words. It sounded like English but it wasn't quite.

'What was that?' she said when his friends had gone to buy a drink. 'Was that English? Why couldn't I understand it?'

'Patois,' said Gus with a grin. 'I'll teach you.'

'There's so much I don't know about you, or about Jamaica,' Beth said in wonder.

'We've got the rest of our lives for you to find out.'

He didn't say he'd done it but Gus must have changed his shifts back because suddenly Beth started seeing him around the hospital again. They were keeping their relationship quiet at work – both at St Catherine's and at Kew – because it seemed unprofessional.

Not that Gus was around the hospital much. One day, though, Beth passed Gus in the corridor.

'Afternoon, Nurse Sanderson,' he said with a little smile as he approached.

'Afternoon, Dr Campbell,' Beth replied, emphasising the 'doctor' because lots of people in the hospital called Gus Mr Campbell which annoyed her.

And then, as they passed, he turned to her and said quietly: 'See you later.' It made Beth smile so widely her cheeks ached. She wondered how it would sound to see him call her Dr Sanderson one day and thought she would like it enormously. She had, once again, applied to university, this time focusing on medical schools far away. She didn't want to be in London where everyone knew her father. She wanted to be Dr Sanderson in her own right, not Dr Sanderson's daughter.

At Kew, Gus was still working on the VDC at different times to Beth. But one Friday, a couple of weeks later, he turned up at the same time as Beth did.

'What are you doing here?' Beth said, delighted to see him. She went to go inside the building but Gus held the door shut, frowning. 'What is it?'

'Your father is coming here.'

'To the VDC?' Beth was surprised. Other than that once, when he'd seen her with Gus, her father hadn't paid much attention to the committee.

'He said he wants to see it because there are so many of us from the hospital that work here.'

'Maybe he's checking up on me?' Beth felt unsettled.

'Possibly there's a bit of that, too.'

Beth groaned. 'What if he says he doesn't want me to work here anymore?'

'Why would he do that?'

'I don't know.' Beth shrugged. 'He's got strange ideas about what women should and shouldn't do. Perhaps he thinks I've got too bold.' A thought occurred to her. 'Perhaps he's heard that I've applied to university again.'

'Would it be a bad thing if he found out?' Gus reached out and touched Beth's fingertips with his own. 'He'll find out eventually anyway, when he has to give his approval to the application.'

'Beth, there you are.' Her father's voice boomed across the gardens. 'I was worried you wouldn't be here.'

'I'm always here on a Friday afternoon,' she said, pulling her hand away from Gus's. But her father had moved on.

'Hello, Campbell,' he said. 'Good to see you.' He slapped Gus on the back in an over-friendly and rather awkward manner.

'Dr Sanderson,' Gus said.

'I've been meaning to say how sorry I was about that business of putting you into the pharmacy,' Geoffrey went on. 'But I've heard you were very useful during the worst days of the raids and we'll get you back on the ward when we can.'

Gus gave him a tight smile and nodded. Beth knew that her father could get Gus back on the wards that afternoon, if he wanted – he was director of the hospital, after all. She lost a tiny bit of respect for him as he pretended it was all out of his hands.

Geoffrey gave Beth a hard stare. 'Beth, why don't you show me this allotment of yours while I'm here? Campbell, you go ahead and we'll see you in there in five minutes.'

Gus nodded. 'Beth has done a wonderful job at the allotment,' he said as he pushed open the door. Beth felt wretched because she knew her father didn't care about the vegetables she was growing; he just wanted to get her on her own.

And sure enough, as they walked across the grass, Beth jabbering about Dig for Victory and the bomb that had shattered the windows of the Palm House, her father turned to her. 'I'd rather you didn't spend too much time with Campbell, Beth.'

Beth bristled. 'Why not?'

'Well, he's from the West Indies, you know?'

'Of course I know.' Beth was short. 'What's that got to do with anything?'

'He's just had a different upbringing from you, Beth. Different culture. Different beliefs. And never the twain shall meet. You understand?'

'Not really.'

Her father sighed and put his arm around her shoulders, squeezing her a little bit too tightly to be comfortable. 'I have warned you, Beth. And I keep seeing you together. Remember who you are, my girl. I'm not saying be rude. Of course not. Be polite, be friendly, but don't get too close.'

Beth stared at her father. She wished she could tell him the truth – that she and Gus were a couple and that she loved him. She wished even more that she could tell her father to bugger off, as she'd done to the woman at the pictures, but she didn't have the nerve. And she hated herself for that.

She just nodded, unsmiling, and pointed to the Anderson shelter. 'That's where I delivered Daisy's baby,' she said. 'Right there.'

Chapter Forty-Six

December 1941

'I can't believe my baby is one already,' said Daisy, looking at Willow as she waddled around the living room of Louisa's cottage, holding tightly to Ivy's hands. 'What a year it's been.'

She smiled at Beth who grinned back broadly. 'Maybe next year will be a bit calmer.'

'Not likely.' Daisy rolled her eyes. 'The County Herb Committees have been such a success that we're expanding. Louisa and I are going on the road, doing talks so they know what to pick and how to dry them.'

'I was talking to one of the botanists the other day,' said Beth. 'He showed me the cards they've had made with the pictures of the plants on.'

'Did he tell you who drew the pictures?' Daisy was so proud she thought she might burst.

'No.'

'My mum.'

'She never did?'

'She's always been a wonderful artist. She kept a diary of her time at Kew, drawing all the flowers and sketching plants. It's such a treasure.'

'You're happy here, then?'

Daisy leaned against the windowsill and sighed. 'I'm not sure happy is the word,' she admitted, thinking about how she still wrote to Rex several times a week. How she still missed him with an ache that, sometimes, she thought would never go away. 'Healing, perhaps?'

'And the panic?'

'It still happens, but much less often.'

'That's really good.'

'I'm glad you could come today,' Daisy said. It wasn't actually Willow's birthday for a few days, but Louisa had arranged a little tea party to celebrate and had made it a Saturday so that Ivy, Jim and Poppy could come. Rex's parents – still grieving and struggling with the bombs in London – had gone to stay with family down in Cornwall, so they weren't there. But there was Beth, of course, and Christopher and Mrs Oliver, who'd become good friends, had said they would drop in. With rationing stricter than ever, Louisa had made a cake with carrots. Daisy wasn't sure about that but it looked delicious and she was looking forward to having a slice.

'I wouldn't have missed it,' Beth said.

'It's a shame Gus couldn't come.'

'He's working.'

Daisy looked at Beth sideways. 'Been seeing a lot of him, have you?'

Beth flushed and Daisy laughed. 'Tell me everything.'

'I will, but not here where anyone could overhear.'

'Are you happy?'

'So happy.'

Daisy thought Beth looked like someone in a painting with her pink cheeks and her dreamy expression. But then she frowned, ruining the effect.

'People are horrible, though, Daisy. We've had someone spit at us when we were walking down Oxford Street. A woman said it wasn't right. My own father told me to stay away from Gus. Lord knows what he would think if he knew the truth.'

'Because he's from Jamaica?' Daisy was horrified for her friend and a little ashamed because she knew, deep down, she'd felt the same when she'd first met him, too.

'We've almost stopped going anywhere together. Gus managed to move out of his digs and into a little basement flat, so we just spend time there. Sometimes we go to the pictures but he always wants to leave before the lights come up, or there's a club in Denmark Street where Gus's friends go. I like it there because he can relax.'

'That's hard for you,' Daisy said. 'You can't keep your romance secret forever.'

'I know.' Beth looked so miserable that Daisy gave her a hug.

'If you really love each other, you can make it work,' she said. 'You'll find a way.'

'I hope so.'

'One of the lads from the village was killed last week,' Daisy said suddenly. 'His mum's in a right state, obviously.' She swallowed. 'It brought it back a bit. When I see the telegram boy, it makes me feel sick.'

Beth made a face. 'I'm not surprised.'

But Daisy wasn't finished. 'I just think, if you've got a chance of happiness, you should grab it so fast, and so firmly that it doesn't get away. Gus is yours, Beth.'

'He is,' Beth said with a determined nod. 'We're just not quite ready to share it with the world.'

Daisy was going to argue but she changed her mind. Beth clearly knew what she was doing. She just hoped it was the right thing.

There was a knock on the door and Teddy went to answer it. It was Christopher and Mrs Oliver, whom Daisy had become very fond of. Daisy beamed to see them arrive and Beth gave her a nudge.

'Is that Christopher?'

'It is,' Daisy said, tugging her hand. 'Come and meet him.'

333

She'd been worried that Beth and Christopher wouldn't get on. There was no real reason for her concerns – it was just something else to fret about on nights when she couldn't sleep. But they hit it off straight away and were soon laughing as Christopher told the story of how Daisy had introduced herself to him.

'I couldn't believe I'd knocked him down,' Daisy confessed. 'And then he revealed that he'd been run over many times before.'

'And once since,' Christopher added with a sheepish grin.

Beth roared with laughter and Daisy was pleased. She wouldn't have liked it if they'd not been friends.

'Daisy?' her mother was there, Willow on her hip. 'Do you think she feels a bit warm?'

Daisy looked at her daughter, who had two very rosy cheeks, and felt panic rising up. What if Willow was really poorly? What if she had a fever and had to go to hospital? How would they get there? What if she died?

She put a hand on the little girl's arm and concentrated on the feel of her woolly cardigan under her fingers. One of Louisa's WI ladies had knitted it for her. As she felt the soft stitches and focused on her breathing, Daisy felt her chest loosen again.

'What do you think?' Ivy said.

With a fair amount of effort, Daisy smiled at her mother. 'I think she's wearing a thick cardigan and we should take it off. It's very warm in here, with so many people.'

Ivy looked relieved. 'You're right. Here, take Willow and I'll go and get Louisa to open a window.'

Daisy sat down with Willow on her lap and started to unbutton her cardigan. 'Are you having a lovely birthday?' she asked. Willow blinked at her, unsmiling. She had a runny nose and her eyes were a little watery. Perhaps she was coming down with a cold, or maybe she was just a little overwhelmed by all the attention.

She pulled off the little cardigan and blew a raspberry on Willow's chubby neck, hoping to make her laugh, but she didn't. She just snuggled into her mother's chest.

'Are you sleepy?' Daisy looked at the clock on the mantelpiece. It wasn't nap time. 'Has it all been too much fun?'

She felt Willow's forehead with the back of her hand. She was roasting hot. She did the same to her chest, which was just as warm.

'Are you feeling poorly?' she cooed. Willow looked up at her, eyes wide, and then she went stiff in Daisy's arms. Her head fell back and her eyes rolled.

'Beth!' Daisy shouted. 'Beth! Willow's not well.'

She stood up with her daughter still rigid in her arms and looked around at the crowded room. 'Everyone needs to go,' she said. 'It's too hot in here and Willow is poorly. Christopher, please run for the doctor. Mum and Dad, take Poppy and go to my flat.'

Daisy wasn't sure if it was the way she'd spoken or what she'd said, but as Beth rushed to her side, everyone did exactly as she'd told them.

'Put her on the sofa,' Beth said. 'Has she been under the weather?'

Reluctantly, Daisy laid her daughter down as Willow opened her eyes and looked up at her, her expression woozy and dazed.

'Hello,' Daisy said, weak with relief. 'There you are.'

Beth was looking at the little girl with a critical eye. 'I think she's got a cold, or perhaps a touch of flu,' she said. 'Some children have convulsions when they have a fever. Let's sponge her down and cool her off. See what the doctor says, but I think she'll be fine.'

As ever, Beth was correct. The doctor arrived and checked her over but other than being sleepy and a bit subdued, Willow was absolutely fine.

It was a bit of an abrupt end to the party, but Daisy's parents assured her they would come down and visit again the following weekend, Beth kissed her goodbye and told her the same, and Louisa and Teddy cleared away all the presents and put them in a safe place for Willow to open on her birthday itself.

Finally, there was just Daisy and Willow in their cosy flat. Daisy put the little girl to bed with just a sheet over her so that she didn't get too hot. She checked all the blackout blinds were in position and she was just making a cup of tea, with Blossom the kitten weaving in and out of her legs, when there was a knock on the door downstairs.

Leaving the bedroom door propped open she trod wearily the stairs and opened the door. It was Christopher.

'Oh bloody hell, you look knackered,' he said. 'Shall I come back tomorrow? I just wanted to check Willow was all right.'

Daisy laughed out loud at his bluntness. 'She's fine, but come in. I was just making some tea if you fancy a cup.'

From behind his back, Christopher produced a tin. 'Mrs Oliver's biscuits,' he said. 'She made them for the party.'

'You can definitely come in, then,' Daisy said with a grin.

They went upstairs and Christopher peeked in at Willow.

'She's fine,' Daisy reassured him again, thinking it was quite sweet that he cared enough to want to check. He scooped Blossom up onto his knee – she looked tiny in his huge hands – and sat down.

Daisy brought the tea through to the living room and they sat together on the sofa, drinking their brew and nibbling on the rather hard biscuits.

'So you must be feeling pretty pleased with yourself after today,' Christopher said, dunking his biscuit vigorously into his tea.

'Pleased with myself?' Daisy was shocked. 'Not at all. What on earth makes you say that?'

Christopher looked slightly alarmed. 'Oh crumbs, I didn't mean to upset you, Daisy. I just meant that you didn't doubt yourself when Willow was ill. You did all the right things at exactly the right time.'

Daisy looked at him in total astonishment because he was absolutely right. 'I didn't—' she said, in disbelief – 'I didn't think twice.'

Christopher nodded with an air of triumph. 'See?'

Daisy went over the events of earlier, thinking about how she'd reacted when she realised Willow was ill.

'I told everyone to leave,' she said. 'I just did what was best for Willow at that moment.'

'You were completely in control.'

Foolishly, Daisy thought she might cry. 'Oh Christopher,' she said. 'I did the right thing and I didn't even think about it.'

'You're healing,' he said. 'You're getting better.'

Daisy leaned back against the sofa. She reached out and scratched the top of Blossom's soft head.

'I told you how awful things were when Willow was tiny, but I didn't tell you the absolute truth,' she said, not looking at Christopher.

'You don't have to tell me anything you don't want to,' he assured her.

'I want to tell you,' Daisy said, realising it was important to her that he knew everything. 'I just hope you still want to be my friend afterwards. I did some awful things.'

Christopher squeezed her hand and feeling reassured, she began telling him about how things started going wrong when Rex was killed and then, not long before Willow's birth, she'd discovered that she was pregnant. How difficult she'd found those early days as a mother, missing Rex, feeling lost, and then the terrible day when she'd left Willow in the church and had stood on the bridge, looking down into the murky waters, thinking how much easier it would be to sink down and let the river take her away from the pain.

When she finished, tears in her eyes, she looked at Christopher and was astounded to see his eyes were teary too.

'I was a real mess,' she said, feeling awkward. 'I was horrible to Beth. I said some nasty things. But she helped me so much. She's the cleverest person I've ever met. She did lots of reading and found some things that helped me cope when I was panicking.

337

And her friend Gus got me some medicine to help.'

'She's a good friend.'

'She is.' Daisy took a deep breath. 'Are we still friends?'

Christopher gave her hand another squeeze. 'I think you're very brave,' he said. 'You were coping with Rex's death, and Willow's arrival, and it just all got too much.' He nudged her gently. 'I've heard Mr Churchill has periods of dark moods. He calls it his black dog.'

Daisy smiled. 'That makes it sound more friendly than it felt.'

'I just mean that everyone has something they have to overcome,' Christopher said. 'Maybe it's my total lack of concentration. Maybe it's your black dog.'

'My mum can't read or write very well,' Daisy said, marvelling at how comfortable she must feel with him, to be telling him things she didn't tell many people. 'She's tried so hard over the years, but she can only read bits and pieces. My dad says it's like she can't see the letters properly.'

'But she's overcome it?'

'Never lets it hold her back.'

'There you go.'

He looked at her closely. 'Maybe this will be something you have to live with, or maybe it'll go away and never come back, but either way you'll be stronger for having been through it.'

'Heavens,' Daisy said. 'How did you get to be so wise?'

Christopher bit into one of the crispy biscuits with a flourish, scattering crumbs all over Blossom. 'I read a lot of books,' he said.

Chapter Forty-Seven

'So, Willow was absolutely fine in the end,' Beth was saying. 'But the thing I can't stop thinking about is how Daisy coped. She was so calm.'

'No panicking?' Gus looked impressed.

'She said afterwards that she was terrified but she just focused on Willow.'

'That's very positive.'

'Living down in Kent has really helped her,' Beth said. 'I miss her, but it was the right thing for her to do.'

They were walking along Charing Cross Road, hand in hand, after an evening at the club. They'd had such fun tonight, dancing and laughing and just enjoying each other's company. Now, with Gus shining a tiny torch on the pavement to light their way, they were heading home. Beth quite liked being out and about in the blackout now, though it had taken a long time for her to get used to it. When she was with Gus, the darkness felt like a warm blanket, protecting them from other people's stares or barbed comments.

It was busy this evening, despite the cold weather. People were waiting for buses and spilling out of pubs. Sometimes Beth marvelled at how everyone had just got on with their lives, despite the war, despite the lists of dead soldiers in the newspapers, despite the bombs and the destruction. Human beings, she often thought, were stronger than anyone could ever imagine.

She turned slightly, intending to tell Gus what she was thinking about, when suddenly she felt a hard shove on her back. 'What are you doing with him?' said a gruff voice. 'Get away from him, will you?'

Beth stumbled forwards but caught herself. She turned to see an older man behind her, hate in his eyes and whisky on his breath.

Gus pulled her back so he was in between her and the drunkard. 'Stay away from us,' he said. He towered over the man, who was smartly dressed but was – Beth noticed with surprise – only wearing one shoe. 'Stay away.'

The man drew his arm back as if he was going to punch Gus, but clearly he thought better of it. He muttered something under his breath and wobbled away.

'Good lord,' Beth said, her heart thumping. 'Are you all right? I thought he was going to hit you. I'm shaking.'

She held out her hands to show Gus her trembling fingers, but as she did, she caught her foot on an upturned paving stone. Having saved herself from falling when the drunk pushed her, this time she fell heavily onto the ground.

'Beth!' Gus was there next to her immediately, shining his faint torch on her. 'Are you hurt?'

Beth felt dazed. She'd hit her head as she fell. She put her fingers to her forehead and felt sticky blood. 'I'm bleeding.'

'Let's find a taxi,' Gus said.

Beth scoffed. 'I can walk home from here.'

'Not with a head injury.' Gus paused. 'And not when it was my fault.'

'I'm fine.' Beth leaned on his arm to get herself up, but as she put weight on her left foot she fell back onto the ground again. 'Oof,' she said. 'No.'

Gus shone the tiny beam of light towards her feet and they both winced as it illuminated her ankle, swelling rapidly and already darkening with a bruise.

Beth's head was pounding and she could feel blood trickling

down her cheek, and her ankle was agony. She sighed. 'I think we'd better get that taxi.'

Gus left her on the pavement, holding the little torch, and flagged down a cab – that was easier in the blackout too. Then, with some difficulty, he helped her to her feet and half carried, half dragged her into the taxi.

'Thank you,' she said as she sat on the seat with a grimace. 'I'll see you at Kew tomorrow?'

'Beth Sanderson, you infuriating woman,' Gus said. 'As if I'd let you go home by yourself when you can't walk and you're dripping blood.'

He had a point. Beth thought about the stone steps that led to her parents' front door. There was no way she'd get up there by herself unless she sat on her backside and bumped up, step by step. And that really didn't sound like fun.

'Jump in,' she said. 'But I'm paying.'

She gave the driver her address and in no time they were pulling up beside the house. Her head was really hurting now, and she just wanted to get inside, wipe away the blood, put some ice on her ankle, and settle down for the night. Gus was chewing his lip, obviously upset about what had happened and Beth turned to him.

'I know what you're thinking, and you have to stop,' she said. 'That man was drunk and he was spoiling for a fight. If it hadn't been you and me together, it would have been the hat you were wearing, or the tone of your voice. Or someone else who happened to walk past at the wrong moment.' She felt quite fiercely protective. 'You did nothing wrong.'

Gus looked at her. 'Do you really think that?'

'I do. Now help me up, for goodness' sake, because my head is pounding.'

Leaning on the iron stair rail and with Gus taking her arm, Beth managed to hop her way up the steps and fumbled for her key in her pocket.

'My parents will be in bed by now, I imagine, but Nessa will still be awake,' she told Gus.

But when she turned the key and pushed the door open, she was surprised to see her father standing in the hall. He was wearing a dress shirt with an untied bow tie draped round his neck and obviously he'd just got back from an event.

'Beth, good heavens,' he said. 'What happened?'

'I tripped over a paving slab or something,' Beth half-lied, limping into the house. 'Hit my head and twisted my ankle.'

Her father helped her into the lounge and onto the sofa. 'I'll get my bag,' he said. 'Let's have a look at you.'

In the light, Beth could see that her ankle had ballooned alarmingly, but her head had stopped bleeding. She could feel the blood drying on the side of her face where it had dripped. She must look a right state, she thought. She was lucky Gus hadn't scarpered.

'Oh,' she said out loud.

Gus darted to her side, where she sat with her leg up. 'What is it? Is it painful?'

'No,' she hissed. 'Well, yes, but that's not the point. You're here, with me. My father's bound to ask what we were doing and why we were together. What will we say?'

Gus widened his eyes. 'Do you think he'll be angry? He's always been nice to me – he promised he'd help me get back on the ward.'

Beth hadn't told Gus about her father warning her to stay away from him, nor had she pointed out that if he really wanted him back on the wards, Gus would be there by now. She hadn't wanted to upset him. Now she wished she had, so he'd be prepared.

'Angry,' she said. 'Upset. Generally horrible.' She sighed. 'I think maybe you should go.'

Biting his lip, Gus nodded and Beth felt awful. She knew they should just be honest about their relationship. Proud even. But it just seemed so hard.

Gus turned to leave, but Geoffrey was there in the doorway, holding his black doctor's bag.

'Campbell,' he said. His tone made Beth feel cold.

'I was just leaving, sir,' Gus said.

'I think you should stay,' Geoffrey said. 'Please wait here. Beth, let me get you upstairs.' Beth exchanged a glance with Gus. He looked nervous and she felt the same. What would her father say to him?

Geoffrey helped Beth to her feet and supported her as she hopped up the stairs to her bedroom. Then, gently, he put her onto the bed and dropped his bag on the floor. He went downstairs again and Beth heard muffled voices. When he returned he was carrying a bowl of water.

'Your head doesn't look too bad,' he said. He came over to her and knelt on the floor next to the bed and began sponging her wound. 'I'll bandage your ankle. It looks like a sprain to me, so you'll be out of action for a week or so, I imagine.'

Beth let him clean her forehead, without speaking. But she felt tense and unsettled so when he had finished, she finally blurted: 'I didn't like how you treated Gus.'

Geoffrey had unbuckled her shoe and was holding her ankle in both his hands, turning it from side to side and flexing it up and down to test her movement.

'Why was he here?' he asked, not looking at her.

'Ouch.' Beth said as a jabbing pain shot through her ankle. 'He helped me,' she said again.

'It's not broken.' Her father sat back on his heels and began digging in his bag for a bandage. 'Was he there when you fell?'

Beth swallowed. 'He was.'

'Why?' Now her father did look at her, staring right into her eyes as if to dare her not to tell the truth.

'Because we'd been out together.'

'As friends?' Geoffrey's tone was icy cold.

'Yes, we're friends.'

'Just. Friends?'

Beth wasn't sure what to say.

'How do you mean?' she stammered, hoping she'd misunderstood her father's question.

'I mean—' Geoffrey said, wrapping the bandage around her ankle. He wasn't shouting. He didn't even seem angry. He just seemed disappointed and cold, and that was, Beth knew, even worse. 'I have seen the way he looks at you, and I have seen how you are always together, and I want to know if you are just friends.'

Beth took a breath. 'No,' she admitted. 'We're not just friends.'

Geoffrey closed his eyes briefly, then opened them again and carried on wrapping up Beth's ankle. He didn't speak for a long time. Eventually, as he tidied up all the debris from his unplanned first-aid session, he looked at her again.

'I can't stop you working at the hospital, because, Lord knows, we're short-staffed as it is and by all accounts you're a good nurse. But you are to travel to and from work with me. I'll arrange your shifts accordingly. Clearly, you can't be trusted to behave in the manner I expect, so I need to keep an eye on you.'

Beth wanted to stick her tongue out at him and say 'yah boo sucks' at him treating her like a child, but she realised that wouldn't be the best way to get him to listen to her point of view. So she stayed still, not knowing how to react.

'And you are to resign from Kew Gardens,' her father went on.

'No.' The word was out of Beth's mouth before she realised she'd said it.

'How dare you contradict me?'

'I love it at Kew. I'm doing a good job. It's important work – teaching people about the Dig for Victory campaign.'

Her father looked bullish. 'Fine,' he said. 'You may keep gardening but you must resign from the drugs committee.'

'But I'm learning so much on the VDC,' Beth said, her words falling over each other in her desperation to make her father understand how important it was to her.

Geoffrey looked down at her, where she lay on the bed. 'No

more drugs committee,' he said. 'You are not to see Campbell again. Have I made myself clear?'

'You can't do this,' Beth said. She felt completely helpless, because she was lying on the bed with her leg up in the air and because she knew that, in actual fact, she had no power of her own. 'I'm an adult.'

'And I am your father,' Geoffrey said. 'And while you live under my roof, you will do as I say.'

'Then I'll move out. I have a job.'

Geoffrey laughed, but it was a laugh without humour. 'You have a job because I arranged it,' he said. 'I could stop you nursing with a click of my fingers.'

'Then I will work full-time at Kew Gardens.'

'I could stop that too,' Geoffrey said with the casual confidence of someone who knew the world worked the way he wanted it to. 'A word in the right ear would do it.'

Beth wanted to scream. At that moment she hated her father so violently it almost frightened her.

'So,' he said, 'have I made myself clear?'

Beth stared at him in disgust. There was so much she wanted to say to him. So much she wanted him to understand. If she'd been able to stand, she'd have walked away but she couldn't. So she turned her face to the wall instead. 'Crystal clear,' she muttered.

She lay there stewing for a few minutes and then – with a horrible cold feeling – she remembered that her father had asked Gus to stay. He was downstairs with him now, saying who knew what to him?

With a great deal of difficulty, Beth eased herself out of bed and hobbled to the door of her bedroom. She could hear her father's strident tone downstairs and Gus replying calmly, but she couldn't make out exactly what they were saying.

She tried to go down but swayed on the top step and, scared she would tumble all the way down, sat instead, straining to hear.

Her father was talking. She could hear his voice rumbling

through the half-open lounge door. She leaned forward, desperate to catch the words, and sat up straighter as he said 'Edinburgh'. What reason would he have to mention Edinburgh unless he knew about her application to medical school? They must have requested a reference, she thought. Her father was clearly listing her faults. Her romance with Gus, her audacity at applying to university . . . all of them like personal insults when none of them had anything to do with Geoffrey.

She startled as her father raised his voice. 'Do we have a deal?' he said.

A deal? What was this?

'Indeed,' said Gus.

Beth had no idea what they had agreed. She sat at the top of the stairs, not moving, as Gus came out of the lounge alone. He put on his hat and adjusted it so it tipped downwards over his face and then he looked up and saw her sitting there.

'I'm sorry,' he said.

Beth's father meant everything he had said – and more. The following day, he told Beth he'd phoned Kew Gardens on her behalf and had told the VDC that she could no longer volunteer with them. And he was planning to have a chat with Matron that very day to make sure she didn't send Beth on any errands to the pharmacy.

Beth was trapped at home with her sprained ankle, forced to help her mother pack bandages for the Red Cross, and to listen to her complaining about rationing, and wishing desperately that she could see Gus.

'I feel like my hands are tied,' she wrote furiously to Daisy. 'Because my father knows everyone at the hospital and people do what he says. I am desperate to go to medical school in Edinburgh or Glasgow, where no one knows Geoffrey Sanderson, but I am worried he has done something to scupper that, too. Why else would he mention Edinburgh to Gus? I am longing to talk to

Gus and to find out what went on but how can I get word to him?'

Daisy wrote back immediately.

'My mother and father thought they wouldn't be able to keep in touch during the last war, because, as you know, my mum can't read very well or write. But they found a way.'

Beth, reading the letter alone in her bedroom, rolled her eyes. Finding a way was easier said than done, in her opinion.

She read on. 'They sent dried flowers and seeds to each other. The Victorians did it, apparently. They used the meanings of flowers and sent messages that way.'

'Oh,' Beth said out loud, thrilled to bits. 'We need a code.'

She slid off her bed carefully because her ankle was still painful, and went to her desk where she had a copy of the little cards that had been produced for the County Herb Committees. She leafed through them, looking for something – anything – that could give Gus a clue about where to meet.

But though she had spent ages in the lab, writing up information about each of the flowers and herbs the committees were collecting, she knew more about their chemical compounds and their medical uses than their symbolic meanings.

'It's no use,' she said in despair.

'What's no use?' Her mother stood at her bedroom door, looking at her curiously. 'Are you studying?'

Beth felt guilty, even though she hadn't yet broken one of her father's rules. 'I've heard that flowers and herbs used to have meanings,' she said, hoping telling the truth, which was surely only of interest to her, would mean her mother went away. 'I was just trying to work them out.'

Her mother's eyes lit up and Beth's heart sank. 'I know about this,' her mother said, almost to herself. She looked distant, as though she was trying to remember a half-forgotten dream. 'I remember this.'

She looked at Beth. 'A long time ago, when we were courting, Henry would send me little posies that meant something.

It was old-fashioned then, so I'm surprised anyone still does it now.' Agatha looked terribly sad suddenly and Beth felt a jolt of empathy for her mother. She'd seen first-hand how Rex's death had affected Daisy. Her poor mother had been through the same thing, and she hadn't ever spoken about it until now.

'You must have missed him very much,' she said.

Her mother seemed quite far away as she answered. 'When he died, a part of me died too,' she said. 'I missed us both.'

Beth reached out and took Agatha's hand, half expecting her to pull away. But she didn't. Beth couldn't remember the last time she'd touched her mother.

'You are so like I was, Beth,' Agatha said. 'Stubborn and single-minded and unafraid.'

Not knowing what to say, because her mother had never seemed to be any of those things, Beth chose to simply nod. Agatha smiled. 'I know that now I fuss about tiny problems, and worry about inconsequential things, but once upon a time I was bold. Like you. I took risks. And then Henry died and the girl I'd been died as well.'

She crouched down next to where Beth sat at her desk and took her chin in her hands. Her fingers were cold. 'Your father is a brilliant, kind-hearted, clever man,' she said. 'But he is not right about everything.'

She stood up again and picked up one of the cards. 'I can tell you what the flowers mean,' she said. 'If you'd like me to.'

'Yes please,' Beth whispered.

Her mother's long fingers leafed through the cards until she found the card with a picture of a rose on it. The County Herb Committees collected rosehips to make into vitamin-rich syrup for children.

'Red roses mean love,' she said, pulling it out of the pile and placing it carefully on Beth's desk.

Beth nodded. 'I knew that.'

Agatha looked at her carefully. 'Is that what you want to say?'

Very slowly Beth nodded. 'But not just that,' she admitted. 'Something about waiting?'

'So then you have to put it with something else,' Agatha went on. She fanned through the cards again. 'Some of these are extraordinary,' she said to Beth, who was watching in wonder. 'Belladonna? Isn't that poisonous?'

'Ever so poisonous. The children aren't allowed to collect that one.'

'What children?'

'The evacuees and Brownies and Cubs who collect herbs for medicine.' Beth wondered why she'd never spoken to her mother about this before. 'The drugs committee at Kew Gardens works out what medicines we need, and then all over the country there are WIs and other people growing the plants to make the medicine.' She beamed with pride. 'It was my friend Louisa's idea. She runs it.'

'Well, I never,' said Agatha, staring at the cards she held in her hand. 'People really are pulling together in the most extraordinary way.'

She took another card from the pile. 'Chamomile,' she said, putting it next to the rose card. 'It means patience.'

Beth put her hand on the two cards. 'This is perfect.' She smiled at her mother, feeling closer to her than she ever had before. 'Thank you.'

Chapter Forty-Eight

Daisy waved wildly as Beth got off the train. Beth waved back and Agatha – who had come down to Kent with her – smiled.

'Hello!' Daisy called as they drew nearer. 'I'm so pleased to see you.' She pulled Beth into a hug.

'We were expecting Teddy to pick us up,' Agatha said. She'd been down to Kent twice since Christmas. She had – much to Beth's surprise – been so interested in the County Herb Committees that she'd asked to visit Louisa. She'd spent hours holed up with her that first time, and she was becoming more and more involved with the County Herb Committees each time she came.

'Teddy's not here,' Daisy said. She stood back and with a flourish showed off Teddy's car, parked slightly askew, outside the station. 'Because I can drive you to the village.'

'You learned,' Beth sounded delighted and, Daisy couldn't help but notice, more than a little surprised.

'Finally,' said Daisy. 'It wasn't easy but Teddy trusts me enough to go out on my own now.'

'How is little Willow?' Agatha asked, climbing into the front passenger seat. Beth got in the back.

'She's really good. Talking more and more now. She calls

Louisa, Weeza, which we all think is very funny. Louisa pretends she doesn't like it, but it's obvious she does really.'

She started the engine and pulled away smoothly, much to her relief. It was one thing driving herself to meet WIs or to give talks to groups about drying herbs, but quite another to carry passengers.

There was no special occasion for today's visit. Agatha had simply announced she was coming to see Louisa to talk about growing herbs in city gardens because she was planning to get some of the London WIs involved. Beth had written to Daisy sounding rather taken aback at this new side of her mother, and Daisy had urged her to come down and visit with her because she knew Beth and Agatha were getting on well now, and she thought Beth would be impressed with Agatha's dedication to the County Herb Committees.

At the village, Daisy parked next to Louisa's cottage and they all walked across the road to the office. Teddy was at his desk in the former waiting room, which had been painted white to get rid of the oily head marks that made Daisy feel queasy. Willow was on his lap, looking at a picture book upside down.

'Hello, all,' he said as they came in. 'Look, Willow.'

Willow beamed as she saw her mother, and Daisy's heart swelled with love. 'Mama,' Willow said, sliding off Teddy's knee and waddling over to Daisy. Daisy scooped her up and squeezed her tight.

'Look who's here,' she said to her daughter. 'Beth and Agatha.'

Willow regarded the women with a serious face and then smiled broadly. 'Bef.' She kicked to get down and ran off into the other room shouting: 'Weeza! Bef!'

'Go on through,' Daisy said to Agatha. 'Louisa's expecting you.' She turned to Beth. 'Fancy a cup of tea?'

With Willow in tow, they went up to Daisy's flat. The women went to the kitchen, while Willow upended a box of toys on the living-room floor.

'So tell me everything,' Daisy said, filling the kettle. 'What's happening?'

Beth made a face. 'I've got good news and bad news.'

'Good news first,' said Daisy.

'I've got a place at Edinburgh university to study medicine.'

Daisy was speechless. She put down the tea tin she was holding and wrapped Beth in her arms. 'Oh my goodness,' she spluttered. 'You did it. How?'

'I actually don't know.' Beth looked bewildered. 'My father had to approve my application and he did. He just signed it and sent it off.'

'Could your mother have had a word?'

Beth shrugged. 'She's being very supportive but she says it wasn't anything to do with her.' She lowered her voice. 'I have to say, I can't believe how different she is.'

'It's because of you,' Daisy said. She'd thought about this a lot, and discussed it with Louisa. 'It's because you reminded her of her younger self and she didn't want you to lose that bit of yourself that she lost. And then you made her see she could get it back.'

Beth looked pleased. 'I think we helped each other.'

'So you're going to Edinburgh?' Daisy said. 'I'll miss you horribly.'

'I'll miss you too. But you can visit. It's such a lovely city.'

'And you really can't think why your father suddenly changed his mind, after all this time?'

Beth leaned against the counter. 'That's the bad news.'

'What?'

'I think's it's something to do with Gus.'

Daisy blinked. 'How on earth?'

'Remember I told you about that awful night when I hurt my ankle and my father found out about Gus and me?'

'Of course.'

'I listened to them talking and I was sure that Father mentioned Edinburgh. I think . . .' Beth trailed off.

'What do you think?' Daisy had no clue what Beth meant but her friend looked pale and upset.

'I think perhaps my father told Gus that he would support my application if Gus stayed away from me.'

Daisy stared at her. 'No,' she said firmly. 'He wouldn't do that. Would he?'

'I think he might.' Beth's eyes were filled with tears. 'My mother says my father is kind but I think he is only kind when things are going the way he wants. And I think he can be ruthless and uncompromising.'

'Oh Beth.'

'I know.'

'What will you do?'

'Go to Edinburgh. Try to forget about Gus.'

Daisy hated that idea. She wanted Beth to be happy. 'Maybe if you speak to Gus—'

'I've tried,' Beth said, sounding resigned.

'You've seen him?'

'No. My father knows everyone. I knew that if I tried to get to Gus someone would snitch, and maybe Gus would end up losing his job. So I sent the flower messages instead, like you suggested. I thought it was the safest way to get a message to him.'

Daisy thought hard. 'Perhaps he didn't get them. Tell me what you did.'

'I went to the gardens really early one morning, pretended I'd left something in the lab and helped myself to some of the herbs.'

'Sneaky,' Daisy said in approval. 'What then?'

I made a little posy of dried chamomile and some rosehips . . .'

Daisy frowned, trying to remember all the meanings her mother had told her over the years. 'Patience?' she said. 'And love?'

'Spot on. I sent them down to the pharmacy at the hospital. We have porters that take notes and prescriptions and letters between wards. I just popped them in an envelope and put Gus's name on the front. That way, if for some reason my father saw it, he wouldn't know it was from me. And to be extra sure he'd know what the posy meant, I added the little cards – you know the ones the County Herb Committees have made? So he could look them up if he needed to.'

'But Gus didn't send a message back?'

'Not a thing.'

'So that's it?' Daisy said. She felt absurdly sad about it all. 'No more Gus?'

'No more Gus,' said Beth.

'You didn't try to speak to him at Kew?'

'I thought about it, but Father knows Dr Bloomberg and I was too worried that Gus would suffer if I tried to get in touch any other way.'

There was a pause as Daisy tried to make sense of it all. 'That's so sad,' she said.

'It is.'

Wanting to lighten the mood, Daisy said: 'But you are going to be a doctor.'

'I am.' Beth gave Daisy a slightly tearful smile. 'So, like I say, good news and bad news.'

Daisy gave her friend's arm a little supportive squeeze.

'What about you?' Beth said, clearly keen to talk about something else.

'What about me?' Daisy picked up the teacups and gave one to Beth. 'Shall we go into the living room so we can keep an eye on Willow?' They went through and sat on the sofa. 'Do you think you could ever fall in love again?'

'I've not given it much thought,' Daisy said, though this was a lie. She had given it some thought. Recently, when she spent time with Christopher, she found herself looking at him in a different way. Admiring how the sun caught the fair hairs on his strong wrists. Or wondering how her small hand would look in his large one. She was confused about it and felt guilty about betraying Rex. She'd loved him so much, but he wasn't here, and

Christopher was. She wasn't ready to tell Beth about it, though, not yet. Because she felt scared and guilty and excited and mixed up and she didn't want to put it into words.

Christopher, she was sure, didn't know how she felt. But she was beginning to get flustered whenever they spent time together and she was worried he'd work it out. As much as he had his head in the clouds half the time, he was an astute observer and understood how people's minds worked, sometimes better than they did themselves. She didn't want him to be embarrassed that she was developing these feelings. So she'd started trying to avoid him as much as possible, which wasn't easy as they spent a lot of time together and now she was fretting that she was going to offend him. It was all a big mess.

Christopher, apparently, had noticed something was wrong. He turned up on her doorstep later that afternoon, when Beth and Agatha had gone back to London, weighed down with plans about how the urban WIs could take on some herb growing and drying.

'Hello,' Daisy said, feeling her cheeks redden just at the sight of him. He looked like a Viking, she often thought, because he was so tall and broad and fair. Today he looked even more Nordic with the spring sunshine making his hair glow.

'I feel like I haven't seen you for ages,' he said. 'And I am at a loose end because our new Land Girls are proving astonishingly capable.' Beech Tree Farm had employed two women from the Land Army to help with the extra food they were growing and they had already made life easier for Christopher and Mr and Mrs Oliver. 'So I thought, as it's a lovely evening, we could go for a walk before Willow has to go to bed.'

Given the way she had been feeling about Christopher, Daisy thought it was best to say no. She would make up an excuse so he didn't feel bad. She opened her mouth to say she had plans but instead she simply said: 'That would be nice.'

She put a protesting Willow into her pram and she and Christopher strolled down the road towards the village green and the duck pond. It really was a glorious spring evening. The daffodils spread across the green in a splash of bright yellow and tulips bobbed their heads in the breeze. Daisy had a sudden pang of longing to see Kew Gardens with its carpets of crocuses and spring flower displays. She said so to Christopher.

'I'd like to see it too. I've never been.'

'It's very special,' Daisy said thoughtfully. 'It's a treasure.'

'And it escaped the bombs? So far, I mean.'

'Not completely. All the windows in the Palm House were shattered once. And there were a few others that fell nearby. But it's solid, is Kew. It feels as though it will always be there, even when everything else changes.'

She glanced at Christopher. 'Do you know that the Suffragettes burned down the tea pavilion at Kew?'

'I did not know that.'

'I don't think they meant it to be destroyed completely. The fire got out of hand. And actually, it was a bit of a mistake because the business was run by a woman.'

Christopher grinned. 'I've always rather admired the Suffragettes.'

'Louisa was a Suffragette. And so was my mother,' Daisy said proudly.

'Now that doesn't surprise me,' said Christopher, chuckling. 'I imagine you would be one too, if it were necessary.'

Daisy nudged him, pleased with the compliment. 'My father brought an acorn back from the battlefields in France and he planted it in the ashes of the tea pavilion. Now there's an oak tree there.'

'That's wonderful.'

Struck with a sudden idea, Daisy clutched Christopher's arm. 'Louisa's going to Kew next week for a terribly important meeting with the VDC. I'm going too. Why don't you come along? I can show you Kew Gardens and the oak tree and the allotment and all of it?'

Christopher didn't answer straight away and Daisy felt silly. She'd obviously overstepped the mark and made him feel uncomfortable and that was exactly what she'd hoped to avoid doing. To hide her embarrassment, she lifted Willow out of the pram and took her over to a clump of daffodils.

'Look at the flowers, Willow,' she said. Willow wiggled down onto the ground and wandered in and out of the daffodils, doing the funny little crouch she did when something had interested her and she wanted to see better.

'I'd like to come.' Christopher was standing next to her, frowning as though he didn't properly understand what he was saying. 'Kew is a really important place to you and that means it's important to me.'

Daisy looked up at him and smiled. 'I'm glad.'

There was a moment as they looked at each other. Daisy could hear the ducks quacking and Willow's babbling, but all she was focusing on was Christopher. He bent his head and kissed her and there was a second when she kissed him back.

But then Rex's face popped into her mind, the way his lips had felt when she kissed him, and the way his hands had felt on her back. This was different. She wasn't ready.

She pulled away and Christopher looked at her, screwing his face up.

'God,' he said. 'Sorry. Did I misread things?'

Daisy touched her fingertips to her lips, trying to make sense of her emotions. 'No,' she said. 'You didn't.'

'But you pulled away.'

'I'm sorry,' Daisy said. 'I thought it was what I wanted but then—' She breathed in deeply. 'It's going to take me a while, that's all. I'm not ready yet, but I might be one day soon. I hope so, anyway.'

Christopher gave her one of his most dazzling smiles. 'So it's not a no?'

'No,' Daisy said, smiling back. 'It's not a no. It's a not yet.'

Chapter Forty-Nine

The trip to Kew Gardens felt a bit like an outing, Daisy thought. She remembered going to picnics on Hackney Marshes with the Sunday School, being excited about what the day would be like and setting off with a real feeling of expectation and excitement. That was how she felt today, which was silly, really, because it was supposed to be work.

Teddy had offered to take Willow for the day, which Daisy was torn about. She didn't like leaving her for too long; she was terrified that somewhere deep inside the little girl would remember the day when she'd left her at St Anne's and worry that Daisy wasn't coming back. But Louisa had asked her to be involved in the meeting with the VDC and she knew it would be easier if she didn't have to worry about Willow. She was so proud of what Louisa had achieved and chuffed that she was part of it. She was very flattered that Louisa wanted her to help give the update to the committee.

And, of course, Christopher was with them. Daisy had worried that things would be strange between them after their kiss, but he was as funny and direct and – well, Christopher – as he always had been. He was excited about going to Kew and had said he would wander around the gardens while Daisy and Louisa were in with the committee. He would go to find the allotment and say hello to Beth.

Even Agatha was involved. She'd come up with wonderful ideas to use window boxes, baskets and pots to grow herbs and flowers, and she was going to present them to the committee too, to show that even people in the cities could get involved. She'd already started the Central London County Herb Committee and was recruiting for women to run committees in the suburbs. Daisy thought, not for the first time, that though the war was awful and changed some people's lives – her own life, for a start, and Willow's – completely, those changes weren't always bad. It was strange how people adapted and made the best of terrible situations.

Christopher had been to London many times, but not for a long while because he'd been so busy on the farm, so he was like an excited child as they pulled into Charing Cross Station.

'There's the river,' he cried. 'Oh look at all the barrage balloons. What a sight they are.'

'Saw one come loose from its tether once,' Daisy told him. 'All the kids were chasing it as it floated over the houses. Think they were quite disappointed when it was fixed again.'

Christopher didn't say anything about the bomb damage all along the river banks, or about the numbers painted on the tube platform, showing where families could shelter, but Daisy knew he was taking it all in, his sharp eyes noting the devastation along the Strand.

When they got to Kew, Daisy drew him a little map on the back of an envelope. 'It's so big, and it's really easy to get lost,' she warned. 'Maybe try to keep to the paths.'

Christopher patted his bag. 'I have a book and some sandwiches,' he said. 'I'll be right as rain.' He turned to her and put his hands on her shoulders. 'Now, you listen to me for a second. I know you're nervous about today but everything you and Louisa are doing is admirable and you should be shouting it from the rooftops.'

Daisy looked up at him, marvelling at his insight. She was so worried and her self-doubt was creeping back. She shouldn't be here, she kept thinking. She didn't know what she was doing. It was Louisa's thing. She would only make a mess of it all.

'You're a vital part of the County Herb Committees – isn't she, Louisa?'

'I'd be lost without you, Daisy,' Louisa said.

'There you are. Just keep remembering that and you'll do well.'

'I can't argue with that,' said Daisy, feeling her nerves calm, just a little bit.

'Right, I'm off to admire this wonderful Dig for Victory vegetable patch,' Christopher said. 'Good luck, both of you.'

He gave them a little salute and wandered off happily in completely the opposite way to the allotment. Daisy thought about shouting after him and pointing him in the right direction but then she changed her mind. He'd find his way there, she thought. He always did – in the end.

Louisa was watching her curiously, a little smile on her face. 'You and Christopher have got close,' she said. It wasn't a question.

Daisy nodded. 'We're good friends.'

'Shall we head over to the buildings?' Louisa said. Daisy fell into step with her as they walked over to where their meeting was to take place. 'I like how you are together,' Louisa carried on. 'Supportive. But quietly so. Like you're just propping each other up.'

'I like that too.' Daisy hadn't thought of their relationship as supportive until now, but she realised Louisa was right. Christopher had helped her a lot since she'd moved to Kent.

'Do you think you could be more than friends?' Louisa asked, sounding very casual.

Daisy looked at her and then back at the path ahead. 'Maybe,' she said, concentrating on keeping her voice as causal as her godmother's. 'One day.'

Louisa nodded. 'Good.'

*

361

The meeting went better than Daisy or Louisa could have dared to hope. She spotted Gus and gave him a little wave. He waved back. She knew he loved the work with the VDC where his expertise as a heart doctor was appreciated.

On the other side of the room was Beth's father. He'd come along to see his wife speak. Daisy glowered at him from the back of the room. She still couldn't quite believe anyone would behave as nastily as Beth thought her father had. And to his own daughter, no less. He looked terribly proud of Agatha but Daisy thought however nice that was to see, it didn't make up for the awful things he'd done.

She looked round as Beth slipped into the room beside her. She was wearing her gardening overalls and Daisy waited to feel the familiar twinge of envy. But it didn't come.

All the bigwigs at the VDC – and the director of Kew, Sir Edward Horton, himself – were very impressed with what they had achieved. Agatha's little talk on city gardening went down a storm. She was so self-assured and confident in front of a crowd that Daisy couldn't believe she was the same person Beth had told her about. There was a bit of a discussion about whether these gardens could be used to cultivate the more poisonous plants – belladonna and foxglove or henbane.

'It would be more controlled than trying to identify them from hedgerows,' one committee member pointed out. 'And we will need more than we can grow here at Kew.' The plans were agreed and Agatha looked as proud as punch. Then Daisy spoke about the sheer numbers of herbs and flowers that had been grown, or collected from where they grew naturally, and those that would be collected this summer.

'The Boy Scouts from Gillingham collected seventy-six pounds of valerian,' she told the committee, pleased that her voice sounded clear, without a hint of the nerves she felt inside.

Louisa reported back on the overall organisation and how the County Herb Committees were expanding, and she ended by talking about the positive effect being involved had on evacuated children.

'I confess I have a personal interest, as my husband is the billeting officer for evacuees in our area,' she said. 'But I have seen children, who are missing their mothers and struggling to settle into their new homes, bloom under the responsibility of growing plants for the war effort, or collecting conkers or picking rosehips. Children whose only experience of plants was the moss on the walls of their houses, or weeds in the cracks of paving stones are now talking confidently about how to identify juniper berries. It's been wonderful to see, and of all the achievements of the County Herb Committees, this is the one I'm most proud of.'

The men – because they were all men, Daisy couldn't help but notice – all applauded and everyone smiled and Daisy was pleased she'd come along today. This was something really important, she thought. Sir Edward cleared his throat and everyone in the room fell silent immediately. 'Along with the opportunity that Mrs Sanderson has provided,' he said. 'I believe there has been an agreement to cultivate belladonna here at Kew Gardens. The plot has been prepared and there are some newspaper photographers waiting to capture the moment the first seeds are sown. So if you wouldn't mind following me.'

They all trooped outside, except for Beth, who hung back so that she could head off to the allotment without being spotted. Daisy knew she felt awkward around Gus and she didn't blame her one bit.

She and Louisa followed the crowd through the gardens and along to a patch of ground where Hetty and another gardener whom Daisy didn't know, stood with spades ready to pose for a photograph. Daisy gave her former colleague a delighted 'hello' and Hetty waved gaily, clearly pleased to be in the spotlight for once.

The little garden was fenced off with a freshly painted white wooden fence and a gate that could be padlocked, for safety, because belladonna was toxic, so it was just Hetty and the other gardener – Ruby – who were inside, along with the photographer.

Everyone else stood to one side, watching. Daisy and Louisa were at the back of the group, while Agatha had somehow managed to position herself right next to Sir Edward and was chatting away to him as if they were old friends. Which, Daisy thought, they may well have been.

'Right, ladies,' the photographer said. 'I just need you to put your spades in the ground and pretend to dig.'

Ruby put her spade into the ground and smiled broadly. Hetty did the same, putting her boot onto the spade to give it more oomph. She stamped down and, suddenly, the whole garden vanished in a flash of blinding light. Daisy felt as though she was flying backwards, all the air sucked out of her body, as she landed with a thump, sprawled on the grass. She lay there for a while, trying to make sense of what had happened. She couldn't hear anything – her ears were ringing – and she couldn't see anything but gritty black smoke. For a second she didn't even know where she was. And then the fog in her head cleared a bit, and the soot in her eyes cleared too, and she remembered. Kew Gardens. The photographs. Louisa. Scrambling to sit up, she looked around. Louisa was lying face down on the grass a little way away. Her dress was torn and her hat was gone.

Daisy crawled over to her. 'Louisa,' she said. 'Louisa?'

She was crying now, tears falling down her cheeks and onto her godmother where she lay. 'Louisa.'

And then Louisa moaned and turned over, her eyes flickering open. Daisy threw herself onto her. 'Louisa, you're alive.'

'What happened?' Louisa looked dazed.

'I don't know. Hetty dug into the ground and then there was a huge explosion . . .' Daisy trailed off as she realised what had happened. 'It must have been a bomb, Louisa, buried under the ground from one of the raids.'

Louisa gave her a confused look and Daisy knew she had to

get help. She stood up, noticing that her back and legs hurt from where she'd landed so heavily on the ground, and took in the scenery around her. Everything was muffled still, and murky with smoke, so it was like being under water. She could see people lying on the ground, and others beginning to move, helping each other. She could hear crying and moaning and from far away she heard a scream. She waited for the panic to grip her, to take her plunging down into despair, but it didn't come. Slowly she breathed out. She had to do something.

'Louisa,' she said. 'We have to move. Let's see if you can walk.'

Chapter Fifty

Beth was helping the lab assistants put everything back as it had been before the meeting. She was just moving a stool back to the side of the lab when the explosion happened. The windows on the other side of the room all shattered, showering the lab in broken glass. Beth and one of the lab assistants – a young medical student called Shaun – both ducked down behind a bench to avoid being hit by the shards, and then, as the dust settled, they stood up again slowly, looking around in confusion.

'What on earth . . .?' Shaun said, sounding very young and frightened.

'Can you telephone for help?' she said urgently. 'Run up to the offices and call nine nine nine. Ask them to send ambulances.'

Shaun turned and fled. Beth stood for a moment looking through the broken windows, her ears ringing, as she tried to get her bearings and work out where the explosion had come from. Close by, she thought in terror. It had to be close to have broken the windows like it had. Almost without thinking, she hurried out of the lab and into the gardens. She started to run. The air was thick with smoke and dust – just like during the raids last year. The trees, which had been budding beautifully, were stark and bare against the grey sky. Small, bright green leaves were drifting down around her like a strange kind of snowflake.

She heard shouts and screams and ran along the path towards

the area where the belladonna bed was going to be. Was it there? Had the bomb gone off just where everyone was? She felt a surge of panic. Her breath was coming in short, panting gasps as she ran, and her legs felt shaky.

She rounded a bend and in front of her there was chaos. Beth had been to see the new belladonna plot that morning. She had admired the neat white fence. Now there was nothing there except a hole in the ground and piles of earth and dirt everywhere. She could see people bleeding, and others crying, while some just lay on the ground. A man she didn't know walked past her, holding his head, and then simply crumpled as his legs gave way.

'Someone needs to take charge,' Beth muttered. She looked around for her father, or Gus, or one of the other doctors, but the air was thick with smoke and dusty earth and she couldn't see anyone. No one was in control. For a wild second she thought about running away, turning tail and racing across the grass to safety, but then a calm came over her. She was a nurse and she was going to take charge.

Someone launched themselves at her and she turned in fright and found Daisy, wide-eyed and covered in dust. 'Beth,' she gasped. 'Oh Beth.'

They held each other for a moment, each pleased the other was there, solid and alive, and then Beth looked at her friend. 'There were about thirty people at the presentation,' she said, trying to keep her voice calm and to make it sound like she was in control. 'Shaun has called for help. I need to find anyone who's injured. Can you help me?'

Daisy looked scared half to death but she nodded. 'Louisa is fine. I think she's broken her arm and she is a little bit confused. I sat her down over there.'

'Good,' Beth said. 'We'll put the walking wounded over there.' She dug in the pocket of her overalls and, to her relief, found a stubby piece of chalk that she used for writing on the blackboard in the Anderson shelter to keep track of what they'd planted where. She thrust the chalk at Daisy. 'Put a mark on everyone when I've checked them over.'

She followed Daisy to where Louisa sat, looking more focused now. Beth looked at her arm and agreed it was broken. 'Stay here,' she said to Louisa. 'Stay with Daisy.'

Daisy put a white slash of chalk on Louisa's dusty forehead. The line stood out brightly against the grey dirt.

'I'll send people to you,' Beth said. 'I need to help the others.'

She set off through the dust and smoke. She found some of the botanists from the VDC, all with cuts and bruises, and helped them over to where Daisy was. One of them had a large splinter from the pretty white fence stuck in his thigh. Beth sat him down with the others and looked at him. 'I'm going to leave that where it is,' she said bluntly. 'If I pull it out, it'll do more damage.' The botanist – a sweet-natured chap called Keith – nodded and then his face went grey and he fainted. Daisy calmly leaned over and chalked his forehead. Beth thought the adrenaline was helping her stay focused and she hoped she wouldn't suddenly panic. But she seemed very much in control as she nodded to Beth. 'I'll keep an eye on him,' she said.

And off Beth went again, her heart thumping. Trying not to think about where her mother was, or her father, or Gus, and trying not to look at the huge hole where, just a few minutes earlier, people must have been standing. She knew Hetty and another gardener – Ruby – had been asked to do the honours and dig into the ground in the new plot. Had that been what had set the bomb off? Perhaps it had been lying under the ground, unexploded, since the raid that had hit the Palm House? Could that happen? She shuddered, feeling sick as the dust and dirt lodged in her throat.

She bent down and helped another – thankfully uninjured – botanist to his feet, and as she did so, she saw Gus coming through the haze. She ran to him and without thinking she threw her arms round him. 'Gus,' she said. 'Oh Gus.'

He hugged her back for a second and then released her quickly. 'Beth, we need to help people.'

'There are some injuries but nothing serious so far,' Beth said. 'I've set up a bit of a system. Daisy's got the walking wounded and I'm sending people to her.'

'What shall I do?' he said.

'I don't know. What do you think?'

Gus shook his head. 'You're in charge,' he said. 'It has to stay that way or it'll get confusing. Where do you need me?'

Beth felt that rush of calm again as she told him what she thought they should do. And together they hurried off, knowing that the closer they got to where the bomb had been, the worse the injuries would be.

And then, like a miracle, she found Hetty and Ruby, both out cold and covered in blood but both breathing. How could that be? Beth blinked into the dusty air and saw the bomb blast hadn't actually been in the belladonna garden as she'd assumed, but slightly further away.

'Oh thank God,' she breathed. 'Thank God.' She ran to them and checked their vital signs as – to her huge relief – she saw two ambulance men coming towards her.

She stood up as they approached and, as if she was filling in a doctor doing his rounds on her ward, she explained concisely what had happened and who needed treatment first.

'This is Hetty and this is Ruby,' she said. 'I think they must have taken the force of it.'

Wiping her clammy forehead, Beth let the ambulance men take over and went to find her parents.

'Father?' she called. 'Mother?'

It was becoming easier to see as the dirt thrown up by the bomb settled but the air was still smoky. There were a couple of small fires burning, and one large oak tree was ablaze, the flames reaching up from its branches into the sky. But she couldn't see her parents. She rubbed her eyes, which were already sore and gritty, and carried on searching methodically through the dusty scene.

'Beth?' Her father was there, thankfully in one piece, though his suit was ragged and his face was bleeding. He was wearing an expression Beth had never seen on his face before and with shock she realised it was panic. He was panicking. 'I can't find your mother,' he said shrilly. 'I can't find Agatha.'

Beth grabbed his arm. 'Father,' she said. 'Daddy?' He looked at her. 'I will find her.'

He nodded and then, gazing around, he pulled himself up a bit taller. 'We need to start helping,' he said. 'Beth, you find somewhere to put the walking wounded.'

'Daddy,' she said, trying to stop him but he carried on.

'We need to tell the ambulance chaps what's going on . . .'

'Daddy, I've done it,' Beth said. 'Daisy's got the walking wounded, and Gus and I are triaging patients as we go.'

Her father looked her, seeming confused for a second, and then relieved. 'What do you need me to do?'

But before Beth could give him a job, there was a call from where Gus stood, only just visible in the smoke from the oak tree.

'Beth!' he shouted from across the grass. 'I've got your mother.'

Beth and Geoffrey exchanged a look. Beth's heart thumped with fear and she took her father's hand, which felt cold in her own.

'I'll go,' Geoffrey said.

'We'll both go.'

They hurried – hand in hand – across to where Agatha lay, unconscious, on the ground. Gus was checking her pulse and listening to see if she was breathing. Sir Edward was there too, conscious and sitting up on the grass, but clearly in pain. Gus looked at Beth and she felt a wave of terror as she read his distraught expression. She wanted to howl and scream but instead she positioned herself between her father and Gus and looked straight at him. 'Daddy,' she said firmly. 'Look after Sir Edward.'

'But—'

'Look after him.'

Thankfully, Geoffrey turned his attention to Sir Edward, and Beth went to her mother's side. Gus looked up. 'She was conscious. She spoke to me,' he said. 'Agatha?'

Her mother didn't answer. Her face was waxy and her lips were blue.

'Agatha?' Gus said again.

'Help her,' Beth begged. 'Help her.'

Gus pushed her mother over onto her front, making Beth shriek. 'What are you doing?'

He didn't reply, but simply pushed down on Agatha's back and then lifted her arms, then did the same again.

'Pumping her heart?' Beth said. 'You're pumping her heart.' She watched, her hand over her mouth, as Gus carried on. And then the ambulance men were there, and they were putting a mask over her mother's face and telling Beth that Agatha was alive. Gus was holding her tightly and she was crying and her father was crying – and then everything went black.

Beth woke up in a hospital bed, Gus by her side.

'Where's my mother?' she said, trying to sit up.

'Easy,' Gus said. He was still wearing his dusty, torn clothes but had found his hat which was surprisingly intact.

'Is she . . .?' Beth swallowed a sob.

'She's going to be all right.'

She leaned back against the pillows. 'Because of you,' she said. 'You saved her life.'

'I did what I'd been trained to do.'

Beth reached out and took his hand. 'Because you're a cardiac doctor, not a pharmacy assistant.'

Gus nodded. 'That is true.'

'It is indeed.'

Beth's father stood at her cubicle, looking pale and tired and ten years older than he had that morning. Gus stood up, letting go of Beth's hand.

'Your mother is fine,' Geoffrey said. 'She's awake and talking.'

'Gus saved her, Daddy,' Beth said.

Geoffrey nodded. 'He did.' He held his hand out to Gus. Slowly, Gus took it and shook it firmly. 'Thank you,' Geoffrey said. 'Dr Campbell.'

Beth wanted to cry. Her father had said 'doctor'.

'How is Louisa?' she said. 'What's happened? Is everyone all right? What about Ruby and Hetty?'

'Everyone's all right,' Gus said, putting out a hand to calm her down. 'Hetty's going to have a rather a nasty scar across her tummy because she was scratched by some flying metal. Ruby—' Gus swallowed and Beth felt afraid.

'Tell me.'

'She's going to lose her eye.'

'Oh Lord.'

'But they're both alive,' Gus said.

'And Louisa?'

'Broken arm. Last I saw of her, she was at the plaster clinic, bossing all the nurses around.'

'Did anyone . . .?' Beth couldn't get the words out but Gus, as ever, understood what she wanted to say.

'The photographer didn't make it,' he said.

'Oh no.' Beth was filled with sadness. 'How awful.'

'It would have been a lot worse if you hadn't been there.'

'I thought you might want to sign my cast,' a voice said and there was Louisa, looking cheerful despite her broken arm. Daisy was with her.

'I'm glad you're all right,' Daisy said, giving Beth a kiss. 'You didn't half give us a scare when you fainted like that.'

'Where's Christopher?' Beth said.

Daisy shrugged. 'Could be anywhere,' she said with a small smile. 'The good thing is, he's very distinctive. I asked the chaps on the gate to look out for him. One of the nurses telephoned Teddy and told him what had happened.'

'Nurses are always reliable,' Beth said with a smile. She glanced round. 'Where are we? This isn't St Catherine's?'

'Paddington,' said Daisy. 'It's where they were bringing all the casualties from Kew Gardens.'

Beth nodded. She looked at Geoffrey, who seemed uncomfortable, shifting from foot to foot.

'Are you all right, Father?' Beth asked. 'Are you hurting? Do you need someone?'

But Geoffrey shook his head. 'I wanted to have a word with you,' he said.

'Go ahead.'

'In private.'

'We'll go,' Daisy said, but Beth stopped her.

'No, stay,' she said. 'I think maybe everyone should hear this.'

Geoffrey gave her a look of frustration and then sighed. 'Fine. Yes, please stay.' Beth sat higher up against her pillows and waited patiently.

'I have done some things that I am not proud of,' Geoffrey said carefully. 'I was blinded by my own prejudice and I was wrong.'

Beth thought that she'd never heard her father say that he was wrong before. She nodded.

'I thought the only people who made good doctors were men,' Geoffrey went on. He glanced at Gus. 'Men who looked like me.'

'There are many who think that way,' Gus said.

'Indeed there are. But that doesn't make it right.' Geoffrey put his hand on Beth's arm. 'Today proved that I am a silly, stubborn old fool. It proved that Gus is more than capable of getting back on the wards as soon as I can make it happen.' He smiled at Beth. 'And it proved to me that you are an excellent nurse and you will make a fine doctor.'

Beth breathed out slowly.

'I need to ask you something,' she said. Her voice shook a little.

'Did you tell Gus that you would approve my university application if he stayed away from me?'

She heard Daisy gasp, but her eyes were fixed on Geoffrey.

Her father winced and he dropped his gaze, looking so terribly ashamed of himself that he couldn't meet her stare. 'Beth, you must understand—'

'Did you tell Gus that you would approve my university application if he stayed away from me?' she asked again, clear and cold.

Geoffrey's reply was so quiet she could barely hear it. 'I did,' he said.

Beth felt sick. 'That was an awful thing to do.'

'It was,' Geoffrey agreed. Finally, he raised his gaze to meet Beth's eyes. 'If you will accept my apology, I promise I will spend the rest of my life making it up to you.' He swallowed. 'I love you, Elizabeth. And I'm very proud of you.' His voice cracked on the last few words and Beth found tears in her own eyes too. She wasn't sure their relationship would ever be as it should be, but she found – almost to her surprise – that she hoped they would be able to repair it, even just a little bit.

'I'm going to medical school,' she said.

'With my blessing.' Geoffrey looked contrite.

Beth wasn't going to thank him. She simply said: 'Yes.' Then she added: 'I think there's something you need to say to Gus?'

Geoffrey looked reluctant but he nodded. 'Dr Campbell,' he said. 'Gus. It was wrong of me to make such a demand of you. I was wrong to force you into such an impossible decision. I apologise wholeheartedly.'

Gus gave Geoffrey a little nod. 'I accept.'

'Gus was so committed to staying away that he didn't even respond when I sent him a message,' Beth said. 'He wasn't going to let anything interfere with my place at Edinburgh.'

Gus looked at Beth quizzically. 'You didn't send me a message.'

Beth heard Daisy giggle. She looked at Gus. 'It was in code.'

'Code? Like a spy?'

Daisy giggled again, and even Geoffrey's lips showed the trace of a smile. Beth sighed. 'I sent you rosehips – which mean love – and chamomile, which stands for patience. And I sent you the Herb Committee cards so you could work it out.'

'That was from you?' Gus looked astonished. 'I thought it was just a mistake.'

Beth fell back against the pillows and laughed. Gus slipped his hand into hers and she squeezed it tightly. 'Are you sure this man is the one for you?' Geoffrey said jovially. 'He's rather slow on the uptake.'

'Daddy,' chided Beth, but she was still chuckling.

Gus turned to Geoffrey. 'There is something I wanted to ask you, sir.'

'Go on.'

Gus took his hat off and held it in front of him like a shield. He looked terribly nervous suddenly and Beth didn't understand why.

'I wondered if, after everything that's happened, I might have your permission to ask Beth to marry me,' he said.

Beth gasped and Daisy let out a little shriek of excitement.

Geoffrey made a grunting sound. 'Marry you?'

'Yes, sir.'

'It won't be easy.'

'No, sir.'

'I expect you to look after her.'

'I think we'll be looking after each other.'

Beth giggled and her father glared at her.

'All right, then,' he said. 'Go ahead.'

'Now?' Gus looked alarmed. 'With all of you here?'

'No time like the present,' Daisy said.

Everyone looked at Gus. He swallowed. 'I haven't prepared anything.'

'Just do it,' Daisy urged. Beth gave her a look that was supposed to stop her interfering but she stuck her tongue out and gave Gus a nudge. 'Go on.'

'Beth,' Gus said. His voice was croaky and he cleared his throat and tried again. 'Beth, I love you,' he said in a rush. 'Will you marry me?'

Beth thought she'd never felt as happy as she did in that moment. The man she loved was telling her he wanted to spend his whole life with her. She had won her father's long-awaited approval. And she had a place at medical school waiting for her. She would be a doctor at long last. Her dreams were all coming true.

She looked at Gus, standing nervously, waiting for an answer, and she took a breath. 'No,' she said. 'I don't want to marry you.'

There was a loud gasp from Daisy, and Gus looked bewildered. Beth reached out and took his hand. 'I think you're wonderful,' she said. 'I love you madly. But I don't want to get married. Not yet. Maybe not ever.'

'All right,' said Gus sounding very Jamaican all of a sudden. He grinned broadly. 'I think I know why.'

Even though they were surrounded by their friends, Beth felt as though she and Gus were the only people in the world right then.

'Because I want to be Dr Sanderson,' she said.

Chapter Fifty-One

Louisa had to stay in hospital overnight, much to her disgust, so it was a weary, solitary Daisy who said goodbye to an overwhelmed, emotional and thoroughly delighted Beth at the hospital.

'Why don't you stay the night with us?' Beth said as they walked towards the main doors of St Catherine's. 'She can stay, can't she, Father?'

'Of course.' Geoffrey looked fit to drop himself but he managed a smile. 'You're very welcome.'

Agatha was doing well, all things considered, so Beth and Geoffrey had decided to go home and get some rest. But though the offer of their spare room in Bloomsbury was inviting, and though Daisy was tempted to jump on a bus to Hackney and go home to her childhood bedroom, she really wanted to get back to Willow. It might be a long train ride back to Kent but she knew it would be worth it when she got there. She wanted to cuddle her little girl and thank her lucky stars that she had made it through today. Plus she had no idea where Christopher had got to. She had an idea that he might have made his way home after the bomb exploded – at least that's what she hoped – and she wanted to check he was all right.

She kissed Geoffrey on the cheek and hugged Beth, and went out into the spring evening. It wasn't even dark yet, which surprised her. She was so tired that it felt like the middle of the night. The thought of trekking across town to Charing Cross was too much. She'd get a taxi, she decided, even though it was a bit extravagant. But then she looked down at herself. Her dress, which she'd chosen so carefully that morning, was shredded around the hem. Her shoes were muddy. Her hair was a tangled mess. She thought that no self-respecting cab driver would pull over for her. She must look like some sort of wild woman. Bus it was, then.

She felt a wave of self-pity as she walked across the road to the bus stop. Beth had Gus, and Louisa had Teddy, who was on his way up to London right that minute, having arranged for one of the WI ladies to look after Willow until Daisy got home. Daisy was all alone. She missed Rex so badly it hurt and she wanted her mum, but she knew she had to go home to her own daughter and the weight of responsibility felt heavy upon her. She winced as she walked because her back hurt from falling when the bomb went off, and she just felt miserable.

Miserable, she thought, as she leaned against a wall and looked for an approaching bus, but not depressed. She tested her feelings, the way Louisa had tested her broken arm when she'd first got to the hospital. There was no doubting she felt gloomy and her nerves were still jangling after the horrible experience she'd had, but did she feel panicky? No. Had she plunged into the relentless darkness she'd felt before? Definitely not. That was something positive.

She wondered again where Christopher was and hoped he'd headed back to Kent as soon as he could. He must have heard the explosion and been worried about them all, she thought. Perhaps he'd tried to find them in the chaos? He'd be worried about Louisa, she knew. She was a little surprised that he hadn't shown up at the hospital. He had his head in the clouds most of the time, but he was resourceful when he had to be.

'You look remarkably cheerful for someone who's cheated death,' said a voice. Hardly able to believe her ears, she turned to see Christopher himself standing next to her, clutching a drooping bunch of flowers.

'I was just thinking about you and you appeared,' she said, absolutely thrilled to bits to see him there.

'Like a genie from a lamp.' Christopher grinned.

They stared at each other for a moment, Christopher's smile slipping slightly. 'I am so pleased to see you, Daisy,' he muttered. 'I was so frightened. I've been all round the hospital looking for you. I found Louisa eventually and she told me you were all right.' He looked stricken. Goodness, when that bomb went off, I was really frightened.'

'I was frightened too,' she said. 'It was awful, Christopher.'

Christopher moved towards her and opened his arms and Daisy stepped into his comforting embrace.

'I felt so bad that I wasn't there,' Christopher said. 'I tried to get to you but almost as soon as the explosion happened, there were people ushering us out of the gardens and onto the street.'

'I was glad you weren't there.' Daisy liked how his arms felt around her, strong and protective. 'The whole time we were trying to make sure everyone was all right and helping people who were injured, I kept thinking thank goodness you were safe. I didn't have to worry because I knew you weren't there.'

They clung on to each other for a while. Daisy felt as though she'd been like that barrage balloon she'd seen that had come unfastened. But now, with his arms around her and the love she could see in his eyes, Christopher had tethered her again.

'We should probably move,' Christopher said eventually. 'I don't think we can stand here much longer before someone complains.'

Daisy looked round and, sure enough, they were slap bang in the middle of the pavement with people veering round them and tutting.

'I don't care,' she said. 'I've had a horrible day and I want to stand here with you.'

379

'I'm not going to argue about that.' Christopher smiled down at her. 'But perhaps we should move a little to the side.'

He half picked her up and shuffled her to the edge of the pavement.

'Now,' he said. 'The thing is, Daisy—'

'What is the thing?' Daisy rested her head on his chest and closed her eyes, revelling in the feel of him.

'The thing is, the way I felt today when I heard that explosion and knew it must have been near you, made me realise something.'

'What did you realise?'

'That I love you.'

Daisy opened her eyes.

'I know that you said "not yet" and I understand that, but I just wanted you to know.'

There was a pause. Daisy moved slightly so that she could see Christopher's face. He still had his arms around her but he wasn't looking at her – he was looking away over her head, his jaw set.

'The thing is,' she said. Christopher looked down at her. 'What is the thing?'

Daisy took a breath. She thought about Rex and the wonderful life they would have had together. Then she thought about how lonely she'd felt leaving the hospital and how, when she'd seen Christopher, something inside her had felt lighter. She smiled at him.

'I love you too.'

Christopher's jaw relaxed. He unwound his arms from Daisy and held her at arm's length, looking straight at her. 'Are you sure?' he said.

'It's funny, because you'd think I wouldn't be sure,' Daisy said. 'Given everything that's happened. But I am quite sure. I don't think I've ever been surer of anything in my whole life.'

Christopher bent his head and kissed her and this time Daisy didn't pull away. She didn't notice the differences between him and Rex, she didn't worry about whether she was doing the right thing, she just lost herself in the moment.

Much later, as Daisy and Christopher walked hand in hand down the lane to the village, Christopher turned to her again.

'I promise this is the last time I'll ask, but I just want to be absolutely certain. Because you've got Willow to think about, and you're still grieving for Rex, and I don't want to push you into anything you're not ready for.'

Daisy laughed. 'Christopher, I'm absolutely certain. You made me happy when I thought I'd never be happy again.'

'I didn't,' Christopher said. 'You did that all by yourself.'

Daisy squeezed his hand. 'All right, then. You showed me there was more happiness to be had.'

'That's better.'

'I want to be with you.' She felt a sudden twinge of uncertainty. Was he trying to tell her that he had changed his mind? 'But what about you?'

'What about me?' he asked.

'Are you absolutely certain? Because I come with baggage, Christopher. Baggage and a daughter.'

'I love you, Daisy, baggage and all,' he said. 'And I love Willow. I even love Blossom.' He paused looking at her critically. 'I do have one condition, though.'

Daisy's stomach lurched. What was he going to ask?

'What is it?'

'You really need to brush your hair.'

Chapter Fifty-Two

Two months later

Beth looked at herself in the mirror and gave her reflection a little nod of approval. She'd found another party dress from the days when she went to lots of parties and Nessa had worked some magic on it; she was very clever with a needle. She'd snipped off the collar, changed the neckline, made the skirt narrower – and it was like a new dress. Just what was needed for a day like today.

She gave her hair a final pat and went downstairs to find her parents.

Agatha was sitting on the sofa. She still looked thin and pale but she gave Beth a broad smile as she entered.

'You look very pretty,' she said. 'Nessa did a good job with that dress.'

Beth gave her a twirl. 'You look nice, too.' She looked her mother over with a critical eye. 'How are you feeling?'

'Almost back to normal,' Agatha said. 'Tired, but I'm definitely on the mend.'

'You've recovered so well.'

'I've got good doctors. At home as well as at the hospital.'

Beth grinned at her. 'Make sure you don't overdo it today. To the church and then home. Not too much standing around chatting.'

'We'll see.'

'Ready?' Geoffrey stood in the doorway, looking very smart in his suit. 'I've got a taxi waiting to take us to Kew.' He smiled at Beth. 'You look lovely, darling.'

Beth bobbed a curtesy to say thank you. 'Gus is meeting us there.'

'He doesn't want us to pick him up?'

'He's coming straight from the hospital,' Beth said, rolling her eyes. 'He wanted to check on his patients before he left.'

'Excellent.' Geoffrey sounded approving. 'I knew he was the right person for that job.'

Beth thought about arguing but decided against it. If her father wanted to take credit for getting Gus back on the wards, then so be it. At least he was there, seeing patients and proving all the people who'd doubted him wrong.

As it turned out, most of Gus's patients on the cardiac ward didn't give two hoots about the colour of their doctor's skin. They were poorly and they wanted to be better, and generally they trusted Gus to help them.

It wasn't all easy. Gus told Beth that often patients spoke to the nurses, or a more junior doctor, instead of to him, if he'd asked them a question. Some people couldn't believe that someone who looked like Gus could hold any authority. Others complained outright and, if they did, they were given a different doctor. Beth didn't like that. Nor did Gus. But he'd told Beth he was focusing on small steps. One day at a time.

Beth was finally starting university in the autumn, leaving London behind for Edinburgh. Gus wasn't going to move with her. Not yet. But one day . . .

'Are you nervous?' Agatha asked as their taxi trundled through London. 'You're all twitchy.'

'I am bit,' Beth admitted.

'You'll be fine.' She patted Beth's hand.

'It feels like an important day, that's all.' Beth thought about it. 'Like the ending of a chapter and the beginning of something new. I don't want to make any mistakes.'

Agatha smiled at her. 'But mistakes are how we learn,' she said. She looked pleased with herself. 'I read that somewhere and I rather liked it. I think it applies to all of us, doesn't it?'

Beth made a face. 'I'd rather learn without saying the wrong thing in church and embarrassing myself in front of all Daisy's family and friends.'

'Do you want to go through your bit again?'

'Yes please,' said Beth, even though she'd read it so many times she knew it off by heart, upside down and back to front.

Gus was waiting for them at the side of the road. Beth tumbled out of the taxi and rushed to greet him. She hoped she'd never stop being pleased to see him. He kissed her hello, greeted Agatha warmly – with an appraising doctor's eye – and shook hands with Beth's father. Geoffrey and Gus were still a little awkward with each other. Geoffrey was overly jovial, all back-slapping and calling Gus 'old chap' and laughing too loudly, while Gus was guarded and distrustful. But, Beth thought, it was an improvement on where they'd been.

Agatha took Geoffrey's arm to walk into church, while Beth waited at the door for Daisy to arrive.

'When Daisy said she wanted to have Willow christened here, I thought she was wrong,' she admitted to Gus. 'For ages I couldn't even look at the church when I walked to Kew Gardens, because it brought back so many awful memories. But actually, I think she was right.'

Gus nodded. 'It feels like everything has come full circle.'

'My mother said it's the end of one chapter and the beginning of the next.'

'She's right.'

'I hope the next chapter will be less dramatic.'

Gus chuckled. 'Now where's the fun in that?'

Daisy took a breath as Jim parked the van close to the church.

'Ready?' Ivy said.

'I'm ready.'

'I think this was a very good idea.' Ivy clambered out of the van and held her hand out to help Daisy down. 'Lay some ghosts to rest.'

'That's the idea.'

Jim had got Willow from the tiny back seat of the van. He brought her over to Daisy and she took the little girl into her arms and stood for a moment, looking at the church. She thought about how she'd nearly lost her daughter – and how her daughter had nearly lost her – and how all the people who'd helped her find herself again were here today, and she smiled.

'Shall we go and find Christopher?' she said to Willow. 'And Teddy and Louisa?'

'Weeza,' said Willow, nodding. She looked very sweet in the little white dress Daisy had made for her from an old pillowcase. Poppy had donated some ribbon that she'd been saving, and Ivy had cut the lace from a tablecloth that had once belonged to Jim's mother, and altogether it looked pretty as a picture. As long as you didn't look too closely at the uneven stitching, Daisy thought, looking at the hem of Willow's dress and wincing.

With Willow in her arms, and with her parents and Poppy by her side, Daisy walked across the green to St Anne's.

Rex's parents were there, thrilled to bits to see Willow but sad, too, that their son wasn't part of the day. Louisa and Teddy were there, too. And Beth and her family, and Gus, looking very smart.

Daisy left Willow being fussed over by all four of her grandparents – and loving every minute – and went to Beth.

'Have you seen Christopher?' she hissed.

Beth shook her head. 'Didn't he come up to London with you?'

'No,' Daisy sighed. 'Because he couldn't leave the farm overnight. He said he'd get the train this morning but he should have been here by now.'

'He'll be here,' Beth assured her. Daisy hoped she was right. Things were going well with Christopher but they were taking it slowly and she was worried that a big occasion like today – seeing all of her family and meeting Rex's parents – would be too much, too soon.

'Perhaps he's had second thoughts?' she said.

Beth bit her lip, thinking. 'I can't imagine he has. But even if he's not coming, it doesn't mean today is spoiled. It's all about Willow, after all.'

'You're right,' said Daisy, forcing a smile. 'Absolutely. Maybe we should go inside.'

Christenings were usually held at the end of the Sunday service, but Daisy hadn't wanted to share Willow's ceremony. 'I'm not being precious,' she had told Reverend King. 'I just feel a bit—' She'd paused, searching for the right word. 'A bit fragile. This isn't a normal baptism and I don't want to pretend that it is.'

As always, Reverend King understood perfectly. He'd arranged for this Sunday afternoon service, after the other worshippers had drifted off home, especially for Willow. Daisy was very grateful.

So when Daisy and Beth went inside the cool, dim church, the only people in the pews were friends. Daisy waved hello to some of the gardeners from Kew. Hetty wasn't there – she was still recovering in hospital – but Ruby was, with a patch over her eye. She was going to grow her hair to hide it, she'd told Daisy who, once more, had been struck by the bravery of the people around her. Her parents' friend Bernie was there, sitting with Louisa and Teddy and laughing at something Louisa had said. Daisy blew him a kiss and he grinned at her.

She scanned the people, searching for Christopher. He was hard to miss in a crowd and quickly she realised that he definitely wasn't there. Her heart twisted with sadness but she pasted on a jolly expression.

'How lovely to meet all your family and friends,' Reverend

King said, coming down the aisle to greet her. 'It's a very happy occasion.'

'It is,' said Daisy. It was. So why did she feel so sad?

'There must be some sorrow, though,' the vicar said. 'I understand it's a day where you'll be missing your husband as well. I'd like to mention him, if that's all right with you?'

'It's more than all right.' Daisy was touched. 'His parents are here and they would like that, too, I'm sure.'

'I was very pleased that you asked to hold the christening here. I remember you saying your parents were married here.'

Daisy looked over to where Ivy and Jim were entertaining Willow. 'They were.' She lowered her voice. 'And, I'm not supposed to tell anyone, but perhaps later ask their friend Bernie over there' – she tilted her head – 'why he has a special place in his heart for St Anne's.'

Reverend King raised an eyebrow and Daisy laughed. It was going to be such a wonderful day, she thought. If only Christopher was there, too.

'Are we ready to start?'

With one final look outside the church to see if Christopher was approaching, Daisy nodded. 'Let's get on.'

They gathered by the font, Daisy and Willow, with Beth, who was to be her godmother, and Teddy, who Daisy had asked to be godfather. They both looked proud as punch, and Beth said all her bits clearly and without stumbling – Daisy thought she'd probably rehearsed.

As Reverend King went to pour the water onto Willow's forehead, Willow said, 'No!' very loudly and arched her back so that she was out of reach, which made everyone laugh. At that moment, there was a thudding sound at the church porch and Christopher appeared. His tie was askew and he was rather red in the face. Everyone turned to look at him and he widened his eyes in horror.

'Have you started? God, I'm so sorry. I forgot to get off the blasted tube. I had to run all the way from Richmond.'

'Why didn't you just get back on the tube going the other way?' Daisy asked. She was smiling, though, because she was simply pleased to see him.

Christopher scratched his head. 'Didn't think of that.'

'Come on,' Daisy said. 'We're almost finished.'

Christopher came and stood beside Daisy and distracted Willow as Reverend King finished the baptism and suddenly everything was perfect.

Later, once the tears of happiness and sadness had dried, everyone trooped outside the church for a photograph. The bells were ringing and Daisy watched as Ivy stopped to listen, a strange expression on her face. 'Memories?' she asked her mother.

Ivy nodded. 'So many memories.' Jim put his arm round Ivy's shoulders and Daisy smiled to see her parents still happy together after so many years. Once upon a time she and Rex had talked about being like that one day. That wouldn't happen now, but she'd been given a second chance. Perhaps she and Christopher would grow old together. She had a feeling that they would.

'Daisy, you in the middle with Willow, and then everyone else gather round,' said Poppy, who had her first camera and was eager to take as many snaps as she could.

When Poppy had taken as many pictures of the group as she wanted, Daisy pulled her aside. 'Can you let Dad take one with you in it?' she said.

Poppy handed over her camera and Daisy gathered her and Ivy and Louisa, along with Beth and Agatha and, of course, little Willow, and they all smiled for the camera.

'It's a new generation of Kew Gardens girls,' Daisy said. 'I wonder what our next chapter will hold?'

> *"Kew is one of the world's most important botanical institutes and this country depends on it"*

Sir David Attenborough, Naturalist

Founded in 1759, the Royal Botanic Gardens, Kew is a world-famous, scientific organisation and leading botanic garden. With its world-wide collections, partnerships spanning the globe, and 326 acre UNESCO world heritage site, RBG Kew is a hotbed of education, inspiration, and cutting edge research. No institution is better placed to demonstrate why plants and fungi hold the key to solving some of the great global challenges facing us today, from food insecurity to biodiversity loss. Kew Gardens is a major international – and top London – tourist attraction, which welcomes millions of visitors each year. Thanks to its incredible work force, it remains a place of nature, mindfulness, heritage, and beauty.

www.kew.org

Reading list

To find out more about Kew Gardens and its history, I recommend *The History of the Royal Botanic Gardens Kew* by Ray Desmond and *The Story of Kew Gardens in Photographs* by Lynn Parker and Kiri Ross-Jones.

Some of the books that helped inspire me while I was writing this story were *The Country Diary of an Edwardian Lady* by Edith Holden, on which I based Ivy's journal, and *My Growing Garden* by J Horace McFarland, which I drew on for Bernie's fictional textbook, *A Year in My Garden*.

To learn more about the Suffragettes I recommend *My Own Story* by Emmeline Pankhurst and *The Suffragettes in Pictures* by Diane Atkinson.

For an evocative account of the Gardens in the early 20th century, *Kew Gardens* by Virginia Woolf is the perfect read.

Help us make the next generation of readers

We – both author and publisher – hope you enjoyed this book. We believe that you can become a reader at any time in your life, but we'd love your help to give the next generation a head start.

Did you know that 9 per cent of children don't have a book of their own in their home, rising to 13 per cent in disadvantaged families*? We'd like to try to change that by asking you to consider the role you could play in helping to build readers of the future.

We'd love you to think of sharing, borrowing, reading, buying or talking about a book with a child in your life and spreading the love of reading. We want to make sure the next generation continue to have access to books, wherever they come from.

And if you would like to consider donating to charities that help fund literacy projects, find out more at **www.literacytrust.org.uk** and **www.booktrust.org.uk**.

THANK YOU

*As reported by the National Literacy Trust